seduced

Also by Nelson George

NELSON GEORGE

G. P. Putnam's Sons New York

seduced

THE LIFE AND TIMES OF A ONE-HIT WONDER

G. P. Putnam's Sons
Publishers Since 1838
200 Madison Avenue
New York, NY 10016

Library of Congress Cataloging-in-Publication Data

George, Nelson.
    Seduced : the life and times of a one-hit wonder / Nelson George.
      p. cm.
    ISBN 0-399-14169-3
    1. Afro-American composers—New York (N.Y.)—Fiction.   2. Afro-
American men—New York (N.Y.)—Fiction.   3. Young men—New York
(N.Y.)— Fiction.   4. Queens (New York, N.Y.)—Fiction.   I. Title.
PS3557.E493S43   1996   95-26606 CIP
813'.54—dc20

Printed in the United States of America
10 9 8 7 6 5 4 3 2 1

Book designed by Bonni Leon-Berman

This book is printed on acid-free paper. ∞

Dedicated to Ann Carli.

Creativity's never had

a better friend.

Contents

Los Angeles, Philly—1985–87

Brooklyn—1987, 1988

"Each woman I do not have is a song I write."
—Antonio Carlos Jobim

Seduced

by Derek Harper

There's times when it's easy to lose control
There's times when you get plain lost.
We all have our frailties
Some more than most
But if you let someone else dominate your mentality
Be prepared to pay the cost.

Seduced by another man's fantasies
Seduced by another man's dreams
I was seduced by another man's fantasies
Until I forgot what's me.

Seduced by another man's image of me
Seduced by another man's feelings
I was seduced by another man's image of me
Until I became his dream.

Seduced
(No More!)

Seduced
(No More!)

Seduced
(No More!)

queens — 1960s, 1970s

"Voices Inside My Head"

My name is Derek Harper, which may mean something to you fans of music trivia and nothing to everyone else. With the exception of roughly eight months in 1988, I've never been a face in a music video, a chart listing in *Billboard*, or a celebrity of any measure. But I'm sure many of you have heard my work.

I've been a songwriter who's been labeled a tunesmith, a hack, an artist, and a thief depending on the year, the place, and the speaker. Personally, I think I'm some kind of channel through which God (or, on occasion, the Devil) speaks. Combinations of lyrics and melodies pop into my head, and I grab them before they disappear. As in that old Police song "Voices Inside My Head," my mind fills up with music and I pour it out. On the subway. Rounding third in a softball game. When dead tired and depressed. It doesn't matter the circumstance or the time. They come to me and I listen.

That's not to say I don't have to work. Often what I receive is a fragment, a sentence, enough notes to constitute a hook. Rarely am I so deeply blessed or cursed as to be given a whole song from stem to stern. But a little bit can be enough if you let it breathe awhile.

My moms hates it when I mention blessed and cursed as if they were just two sides of a coin. She thinks songwriting is something I could only be grateful about. I love her, but she doesn't know all that has happened to me because of these voices. She doesn't know all I've seen or what I've done. Sometimes this blessing has led me astray. Joy and pain, as Frankie Beverly sang. Joy and pain.

"Bring It on Home"

In the mid-sixties, black folks made a little mecca for themselves out in Queens, New York—a place best known for the Mets, Archie Bunker, and JFK airport. In the working-class neighborhoods of Jamaica and Hollis, and the more bourgeois areas known as St. Albans and Cambria Heights, blacks looking to stretch out from the tenements and concrete of Harlem and Brooklyn found their little piece of suburbia in places that were a bus and subway ride from Manhattan (what's known as a "two-fare zone"). Though this made commuting a hassle and more expensive, it gave these neighborhoods a distinctly middle-class, un-urban, self-contained ambiance.

Like their white neighbors, these Queensites treasured their tree-lined streets, tidy lawns, and backyards made for barbeque, portable swings, and plastic wading pools. On Saturdays, fathers wore knit sweaters and Kangol caps while they washed their Cadillacs and sipped the local beers, Reingold or Schaeffer. Mothers stuck their heads outside wearing pink foam curlers to pull the latest *Jet* and *Ebony* out of the mailbox as Sam Cooke played softly on the hi-fi. Boys climbed into the back of Chrysler station wagons as they waited to be driven to Baisley Park for Little League games, while their sisters bounced from house to house playing jacks, practicing the camel walk, and swooning at the Miracles' latest slow jam.

Black celebrities dotted this part of Queens. James Brown, John Coltrane, and Count Basie all kept houses around the way and everybody knew where. If you waited patiently and stayed off the grass they'd scribble an autograph and, if you looked pitiful enough, they might slip you a quarter for ice cream.

City workers—bus drivers, school teachers, meter maids, nurses, cops, corrections officers, and bureaucrats of various titles—were the backbone of black Queens. These were men and women who were direct beneficiaries of the civil rights movement, New York's longstanding commitment to unionization, liberal mayors Robert Wagner and John Lindsay, and their own hard years of toil. It was a kind of black middle-class heaven, a place where bourgie groups like the Links and Jack & Jill thrived. On Sundays, while mom and the kids were at church, many overworked daddies sat in their brown slippers in their backyards reading the *New York Times* while puffing on Dutch Masters cigars.

Harlem and Brooklyn were known for their vibrant, contentious black communities, but few outside of Queens seemed to know this world existed, which was fine by most of the black home owners. Year after year white folks trickled out of Jamaica, Hollis, and St. Albans, running away from darker neighbors who shared the same values, religious commitment, and economic class. Problem was, we just weren't white. By the time I got to Andrew Jackson High in St. Albans, it was the first all-black high school in the borough, and it wouldn't be the last.

Pops didn't care. White folks fleeing didn't bother him since they rarely utilized his services and Pops was always about business. A stern, stocky man with a slight Chinese slant to his baby browns. It's my father's hands I remember mostly: firm and always well manicured. He had a quiet confidence that came from understanding his place in the world. My father was, is, and always will be an undertaker, and his love of his profession profoundly affected his worldview and our family. First of all, death held no mystery in our lives. It was constant and inevitable. Or, as my pops often said to the bereaved, "It is the sad period at the end of a long eventful sentence." (Yup, he talked that way.) So when my pet hamster, Susan, died and Moms' cat, Fluffy, got coldcocked by a flying garbage can, we Harpers took it in stride. They were mourned; they were buried; life went on. It was all very matter-of-fact. And this outlook didn't apply just to pets. Hardly. I remember the night Dr. King was assassinated—I was about eleven—my mother and father were stoic when most of our neighbors were either outraged or teary. Conversation at our dinner table centered on the autopsy, the embalming, which Atlanta funeral home would land the contract, and how this prestigious job surely secured their future.

You see, being an undertaker is one of the best damn jobs a black person can have. Always has been. Back in the old days down South it was one of the few lucrative professions blacks could enter with little fear of white resentment or interference. The last thing a redneck wanted was to deal with dead black bodies (except, of course, at the odd lynching). This rather ironic freedom allowed black undertakers to ply their trade without fear. Between white sheriffs, moonshine, juke joints, old age, pork, and high blood pressure, black undertakers always had a steady cash flow. Add to that heroin, angel dust, crack, etc., and the money still flowed on. Undertaking is what my grandfather on my pops' side did back in Newport News, Virginia, and so it's no surprise that Pops continued the trade up North. We lived well because of it. I never wanted for much materially. I always had cash for movies and comic books and, as time passed, for records of every description. Pops was a big man in our black middle-class community. A role model in the classic sense.

I had, and still have, no beef with how Pops ran his business. He was on it. The problem in the Harper house was that Daniel Harper was an undertaker even when he was home with me and Moms. The work consumed him and eventually consumed those who depended on him. Death, often violent and at night, haunts African-American neighborhoods and Pops was always on call. My childhood was scarred by trips canceled or delayed. Parents' nights were attended by my moms alone. There was the vague sense I was bothering Pops whenever I asked him to look over my algebra.

It was really hard on Moms, who, as time passed, seemed to shrink into my father's shadow. A chubby, clear-eyed woman with a beguiling warmth and an introspective nature, she held a belief in God's will that helped her fill the vast space between her girlish ambitions and the adult reality she accepted. They'd come up from Newport News after she'd graduated from Hampton Institute and he from Virginia Union. Pops' father had staked him with some cash and Moms' father cashed in a savings bond as a wedding gift. So when Pops opened the funeral home she had almost as much money invested in it as he did. Apparently they'd worked as partners building it up in the early years. Then I came along and she stayed home. If I do say so myself, I was not a high-maintenance kid. Yet once I was born and, after the miscarriage, her involvement was limited to Saturday visits to check the books.

The miscarriage happened when I was five. I remember it kinda in snapshots. It was a Sunday night. I'd watched "The Wonderful World of Disney." I'd taken a bath. My mother had tucked me in. I was awakened by a sound. It wasn't a shout. It wasn't a scream. It was some other sound, some primal thing so dark it sounded like nothing but fear. I moved toward the bathroom. Don't know if I walked or ran. I was just there at the doorway and there was crimson fluid on the floor and Moms was soaked in it, her blue night gown was drenched, and my pops had towels in both hands. Peeking unformed from the toilet, there was my little sister who'd never be.

I wish I could say more, but I'm probably lucky I can't. There was no funeral. There was no explanation given me. Apparently very few of my relatives were told. Except for my memory, there is no documentation of this Harper family tragedy.

Yet there was mourning, mourning that I think has never ended for my Moms. It figures that my father buried Penny the girl and, drawing on his professional experience, somehow moved past the grief and slowly, internally, let the wound heal. My moms had no such control mechanism. You'd just never know when she'd burst out into tears at the sight of a little girl. She cried at Radio City when the little girl in *Mary Poppins* sang "Spoon Full of Sugar." She cried when ads for black dolls first appeared in *Ebony* magazine. She cried during my fifth-grade parent's night when she saw the self-portrait one of my classmates drew of herself and her mother that hung over a radiator.

I'm not saying my moms was constantly breaking down—that's not the case. But her grieving over this particular death lingered. Like my Pops, she managed to brush aside all the work done at the funeral home, but this grief was too deep to be dealt with. Moms was never pregnant again. Whether this was because of Penny's death or some physical ailment, I don't know, and I've never had the guts to ask.

Now regardless of whatever ailed Moms, she was always warm and accessible to me. She was there for me when it came to homework, runny noses, and those existential questions that kids ask, like "Why is the moon white?" Pops, in contrast, had no interest in any of that stuff on a day-to-day basis. If Moms was the micromanager, Pops was concerned with issues of macromanagement. He wanted me healthy and happy. No question about that. He just felt providing a big house, a steady (though modest) allowance, and a stable environment was enough. And basically he was right. I'm not a stick-up kid. I never stole anything except the occasional Captain America comic book and never really liked getting high. I knew better. My life has probably been easier than 90 percent of the little black boys born in this country.

Still I wish he'd been a bit more attentive. I'm not mad at him but, sometimes, just sometimes, I felt neglected. When I was nine, Pops helped organize a neighborhood outing to Bear Mountain in upstate New York. Neighbors, church folks, and a few relatives all boarded rented school buses to burn meat and swill beer. I learned to shoot a layup that day. Pops was supposed to teach me. He'd seen me play a couple of times and said I needed some pointers. I looked forward to this lesson for two weeks. The day of the outing it was an unusually hot one for April. Still I was ready for a full day of sweating. Getting off the bus I immediately planted myself on the basketball court, which was just a long jump shot from the barbecue pit. I waited for him right near the top of the key, loosening up.

Some other kids wanted to play, but I told them I was busy. They organized a three-on-three at one end while I waited anxiously at the other. Pops was busy. He was barbecuing. He was barbecuing for everyone. He announced, "I know how to handle dead meat," and everybody laughed. He was hosting the affair. I guess I should have gone over there, tugged at his barbecue-stained apron, and made him fulfill his promise to me. But I didn't. I just stood at the top of the key and watched Pops barbecue with my lower lip poked out.

"You wanna shoot some hoops, youngblood?"

From out of nowhere Uncle Mike stood next to me. He was Pops' little brother and the Harper family's self-appointed renegade. Where Pops was straight-laced and a touch corny, Uncle Mike was happy-go-lucky and willfully hip. If Pops was as stable as stone, Uncle Mike was as elusive as sunlight in Seattle. If Pops' reasoning was as precise as a Nikon camera, Uncle Mike's worldview was marred like thumb prints on a negative. Or, as Pops would say of him with a sarcastic smile, "Your Uncle Mike is the jack-of-all-trades but the master of none."

I answered Uncle Mike's query with a shrug of my shoulders. He peered over at his brother and shook his head. "Your father is running shit again, ain't he?" I shrugged again. "Supposed to be playing ball with you but he ain't, is he?"

"He promised to teach me the right way to make a layup." My lip was way out now.

"Well," Uncle Mike replied, "do you wanna learn or are you gonna wait on him? I know I used to until I figured I had to find out things my own way."

A few moments later I was dribbling and then leaping awkwardly up in the air. "Nope," Uncle Mike said. "That ain't it, youngblood." For the next half hour Uncle Mike led me through the intricacies of the layup. Dribble. Step. Dribble. Step. Right leg up. Right arm up. Left leg straight with a slight bend in the knee. Flick with the right hand. Land. "All in rhythm, youngblood."

"Okay, Uncle Mike."

"All in rhythm."

"Okay!" I shouted back. I wasn't mad at him, of course. I was slightly mad at myself. My dribble was unsteady and my right-hand flick was like a throw that made the ball bang like a brick against the backboard. But my real irritation was aimed at Pops who, after supervising the barbecue pit, came over to the court with a Coke in his hand. I was drenched in sweat and frustration, so I didn't acknowledge him.

He walked over to where Uncle Mike stood and belched. Out of the corner of my eye I watched the two brothers talk. Pops was stocky and barrel-chested; Uncle Mike was taller with wide shoulders. Brothers, yes, but different. Their voices grew louder. I turned. Next thing I knew Pops had snatched the ball from me. He and Uncle Mike then squared off for a game of one-on-one. At first I was like "Yeah, Uncle Mike, kick Pops' ass." Then I relented. If Pops lost he'd be evil for days. Maybe Pops should win, I thought, but it should be close enough that he'd be a little humbled.

I desired high drama. What I got was the underwhelming spectacle of two out-of-condition men going, sloppily, after their memories of macho. Air balls missed the rim. Layups were blown. Dribbles bounced off feet. Pops breathed heavily like an ox wading through mud. Uncle Mike was as hectic as a dog shedding water. Real fast the game petered out into the listless punch, counter-punch of a bad heavyweight fight. Watching them I knew there wasn't a hint of athletic ability in my blood.

There was one ray of happiness. Pops tried to go around Uncle Mike and kicked the ball off his knee. I grabbed it in stride as if it was a pass. Dribble. Step. Dribble. Step. Dribble. Step. Right leg up. Right arm up. Left leg stiff with a slight bend at the joint. Flick. It flowed like Walt Frazier running the backdoor play with Bill Bradley. Uncle Mike said, "Right on, youngblood," and Pops said, "Looking good, son," and it was just a magic moment. With that layup I was, momentarily, the center of the Harper family universe.

Then Uncle Mike smiled and told Pops, "Let's get us some brew."

"No, thanks," Pops replied, "I'm having a Coke."

"If you're gonna belch," Uncle Mike shot back, "then do it for a good reason."

My moment was over. They were back doing their thing—engaged in some argument that started before I was born. They'd almost left the court when Pops yelled over his shoulder. "Derek," he said, "you better come and have some of this barbecue." But I didn't want any barbecue. I had wanted some time with him on this day, but that was all I was gonna get.

"Charlie Brown"

In light of my rather dour family history, I think I should tell you how much I loved music. From the time I was very small I remembered songs with remarkable clarity. When I was two and a half, my Moms says I'd wobble around the house singing, "Who walked through the classroom cool and slow/ who called the English teacher Daddy-O?/ Charlie Brown!/ He's a clown/ That Charlie Brown!" I must have heard the Coaster's record on the radio, since my Moms declares never to have owned a copy.

Picking up on this as I grew older, Pops gave me trumpet lessons (he loved Louis Armstrong), violin lessons (he thought it would give me class), and the basic piano lessons any little kid of middle-class upbringing must be subjected to. The latter were marginally successful. I learned A flat from D sharp and chords from choruses, but my ability to execute at the keyboard was limited by my small fingers and a profound lack of discipline. I spent more time at the piano teacher's house reading her daughter's Curious George books than playing the scales. I already had an ear for melody, but actual chops, my dexterity, never really caught up to my sometimes wavering ambition.

In the junior high band I was stuck with the baritone horn. Now the baritone horn might have been all right if someone, particularly the music teacher, had a clue as to how the damn thing was supposed to sound. Once he mentioned that it should "resonate as a trombone does," but that was as close as he came to instruction. The baritone horn looks like an underweight tuba, though it lacks the foghorn power of its big brother. Because it was cumbersome to carry and totally lacking in status, I took it home only once to practice—and I was a kid who loved music. My crowning achievement on that marvelously obscure instrument was splitting a two-bar solo with my fellow baritone hornist Nathan Silverman at the seventh-grade concert. A grand moment, indeed, since for most of the night Nathan and I had just fingered our instruments without blowing into them, thinking, quite correctly, no one knew (or cared) how we sounded anyway.

Despite this setback, sound still obsessed me. Choruses, bits of lyrics, melody lines, drumbeats, vocal riffs all stuck in my brain even as algebra computations and females' telephone numbers eluded me. Sometimes I could feel the melancholy of the Temptations' "Just My Imagination" and the Chi-Lites' "Oh Girl" right in my skinny bones. I began fantasizing about climbing inside my favorite songs. I'd let the music wash over me, I'd be swallowed whole inside the melody, and my skin would evaporate into the harmonies. Listening to the Temptations' "My Girl" or Simon & Garfunkel's "Feelin' Groovy," I felt as if I'd melted into a way of seeing the world that was a world itself. The very intangibility of music, the way it can seem so complete and to exist all around you yet be totally fluid, pleased me deeply. Music can be contained on a record, on a tape, on a CD, but it can never be held, never really grasped.

As an adolescent I got into the habit of staying up late and listening to my AM/FM radio real low after my parents had gone to bed. On a good night I could hear Delaware, Montreal, Boston, and other cities that would blast through the static as I lay in the darkness with the bed spread on half my body and half on the floor. Voices of deejays rapping about sales at brake shops and shoe stores at malls I'd never heard of in suburban townships I'd never want to visit. The records, however, were all the same: tinny anthems of love and lust that were as familiar as the water stains on my ceiling. These were songs that helped fill in the fabric of life, yet they were in themselves nothing you really cared about.

At two or three in the morning the shifting frequencies sounded incredibly loud. Switching dials. Sampling fragments of sound. Zip. Blip. Zip again. I'd wonder if my slumbering parents were rolling over in their bed, suffering inexplicable irritation caused by vibrations from my radio. But in the house all that was conscious was me, my moving dial, and "Let's Stay Together" and "American Pie" and "Fire" and "I'll Be Around" and "Knock Three Times." Night after night I challenged the AM stations to play that one disagreeable record that would literally turn me off.

But late-night radio never does. In bed it all sounds like it should. Just one more, I'd promise myself. Then I'd wait another three minutes, my body tired, my mind sluggish, yet something pushed me to listen until blue light curled under my curtains. In the blessed darkness the dial glowed, red numbers surrounded by black, but once daylight entered the room, the radio was nothing special and I would give in to slumber.

I might have just stayed a weak musician and never become a songwriter if I hadn't become obsessed with Stevie Wonder's "Living for the City" when I was about fourteen. I'd sit in front of my pops' component set and play Wonder's masterpiece over and over. I loved all of *Innervisions* but "Living" really spoke to me. It was as if *Native Son* or *Manchild in the Promised Land*, books my Moms had given me to learn about "our less fortunate brothers and sisters," had been given tempo and tune. Epic in scope, intimate in detail, ominous yet stirring, "Living" set me daydreaming about its characters. The kids from Hardtimes, Mississippi, in the opening verse. The journey of one little black boy to New York City and the mistakes that destroyed him. In a voice that was colorful and tortured, this kid told a sad, brutal tale of dashed expectations. It wasn't my family's life but it still felt real close to me, like if Pops had gone left instead of right when he first got off the bus in New York.

This idea that life didn't merely glide by, that it had fateful moments of decision, and that a song could be carved out of this material moved me to begin writing stuff down in a spiral notebook I carried everywhere. Just things I saw or people I met. I'd show my words to Moms, who suggested I try putting them to music. The thing was, what she wanted me to do was write love songs, not story songs, so "they'd be like most things on the radio." It sounded like good advice. Whenever I was in trouble creatively, I'd just go put the needle back on "Living for the City" and let my mind wander as that ominous keyboard intro filled our living room.

"You Really Got a Hold on Me"

Fourteen was a real key year for me. It was the same year I had my cherry popped. Unlike most love songs, it wasn't romantic and it wasn't that much fun. It was quick, and it was kinda nasty. And it happened over at Aunt Alma's house.

Aunt Alma lived over in the Samuel J. Tilden housing projects in a funky part of Brooklyn called Brownsville. She was my mother's sister and had moved to New York not long after my parents had, but her sojourn had not turned out as well. Her husband, Teddy, had worked in the shipyard of Newport News and thought getting work on Manhattan's docks would be just as easy. In Newport News there was a long tradition of black employment in the nautical trades. In the Big Apple it was all controlled by the Irish and Italians, and the few "good" Negroes they hired never had any job security and always had to take racial slurs in stride. Uncle Teddy couldn't quite get the hang of being an Uncle Tom, even if it meant feeding his family, so he didn't work much. On several occasions, Pops offered him a gig at his funeral home, but a combination of pride and disgust at Pops' profession kept Uncle Teddy saying no.

Aunt Alma worked as a registered nurse at King's County Hospital where, through layoffs, budget cuts, and mismanagement, she persevered and even thrived. Over the years, their family grew with the additions of Anna, Alla, and Alice—cute girls born two years apart—and the pressure increased on Uncle Teddy with each birth.

Still Uncle Teddy's economic failures continued. Like a lot of men of his time, he saw wine as the way to smooth over his troubles. Regularly he'd disappear, only to be found days later sleeping in some stairwell or bench around the projects.

Uncle Teddy's heavy drinking made trips to Brownsville tense for my parents. Moms was always there for her sister: loaning her money, sharing her tears, filling her with hope. Pops, basically, did the right thing by his wife's sister but without tremendous enthusiasm. I mean, if Moms was upset, then Pops was upset, too. Still his overall philosophy was simple: "If Teddy don't wanna act right, what can I do?" He got tired of offering Uncle Teddy a job. He got tired of searching around Brownsville in his Caddy for his brother-in-law. He got real tired of slipping Aunt Alma $100 every time Moms dragged him over to Brooklyn for Sunday dinner. In the car driving from Queens to Brooklyn he invariably used to mutter, "One day I'll get my hands on Teddy," and that he meant it in a professional sense really pissed Moms off.

Now for me visiting the Tilden Projects was big fun. Unlike Queens, where everyone on the block knew you, people in the projects tended to be close only to folks on their floor. Otherwise you were semi-anonymous and to me anonymity meant freedom. You could play stickball in the street while dodging cars, or slip comic books into your pants and run like hell out of the corner candy store or you could drop water—filled balloons out of hallway windows—at old men with groceries. Best of all, you could feel up girls in the staircases and they'd feel you back.

I had some real advantages in this area over the local guys. My clothes were a touch more expensive than what the project boys wore. I had a weekly allowance, which meant I could buy more Wise potato chips and watermelon candy. I was from Queens, which sounded vaguely exotic to girls who'd never left Brownsville, much less Brooklyn. And I had Anna, Aunt Alma's oldest daughter, on my side.

Anna was tall, boney, and gap-toothed, but she had these really bright eyes and loved to dance. If she wasn't the most popular girl in the projects, she was pushing hard for the number-two spot. She was the only reason my Pops got any pleasure out of visiting Brownsville, since Anna always got him out his seat and made him learn the latest dances, to the delight of Anna and the hostile laughter of Uncle Teddy. Moms liked her, too, though sometimes I'd see Moms look at Anna with this weird intensity. It came and went, and when Moms saw Pops watching her she'd just smile and play it off. Anyway, with Anna's aid my comings and goings were always announced to her cutest friends in advance, so there was an air of anticipation about my appearances. Anna hooked me up better with women than any guy ever had or would.

Which is why I lost my virginity one Sunday afternoon on the roof of 315 Livonia Avenue. Downstairs, my moms and pops were lecturing Uncle Teddy on the evils of demon rum while Aunt Alma cried. Up on the roof, which was something of a ghetto lovers' lane, Becky Jones, a buck-toothed fifteen-year-old with mocha-colored skin and slanted Chinese eyes, was hopping up and down on me while my three cousins giggled behind the door to the roof. I thought Anna had just arranged for Becky and me to go up there and kiss, but homegirl quickly grabbed a hold of my happy young manhood and manipulated it to attention. Once it became clear we were going further than hickies, I tried to play the aggressive male role. Becky, however, wasn't having it. Suddenly I was on the bottom with the seat of my good Sunday school pants becoming filthy as they rubbed against the rooftop's tar.

I was on punishment for a week for ruining my pants, but that seemed the least of my worries. Anna called me a couple of times that week, telling me Becky thought she might be pregnant. Initially I was stunned and then filled with that kind of deep suicidal fear adolescents specialize in. Lucky for me, I was a reader. I scoped out some sex-ed books in the library and figured that Becky was clearly out of her mind. I vowed then never again to mess with a girl from the projects, a plan which lasted, oh, a couple of months. More important, I got my first package of Trojans.

Back in the seventies you'd carry a condom for a number of reasons. You carried them in case you stumbled into the miracle of a one-night stand. You carried them for girls you thought nasty. You carried them for girls you thought were easy. And, perhaps most important, you carried them to show other guys you had them. Back then, condoms were considered far from mandatory by many brothers. I mean, bloods who had no fear of making babies didn't give a damn. For guys like me, though, who were basically nice guys who aspired to roguishness, condoms symbolized our thwarted desires on several levels.

There was, for example, the sorry phenomenon of the unused condom. Initially, buying a condom was a high. You got one of those three-packs of Trojans from the drug store, then slid one in your wallet and smiled as it bulged out right where your Merry Marvel Marching Society membership card used to be. However, as time passed, it seemed to grow in size until it filled the whole damn wallet, a manifestation of your failure as a mack, seducer, and all-around love man. The condom would be in there so long that the imprint pushed right through the wallet's leather, creating the impression of a zero that summed up your love life.

I'll never forget the afternoon I finally got to unleash that first condom. Pam Washington was up for the summer from South Carolina and was staying two doors down. She had big red gums, a silly laugh, and a glorious untrained voice I fell for immediately, so I decided to seduce her. I played a few of my songs for her on the ragged piano we kept in the basement and she really liked them. When she sang those painfully adolescent love songs with so much commitment, I suddenly felt like Smokey Robinson. We could have been the next Ashford & Simpson if my condoms hadn't intervened.

We'd sing my songs and snuggle up afterwards on the sofa bed. One afternoon the snuggling got crazy cozy and she was wiggling below me and I opened my wallet. We were both horny after a summer of snuggling and, goddamn it, I ripped open my lonely condom and there it was in all its spermicidal glory. Problem was the condom was as dry as sandpaper and just as flexible. Pam giggled her silly, girlish, South Carolina giggle and my pride shriveled up with my condom. I was so embarrassed I chased her out of my basement and out of my life. I wouldn't speak to her. I couldn't face her. I'd tied up a dream in that piece of lubricated rubber and just was nowhere near mature enough to see the humor in its failure. It was my first experience in the sometimes evil alchemy of a woman's laughter and a man's sexuality, and I took it real hard.

But condoms weren't through with me. Three years later, during my freshman year in high school, I was hooked up with Carlene Mathews by a friend who was seeing her older sister. Carlene was slender and buxom. Her eyes were hooded and sleepy and maybe a little too child-like for her own good. Carlene was not the brightest person I'd ever know, yet on certain crucial topics she was way more sophisticated than me. A couple of weeks into the relationship she called me on a Friday night. I was working on biology 101, but her conversation was much more educational.

"I need some vitamin D," she told me. Then she said it again as I, stupidly, advised her to stop by a drug store. I wasn't that naive. However, I was really stunned. No woman had ever come right out and said, "Yes, not only do I like sex, but I want to have some with you." This was new ground for me. "When can I get some?" she wondered. Well, my Pops would be at the funeral parlor all day and my Moms would be visiting my aunt in the Bronx that afternoon. "Bet," Carlene said, "I'll be over tomorrow afternoon."

After she hung up I sat there with a worried face and a hard dick. This was real adult stuff. I pulled out my condoms, counted them, and lined them up on my desk. I did sit-ups and push-ups. I changed my sheets and my underwear. I put away my *Players'* magazines—after I'd jerked off to my classic Pam Grier issue—and I slept fitfully, getting up every hour or so, anxious for the dawn.

In the morning I ate four scrambled eggs and a bowl of Raisin Bran for extra potency. I checked the water in my pops' car and I walked my mother to the bus stop. Then I took two showers, put on Ban roll-on deodorant and my pops' Old Spice aftershave and clipped my nails, even my toenails. I mean, this was serious business. About two o'clock, Carlene appeared at my door in a loose-fitting top, jeans, and sneakers. She had a little more lipstick than mid-afternoon required, and her usually docile eyes were more intense than I'd ever seen them.

She flopped down on the living room sofa. I slid the new Ashford & Simpson LP on the turntable. She looked at me. I stared at her. Next thing I knew we were rolling on the floor. After bumping my knee on the sofa, I guided her down to the basement. Carlene undressed quickly and stretched out on the pull-out sofa like a *Players* magazine centerfold. I pulled out my most recently purchased condom—I'd learned that lesson—and ripped it open like a bag of Wise potato chips.

I thought I was calm. I wasn't. I could not get the condom on. It would not roll down. I tried to loop it over the tip, just as they taught in sex-ed class, while Carlene looked on impatiently. Frustrated, I decided to yank the condom on and ripped the latex from the circular rim. It was a disaster in the making. Quickly I slid out another condom. My member was still erect, though my technical difficulties were making it quite unhappy. Again I ripped open a package, but my anxiousness got in the way again. I got an air bubble in the condom. I mean, I had the damn thing on but there was a substantial pocket of air on the left side. By now I was insane with lust, so I just tried to jam the whole thing, air pocket and all, inside Carlene. Maybe I got the head in before she pushed me away.

I still had more condoms and we still had plenty of time, but the intensity was gone and we never recaptured that excitement. On and off for the next two hours I'd get hard and she wouldn't be aroused. Or she'd be ready and I'd be lukewarm.

It was a painfully unsatisfactory afternoon. I walked her home in silence, but I was determined not to let this one afternoon ruin a good thing. We did have a few more afternoons together, none as lustful, though. Unfortunately, not long afterwards, she got a job at an upstate summer camp where, to the chagrin of her parents and myself, she got into a torrid affair with a thirty-year-old counselor.

Yet ultimately my time with Carlene taught me some very important stuff. Number one, never allow yourself to be intimidated by aggressive female sexuality. A woman such as Carlene knows what she wants and who she wants it with, just like any man. With Carlene there would be no misunderstandings, no miscommunications, at least not when it came to sex. She was a straight shooter and, in a world where women are trained to be timid, I had to learn to treasure that.

Number two, I figured I had to learn the zen of condoms. If I was never going to be handsome or slick enough to avoid using them, then condoms and yours truly had to become friends. In between classes and songwriting, I'd practice putting on condoms, so that from opening the package to putting them on, everything happened in smooth easy movements. I experimented with different types—lubricated, dry, ribbed, flavored, etc., until this trumpeter around the corner who'd toured in Japan with the Ohio Players gave me some lambskins.

They came in little blue capsules and were moist as Sunkist oranges and gave you the illusion you weren't wearing a condom. A very nice trick indeed. As disastrous as sex on ghetto rooftops and my comfy basement had been, it all paid dividends by preparing me for the first great love of my life.

"Do You Know Where You're Going"

Candi Evans used to sit across from me in sophomore English class. I spent half my time watching the board and half my time gazing rapturously at her. I admired her mind and dreamed of her body from across the vast distance of a high school classroom aisle. Her nose was small; her lips slender; her eyes wide and generous. She usually wore her hair straight on top with two curly Afro puffs on either side, which made her face seem small and very feminine. Her breasts pointed straight out, and I'd fantasize making vowel sounds around them with my mouth. To me, Candi's most alluring feature, though, was her voice. She possessed a pretty singsong quality that made her overemphasize certain words. Her conversation sounded like a melody. I'd just sit there cataloging all that was wonderful about Candi in class and then that night recall every detail in the darkness of my bedroom.

One day when it finally got to be too much, I asked her out. My question was more defensive than aggressive. I said, "How's about taking in a flick with me?" I didn't request a particular day or time, as if I expected to be told no. She was noncommittal. She had "to think about it," which meant she probably had a boyfriend. She didn't, however, say that, which would have been a simple way to terminate my hopes. Instead she left her options open. This all happened on a Monday. She was vague about it until that Thursday when she said, "What about Sunday afternoon?" Unlike a Friday night or Saturday date, it cut down the chances of us staying out late or of any tricky improvisations on my part. There was church in the morning and school the next day, which limited our time together. It also meant I had to wait all weekend for my shot, all that time being very careful not to blow my allowance on Friday or Saturday. I was going to argue for a better day but something said "Relax," so I tried to.

Friday night I played basketball after school and stayed home watching the Knicks play Boston. On Saturday I did my homework, brought the mail over to my father at the funeral parlor, and then sat at home, tortured the rest of the day as my friends went into the city to see a Bruce Lee movie while I, holding onto my dimes for Sunday, stayed stuck in Queens. I woke up Sunday morning to see three inches of fresh white snow filling the Queens streets. For those of you unaware of Queens' relationship to snow, the borough is notorious for being the last of New York's five boroughs to get its streets cleaned during a winter storm.

That afternoon I watched the Jets lose to New England. I was constantly checking for Candi's call, but my moms was on a Sunday talking binge. Would she get through when she needed to? This was in those primitive days before call waiting, so my anxiety built. Finally, while roasting a turkey, the oven overheated and Moms, who rarely saw any reason to hang up on a Sunday, took a phone break. And, just perfect, Candi called. I was doubly blessed when Candi, despite the snow and the difficulty of travel in Queens, said she still wanted to go to the movies. Even better, she wanted to see *Mahogany*, which was playing at the Jamaica Theater on Jamaica Boulevard, the heart of the area's business strip and one bus ride from her house. "Right on!" I thought to myself. "Right on!"

There was a layer of ice on Jamaica Avenue about a half-inch thick, so Candi and I didn't so much walk, as glide down that wide boulevard. We navigated by grabbing onto garbage cans, parking meters, and the thick green pylons that held up the elevated train. Mostly, however, I found myself hanging onto Candi. That is when she wasn't being playful and pushing me so that I'd go sliding across and, occasionally, falling down on the ice. That singsong voice of hers giggled at me and no amount of embarrassment at my gawky awkwardness could take away my joy. When she finally fell—after a strong shove from me—I marveled at how pleasantly her butt bounced against the ice. Apologetically I pulled her up, just to have her push me back down again and laugh that sweet singsong laugh.

Sore and sweaty we camped in the Jamaica Theater balcony. Slowly we unburdened ourselves of all our winter clothes and purchased provisions: popcorn without butter, red Twizzlers for me, black licorice for her, and a giant 7-Up with two straws for us to share. Diana Ross was on the screen in several wild, self-designed outfits as a hot black model, Anthony Perkins was a collection of kooky-acting tics as a fey fashion photographer, and Billy Dee Williams—oh, Billy Dee—was making Candi swoon.

I tried not to be jealous. I really did. But to have her attention turn so lustily from me toward this mustache-wearing old man peeved me. When Diana left Billy Dee in Chicago to pursue her modeling career I said, "Good move," which led Candi to hit me in the ribs and shush me, as if I'd blasphemed in a church. Then I got a little obnoxious. I shifted in my seat, humming the theme to *Mahogany*, "Do You Know Where You're Going," in her ear. Spilled pop corn sloppily on the floor. All of it to draw her attention back to me.

I could have blown my relationship with her right then in a fatal blast of adolescent ego. Thankfully some latent romanticism surfaced to save the date. I said, "Candi, if you become my Diana Ross, I'll be your Billy Dee." Yup, it was corny, and over-the-top, but it was the kind of thing a teenage guy says to a dreamy-eyed teenage girl on a first date. That was a key moment in my life. If she'd laughed or just brushed the comment off, I probably would have continued being obnoxious and blowing the relationship. But it worked. "That's so sweet," she said, and laid her head back against my right shoulder, snuggling up against me. Candi sat like that the rest of the movie and even when my right arm went numb and the feeling in my fingers disappeared, I didn't move another muscle until the final credits.

Candi infused me with a confidence in words sentimental and direct that hasn't left me. Billy Dee uttered the immortal line, "Success means nothing without someone to share it with" to Diana early in the film and, eventually, Diana came back with it in the big finish. It was as corny as what I'd said but, on screen at least, equally effective. That Berry Gordy had penned that one-liner—sort of an outtake from a Supremes song—only confirmed that there was something strong and true about it.

When we went out on Jamaica Avenue later, the temperature had dropped and the ice was no longer fun but treacherous. Arm and arm, we navigated, walking toward the bus depot on 165th Street. We moved in concert, like a piccolo and a flute in a concerto, and it felt as natural now as our earlier walk had been funny. When I got home there was a little homework left to do and Moms had left a plate of pork chops and cabbage on the stove. All I could do was stare into space and realize I'd had a good date with Candi Evans and that she wanted me—me, the nerdy kid from English class—to be her boyfriend. Thank you, Billy Dee, I kept thinking. Thank you.

"Betcha By Golly Wow"

Candi had wanted to see *Thomasine & Bushrod* with Max Julien and Vonetta McGee. It was a black Western and a love story. I wanted to see *Three the Hard Way* with Fred Williamson, Jim Brown, and Jim Kelly, the black kung fu man, battling an evil scheme to poison black America's drinking water with sickle cell anemia. Romance prevailed, and I sat quietly through the damn thing, more than satisfied with copping a feel of Candi's pert right breast and tongue kissing all through the middle of the movie.

After the film we walked hand in hand down Seventh Avenue from Times Square to Herald Square and then, with no particular destination in mind, angled over to Sixth Avenue and moved downtown toward Greenwich Village. We strolled slowly through the early spring evening and every now and then a breeze would blow up Sixth that wiggled Candi's Afro puffs. It felt so good being with her that I ignored the lower back pain my black platform shoes were causing me.

Sixth Avenue on a Saturday evening was empty for long stretches. All the flower and plant shops were shuttered. So were all the tiny, dingy delis that catered to the flower shop trade. Now and then a fleet of cars burst out of the Village bringing with them a brief wave of light and noise. I started singing the Stylistics' "Betcha By Golly Wow" to Candi and she told me I had "a nice voice," which was cool, though I would have preferred her saying I had a "sexy voice" or a "beautiful voice" or a "strong voice." I fought off my mild irritation by squeezing her hand tighter.

Just above Fourteenth Street we walked past a McDonald's with a water fountain built into the front. Red and green lights surrounded the fountain and colored the water. Inside were bits of faux Spanish decor.

"Tacky," Candi decided.

"Some might call it fast-food elegant," I foolishly suggested.

"Nope," she said. "Tacky is the word."

"Except for hamburgers, right?"

"But," she said firmly, "we're not gonna have any tonight." We kept on walking.

We were in the Village now, following in the footsteps of so many young people in search of something we'd never seen before. Such as the group of young white men in tight-fitting leather biker outfits holding hands as they strolled by. Or the Pink Pussy Cat sex shop I threatened to drag Candi into, even though I was scared to go in myself. Or the dark, funky little restaurants that lined the streets and that all looked too chic, too adult, and too expensive for my little condom-marred wallet.

"Where do we eat?" she wondered.

Perplexed and intimidated by the variety, all I could say was, "Good question." Candi answered it for me by picking out a homey-looking Italian bistro across the street. Inside I was reassured when I looked at the menu. I figured out we could even have dessert and still have train fare back to Queens. Relieved, I went back to groping Candi. There's something about being a teenaged male on a date that turns a nice guy into an octopus.

We ordered a carafe of red wine and clicked glasses over the candle. After two glasses, Candi told me, "I wish we could go somewhere private." I agreed and, with a smirk, said, "Your place or mine?" This movie-derived witticism didn't get a smile from her. It wasn't easy to sneak off from our parents, and since Candi was on the fast track to the honor role, her parents were that much more mindful of what she was doing and where she was going. It was frustrating, but that's the way it was.

Candi asked if I wanted to play a game and then pulled a blue Bic pen out of her pocketbook. On her napkin she drew the straight crisscrossed lines of tic-tac-toe.

"Not tic-tac-toe."

"No," she whispered. "Candi's tic-tac-toe."

Instead of the traditional two horizontal and vertical lines, Candi drew three intersecting lines that created four spaces in every direction. Three in a row didn't win the game. It got you one point. Four in a row won you an additional half a point. Whoever got the most points won. Candi was X and I was O. The resulting game ended in a two-two tie.

I think she was toying with me that first game, because she won the next three easily before I quit.

"I don't wanna play anymore."

"Sore loser."

"I guess it's not the game I really wanna play with you. That's all."

"Okay," she said, putting her napkin in her purse, "I can't argue with that."

We squeezed hands over the subway tracks running back to Queens. I told her, "You know, I like you a lot" with a sincerity usually reserved for "I love you." She responded in kind. Then there was a lengthy silence broken by Candi. "Nobody," she announced, "will be at my house next Saturday but me."

"That's good," I said. "That sounds real good."

"Okay then," Candi replied, as I could feel her hand growing warm.

"Are you scared?" I asked.

"Anticipation, Derek. Anticipation."

Right then I vowed not to let anticipation mess me up as it had in the past. I had a whole week to be ready this time and I would be. For seven whole days I didn't masturbate. I ran around the Jackson High track every day after school. I went to sleep by eleven. My moms wondered if I was going to try out for the track team. I just said I was building up my stamina and left it at that.

Nine days after that evening in the Village I sleepwalked into Jackson High and made a left turn in the direction of the guidance offices. Being a Monday, I was dazed and grumpy. I've never been a morning person so I'd already seen two people I knew and ignored, simply to avoid the burden of communication. Still, this wasn't a typical Monday. This Monday was different from all the Mondays that had come before because just two days earlier I'd had sex with someone I had serious feelings for.

Candi was standing in the guidance counselor's doorway talking to Andre, a six-foot-four-inch guy in red and white Converses, who was telling her he was a lock to make the basketball team and how good it would be to have her cheer for him. I could tell she was half listening, her Afro puffs moving up and down, her singsong voice going "That's nice" and "Uh huh." When she saw me I had this deep urge to turn around and sprint out of the building. Too late.

Softly she said, "Good morning."

"Let's go somewhere more private," I said and she scampered off to grab her books. She kissed my lips lightly as Andre stood by gawking jealously. Ordinarily I would have basked in having this audience for Candi's devotion to me. This Monday morning all I could think was "Why am I suddenly so scared?" As Candi and I walked down the hall I blurted out, "I'm sorry," and she asked why.

"I wasn't—" No, that didn't sound good. I tried again. "I kinda rushed out on Saturday so I didn't, you know, talk." She smiled and squeezed my waist. I was trying to apologize for not calling on Sunday, but I kept getting flustered, which she found funny.

When I wanted to know why she was laughing, Candi said, "Remember, the phone works both ways." I wasn't quite sure if that meant no calling had been okay or that she purposefully hadn't called me either. I was gonna ask for some clarification, but Candi was already on to the next subject. She asked, "Did you mean what you said?"

"Which thing?" I replied stupidly.

Now she acted a little upset. "You know which thing and you know when you said it."

Getting stupider by the second, I replied, "Did you?" This was a delaying tactic, but Candi wasn't about to be distracted.

"Yes," she said confidently, "I meant what I said. I always mean it when I say I love somebody. Don't you?"

Well, I just grabbed her sweet face in my hands and kissed her hard and sloppy. It wasn't that I was overcome with emotion. I just didn't know how to answer her question. Kissing seemed like the thing to do. Kissing Candi made me feel like we were back in her bedroom with incense burning and Barry White on her eight-track real low, when the "I love you's" flowed like water.

But this was a Monday morning, a school day when her parted lips demanded words, not romantic deeds. A long kiss was not enough on a Monday morning. "Let's not talk about this now" had to be the goofiest transition out of a kiss ever uttered. And, unfortunately, I said it. As Candi's face registered her dismay, the passing bell rang, the hall filled, and she moved away from me into the flow of our classmates.

I told myself, "If she wants every guy who screws her to love her, she's in trouble." I liked her a lot. But did I love her? I did say I did. She said so, too. I mean, we both obviously had wanted to sleep together and she was a virgin. That made it special for her, and it was supposed to be special for me, too. Maybe I didn't understand how important this was for her. Or did I understand and not want to admit it in the cold light of Monday?

Four hours later I watched Candi's ass twist left, then right, and then slide down onto the cinder track of Jackson High. She was first and then the other green-skirted rumps under her command slid down, mirroring her move. When they had all finally landed upon the track Candi led a cheer of "JACKSON!" and she and the other cheerleaders twirled their pom-poms and made a V with their arms. They held this pose for two beats and then Candi called for a break.

As the cheerleaders dusted off, I walked down the concrete stadium steps and made eye contact with her. Candi walked through the black metal gate that separated the track from the stands, came up the steps, kissed me, and hand in hand we walked to the very top of the stands. Candi got right down to it. "I think I went too far in what I said this morning."

"No," I interrupted, "it was me. I didn't go far enough." With the clumsy enthusiasm of a baby snatching a rattle I embraced her. She tried hard to squirm out of my arms, but I wasn't letting go. It was as though I wanted to communicate my love through the warmth of this hug, as if words were really inadequate to the feelings I had. Then I went for it. "Candi," I said, "I was there, too. I don't want what we did to become something bad for either of us. I want it to grow, and I think that's what you want, too. That's why you asked that question. You weren't sure about me. You wanted to know you could trust me. You're my lady now. That should answer your question."

I can be so damn corny. But as at the Jamaica Theater, it was corny from the heart, which I figured was the thing that made it all right.

And good love songs are corny in this way. My statement finished, I loosened my hold on Candi and she stared off into the distance. I guess she was gathering her thoughts. Then she was all over me, kissing my face, licking my embryonic beard, and running her hands over my bony ribs. When she licked my ear behind closed eyes, I whispered, "You can put that in my mouth if you want to."

"What? And spoil you again? You already think you're Richard Roundtree now. Next thing I know you'll be wearing leather jackets and turtleneck sweaters." I laughed and Candi hopped on down the steps, called her cheerleaders together to work through their routines again.

I sat there watching Candi feeling very relieved. I'd never made love to a virgin before and, though I didn't know it then, I never would again. This was sex with emotion, sex with love, sex as pleasing and complicated as anything I'd felt up to that point. That felt cool to me. I sat watching Candi lead the Jackson cheerleaders the rest of that afternoon, positive there was no more important thing in the world.

"Turn Back the Hands of Time"

When r&b was still called soul it was the soundtrack of black working-class life. It was Gladys Kinght & the Pips that Atlanta mothers listened to on transistors when they picked up their kids from elementary school on Auburn Avenue. It was the Four Tops emanating from the speakers of an off-duty Detroit policeman's electric blue Cadillac whose tail fins threatened to send his ride flying across West Grand Boulevard. It was the voice of the Impressions featuring Curtis Mayfield gliding out of a Motorola Hi-Fi, as a little boy in Baldwin Hills reluctantly took out the garbage. It was the sound of an optimistic, Christian, God-fearing, much-repressed but never-broken people who saw freedom in government work, picket signs, and the sweet textures of female background singers swaying on the two and the four.

Soul was the music of Mr. Walt's barbershop on Hollis Boulevard in Queens in the years I was growing up. There was a large jukebox in the back of the place, right next to the one restroom and the life-size cut-out of a brown-skinned, bikini-clad sister holding a bottle of Wild Irish Rose. The bass knob was always at 10, so you'd hear the fingers of Duck Dunn, James Jamerson (and later James Jamerson, Jr.), and Bootsy Collins competing with the voices of soul singers from the metropolises of Memphis, Detroit, and Cincinnati. No one seemed to mind the sonic imbalance, though. For nearly twenty years I got my hair cut to the throb of bass lines that flowed from the jukebox through the clippers and right into my scalp.

Everything in that room had a pulse to it—the way people flipped through *Jet*, the way mothers popped their sons on the side of the head for fidgeting in the barber chair, the way strokes of Mr. Walt's clippers sent two weeks of bushy Afro floating earthbound, and the way his son, Little Walt, guided his broom across the light beige linoleum, pushing masses of dirty, dandruff-infected hair into the corner, and the way scissors put the finishing touches on yet another beautifully sculpted head. When Mr. Walt was on his game, brothers and sisters left his establishment with wondrous black halos that put a bop in their step, a sway in their hips.

Not only was Mr. Walt's place as funky as fatback in August and his skills as precise as the right amount of vinegar in pigs' feet, but he was a joy to be around. Not that he was a talker. On the contrary, Mr. Walt was a conversation facilitator. It was all "Mmmm hummm" and "Ah ha" and "You don't say" and "How 'bout that?" and "I read somethin' 'bout that in the *Daily News*" and "Goddamn!" and, when he was really excited, "Goddamn" twice with more emphasis on the second "damn." Whether you were in the barber chair or sitting on one of the brown and yellow checked vinyl kitchen chairs he used for seats, Mr. Walt was like a laser that moved about the shop seeking out the voice that could keep the flow going. There were other barbers there—his cousin Big Al and a kid named C. C. from Tennessee—but if Mr. Walt took a day off it was like the tempo was off, as if Booker T. didn't show up for a Stax session with Otis.

Like most everyone in St. Albans I liked Mr. Walt and often stopped by to hang out. Mr. Walt discouraged this practice. He'd say firmly, "I don't want no idle Negroes turning this shop into a street corner." But Mr. Walt loved that I read the back of album covers and knew that the bass player in MFSB (Ronnie Baker) also played with Salsoul Orchestra and that the same guy who produced "Just My Imagination" (Norman Whitfield) made the *Car Wash* soundtrack. He even murmured "Ah ha" and "You don't say" to me just like I was one of the neighbor elders, which, of course, I loved. Which, of course, made his son hate me even more.

Little Walt and I had never really seen eye to eye. Back in kindergarten we'd argued over who got to use the Playdoh first and he'd ended up trying to stick a big aqua pile of it up my nose. It never got any better between us. To me, Little Walt was a sullen, withdrawn, sad-eyed lump. Like his father, Little Walt didn't have much to say—he just didn't have the savvy to turn it into a virtue. He brushed fallen hair into corners and watched people talk through envious dark brown eyes.

Topics varied from Walt Frazier versus Jerry West (the nod always going to Clyde), the perpetually sad state of Queens' sewers, whether the Mets' Tommy Agee could be compared to Willie Mays (a joke, of course), who was finer, Pam Grier or Cicely Tyson (I went for "Foxy Brown"), whether the young Cassius Clay could beat the older Ali (a toss-up), and whether disco was some plot to destroy black music ("probably" was the consensus). Sports, women, politics, and money were the anchors for all talk, and I soaked up tons of barbershop wisdom. Older brothers were real suspicious of their women's motives for loving them, which was strange since, judging by the general lechery of the conversations, their women had a lot more to worry about.

White people, as a general concern, came up only in relation to specific instances (a boss who harassed his black workers; a cop who made his ticket quota in our neighborhood), but otherwise white racism was so much a given that only a shocking new outrage really excited the customers. Most folks were too busy trying to keep up the mortgage, their kid's ever-changing shoe size, and taxes to ponder the white man. So I made it my business not to worry about what white people thought about me and kept my mind on what I was trying to do. It just seemed practical.

The only bad thing about Mr. Walt's was that conversations about money too often turned to my pops. As I said earlier, undertakers have a special place in the black community. Sooner or later everybody deals with them and never under the best circumstances. While their work commands respect, nobody really loves an undertaker and, just below the surface, everybody thinks there's something ghoulish about the job. But some folks in the community had a deeper beef with Pops. Rumor was that he overcharged. That the white man on 155th Street, O'Malley, gave folks a better price.

John McCoy was a stocky and stupid sanitation man whose eldest son had been tragically killed by a drunk postal worker while chasing a softball in the street. McCoy beefed about the way that Pops wouldn't cut him any slack on the coffin he wanted. In fact, he had the nerve to claim Pops raised the price on the carnations in the viewing room out of spite, thus forcing the McCoys to bury their son at O'Malley's. When I brought these accusations home to Moms she'd just say, "Don't bother your daddy with this street talk." So I didn't.

Then one hot afternoon at Mr. Walt's, McCoy happened to come in for a shape-up while Pops was in the chair. I was standing by the juke-box dropping in a quarter to hear Tyrone Davis' "Turn Back the Hands of Time" when Little Walt whispered harshly, "Your daddy's gonna get his ass kicked."

McCoy sat his fat sanitation department booty right across from the barber chair and picked up a *Jet* with Bill Cosby and Sidney Poitier grinning on the cover. But he didn't look down. McCoy stared at Pops while Mr. Walt talked about the difference between Virginia and South Carolina porgies with C. C., quite mindful of McCoy's bad attitude.

McCoy quickly managed to connect dead fish with dead people. "You better watch your blade with Harper there, Mr. Walt," he inter-jected. "You cut that cat too close and you won't be able to pay for your own funeral. Liable to have to bury yourself right there under your barber chair." That produced a good-natured laugh from a few people. It was a little needle. Things could have ended there. Then McCoy pushed it. "Had to bury my son with the white man, Walt. An Irishman, at that."

Mr. Walt came back with, "Ain't your name McCoy?"

"Yeah," the sanitation man replied.

Mr. Walt said, "Well, all right then," and chuckled.

Pops raised his hand for Mr. Walt to stop cutting. Sitting forward in his chair, he squinted at McCoy like he was far away. "Your grief is deep, McCoy," he began, "so deep and genuine I don't expect you to hear what I have to say. So I don't say this for you. I say this now, so that it wasn't like your concerns were never answered. But, as I say, I don't expect you to hear me.

"I treat the deceased with all the care I can. I am one black man. Like Mr. Walt here I serve black people only. Not because I tell white people not to come to my place of business but because they don't. That means I can't get the Bernsteins or Rizzutos or, no disrespect intended, the real McCoys, either. My clients are a select group, just like Mr. Walt's. Mr. Walt charges six dollars for a shave and a cut. I know other barbers who charge one dollar or a dollar fifty less. But Mr. Walt serves this neighborhood, and to serve this neighborhood, which means us—us being all black people 'round here—the man has to stay in business. The rent man, the gas man, the taxman know only one color. I was disappointed I didn't serve your family in a time of need. That's the truth I'm speaking to you, McCoy." He hesitated a moment. "But I'm trying to stay open for everybody who might need me. Everybody. That's really all I have to say." Pops sat back in the chair and asked Mr. Walt to resume his cutting.

It was quiet as McCoy's face squirreled up into a knot and his analytical powers, which I could tell were limited, tossed around Pops' words. Finally McCoy stood up and yelled, "Are you comparing my son's death to a hair cut?!"

I got filled with that most dreaded of childhood fears: the thought of my father getting beat up in front of me. Pops didn't move a muscle. It was as if McCoy's remark was beneath him, a quality that probably irritated McCoy in the first place. Mr. Walt quickly moved to intercede. "I will not have any confusion in my shop, McCoy," he said, clippers buzzing in his hand. This could have been a bad moment. Pops was acting a bit too regal. Mr. Walt was being too nice, and McCoy was angry as hell.

At that moment Edgecombe Lennox sauntered in through the door and everything was all right. "Well," his melodious baritone announced, "it sure is hot in here today." He strolled into the middle of the room, took off his beige Kangol cap to wipe his brow with a sky blue handkerchief, and positioned himself between Mr. Walt and McCoy, with his back to the uptight sanitation man. Ordinarily, I suspect McCoy would have rolled right on, but Edgecombe was quite a sight.

Six foot four with broad shoulders and a large round head, Edgecombe was garbed in Kangol, leather pants, a silk shirt open to his belly, three slender gold chains, and Bally Loafers, all of it a bone-colored shade of beige. In his right hand, wrapped in two diamond rings so bright they'd blind a manicurist, were a stack of 45s. I'd heard Edgecombe spoken of, but this was my first time seeing him.

As I looked on in awe, Edgecombe greeted Mr. Walt and introduced himself to my pops who, for all his outward detachment, had to be genuinely relieved at the distraction. However, Edgecombe was to be more than a delay in the proceedings—the man was a full-scale interruption. "I didn't bring these around here for my health," he announced, holding up the stack of vinyl. "I got the new Millie Jackson record right here. That is they're here for anybody who likes free records." A gray-haired Grandma with two anxious eight-year-olds in tow, grabbed two and said, "I love me some Millie Jackson!" Edge leaned over to the kids and held out two quarters in his free hand. Both quarters were painted red, which struck me as peculiar. "Why don't you go tell some folks they giving out free records over at Mr. Walt's," he suggested as the quarters were removed from his hand and the eight-year-olds scampered out the door.

McCoy was already looking a little befuddled when Edgecombe handed him a record and said, "It's Millie Jackson's follow-up to 'Caught Up.' She may not be your thang, but I bet your woman will enjoy it." When McCoy replied, "Thanks," I knew his anger had been defeated. A few more kids ran in, followed closely by their mothers. Edgecombe was at the center of the room and they all crowded around, creating a demilitarized zone between Pops and McCoy. Mr. Walt cautiously resumed cutting Pops' head and McCoy, slowly, like water on a sidewalk in June, evaporated. By the time Edgecombe had (with my gracious assistance) opened the jukebox, inserted Millie Jackson's latest, and played it twice for our edification, McCoy was gone and Pops was well shorn with no loss of dignity. He split to check out Moms' doing the books at the funeral home and I stuck around Mr. Walt's. That aborted confrontation, a moment maybe when I should have gotten more insight into my pops and his thinking, went right past me at the time. I remember it clearly now, but Edgecombe Lennox was all I thought of then.

You see, Edgecombe Lennox aka Edge, which his main men called him, was the first person I met who was in the music business, and the impact of that obscured what came before. The man was clearly cool in dress and manner. And Edge was a talker, a man ready to spin a tale of rhythm & blues at the drop of a needle. After dispensing his free records, Edge spent the afternoon talking about the Apollo Theater and Millie Jackson and Joe Simon and James Brown and other stars he'd worked with.

Edge explained to me that a promotion man did two things. "I get records played on the radio." Then he shoved another red quarter in the jukebox to play Millie Jackson's record again. "I bring them over to the station, talk to my friends there, and they play them. I'm friends with all the deejays, ya understand. Now part of getting them on the air is to get people buying the record before radio even plays it. That's the second thing. Mr. Walt's is one of those places where black people congregate. So I give him a few of my special quarters to play my records when the place is crowded and I give him a few free records for the jukebox. It's as simple as that, youngblood." Of course there was a lot more to it than that, but I guess he figured the basics were enough for a teenager.

He wondered why I was so curious. I told him I was a songwriter and wanted to be like Stevie Wonder. He said, "Keep writing songs. That's good you're doing that." Then he smiled and added, "Get with one of these little bookworm kids around here that's going to law school and hire him." I wondered why I just couldn't get a big-time lawyer now. "Well, it's all about trust, youngblood." This was all a little too vague for me so I really started peppering him with questions. I followed him out the door where a bone-beige Coup de Ville that matched his ensemble sat parked next to a fire hydrant. As he got in his Caddy I made an innocent query: "What should I do now, Edge?"

He turned to me and, with what I perceived as the utmost sincerity said, "Write songs. Write a lot of them since it takes awhile to hit. In fact, write twenty songs. Write twenty of the best songs you can. Then listen to them and when you know what's wrong with them, throw them all away. All twenty. Then write twenty more. When you understand what's wrong with that next twenty, you sit down and make them better. Once you've done all that, then you give me a call." He held out his card, moving it in front of me as my eyes followed it like a healthy sister's behind. "Don't call me until you know how to fix that second twenty 'cause you won't be ready until then. You understand?"

I nodded my head affirmatively and palmed that card and felt like the lyrics in my notebook would soon be gold. I know now, of course, that he was humoring me. It didn't hit me until Moms came upstairs with my trashcan the next day, wondering why it was filled with all these crumpled little white balls of paper. After listening to my earnest recitation of Edge's advice, Moms told me, "I think you're rushing things, son. You see, what Mr. Lennox was getting at was that it takes time to understand how to write songs. You have to write a lot of not bad but incomplete songs before you really get the hang of it."

I asked her, "You think he wants me to write bad or incomplete songs on purpose? You know, just to learn what not to do?"

"No, Derek," she said. "Don't make it sound so complicated. He just doesn't want you to rush into it. Take your time. Learn. Where's that card he gave you?" I showed it to Moms and she suggested she hold onto it. I didn't much care for that idea figuring, quite rightly, I'd never see that card again. But I'd already memorized what it said:

EDGECOMBE LENNOX
Promotion Director
Spring Records
729 Seventh Avenue
New York, NY 10000

Still, I took her words to heart and uncrumpled all the little white paper balls. Every time I went to Mr. Walt's I asked about Edge, but I was always just missing him or he was coming much later, until one day Mr. Walt said Edge had gotten a promotion. He was vice president over at Spring now and he wouldn't have time to visit anymore. Little Walt came over holding two tickets to see Tyrone Davis and Millie Jackson at the Felt Forum. "Edge left them for me and my father," he teased. "Then we're all going to a party at Leviticus disco." Leviticus was the black disco in Manhattan in the seventies. Jealousy overwhelmed me. Had I made a bad impression? Maybe if I'd been a singer he would have been more interested. As teenagers will, I tortured myself over this "rejection" for several long nights while listening to AM radio. I even made one of those juvenile vows that whenever I saw Edge again I was going to have a song ready for him. Yes, indeed, I'd have a song ready.

"I Love Music"

After meeting Edge my musical ambitions really kicked in. Running track was out. Studying was de-emphasized. Even Candi was pushed back. During my junior year I fell in with a snobbish clique of musicians, all seniors, who used the Jackson High band room for unauthorized jam sessions, while viewing many of the music teachers with contempt. They were notorious for dropping "Three Blind Mice" into a concert performance for the entire school of "Battle Hymn of the Republic" as a commentary on the unadventurous instruction they were receiving.

The clique's leader was Donald Dillon, a demon bassist who sported a goatee à la Mingus, though his immediate idols were Weather Report's Jaco Pastorious and Return to Forever's Stanley Clarke. This was bass playing for bassists who envied lead guitarists. It was noteworthy for its high-pitched tunings, long and plentiful solos, and disdain for the in-the-pocket bass aesthetic of r&b. In the years after Miles Davis' *Bitches Brew*, jazz fusion's pyrotechnic flash was what cool kids were into, and Dillon, light-skinned, bushy-haired, and vain, saw this music as a logical extension of his "look." Abdul Hazzard on drums, Galyn Jones on piano and electric keyboards, and B. J. Timmons on guitar and vocals were the other core members. Timmons was the least musically pretentious of the crew's members, which was why he brought me, a hardcore r&b man, into their circle.

Initially I was optimistic these guys would help me with my songs. Be my muse, so to speak. Every now and again I'd get them to try out one of my tunes. They'd noodle around with the song a little, and make the odd good suggestion. But Dillon's heart was never in it. He'd say, "It needs more work," and then put down his lead sheet and play some complicated Weather Report riff as if to cleanse his fingers from the taint of my music. Sooner or later the other guys would join Dillon and so I'd be left to gather up my lead sheets and sit quietly in a corner. This happened three or four times before I realized this was not my backing band to be. I could have walked away then and sought out some younger, more respectful musicians. But this was the best band in my age range in St. Albans, which is saying a lot since in every other basement in that part of Queens kids had musical equipment. Plus, I'd never been around a band before and the romance of the thing seduced me.

Though they saw themselves as progressive jazzmen, on weekends they'd play gigs as the Contemporaries. Their card read, "If it's contemporary, we play it." Wedding receptions. Birthday bashes. Bar mitzvahs. The works. They liked the checks, had contempt for the audiences, and always stuck some jazz instrumentals into the mix for themselves. I wanted to be down, so I became their roadie. I'd haul equipment from Timmons' father's van to the gig. I'd drive the van. I even wore sunglasses at night to give off that bodyguard look when they were collecting cash. Still, I didn't get to play much. Every now and then I filled in as second keyboardist on certain songs. Acutely aware of my instrumental limitations, I never overplayed my hand. However, my being humble didn't move Dillon, who seemed to view timidity as weakness. At best they'd let me play on Stevie's "Superstition" because I knew the song so damn well. If a gig called for all jazz, I'd be a mule all night. Maybe I'd get a piece of Herbie Hancock's "Chameleon," but on something traditional like Miles' "All Blues," Dillon's eyes would get all big if I even looked at the electric piano. Timmons was sympathetic, arguing that I wouldn't ever get better if I didn't get a chance to learn, but Dillon's views were law with the Contemporaries.

In seventy-six, the Bicentennial year, I got my revenge on Dillon. It was called disco. P-Funk, Earth, Wind & Fire, the Commodores, and Cameo had been all right. It was funky. It was melodic. It was band music. Of course, we didn't yet know—no one knew—that this was the last era of band music in black pop, but it was clear something was changing. Disco, a highly produced, soft dance music was starting to dominate New York's radio and clubs and people wanted it for their social events. Dillon damned it as too rigid, too predictable, too stupid. By spring seventy-six, disco was hot enough around town that disco deejays were starting to scoop up gigs. The turning point for the Contemporaries occurred in March when we lost out on an engagement party to a deejay who—was this possible?—talked over the records!

After that, Timmons called an emergency meeting of the Contemporaries. "I don't love this music," he began, "but money is money. I was counting on us earning enough money this year so that I could buy a new ride to take with me to college. I'm going to UCLA and no ride out there means no pussy. Simple as that. I got to have a new ride. We got to make some money this spring. The Contemporaries have got to play some disco." Timmons then presented a list of tunes people had requested that the Contemporaries were going to have to learn to play. On that list was Silver Convention's "Fly Robin Fly," K.C. & the Sunshine Band's "Shake, Shake, Shake (Shake Your Booty)," George Mc-Crae's "Rock Your Baby," Double Exposure's "Ten Percent," The Trammps' "That's Where the Happy People Go," Tavares' "Heaven Must Be Missing an Angel," and Van McCoy's "The Hustle." Dillon looked like he was going to cry. "I don't wanna play this crap, man. I will not play shake your booty."

"You think I want to?" Timmons replied. "I love what we play in here. But the Contemporaries weren't created to be a jazz band, Dillon. We play for Grandmas and little kids and shit. They wanna hear what's on the radio and our problem is that we just happen to be in New York, the damn disco capital of the world. Either we play it or become a straight-up jazz band. My heart is with that. But my dick is telling me get a car, baby."

Dillon just sat there, plucking his bass strings and fondling the instrument like it would ward off evil.

"Come on, Dillon," Timmons pleaded, "we can't do this without you, brother."

"Okay," he answered finally. "Okay. I'm not arranging this mess, though. I'm not spending that much time listening to it."

"I'll do it," I volunteered way too cheerfully. "I actually like a lot of those songs."

Dillon just rolled his eyes and said, "That figures."

Along with Timmons, I wrote the lead sheets and worked on how our little band could approximate some of these overwrought disco productions. Listening to these records was painful for Timmons. I could feel his condescending stare on the side of my head when I got excited about "Heaven Must Be Missing an Angel." I didn't care. I'd already figured something out—something that would work for me the rest of my career. Disco was, from the perspective of song structure, not that different from r&b or soul. It usually went verse-chorus-verse-chorus-verse-bridge-chorus-tag or verse-verse-chorus-verse-chorus-bridge-chorus-tag just like hundreds of songs before it. It was just that the tags went on and on long after the vocals had faded. Lyrically speaking, the O'Jays' "I Love Music" or Carol Douglas's "Doctor's Orders" still used metaphor and story techniques right out of Motown. Disco songs were pop songs no sillier than the Miracles' "Mickey's Monkey" or Shorty Long's "Function at the Junction." Disco songs were longer because dancers wanted more dance time and records were now physically longer. If they'd had 12-inch singles when the Supremes made "I Hear a Symphony," Diana Ross would have been cooing for seven minutes instead of three (see "Love Hangover" for a reference point).

Song structure doesn't change. Melodies evolved though the classics are always recycled, as they often were. But rhythms will always be fluid. Dancers are a restless bunch. Always on the hunt for a new reason to grind their hips. The instrumentation of one era gives way to the instrumentation of the next. Listening to Gloria Gaynor's version of "Never Can Say Goodbye" is all about this lesson. The Jackson Five original is a legitimately great record. Michael declares his devotion to his girl, the arrangement had real drama, and the whole thing was kind of gently heartbreaking. Gaynor's record was long and bright and happily monotonous, which made it a perfect artifact for its time. I took pleasure in thinking a purist like Dillon, for all his damn chops, would be trapped by them into wanting music the way he wanted it. I'd do what dancers demanded and always find work.

So we started doing disco and it helped. Still, it didn't save the Contemporaries. People wanted to have a guy with records and two turntables come to their wedding reception and play MFSB. The killing blow was a reception at Flushing Meadows Park. The family had hired a deejay to play between our sets. What a disaster. The floor was filled every time he threw on the latest disco jam. People were hustling their asses off. Next to real disco we sounded fake. Dillon began consuming bottles of Heineken at a rapid rate and managed to pop a bass string—a real musical rarity. In the van on the way back to St. Albans he quit the Contemporaries. Timmons thought he'd change his mind after he'd sobered up. Next afternoon, in the clear light of day, Dillon didn't waver. "I'm just gonna be the new Jaco. Disco," he spat out, "was soul-killing music."

The other guys were devastated. Me, I was pissed. After all, I was just getting to play regularly. Still, just being around a band, working on arrangements, and playing in front of people had helped me mature. There probably wasn't much more for me to learn from this particular band. The next lesson in my musical education came from Vernon Jackson, and the fruits of our partnership would be much more tangible.

Traveling the Highway to Heaven (Part 1)

I first encountered Vernon Jackson in Sunday school when I was eleven and he was nine. Vernon had a voice blessed by God and an intense desire to be heard. Without that voice he'd have been just another little religious black boy from a big family in Jamaica, Queens. He would have dumped his weekly quarters in the collection plate, sang "Yes, Jesus Loves Me" once a week, and played softball in Baisley Park. However, Vernon's blessing gave him a very different kind of childhood.

By ten, Vernon was vocalizing with the main choir at his church. By eleven, he was soloing, and by thirteen, he was an attraction that toured around the city. He had women pinching his cheeks, older men envying his skill, and never had time to play ball between rehearsals and Bible study. By sixteen, when he re-entered my life, he was a minor legend among the church people in New York City and was quietly going out of his mind.

Child stardom is one of the nastiest tricks God can play on a kid. The Lord gives you a gift beyond your years that elevates you, advances you, and eventually traps you. It brings your parents money, your family prestige, and invests you with a specialness everyone craves and that you never forget.

Which is the problem. Time passes, hormones kick in. In the course of one summer you grow four inches. Vernon Jackson, a cutey at eight, was by sixteen acne-scarred and roly-poly, trapped between a beautiful child life and an uncertain adult existence. He could still sing, though his voice had darkened and now often sounded better sour than sweet. There were many new angelic singers younger than Vernon, and he looked upon them enviously, that is when their very presence didn't make him cry.

At Jackson High he hung with a clique of pious born-again kids who'd sing gospel songs in the cafeteria to drown out boom boxes broadcasting "offensive" songs, and for the most part, Vernon's world and mine didn't intersect. It's strange really. I was the son of an undertaker and he a gospel singer. Seems like we might have hung. We had God or at least death in common.

So when Moms brought him over for dinner one Sunday night I hadn't said much more than a hello to Vernon since our Sunday school days. He had a round body, a small head that looked sunken amid the cluster of jheri-curls encircling his face. The curls were well maintained, but his skin was unruly, marked by pimples and black heads that resulted from his misguided attempts to bust the pimples. Even at dinner, where he displayed impeccably good manners, his hand regularly moved to his cheeks and chin to squeeze offending bumps. If he weren't so earnest (and I wasn't sitting with my parents), I would have been laughing at him.

It wasn't strange that Vernon was a dinner guest. Since Pops was on the stiff side, and churches are to funeral homes as pitchers are to catchers, good relations with the religious community was essential. Moms was always inviting church people over—ministers, deacons, choir leaders, the ladies who baked pies for church sales. Anybody who attended services at a Christian church in South Queens could end up eating the Harper family chow come Sunday. But her favorite church was the First Baptist of St. Albans, a brick building with modest stained glass and old ratty hymn books, but that always had the most intense choir in all of black Queens. It was fronting this choir that made Vernon a star, and it was because of that stardom that he ate with us that Sunday afternoon.

"Derek," my moms started, "I've been telling Vernon that you've been writing songs."

"Yes," Vernon chimed in. "Your mother tells me, you've written a lot of songs."

"Yeah," I admitted. "It's fun, you know. It's like a puzzle. Putting words and music together."

Then my pops cut in, "Puzzles are games. Games aren't what life's about. I guarantee you that." This was really the first time Pops had spoken about my songwriting. He'd heard me mention it at dinner before, but this was the closest thing to an opinion he'd offered. Though he certainly didn't seem too enthused, Pops' input on something outside of business was rare.

"Well, that's only if it's a playful song, honey," my moms replied.

Pops wasn't gonna keep her from her agenda. "If the songs he writes are about something meaningful, and they touch people, then they aren't games. They become more than that."

"Yes, Mr. Harper," Vernon added. "The gospel song is a song of good news. It brings people closer to their final union with our savior Jesus Christ." Then his focus turned to me. "Your mother has shown me some of your lyrics." I cut Moms a dirty look she ignored. "You have a gift, Derek. I've been singing since I was eight. I know a good song." He reached into his jacket pocket and pulled out an extremely wrinkled piece of paper. He started sing-saying the words "Let love flow," stretching out the last word by adding a lot of "ooooo's." Then he sang the verses "Let it fall all over me like a river and let it roll across my skin for days."

"Hey, I wrote that!"

"I hope you don't mind, Derek. I let Vernon look at it."

Mind? Hell, no. I couldn't believe my ears. It was an incredible feeling to hear my words being sung by such an amazing voice. So I said, "That sounded beautiful."

"Thank you," he said. "Did I get the melody right?"

"Pretty close."

"Thank you again. But one thing was wrong, Derek."

"What?"

"It wasn't written in praise of the Lord."

"That's right," Moms spoke with righteous glee. "It would be great if you worked with Vernon to write some gospel songs. Don't you agree, honey?"

Pops seemed as surprised by this suggestion as I was. And, just as plainly, my moms thought it was a great idea. So Pops said, "I imagine I do agree." I got the feeling he wanted to add, "It might be good for business," and if Vernon wasn't at the table I bet he would have.

Vernon upped the ante. "You see, Derek, there's a city-wide gospel singing competition in May, and I'm scheduled to compete in the male gospel category. It would be a bonus to debut a new song there. I have some ideas, but I need some help. Your mother suggested you. After reading some of your lyrics I was impressed enough to come here tonight and offer you the opportunity to have some of your music performed and to praise the Lord. What do you think of that, Derek?"

Vernon was a very persuasive talker. I didn't even think about how strange it was that a certified gospel star was approaching a relatively immature talent when established songwriters should have been jumping at the chance. Two writing sessions later I understood why. Number one, Vernon was a very undisciplined singer. It's one thing to shout and scream with a choir, a booming Hammond B3 organ and a congregation goading you on. It's another to be in my basement on a Thursday evening shouting as I hum a melody line. He'd start off all right, but midway through his internal accelerator would kick in and he'd start speeding up. If you've ever seen Patti LaBelle or Mariah Carey deconstruct a song in concert, you get the picture.

This man-child was also extremely bitter. Vernon was mad at his parents for making cash off his talent. He was mad at church people for once praising him and now treating him as a has-been. He'd start, "I was a cute kid. Some people thought I was beautiful." Then really wallow in it, "So now they whisper that's all it was. That I looked like Michael Jackson then and just like Michael Jackson, now, I have pimples and no future." No one remembers now, but in the mid-seventies there were two or three years when Michael wasn't happening and his future looked cloudy. Vernon was always alluding to Michael Jackson which, at that particular moment in time, meant child brilliance and teenaged confusion.

One other thing about Vernon that was disconcerting was his sexuality, or lack thereof. He'd refer to "the Lord's admonitions against carnality" and "the flaunting of the flesh" and "the visual blasphemy" of halter tops, hot pants, and spandex pants. Preachers spewed that stuff like brown leaves from October trees. Never had I heard it from a teenaged male, never from a boy younger than me. So Vernon had his problems, but the boy could sing real pretty. I'd sing along with him—which was like a house cat roaring with a lion—and I'd feel the force of his sound vibrate my damn chair. For all our differences, I'd never felt such a connection with someone through music.

Vernon knew every gospel song ever written. I'd hum something, or try an idea on the piano, and he'd name a song it sounded like. And happily for me, Vernon was impressed that I knew so much about black pop. We'd sit down there and I'd play him some r&b and he'd play me some gospel. If we never got a song out of the experience I figured we'd both end up knowing more music.

I particularly enjoyed hymns like "Peace in the Valley" and "Precious Lord." Old songs. Dignified songs. Not ageless maybe but truly timeless. Vernon grew partial to a song on the O'Jays' *Family Reunion* album called "Stairway to Heaven." The title first attracted him. Once drawn in, Vernon got caught up in how Gamble and Huff built drama into the orchestration and how Eddie Levert got off in the last third of the song and, finally, the mixed metaphor of climbing to a height of spiritual and sexual ecstasy (though he wouldn't admit it).

Somehow my affection for hymns and his for that O'Jay's song came together to produce "Traveling the Highway to Heaven." Here's a taste.

Traveling the highway to heaven
And now my feet don't feel a thing.
Traveling the highway to heaven
And now my vehicle is the praise I sing.
Traveling the highway to heaven
And my journey is to see the king.

It was an old-fashioned sing-a-long that the church ladies could clap to. At one point I had some shame and wanted to change highway to road, but Vernon wasn't going for it. Once that was settled, Timmons stopped by with his axe and we cut a demo version in my basement on a four-track machine he had. It was really sweet to hear my piano, Timmons' guitar, and Vernon's voice in harmony. I got such a thrill at that moment. It was the first time I'd ever heard anything I'd worked on sound so complete, so strong. It was the first truly satisfying artistic moment of my life and, like in that song by the Four Tops, I felt my nature rise. In some teenage sense I saw why artists neglected their lovers, their family, and the world.

Then the magic was over. We did three slightly different versions of the song. I ran off a copy for myself and then, with the desperation of a malnourished child, Vernon snatched up his cassette and rushed out of the house. This was a Saturday afternoon and it was the last I heard from him for a week. He didn't show up at church the next day. Didn't see him at school either, which was weird since church kids almost never cut school. When my moms called over to Vernon's house, his parents said he'd been in the city most of the week with his godfather. The competition was that next Sunday at Bibleway Church in Brooklyn and we'd have no time to write an arrangement. No time to rehearse. The anxiety was killing me.

A week after that glorious afternoon. Vernon showed up at my front door with two older men in suits. One was Jackie Ebets, the owner of Reach High Records, an indie label that released soul and gospel. He was a balding white man with intense eyes and the most patently fake smile this side of Ronald McDonald. The other, Zeke Rider, was a short, squat, dark-skinned man who looked beaten down by life. He was Vernon's godfather and new manager. Moms was on her way to look at Pops' books when they arrived, but she'd forgotten her number two pencils so she'd doubled back. In retrospect, I'm sure they'd waited for Moms to leave before ringing the buzzer. At the time I'd just thought it was a coincidence.

Vernon had played them the song and not only were they confident they'd win the competition, they thought "Highway" had the potential to become a gospel standard like "Peace in the Valley." Even better, in the short run, was $500 in cash and $1,000 in a check they offered me to control the publishing rights for my half of the song. Rider, who did most of the talking, said without such a contractual safeguard he wouldn't allow Vernon to perform it the next day. "Expose a song like that without it being signed to a significant publishing company," he said gravely, "and God knows who'll be recording it without permission tomorrow. No blasphemy intended, of course." Vernon nodded like he understood.

Neither my moms nor I knew all the implications of the offer, other than $1,500 would be great to have in the bank toward college tuition. My Moms should never have signed it or allowed me to without benefit of a lawyer (something Pops pointed out, quite loudly, that night over dinner). Still, Vernon, a true gospel child, endorsed Rider and Ebets and that meant a lot to her. The one wise thing Moms did was to cross out, almost on instinct, all option clauses.

"If they write more together and you gentlemen want to come back with a bigger offer, that's fine," she said. "But this song was written expressly for Vernon and we'd do nothing to stand in the way of his performing it tomorrow." Rider pressed for more options on whatever other songs we'd write together. Every time he did this beads of sweat formed on his nose. Ebets let Rider carry the ball on this, though I think he was the brains behind the deal. He was the one who finally ended negotiations by offering Rider a hanky to dry his nozzle.

Vernon's role was simply to smile at Moms whenever doubt flashed across her face and call me "my God-blessed friend." After we'd signed, Ebets pulled out an acetate copy of a 45 and asked if he could play it. The melody of "Traveling the Highway to Heaven" filled the living room. Instead of just a guitar and piano, there was a hefty-voiced choir, lots of hand clapping and foot stomping, and hyperactive rhythm arrangements. Vernon was singing all over himself again.

It wasn't bad, just too typical, with no build and no tease. Just unearned ecstasy all over the place. "See," Ebets boasted, "what a professional arrangement sounds like," as if I should have been grateful. It was apparent what Vernon had been doing all week.

At the competition, "Heaven" was even more boisterous and less nuanced. The drummer was heavy handed and made the rhythm gallop. Vernon garbled my carefully worded lyric with lots of gasps and shouts. I sat with my parents and Candi while getting deeply pissed off. The crowd got into it, but they got into most of the performances. A gospel crowd is extremely emotional and if you have a real commitment to God, one they can feel, the gospel crowd will rock with you all night long, even if the musicianship is shakey. What our version of "Heaven" would have done was soothe them and, I believe, stuck out more. Despite my reservations, Vernon still came in second among some very talented singers. But he lost out to an eleven-year-old boy preacher named Rev. Daniel Amos Robinson from the Bronx. Standing next to the young Reverend receiving the first-place trophy, Vernon looked like he'd seen the devil. The look of contempt etched on Vernon's mug was clear from the balcony and was not considered in keeping with the spirit the elders expected.

I tried to console him afterwards, but his anger at the gospel community seemed a permanent black spot on his once-clean soul. He vowed not to perform in New York again, which I told him was extreme, but he said, "They don't want me anymore. They don't like who I am now. Why should I sing praises before them? When I pray to myself, they don't hear. No one criticizes me then. I don't need them. I need Him."

Ebets was pissed when Vernon told him about his "retirement," but the engines of commerce roll on. Reach High records wiped Vernon's voice from the tracks and, in your classic ironic twist, Vernon's wet-nosed godfather got that young Reverend from the Bronx to sing on it. "Heaven" never became a gospel standard, but it was a minor hit on gospel radio throughout the Northeast and a few small royalty checks ($300 there, $250 there) started trickling in from the surprisingly honest people at Reach High.

I saw Vernon around school a lot the rest of the semester. He looked fine but seemed preoccupied. Word was he was moving to North Carolina over the summer to live with his grandparents. Moms was disappointed that I wasn't writing more gospel songs, but without Vernon's input I didn't think in those terms. Moms didn't give up easily. One Sunday I wandered in the house and there was Vernon Jackson at the dinner table. After dessert, Moms guided us back into the basement and, at her request, I played a couple of my half-assed gospel tunes for Vernon. "Your heart's not in that, Derek. Put in some worldly lyrics and then they'll work." Good advice. Then I made him an offer.

"If you sing them I'll change them. Come on and sing popular music. Do like Sam Cooke and Otis Redding and all those guys and come make this kind of music with me. I know we'll make money. Get college tuition. Get new cars. We'll have our own apartments by twenty-one."

Vernon sighed and then kind of batted his eyes at me. "I'd like to make you happy, Derek." There was a wan smile on his lips and worry lines in his brow. "But I can only sing about God. If I can't sing about Him, then I sure can't see myself singing about 'her.' Singing about loving her and wanting her would be a lie and to lie is to sin." Then he smiled all pretty. "You know I've never been with a girl." I told him I suspected he hadn't. "So how could I sing about loving a woman when I don't know anything about it?"

"But you know about loving Him?"

"That's all I've ever known."

That was a real emphatic sentence. Vernon looked at me hard and strong when he said that. But he made no other move and I didn't ask for clarification. All I could think of to reply was, "As long as you're happy." Then Vernon was gone, out of the basement, the house, and that phase of my life. In July he moved down to Winston-Salem, North Carolina, to be with grandparents and with God.

"Dazed and Confused"

No funeral ever affected our family as much as the one held August 1975. It was a small and intimate funeral that was held in room B, one of my Pops' more modest rooms. But this was no ordinary funeral—this was a death in our family. Uncle Teddy had gone out drinking on a Friday night and, as was his habit, he'd fallen asleep on a bench in the Van Dyck projects, a public housing complex across the street from the Tilden houses. Nothing new. He'd done this scores of times since moving to Brownsville in the early sixties.

But Brownsville, which had been a ghetto since the Jews moved in during the thirties, was now turning into something harder, something more vicious than it had been before. Some say it was a newly strung-out junkie who'd slashed his throat. An old lady who'd been up late sewing hems in a new dress swore she saw several young men wearing sleeveless, inside-out dungaree jackets of the Tomahawks gang dashing away. The housing police who called Aunt Alma to identify the body at 2:43 A.M. said there was no sign of a struggle, suggesting the killer slashed Uncle Teddy's throat and then, while his blood spilled, rifled through his pockets. I'd like to tell you more about who did it. However, only the killer and God knows who it was and neither has revealed himself. Vengeance was not ours. We had a dead father and husband and his family to contend with.

A few days after the funeral, Pops sat down with Aunt Alma and Moms in our living room to outline a family plan. While my cousin Anna and I listened in the kitchen, he said, "You could stay in Brownsville, Alma, and raise your girls there without a man. A lot of women do it." Then he paused and let the idea of her family alone in the projects without a male presence sink in.

"But," he said now, "I think I have a better idea, one that'll benefit everybody in the family." Pops' proposal was this: Aunt Alma would move back to Virginia with the two youngest girls, Alla and Alice, where, at least initially, Aunt Alma could work at his father's funeral home. "He's moving a little slow and could use some young legs around the office," Pops explained, "and it would be keeping that money in the family plus I know how he feels about you and the girls."

Aunt Alma asked, "But what about Anna?"

"Let Anna stay with us," he said cautiously. "It would be too far for her to commute to Brooklyn, but she could go to Jackson and her credits would still be good. Transferring New York credits to Virginia could be difficult, Alma. She wants to go to college up here, so she could still do what she needs to get into NYU or St. John's. And she could work at the funeral parlor after school and earn a little of the money my son isn't getting. You know how we feel about her, Alma. You know she'd be treated like a daughter."

Aunt Alma found Pops' logic sound, but she hesitated. It made sense to her; after all, Pops was great on practicality—but emotionally it was hard.

"I like the idea of going home and raising the little ones down

South. New York sure has taken from me more than it's given. You know that. But I'm not sure it's good for Anna to be separated from us so soon after Teddy's passing."

"That's true," Moms agreed.

Then Anna tapped me on the shoulder, whispered, "Move over," and walked right pass me into the living room. The girl just went right in there and imposed herself on grown folks' business. My moms used to say certain young people have an old soul and I guess this is what she meant. Anna walked right in and announced, "Excuse me for interrupting. But Ma, I wouldn't mind staying with Aunt Carrie and Uncle Elmer. So much has changed with Daddy gone. At least I could stay in New York. Like Uncle Elmer said, it would keep me from having to change what I was studying and make it easier for me to get into a school up here."

When she'd finished, Pops cocked his head sideways toward the kitchen and said, "Well, Derek, what do you think? I'm sure you have an opinion." Sheepishly I shuffled out into the living room and told everybody Pops' plan was "da joint," a response that, once translated for Pops, made him happy. Aunt Alma's reservations remained, but the sheer earnestness of Pops' logic overcame her unease. After Aunt Alma gave her consent, Pops got his Caddy and drove us all out to Coney Island where the girls rode the Wonder Wheel, my moms enjoyed screaming on the Cyclone roller coaster, and I wolfed down three large orders of fried shrimp with tartar sauce. It was a bittersweet night for a family that would never be quite the same. Uncle Teddy's murder had started the process, but now we Harpers were doing the heavy renovations ourselves.

The ramifications of that day wouldn't be clear for years. In the short run, however, it meant Anna became the daughter Moms and Pops had and lost. Her vitality brought a brightness to the dinner table that hadn't been in our home before. Coming from the projects in Brownsville to the middle-class haven of St. Albans, Anna saw everything with new eyes. She cracked us up at dinner talking about how stuck up the Cambria Heights girls were, or how corny the raps of Andrew Jackson boys were. Moms took her shopping for school clothes at Bloomingdale's but, after Anna had finished breaking down Moms' style, it was Moms who ended up with espadrilles, new bell bottoms,

S
E
D
U
C
E
D

and a sexy halter top. Pops, to my amazement, loved her new look, though he begged off at being made over himself. It would be easy to suggest that Anna's presence satisfied Moms' lingering despair over her miscarriage, but I'm just not sure that's true. After all, Anna was her sister's daughter, not hers, and she wasn't a small bundle of joy but a lanky, soulful teenager with a strong, independent way of looking at things.

Anna's presence on Pops (and Pops' on Anna) was probably more profound. After years of having to pick up after erratic Uncle Teddy, suddenly Anna was confronted with a male figure as consistent as Walt Frazier's jump shot. When Pops said, "I'll pick you up from school at three-thirty," he didn't mean 3:45 or 4 o'clock. He meant the Caddy would be purring outside the front gate at 3:30. This concept of male punctuality was as much a culture shock to Anna as having her own room. When late as usual, she would finally exit the school building, Pops wouldn't bark at her, as he had done so often with me. Instead, he'd be indulgently exasperated, upset but never mean. I noticed all this and was, of course, slightly jealous. If Anna had been a boy, I might have really flipped at the direct competition. As it was, I occasionally gritted my teeth and tried to understand.

What I couldn't understand, however, was Anna's horrible taste in men. Not two weeks into the school year Little Walt came walking in the door with Anna's books under one arm and her hand in the other. My immediate analysis was painfully simple: semirich middle-class boy wants to knock off semighetto pussy and tell everybody at Mr. Walt's about it, casting me in shame and putting my family's integrity on the line, so I'd have to fight the nigger. Then I'd never be able to get my hair cut at Mr. Walt's again. That's what I told myself.

Yeah, this was a rather self-centered, immature, and bugged view. I know this to be true because that's what Anna screamed at me in the basement the day she found out I'd warned Little Walt to leave her alone. It was our first argument ever and—can you believe it!—it was over that punk Little Walt. He became a regular on the Harper family sofa, a veritable staple at dinner just like corn on the cob and cabbage. And, if that had only been the extent of my woman problems that semester, I could have dealt with it. But things got more serious than Little Walt eating what normally would have been my second helping.

"There Goes My Baby"

Candi moved to Brooklyn. East Flatbush to be exact. It wasn't the end of the world, but it felt like several countries had disappeared. Her parents separated in a nasty parting. She'd told me that things weren't great at home—lots of late-night arguments and silent break-fasts—but I'd been too much into my music thing to pay enough atten-tion or be of comfort. Even when I was with her I often found my mind drifting back to the basement and my piano. I'd be carrying her tray through the Jackson High cafeteria or walking hand in hand down Linden Boulevard and some song, maybe the Isley Brothers' "Summer Breeze" or Bill Withers' "Grandma's Hands" would get caught up in my head and I'd float away from her, falling into the melody, my mind dancing atop the chords.

It wasn't just my mind that drifted. I even began slipping out to par-ties by myself. I couldn't decide why, though. Was it to find a new girl, or was it to feel the music without having to entertain Candi? Either way, I found myself flirting wildly with other women.

It was later the same week Pops made his proposal to Aunt Alma that Candi delivered the bad news. We sat on her porch and held hands and she cried into the folds of my green New York Jets football jersey while I felt like I was about to die. Her mother was escaping Queens. Couldn't afford mortgage payments alone. Family members would take her in and she'd save cash. Candi's college attendance would be endangered otherwise. Like my pops' suggestion to Aunt Alma, it all made sense.

Of course there was more to it. The pain Candi's mother felt at the separation had affected her daughter. During the spring of seventy-six, when I'd been discovering my musical self, my girl had seen the flip side of devotion up close. One reason she'd tolerated my emo-tional absence was that she'd been as preoccupied as I'd been but in a much more painful way—mourning her family's destruction. This all kind of hit me sitting on her porch that evening in Queens. And, of course, by then my understanding was too late to be of any real comfort.

The next time I saw Candi was in a cluttered living room in a modest two-story home just off Brooklyn's Kings Highway. Her three-year-old nephew Willie wandered around talking incessantly to us, himself, and the television as Leslie Uggams sang on the Mike Douglass show. In the kitchen, separated from the living room and us by multi-colored beads hanging from the doorway, were Candi's mother and her aunt Nadine. They were talking while snapping stringbeans and then dropping them into a big gray pot of water. From upstairs came the odd rhythms of little kid's feet stomping on the floor. Candi's Uncle Cecil slept in his easy chair not ten feet away, with *Ebony* magazine laying against his chest.

There was no porch outside but there were red brick steps. We couldn't use them, though. "Just because you're in Brooklyn," Candi's mother said, "it doesn't mean you have to act like it." So Candi and I sat trapped in her relatives' crowded house, feeling comfortable holding hands but not speaking too loudly or too deeply. I suffered through a few other equally constrained visits to Brooklyn that fall. When winter came Candi and I communicated via the phone. I kept her up on the doings at Jackson and she told me of life at her new school, Tilden High, where the presence of Caribbean immigrants was scaring away Jews and Italians in the school's hallways, and beef patties were usurping knishes as the quick treat of choice in East Flatbush's streets.

In those first few months her conversation focused on Queens, the world she'd left behind, and the crowded conditions she now lived under with Uncle Cecil and Aunt Nadine. We spent a lot of the holidays together—she had dinner at my family's on Christmas and we brought in 1977 at an all-night hustle contest on Jamaica Avenue.

But once the new year settled in, with college admission forms flying out and final exams hanging over us, the calls tailed off and when we did talk, their content had changed. Candi asked infrequently about our mutual friends and talked more of Brooklyn streets, Brooklyn parties, and Brooklyn friends. Surely all these new places and events would have something to do with Brooklyn men. I began listening for and half expecting her to tell me she was now seeing some dude out there, and that it was over between us. I even began pushing the issue when she kept talking about this deejay named Delroy aka Dee Love who had a sound system and played Caribbean dance music around Flatbush.

"He's a great deejay," she mentioned one time too often. So I said, "What? You like that monkey music now?" using the slang we natives sometimes employed for folks otherwise known as West Indians.

I thought she'd get mad and reveal her feelings for this Dee Love character. Instead of getting mad she just threw that singsong giggle my way. "You're not jealous, are you?" Of course I denied it, which only delighted her more. Finally she cooled out by announcing, "I'll have the house all to myself next Saturday afternoon. I think you should come over. Unless you're too jealous. Wouldn't want to make you waste your time. Maybe Dee Love is free."

"It won't be necessary to do that. I'll come over."

"Thought you might."

I was there like clockwork. Her family split for Rye Playland at 11:58. I walked in the door at 12:10. It was as good as that first time in Queens. We didn't have long, but that made the time in her bed more precious, more passionate. When Candi got up to go to the bathroom, she suggested I start getting dressed. "It would be real bad for me if you got caught here." I agreed and slid on my underwear and pants before she left the room.

Then curiosity—that suspicious, sneaky thing—began burning inside me. First I went over to her dresser, surveyed the contents of her beauty box, and quickly glanced through her blue Tilden book bag. Nothing incriminating. I felt bad about what I was doing. So to make it right I decided to change Candi's soiled sheets. There was fresh linen in her closet. Right underneath that fresh linen was a box that originally housed Hallmark greetings cards. Now there were paper scraps of Candi's tic-tac-toe games. All of them had the initial C for Candi next to one of the contestants. Initials of various kinds were next to her opponents' scores. Evidence, possibly, but of what? No way of telling if these games were played with other guys or girls, or even if they were played before or after she'd left Queens.

I found a couple of games with my D scrawled next to them. I was genuinely touched when I came across the games we'd played that sweet, anxious Saturday night in Greenwich Village. Then my romantic nostalgia faded when I came across three other games marked D in another's handwriting. Moreover these games were written on the back of stationery from the desk of a Tilden High guidance counselor, Mr. Harvey T. Wineblatt. She could have been playing against a Donna or Darlene or Dinita but, in my mind, this D could only have been Delroy.

"What," she shouted, "are you doing?"

"No," I said quite unreasonably, "what are you doing?"

She accused me of invading her privacy. I accused her of cheating on me. Though her charge was grounded in reality and mine in spiteful self-delusion and suspicion, I didn't back down.

"You've been playing your game with that Delroy guy, haven't you?"

"It's my game. I made it up. So I can play it with anybody I like."

We were still pursuing this argument—me without my shirt on, Candi without shoes and her hair wet—when her mother and aunt Nadine suddenly stood in the doorway. This turned out to be a bad thing for both of us. Could I blame Candi's mother from banning me from her daughter's life? The facts were ugly: caught her daughter, "a good girl," half-dressed with a boy in her sister's house right after breaking up with her husband. She flipped on Candi. No parties. No after-school activities. No dates. No calls or letters from me. More than me, though, Candi's mother blamed it on Brooklyn. "This wouldn't have happened in Queens!" was one of the things I heard her yelling as I threw on my shirt. She also blamed Candi, feeling her confidence in her daughter had been betrayed. I was, I guess, just some long-legged instrument of evil.

Candi's mother didn't call my house. That was the only favor she did for me. So my parents never knew what happened. Yet the incident haunted me anyway. Stupidly I told Anna who, while sympathetic, would bring it up whenever I criticized her relationship with Little Walt. "How can you be mad at me for dating Walter," she argued, "when he's been sweet to me. And not once has he tried to take advantage of me." She also found it funny I'd gotten busted in Brooklyn. "Something about that place and you, Derek," she'd giggle.

"Kashmir"

So in my senior year things should have been coming together, but they were really breaking apart. Anna was ridiculing me and Candi was kept from me, and both took their toll. I grew very withdrawn. I'd put on earphones and sit in my room for hours listening to Funkadelic's *America Eats Its Young,* Santana's *Abraxas,* James Brown's *The Big Payback,* and when I was really feeling out there, the Jimi Hendrix's *Are You Experienced?* damn near 'til the needle rubbed the vinyl white. I started experimenting with herb after I ran into this white kid, Richie Abbatello, at J&R Music World, a hip record store near City Hall where hard-core vinyl junkies got their fix on Saturdays.

Richie saw me buying Harold Melvin & the Bluenotes' *To Be True* and Hendrix's *Axis: Bold As Love,* which blew his mind. Couldn't understand how, "Any black dude groovy enough to buy Hendrix could even stand listening to a bunch of corny guys in suits." Richie, in his black, white, and gold Pittsburgh Steelers uniform, dingy jeans, holey Adidas, and stringy black hair, was rock 'n' roll all the way. Turned out he played second guitar in a heavy metal cover band that played Hendrix, alongside Deep Purple's "Smoke on the Water," the Rolling Stones' "It's Only Rock 'n' Roll," Led Zeppelin's "Dazed and Confused" and "Stairway to Heaven," and other staples of mid-seventies whiteboyism.

One Saturday I somehow ended up at Richie's house in Astoria, along with a bud of his named Roland, listening to Led Zep's *Physical Graffiti.* Let me paint this picture: Zodiac black posters of various couples screwing, posters of Hendrix, the infamous Blind Faith poster with the topless adolescent and one huge banner bearing the Aerosmith logo. He had two white canaries in a cage that he set free as he loaded up a marijuana pipe with a blend of smoke and hashish. Then he put the needle on "Kashmir," an epic of faux-Arabian motifs, Robert Plant's wordless emoting, and John Paul Jones' loud, regal, mountainous keyboard riffs. As the blended herbs filled my sinuses, one of his canaries shitted on my head, but I was so high I didn't care. That night, back in the safety of my bedroom, I put on Aretha

Franklin's *Amazing Grace* to get back my spiritual grounding and wash away Led Zep's demonic vibrations.

That was the heaviest drug trip of the period, but it was representative of where my head was at. Experimentation. Loss of focus. Boredom. Frustration. Even my songwriting was falling off. I'd still go down to the basement and bang on the piano. Timmons and I would jam a bit. But I couldn't get to Candi and it made me morose in the way only a seventeen-year-old can be.

My lethargy started to worry Moms, but I didn't feel comfortable or even able to articulate my feelings to her, particularly since the root of my malaise was in sexual frustration. Pops didn't pick up on it until it came time for me to submit my college admission forms. I didn't know where I wanted to go. Didn't really wanna think about it. Pops, I'm sure you won't be surprised, had some very definite ideas. "At one time I had hopes you'd go to Columbia or even NYU," he commented one night over dinner. "Then I thought maybe it would be good for you to go down South to Howard or Hampton Institute. But your marks have fallen off." He took a big hunk of a well-buttered biscuit and with his mouth still full said, "Now I think St. John's would be a good place for you. It's close to us. It's a private school, so the standards are higher, and I understand they have a Martin Luther King scholarship that almost all its black students get. Considering my income, we got no chance of getting any of that free money Carter's giving out, so anything I can get will help. What do you think about St. John's, Derek?"

"It's got a good basketball team," is what I said. Pops didn't appreciate that reply, but before he could say anything Moms took the floor.

"Derek, have you read the college catalogues?"

"Well," I mumbled, "I glanced at them."

"Glanced?" Pops again. "Derek, this is your life. This isn't a game or some kind of musical foolishness." By now Pops had decided, after once being neutral about my music, that my songwriting was a distraction. "Wherever you go," he continued, "you have to have a major."

"That's true, Pops."

"So what's yours gonna be? Choosing that will help you narrow down the schools."

"Well." There was a long pause as I studied my mashed potatoes.

Then I told him, "Most likely it'll be English." I knew if I'd said music Pops would have choked on his biscuit.

"What about accounting?" This was Moms talking.

"I'm not a numbers type of guy, Moms."

Now in a house built on numbers—the numbers of the dead, the numbers on insurance policies, the model numbers of inventory coffins—my comment was kind of heresy. There was a chill in our dining room. Moms and Pops both knew I was different from them. Now it was clear I might even be some kind of alien, some foreign organism that slid into my skin and seemed to very much resemble them.

But I wasn't through upsetting their digestion. "I've really been thinking about going to CCNY." City College of New York had been the flagship of the public university system since the thirties and still had some of the best professors in town. It had a very aggressive black studies department that I'd read about in the *Amsterdam News* and it was on 133rd Street, deep in the heart of Harlem where there were still bars and after-hours clubs. Bands played all forms of black music and, probably what made it most attractive, it was much funkier than any other college I could have gone to.

Looking back, I know my talk was some black version of teenage middle-class rebellion. I was making this up as I went along. I needed to have a response for my Pops and this was it. Moms seemed to sense this. "If that's what you want," she replied smoothly, "we'll support you." I got the feeling she was just humoring me.

"CCNY, huh," Pops said. "You know, Derek, I've worked very hard to get to a position where you could go anywhere you wanted." His tone surprised me. He sounded almost humble. "I know I mentioned the Martin Luther King scholarship at St. John's. Now don't take that to mean we can't afford to send you to private school."

"Oh," Moms cut in, "I don't think Derek thinks that. Do you, honey?"

"It's not about money, Pops. It's just where I'm interested in going."

"Then," he said with some real heat in his voice, "I don't understand why you'd wanna get on the subway—cause you're not driving a car of mine up there—and ride all the way up to Harlem just to go to a school any child in this city can attend. You could leave New York. You could drive to St. John's, a school with good values that's right up the road. Honestly son, you're not making any sense to me. Do you understand?"

About that time, as I stumbled for a reply, Anna walked in. She'd been up at Jackson meeting with a guidance counselor. As usual the tension in the house was eased by her arrival. Unfortunately for me, Anna then pulled out a catalog from Pace University, a private school down in the City Hall area that specialized in business. Oh, no. Anna, in that charming way of hers, started talking about Pace and financial aid and dorms, while I wolfed down the last of my mashed potatoes and tried to disappear. I told Anna how good it all sounded and excused myself. Pops, perhaps for his own mental health as much as mine, turned his attention to my perky cousin. And Moms, my loving moms, watched me walk out of the dining room, her eyes trying to figure me out like I was a puzzle with a key piece missing.

June 1977 was basically an awful thirty days. Candi's mother still didn't like me (and wasn't too crazy about Candi, either). So I was banned from her prom and her graduation. We were supposed to get together the night of her graduation from Tilden, but she went to a Brooklyn party—one deejayed by Delroy—and we didn't hook up. Yeah, we got together a few days later for a day in the City, but I'd missed that important ritual just as she would miss mine.

While Anna and her "Walter" slow danced, me and the briefly reunited Contemporaries played Heatwave's "Always and Forever" in tribute to our memories of Jackson High. At graduation Pops squirmed as other parents talked of UCLA and Morehouse and Michigan and Spelman and Cornell. I felt for him, but I'd dug my heels in on CCNY after that dinner and vowed to stay at least one semester.

The one good thing about the Jackson prom, maybe the only good thing about that entire hot-ass month, was that the Contemporaries played a ballad I'd written for the occasion. Even Dillon, now sporting a full beard, had been impressed with that Vernon Jackson single. So, with some real enthusiasm, they let me teach them "Something That Will Last." I sang the lead in my best mid-range tenor, careful not to try to mimic Teddy Pendergrass' growl or Smokey Robinson's falsetto. I mean, I was no Vernon Jackson, but it sounded good. I got the tapes to prove it. Even Pops, who stood at the door so no non-Jacksonites got in, could be seen smiling when people complimented me on it. So I tried not to dwell on all the negatives that filled my life that last year of high school. Just like the song said, I was going to build something that would last. At least that's what I wanted, though, like most high school graduates, I had only a vague idea how I'd do it.

manhattan—1983

"Any Day Now"

It was the last set at Sweetwater's and the audience in the cabaret seating area had thinned out to a few diehard Chuck Jackson fans. Jackson, the dark-toned baritone crooner, who had big hits with "I Don't Wanna Cry," "Any Day Now," and a few others back when I was still wearing a bib, was emoting in the direction of two late-fortyish black women. Meanwhile, I tinkled the ivories of the closing verse of "The Greatest Love of All" and gazed over toward the glass partition that separated the bar from the cabaret. Behind the glass men and women did that late-night slow dance called drink, conversation, and desire. I was hoping there would be someone special, someone sweet, someone available awaiting my touch after Jackson had rekindled his last memory.

I was working this gig on the recommendation of my homey Timmons who knew the musical supervisor, a bass player named Russell Harrell. The night had gone smoothly. A couple of adult contemporary standards slipped in with oldies. It was like this whenever you played an oldies gig, a medley of the past for baby boomers spiced with the kind of songs you'd hear under anesthesia at the dentist office. You played these gigs with a fixed grin in deference to the faded star and for his audience while your mind drifted to sleep.

In the last two years I'd played behind the Coasters, the Drifters, Martha Reeves, Dobie Gray, and Chubby Checker. I'd sit behind any keyboard, read off the charts, and play some of the melodies that had enthralled me as a child and watch the spreading butts of singers once celebrated but now relegated to the background of pop music. None of these folks were one-hit wonders. After Chubby had "The Twist," he followed with "The Peppermint Twist" and after Dobie Gray had "In Crowd," he hit years later with "Drift Away."

They'd been touched by the sweet side of God's hand more than once. Yeah, they were at Sweetwater's tonight and the Rochester Lounge two days later, playing right opposite the pool room. But they'd been there before and been backhanded by God and then risen again. For them obscurity was only a pause, not a phase. These singers balanced bitterness and hope on their internal scales. They'd sit on the dressing room stool or lean on Sweetwater's bar relating all the bad breaks, lousy gigs, and thieving managers into a big, fat dossier of thwarted ambition. "Record industry politics" were invoked like a chorus and small royalty checks were the trickiest of verses.

Still, within them was this yearning kernel of optimism. "One good song." "A real smart manager." "A record company that believed." When they found out I wrote songs, they'd put out feelers. "Could I hear the demo?" "I got connections ready to record me with the right material." "You got anything that sounds like Prince?" "Quincy was ready to put me in the studio but Michael heard about it and vetoed the deal 'cause he doesn't want me back in the game."

I was as polite as I could be, but none of these folks were gonna get a taste of my stuff. At the end of every night I wished them good luck and stood at the bar, watching for available women and waiting on my money. And that's what I did after "Any Day Now" was through and the instruments were packed and the trickle that was the crowd had either split for Queens or was fishing around in their pockets for cash. No superstars in the house tonight. Just regulars and a waitress named P. J. with big eyes and killer hips who was with it, but I remembered one thing I'd heard the old men at Mr. Walt's say: "Never shit where you eat." I was tempted to violate that rule with P. J., but instead I sipped the last of my Harvey's Bristol Cream and headed home.

I stepped out onto Amsterdam Avenue and the late autumn wind whipped past me on its way uptown. I turned up the lapels on my leather jacket, got a grip on my keyboard, jaywalked across the avenue, and cut across Sixty-eighth Street to Broadway. It was after midnight and a Thursday night. Broadway in the fall is always lively. Across Broadway the late show at the Cinema Studio was letting out at

Sixty-sixth, and studious-looking film buffs were exiting Truffaut's *The Woman Next Door.*

On my side of Broadway the white marble structures of Lincoln Center loomed over my shoulder. Julliard School of Music. Avery Fisher Hall. The Metropolitan Opera house. The ballet building. That lovely fountain nestled in the center of it all. This was a place of high art, a place where white folks celebrated the best parts of themselves, a place songs and dances as old as Europe's great cities were performed. The only African-American music to be heard with any regularity were jazzmen who played the music of my father, which was cool but didn't give me much chance of performing in these hallowed halls.

Sporadically an r&b show would be booked into Avery Fisher and, actually, one had made a deep impression on me. For my twentieth birthday, Candi got tickets for us to see Teddy Pendergrass at one of his "for women only" concerts, but Candi knew I'd love being in a room full of horny sisters. Teddy performed with a ferocious vigor in slacks and a light beige silk shirt, two slender gold chains, and thick, imposing beard that made me deeply envious. Women screamed and panties went flying toward the stage. When Teddy pleaded, "Let me do what you wanna do, and all I wanna do is make love to you" on the tag of "Close the Door," the smell of sex, the bouquet of lust-filled women, caressed my nose.

It had been a sweet night at the end of a bittersweet day. Candi was returning to Howard the next day for her junior year and my depression at that had me melancholy until Teddy rocked the house. It struck me as quite ironic that all this passion was identified in my mind with the otherwise sterile, pretentious atmosphere of Lincoln Center.

At Lincoln Center, Broadway and Columbus crisscross with Columbus turning into Ninth Avenue as you head downtown. Instead of following the traffic down Ninth, which was my ultimate destination, I crossed past O'Neal's Balloon (where Woody Allen and Diane Keaton ate their farewell lunch in *Annie Hall*) to get back on Broadway. I passed the Lincoln Center cinema, the Paramount Theater, and the Gulf & Western building that stood over it, and the Coliseum, an ancient, dingy gathering place that anchored Columbus Circle.

At the end of Columbus Circle at Fifty-eighth I decided to head down Eighth Avenue where my eyes filled with raunchy images of commerce and sex. Hookers—twitchy, anxious, and bored—presented their merchandise. A few black men with dead, red eyes scouted the terrain from doorways and parked cars. At Fifty-first I passed the Adonis Theater, an old movie house that specialized in gay male fare, where couples were exiting from a showing of the double header *Densely Packed* and *Butt Buddies*. Whatever gets you through the night, but I did pick up my pace whenever I went down the Adonis' block.

Walking through the upper Forties I could feel the pulse of Times Square teeming across Broadway. At Forty-fifth I turned right, going past the Martin Beck Theater across the street and the Camelot, a doorman building where I'd often spied cute young ladies walking in too late at night, young ladies who had the look of "hyphen girls" (singer-dancer-actress-waitress) coming in from gigs just like I was. No luck tonight, though. All I made eye contact with was the doorman, a fairly young Puerto Rican guy pouring over *Hi-Fidelity* magazine.

On the corner of Ninth, there were two institutions that defined my reality at twenty-three. On the southeast corner was Jezebel's, a restaurant that didn't advertise its existence. The windows were covered with heavy drapes. The only sign was a bronze plaque that had the name Jezebel's written out in very stylish script. Owned by a willful, striking dark-skinned woman named Alberta, it was as intimate and ornate as the New York City apartment of my dreams. There were Mary Jane candies in porcelain bowls by the door, Andy Warhol silkscreens of Muhammad Ali and Miriam Makeba on the walls, seats suspended like children's swings from the ceiling, a thicket of palms and trailing vines, intricate Persian rugs, and a lighting design that gave the space a sophisticated, romantic ambiance.

On this night, as on most others, I stood in front of Jezebel's, yearning for the cash I needed to eat one of its Creole meals, and then crossed Ninth to the southwest corner where Smiler's, the twenty-four-hour deli was, where I usually purchased my late-night dinner. Large Tropicana orange juice, big bag of chips. Corned beef sandwich on white bread with mustard. Nothing like a nutritious repast at 1 A.M.

Then I crossed my last block, going over to the uptown side of Forty-fifth and the Chatworth, my Manhattan home away from Queens.

No doorman, but it had two heavily locked doors and a hardcore group of longtime residents waiting for the building to go coop. I'm in the back apartment, 3J, with a terrific view of a brick alley, visible daily through the gray bars on three windows.

The apartment consisted of a small kitchen, a bedroom, living room, and a bathroom. My black futon was in the center of the living room, while the fragile glass coffee table, the stereo, the portable color TV, my electric piano, and the long rows of albums and cassettes were all squeezed against the walls to create the illusion of space. After waking up, usually after noon, I'd roll up my futon and readjust the pieces in the main room, giving it the vague sense of a living room for the evenings when I fumbled at my keyboards and struggled for inspiration.

In case you wondered, the bedroom belonged to someone else. Yeah, this was my Manhattan home, but it wasn't my apartment. The whole damn thing was in the possession of Walter Gibbs who was, as usual, somewhere "out there," somewhere in America, acting as road manager for a funk band, the Spacious Vibe, that was touring with the Commodores and Maze featuring Frankie Beverly.

I met Gibbs in the City College cafeteria my junior year. Bad time. Real bad. Anna got engaged to Little Walt, whom she now demanded I call "Walter." Candi was down in D.C., then pursuing her undergrad degree. Pops was still pissed at me for attending CCNY despite his offer of a new car if I transferred to St. John's.

I was sipping a Coke and reading Albert Murray's flavorful view of the role of blues music in black social life, *Stomping the Blues,* when I noticed this heavy-set brother blowing smoke at two cuties—one of the girls was short and compact with her hair in tight braids and a scowl even tighter, the other was tall, lean, and sillier looking than I'm sure she wanted to be.

"You want a deal and I can get you one." He sat facing them with his arms folded, looking back and forth at them like a stern father. "You want to make records, I'm your man." From under the table Gibbs picked up a big battered JVC boombox. He pressed Play. A chunky lock step rhythm built around a funky clavinet figure blasted out and then a high-pitched voice—obviously a man singing falsetto— sang a strong, repetitive melody about "love ain't free, you pay with pain" that I liked, despite the strained quality of the delivery.

"This track is hot," commented the taller cutie and he grinned, as if to say "Well, what did you expect, anything else?" I should have been in my mass-media class but the brother's game was so strong I had to see his closing move. The guy played two more tracks of similar quality—good music, perky melody, this guy's falsetto. After the piece, he announced, "There's only one thing wrong with these songs. You ain't on them and you could be. So do you wanna 'do the do' or not?" Next thing I knew he whipped out two blue index cards and gave them to his listeners. "That's the time. That's the place. Bring your voices and no bad vibes."

"I'm bringing my boyfriend." This was the stern-faced short girl. The guy ignored her and looked dead at the taller girl.

"Bring your daddy, too. This is all about business. This is about your voices, not your booty."

The short girl with the boyfriend didn't believe him and neither did I. I could tell by the look in the taller girl's eye (and the fact she was still humming that first tune's melody) that he had her hooked. She'd go wherever this music was—a recording studio, an office, the guy's living room—'cause the music had moved her. She was primed because of his sounds, like he'd opened the right door at "Let's Make a Deal." When the girls stood up to leave I made eye contact with him. As we both watched them walk away I spoke in his direction. "You better hope the short one's not too persuasive."

"I'm not worried about that," he said with utter confidence. Then he turned and finally looked my way. "I know the tall one's coming and I'm betting the short one will come to look out for her friend. And she won't bring her boyfriend. She thinks she showed me she was shrewd with that boyfriend mess. Now that she put me on notice, she'll be so busy looking out for her friend, I'll get her to sign a contract and likely the poontang too. Plus she's got the better pipes."

"You that bad, baby," I asked him.

"I've always been able to get to first base, home slice." Then he grinned and a little boy emerged out of his arrogance. "My only problem is that I always fall down rounding third."

The cockiness was gone. It even felt like he needed some reassurance. In that spirit I volunteered, "I thought those were good songs."

"How," he asked matter-of-factly, "would you know?" The arrogance was back, so I answered accordingly. Told him about his simple-ass chords, his unadventurous melody, and that "basically, my man, you've written the same song three times over, but it's cool, man, 'cause it's what's happening now."

"What's your name, brother?" I told him and he replied, "I'm Walter Gibbs."

Gibbs was truthful. As a songwriter-entrepreneur the man always got past first base. He could hustle up anything. He could get free studio time. He could get a&r people to listen to his demos. He could get his name mentioned in Dwayne Robinson's *Billboard* black music column. From that day on I was charmed by the arrogance and the commercialism that oozed from him. I watched him, sometimes with real awe, and imagined I was down with a young Edgecombe Lennox or even, in the deep recesses of my mind, an eighties Berry Gordy.

Too bad Gibbs was being so real about his shortcomings about rounding third. The free studio time was always being yanked after a half hour when a paying client would appear. The tapes given to a&r people either broke, jammed, or picked up an irritating buzzing when he made copies on his boom box. *Billboard*'s black music editor would get the information wrong. I watched him at these moments with sorrow and pity, sorrow that this man was truly snake bit, and pity that I'd befriended such a loser.

Sometimes his bad luck would contain a sliver of good fortune. Brooklyn Promenade, a five-piece band from Bed-Stuy that Gibbs had developed, co-written most of their songs, and gotten signed to Capitol records, had their record-release party at the Parker-Meridien in a big suite with a nice view of Central Park. Should have been a night of triumph. He'd finally taken an artist all the way, from bars and basement rehearsals, from crappy four-track demos to the Power Station where they cut their self-titled debut.

The band's lead guitarist and vocalist, Bobo Brewster, was a slender, bearded guy who resembled Bill Cosby, circa "Uptown Saturday Night." He was laughing and taking pictures and drinking. Drinking a lot. Bobo dived into the open bar like salmon swimming upstream. The party had begun at seven, Bobo started drinking at 7:15, and by 8:45 he was dancing. By 9:15 he was spilling bourbon on writers from *Right On!* magazine. By 9:43, Bobo was holding a glass of Jack

Daniel's in one hand and a Kool cigarette in the other. He was listening to his music, grooving to his voice, right by a big picture window when, in a grand gesture, he swung his body backwards, just as he would on stage, fell backwards over a stool, and went right through the window and down, down, down to Fifty-seventh Street. Needless to say this put a crimp in Capitol's promotional plans for Brooklyn Promenade.

You're wondering about this sliver of good? Well, Bobo was the one who originally had this apartment. A week after his death, Gibbs and I stopped by to pick up his clothes for his family. The Chatworth's landlord, a middle-aged Jewish gent named Samuel L. Simon, was as nearsighted as Mr. Magoo. When Gibbs and I went over there, Simon was sweeping near the front door. "Good morning, Mr. Simon," Gibbs said.

"Good morning, Gibbs," he said. Then he added, "Hey, how ya doin', Bobo." Then he continued sweeping. Gibbs nudged me and then whispered, "Tell him good morning." So I did. He hustled me into the elevator but didn't press a button.

"Go ask him when the heat's coming on."

"Why?"

"Because," Gibbs answered, "he thinks you're Bobo."

"That's sick."

"Maybe," he said. "Maybe not."

I went back into the hallway and asked about the heat. Simon stopped sweeping and focused his squinty eyes upon me. "It's been on for a week, Bobo. You don't feel it?"

"You know how cool I am, Mr. Simon."

"Mr. Simon? Why so formal, Bobo?"

"Just playing. That's all. Talk to you later."

I got in the elevator and we looked at each other. "Blind as a bat!" we said simultaneously.

Within the week Gibbs moved in and, after much conversation, he got me to move in from Queens, too. I felt like a ghoulish bum rushing Bobo's place. But then a clean apartment in a convenient midtown building was a rarity for a brother. Why let it out of the race? Gibbs needed me to front as Bobo, at least until Mr. Simon got new glasses. This was my senior year at CCNY and the commute was kicking my ass. Moms didn't like the idea, but Pops was with it. I'd already made clear my independence, so why not go all the way? On some level he was proud I'd gotten a Manhattan apartment, even if he wondered how I'd obtained it and why Bobo's body was interred by Bentas, the big black Harlem funeral home, and not by him. In the corner of the main room Bobo's guitar and a copy of the Brooklyn Promenade album sat in tribute to our ill-fated benefactor.

After Bobo's tragedy, Gibbs landed a job as road manager for Cameo. Then he worked with the Bar-Kays. And, now, with Spacious Vibe. These gigs, back to back to back, had taken him all over America, strengthening his contacts with concert promoters, club owners, radio deejays, and hotel personnel. Now he had a national base of relationships. Problem was he wasn't sure what the hell to do with them. Anyway, Gibbs had become such a Gypsy we never knew when he'd be in the Apple. I agreed to let him have the bedroom, so he could roll in and out with a minimum of disruption.

So this was my world, more or less, in the fall of 1984. A year after its release Michael Jackson's *Thriller* was still selling. Prince had a hit soundtrack and movie named *Purple Rain,* music videos were going nonstop on this brand new thing called MTV, and I was coming to a dead man's apartment on Forty-fifth Street, playing my songs and, unfortunately, spending too much time thinking about sex.

With Gibbs splitting the rent, money from my gigs, and generous "loans" from Moms, I was getting by financially. But I was bedeviled by my sex drive. Candi was in another city and I had a midtown location and an infrequent roommate. Yet something wasn't clicking. Maybe I felt guilty because I was in love with Candi and didn't wanna cheat. But my sporadic visits to D.C. weren't doing the job. I was alone with my keyboard and my *Players* magazines way too often. You know at twenty-three, if the wind blows you get an erection, and I felt like there was a hurricane outside. What was I doing wrong?

"Sketches of Spain"

As you know, I revere the lyrics of r&b love songs bequeathed to writers like me. The wordplay of Smokey, the earnest heart of Mayfield, the manly desires of Gamble & Huff, the devotion of Ashford & Simpson have all brought me joy. Unfortunately, when it came to good love-making music, I found that my enthusiasm wasn't shared by the women I was meeting. I loved the words of r&b so much that I made a "love tape" that had Teddy's "Love TKO," Marvin's "Sexual Healing," "Climbing the Stairway to Heaven" (O'Jays' version), and several other choice selections of gutty vocals, strong choruses, and devotional and/or heartrending lyrics that I assumed was the ultimate tool of seduction. Surely these music selections would lure the fairer sex more readily into my futon. Sadly, the results were inconclusive. My ability (or rather inability) to seduce women seemed neither hurt nor enhanced by my tape. I employed it repeatedly over the course of eighty-four and can report that the only bras that came off in my apartment were unlatched by me, not the music.

The error in my ways was illustrated by Trisha Brown, a journalism student who lived with her sister in Brooklyn's Crown Heights, whom I'd met at the bar in Sweetwater's after gigging with Martha Reeves. Trisha was a very serious-minded woman with a dour round face, thick glasses, and a close-cut Afro. These possible negatives were offset by her appreciation for Anaïs Nin, a big hearty laugh that belied her regular expression, and one of the most perfectly formed behinds I'd ever had the pleasure to fondle.

The enduring significance of Trisha and my bedroom exploits was that she would only start foreplay after we'd closed the door to her bedroom and she'd clicked the radio on to WRVR, then New York's flagship "jazz" station. I say "jazz" with disdainful quotation marks because it programmed so much fake jazz. Grover Washington, Jr., Stanley Turrentine, Bob James, etc. All these gentlemen began their careers playing the real thing and were now making ultramellow instrumentals with the odd eight-bar improvisation thrown in for effect. Every now and again 'RVR would dip into the vault for Coltrane or Mingus, but Trisha wasn't concerned with the music's purity, only that the music enhanced her sensuality. Don't get me wrong—I'm far from a jazz snob. I mean, I'm an r&b man. But just as I knew true soul from pseudosoul, so it was clear to me listening to 'RVR who had real chops and who was chopped meat.

Reluctantly I bought a couple of those fake jazz records for my apartment. Something sultry by Gato Barbieri, I think, and found that, yes, they did enhance my shooting percentage much more than my treasured love tape had. Still, the inauthenticity of this music rankled me. Soon as we were through I'd roll off my futon and scamper over to the stereo and flip on a record that wouldn't mess with my afterglow, something like Aretha's *Sparkle* or Marvin Gaye's *Let's Get It On*.

This tragic flaw in too many young black women's musical taste (and a bunch of brothers, too) was never clearer to me until two strange nights that summer at the Bottom Line. At Trisha's request we checked out Kenny G. This curly haired white saxophonist was the inheritor of Grover Washington, Jr.'s mantle as pop-jazz king, so it wasn't a surprise that the club was packed. The shocking part for me was that the joint was overflowing with young black couples. In cool sweaters and soft blouses, these cute urbanites appeared enchanted by the boring bull of this marginally talented saxman. For me, Kenny G was an excruciating bastardization that was neither jazz nor Muzak. For Trisha it was smoothing and seductive, and later she really showed her appreciation.

Two nights later I was back at the Bottom Line, this time alone, to see Branford Marsalis. The cabaret was just as crowded for Branford as for Kenny G. The stunning difference was that Branford's crowd was as overwhelmingly white and Asian as Kenny G's had been black. Blowing with the blues understanding granted by his New Orleans pedigree, an appreciation for soul, and his own witty intelligence, Branford was in grand form. It was "real" jazz that challenged the mind as well as the soul, the kind of jazz that apparently repulsed Kenny G fans.

In truth, I was distracted by the musical dilemma this Kenny G –Branford Marsalis dichotomy presented. I could have ignored my taste and only programmed Kenny G like pap (the Yellowjackets, anyone?) whenever a woman stopped by. It was the safe move. It was the doggish move. Yet I couldn't turn off my taste, and eventually I threw out all my crap jazz records as a sign of respect for real jazz. Feeling profoundly conflicted, I called my Uncle Mike in D.C. for a consultation. Longtime veteran of the sex scene (with the five scattered children to prove it) and former jazz bassist turned Maryland toll collector, Uncle Mike was always good for astute romantic insights.

"So you wanna drop them drawers, quick, fast, and in a hurry?" he growled over the phone.

"Something like that, I guess."

"Look, either you want the drawers or you don't."

"Yeah, I want the drawers."

Uncle Mike laughed at that. He loved it when he could get me to drop my rather proper speaking voice and give up the funk. "Your father," Uncle Mike asked, "he never told you about Miles?"

"Well, you know Pops, Uncle Mike. He doesn't care anything about music except who's playing the funeral march today. You know how he is."

"Believe me, I do. Believe me, I do."

"So what are we talking about? Miles Davis?"

Uncle Mike grunted and said, "Miles Dewey Davis to you, son." That was the introduction to a long, rambling dissertation on Miles' role in baby making in the fifties and sixties ("before he began making that damn fool electric shit") when the ebony-skinned trumpeter's muted, silky tone was one of the age's chief erotic instruments. "Yup," Uncle Mike rhapsodized, "when Miles played 'My Funny Valentine,' women swooned, men felt like Clark Gable, and time stood still, like it should when the loving is good."

"Miles was all that, Uncle Mike?"

"Is still all that. Just the other night I played *Sketches of Spain* for my new woman—thirty-eight and fine—and she just about chewed my toes off. Listen," he said with great urgency, "Miles taught me how to say what needed to be said without words. Catch my meaning?"

Honestly I hadn't, but damned if I was gonna tell Uncle Mike that. CBS, before it was Sony, started reissuing a lot of the vintage stuff in the original jackets, which showed real respect for history, though I hated the *Sketches* cover because it had a bogus "Man of LaMancha" motif of a Miles caricature playing against a yellow and bronze backdrop. Looked cheesy to me, but if Uncle Mike said it was a panties dropper I was willing to risk the cash.

I put it on. The first sound you hear is castanets, clicking like crickets in the foreground and then behind them the spiraling sound of flutes and French horns and oboes. Listening in my cramped little apartment I felt like I was walking through some very progressive Moorish temple. *El Cid* filled my mental T.V. screen. Was Uncle Mike's hype just about a Charlton Heston film soundtrack? Then the arrangement pulled back and Miles, with a delightful touch of whimsy, took center stage. Low, muted, in control, calm, he filled in the center of Gil Evans' orchestrations with his personality, making this retro-medieval music urban and smart and dramatic. Pretty soon my critical facilities lightened up and I was grooving with it, caught up in the classical textures and the ability of Miles' trumpet and cornet to dance through them. It seemed to me Miles played amid these Spanish melodies with the intense nonchalance which is, at least part, of what being cool was all about. The pretension of the concept and Miles' wit within it, made *Sketches* intoxicating. I could see why some women swooned. Myself, I was feeling weak kneed at the possibilities.

I tried it on Trisha first. I got her to stop by on the pretext that we'd go dancing at Leviticus. Tried not to give it too much buildup. Even put a (God forgive me) Chuck Mangione album on first to relax her. Then Miles came on and the air in my apartment stood still.

"What's this?" she asked.

"*Sketches of Spain* by Miles Davis. Do you like it?"

"It's different."

"Yeah? How?"

"I don't know," she replied. "Kind of exotic."

"Yeah. Just like making love to you."

"Stop," she said.

"No. I won't stop."

Between the compliments and the Miles and her sexy-smelling perfume, we ended up rolling out the futon, pushing back the other furniture, and making love until the break of dawn. Whether this was the Miles or the confidence Miles invested in me, I'm still not sure, but it was our best sex ever, like we'd finally found our rhythm, not one defined by me looking at the black numbers on a block radio.

In fact, lying next to Trish the next morning I felt like I'd gone too far. Inspired by this music, I'd pushed my relationship with Trish to another level, one I hadn't really thought about going to. My heart, in all its hypocrisy, still belonged to Candi. Or at least my idealized version of Candi. In some ways our distance had made loving her an abstraction, some projection of my desire, which was more comforting than the young woman who lay next to me.

I'd turned to Miles for sex and ended up with some insight, insight I didn't necessarily want. However there's no way to censor such self-knowledge. You just have to acknowledge it and move on. Within two weeks I'd broken up with Trish for some cowardly reason, like I needed more time for my work. Maybe if I'd kept Trish and still been listening to *Sketches* I'd never have been turned out by Ruthie Lee.

"Freaky Body Baby"

Ruthie Lee was from Dallas but her accent always sounded fake to me, like she'd learned it from sitcoms. There was some real Southern honey in it, I suppose. It was the calculation in it, her constant measuring of its effect on you, that made it sound manufactured. When she asked, "How are you, baby?" she really meant "How much do you want me today?" and, for a long time my answer, "So much, Ruthie Lee. So much," told her I was open to whatever game she was playing that day.

Ruthie Lee was a dancer turned model turned singer, one of the thousands of artistically inclined young women struggling through New York life in search of truth, justice, and creative fulfillment. And, if that didn't work out, money. We'd met through a mutual friend, Tamika, at his demo studio out in Long Island City. A yellow gal with hazel eyes and brown hair and a voice. It turned out she lived on Forty-fifth Street near Eighth Avenue at the Camelot, just a two-minute jog from the Chatworth, so we rode back to the city together on the E train. During the ride I got the abbreviated life story: artistic daughter of a middle-class family, got a dance scholarship to Julliard, though singing was her passion and, between dancing in videos and in shows around town, that's what she'd been pursuing. I figured that meant she had to have some other source of revenue. Most likely her parents. Maybe a man, too.

As we got off at Forty-second Street I offered to walk her home. I didn't think she was gonna invite me up but, hey, you never know. Standing in front of the building was that anxious little Puerto Rican doorman I'd spotted reading *Hi-Fidelity*.

"Oh, Ruthie, there's been a robbery. I am so sorry!" Upstairs we found her door kicked in. Considering the fury necessary to dent the metal door, the apartment wasn't in bad shape. In fact, it was the kitchen that was ripped apart. Pots dented. Plates smashed. Shelves disshelved. "I'm sorry I let him in, Ruthie," the doorman continued.

"Didn't I tell you I'd changed the lock?" she demanded.

With an innocent face he replied, "No, Ruthie, I do not know that." I laid back, trying to be supportive and listen without judging. Sounded like the door breaker had been asked to leave, yet expected to return. Probably just days ago. Ruthie Lee seemed surprised, not scared.

Her apartment was a spacious studio with a kitchen and a closet-size bathroom. Lots of records. An amplifier with a mike attached. Clothes in sloppy piles. Cluttered looking. Not traditionally feminine. In fact, it looked a lot like my place.

"Police been here," the doorman said and handed her a detective's business card. "He say, 'Call when you get in.'" Ruthie Lee got an "I-don't-wanna-answer-questions-now" look on her face and stared off into space. I asked where she was gonna stay and she sighed. The doorman said someone would be by in "a couple of hours" to fix the door. I gave the doorman my number and took her by the hand.

An hour later we sat on my sofa drinking white wine. I didn't ask her about who "he" was or why he broke her door and tore up her kitchen. Figured I'd know at some point. I told her my life story and then I played her some tracks I'd written recently. Ruthie Lee took a liking to an up-tempo, disco thing titled "Freaky Body Baby" with some preliminary lyrics about dancing the night away or some crap like that. In my opinion it was garbage. Commercial garbage, but garbage nonetheless. Still she raved about it. My desire to have her faded a bit with the realization she had bad taste.

Not long after listening to the track, Ruthie Lee laid her head on my shoulder, her brunette hair spreading down onto my chest. There was some rather inconsequential conversation. Finally I asked, "Do you want me to call the doorman? See if the door is back on?" She was quiet. I thought maybe she was asleep. Then she sat up. "Can I stay here tonight? I wouldn't feel safe back there tonight. You understand?" Absolutely, I replied.

I slept uneasily on the sofa. She was in my bed in a red Stax Records T-shirt and baggy Knicks shorts. My phone rang about 8:15 A.M. The door had been fixed and her new lock was in place. The doorman was very apologetic.

Ruthie Lee had had a restless sleep. The sheets were off the bed and she laid contorted, pretzel-like, diagonally across my bed. Her legs were muscular and lean, and her auburn hair fell about her face like feathers. The T-shirt had bunched up in the middle and her flat stomach was exposed. I was enjoying this view when from underneath her hair that voice asked, "Was that Ramon?"

"Is Ramon the doorman?"

"Ah, huh."

"Yup. Your door's straight."

She shifted her hair from her face and looked up at me. A gentle smile graced her face. I said, "All this on a first date."

She raised herself up on her elbows and laughed. Her legs were wide apart and I could see the mounts of her ass buried in my shorts.

"I don't have any coffee, but I do have some orange juice. Want some?"

She said, "Sure," and I went into the kitchen. I expected to hear her moving about, picking up her clothes, etc. But I heard nothing but the rustling of my sheets. When I went back in my bedroom she had the covers up to her waist and her head against my pillow. She sat waiting for me. I handed her the O.J. and then sat on the edge of my bed.

"You still afraid to go back to your place?"

"No." She gulped down some orange juice. "I'm just real comfortable right here."

"Oh, I don't wanna get you in any trouble with your—"

"Ex."

"Husband?" I asked. When she didn't answer but continued sipping the juice, I assumed my question was the answer. Then, her honey-dipped voice replied, "We're separated. About six months. He still has some stuff there and I felt the time for us to get back together had passed.

"But he didn't think so."

"No." Another sip. "He gets angry. But he'd never hit me. He does get physical with objects, though."

"I see.

"You know you're sweet."

"Thank you."

"And talented."

"Double thanks."

Standard show-biz palaver. At a promo party I would have let it wash right over me. But this was my place, my bed (actually Gibbs' bed) and my Stax T-shirt. I kissed her lightly and started to pull back, to gauge her reaction. She wrapped her arms around my neck and then she kissed me. Her taste was red wine and orange juice and morning breath. Not the sweetest nectar. Still, here she was and she had said I was "sweet" and "talented." Bad musical taste aside, we made love twice before noon and once more that afternoon.

That evening she kissed me good night with Ramon watching impassively in her lobby. Back at the Chatworth I called Tamika out in Queens. I told Tamika the story (leaving out the sex part) and he said I was smart not to have had sex with her. Partly because he wanted to. Partly because her ex-old man was Otis Clyburn, an old Motown arranger-producer with a bad reputation for knocking out niggas when agitated. Berry Gordy had banned him from their L.A. studio after he took a swing at Jermaine Jackson for chatting up his first wife. Seems old Otis' combination of talent and mentoring attracted young women, but couldn't keep them. He'd apparently met Ruthie Lee soon after she hit New York. Tamika didn't know if they were legally married, but they had lived like it and that's what mattered, anyway. A sexy, insincere-sounding woman and a jealous ex-lover. This was dangerous. My rational side advised me to leave Ruthie Lee alone. But I was young and the air of danger was as seductive as the sex.

A couple of days later she called about 11:30 P.M. She said, "Come over" and bring "your freaky body baby." I was working hard on a lyric, but that honey dipped voice drew me to her. In a tight pink slip she bounced around her studio with the lyrics sheet, singing along to the track. I sat on her sofa bed undressing. Her voice was passable, though I'd originally written this crap with a big-breasted, big-voiced, gospel-trained, gay diva–type vocalist in mind. Still it suited her and I was already sure that when she asked for it, I'd give it to her.

After singing it several times, Ruthie Lee sauntered over to the bed and melted on top of me like butter. That first day we'd made love, our activities had been fairly conventional. I mean, we'd moved around a lot, but nothing too creative. After all, I considered myself an r&b songwriter. In the tradition and all that. Ruthie Lee, however, was far from a conventional woman.

"I want you do something to me." Her face was above me, inches away.

"Okay," I answered. "Let me know. I'm not a mind reader."

"I want you in my butt." My face surely betrayed my shock because she started laughing. "Don't be afraid. I said do me. I'm not gonna do you." I'd heard her the first time and I was upset. Not since Candi had I been this shocked by a woman's request.

Anal sex was something I connected in my brain with decidedly unmanly behavior. Obviously homosexuals did it and, if you were real tight with a brother, he might admit to making a chocolate run with a hooker. You didn't do this with your woman. Brothers from Queens just didn't do this with their regular sweetie. I wanted to tell Ruthie Lee this. But words escaped me at a crucial moment. She scooped KY jelly out of a jar under the bed and ladled it on my dick with swift, firm motions. Then she flipped up her pink slip, bent over the bed, and offered her ass to me. I followed my instincts and slid into her vagina. This seemed to be cool for a minute. Then she began demanding I put it in her ass. "Do it! Do it!" At this moment I didn't question the sincerity of the request.

So I pulled out of her vagina, my body awash in KY jelly and her juices, and put myself where she wanted me. It wasn't as tight as I expected it to be, though that wasn't my first thought. I was just appalled at what I was doing. I felt dirty and sick. Ruthie Lee didn't care. Her anus squeezed around me and she writhed under me, demanding I thrust hard and deep. She glanced back at my face and I'm sure she saw my turmoil.

Still it didn't faze her. She called for more propulsion. I could feel a quivering in her torso that grew more violent. Her back arched like a cat's and her legs flipped over my ass, so that only her hands and face touched the bed. I wasn't sure what was gonna give out first, my back or my dick. I came with a shout and she with a swooshing sound, much like a sports car blazing past a street corner. Her legs fell from my butt to the bed and, as if pulling pearls from oysters, took my dick from the dark hole it had inhabited.

Ruthie Lee seemed happy enough, so I didn't say a word. I strode into her bathroom, wet a wash cloth, stuck the biggest piece of soap I could find in the heart of it and washed my groin with vigor. I'd never quite had an orgasm like that. It was intense, strange. And I felt as if I'd suddenly become a character in some raunchy Richard Pryor routine. When I turned around there was Ruthie Lee, smiling demurely with her hand out. "Towel, please," she said.

Later that night Ruthie Lee told me she often dreamed of dolphins. An empty Caribbean beach, bright aqua blue water, and a nude Ruthie Lee walking slowly into the surf where a long, gray-skinned dolphin waited to kiss her. Their mouths would meet and she'd sink down into the ocean foam with her dolphin lover. Then, with a smile etched upon her face, she fell asleep in my arms.

A couple of days later Ruthie Lee's request was still on my mind. It was like she'd opened up Pandora's box. Once you open yourself to sexual freakiness, you just don't close up immediately. And that woman had gotten me into a freaky frame of mind. I was thinking about acts I never had before, things I usually suppressed. I felt challenged by her sexuality and wanted to know what I could do that would get to her like she'd gotten to me. I sought my answer in Greenwich Village off Sixth Avenue at a place I'd passed hundreds of times since high school, the Pink Pussycat boutique. This night I went in.

I moved slowly, a bit bewildered, amid the inflatable dolls, the leather handcuffs, jells of various flavors, and porno mags. But I finally stopped at the glass case of dildos which drew me near. Some were rubber. Some plastic. Some metal. All erect. My eye was caught by one shiny ebony, battery-operated dildo that resembled my own organ in color and shape. It made an insistent buzzing sound that I must admit I found charming. The transaction was made quickly. I stuffed it in my leather bag with a smile.

On the A train uptown I had second thoughts. Wasn't this thing just a bit too freaky for a real black man to have? Then I got a note on my mental screen. It read as follows: "Every foul thing you can imagine has been practiced, often joyfully, by somebody sometime. Every violation of the body. Every disaster of the soul. Every dark, disgusting, degenerate notion that's crossed your mind one night in the dark has been done by somebody proudly in the bright light of day. Done with glee, mind you. Don't be afraid of offending God, my man. All you did was buy a dildo." Feeling much better I patted my bag and thought of Ruthie Lee.

Back in my apartment I placed the dildo on top of my electric piano and studied it. Then I turned it on. It buzzed insistently on my instrument. Reminded me of the sound of Mr. Walt's clippers at work. Or Pops' hedge trimmers. These metaphors amused me and a rhythm came to mind. I might have written a song right then if I hadn't been obsessed with getting a hold of Ruthie Lee. She didn't return my calls and the Puerto Rican doorman, who surely knew who the hell I was, gave me blank looks and no answers about where she might be. I'd bought a toy for her and I wanted to play.

As days passed, I found myself lingering around her apartment over near Eighth Avenue. I drank orange juice at the diner across the intersection. Munched California rolls at the Japanese restaurant down the block. Mingled with the theater crowd across the street at the Martin Beck Theater. I guess I was "stalking" her. I had no plan, mind you, and no anger so far as I could tell. I just wanted to give her the toy, so I carried it around with me, either in a bag or stuffed into the front of my pants.

Then, after a week of nothing, she appeared. I was coming in late from a Sweetwater's gig and she came up behind me as I entered my building. She looked a bit disheveled and drawn. Her honeyed voice wasn't sweet; it was raspy and a touch bitter. Still my excitement at her presence clouded my vision and I embraced what I wanted to see. And what I wanted to see was her naked in my bed playing with my toy as I ordered her to. In retrospect I think she obeyed me so quickly because it prevented me from asking questions.

What mattered then was that she did as I said and fell asleep in my arms after play had ended. I thought of her and her dolphins before nodding off myself. I woke up about 4 A.M. and heard her whispering into the phone in the living room. I listened to her voice—low, furtive, weary—and then drifted away. I dreamed of being dressed up in my best summer suit, bathed in a light, singing on stage with the Temptations. I was doing the Temptations' walk between Eddie Kendricks and David Ruffin. It was a wonderful dream. I woke up about ten. Ruthie Lee was gone and so was the dildo. Strangely, *Sketches of Spain* was playing low as a whisper on the stereo. Ruthie Lee's smell hung in my bedroom and I laid there just breathing her in. I scrambled two eggs and burnt some toast. Spent most of the afternoon noodling on the piano. I had an idea for a song called "Love Moves," using an insistent rhythm inspired by the sex toy. It was about 3:15 that afternoon when someone pressed my apartment buzzer. I clicked on the intercom. "Is this Derek Harper?" The voice was flat, bored, bureaucratic, and white in that undefinably ethnic New York way. "Yeah," I answered, dragging that one word out slow as a waltz. I remember the cadences of that exchange so well, because it was the last moment of normalcy I'd experience for several months.

"Thin Line Between Love and Hate"

At my door were detectives, officers duly sworn by the city of New York to investigate assault, mayhem, and murder. At first, Dets. Petrocelli and Christie didn't tell me why they wanted to talk about Ruthie Lee. How long had I known her? Were we sexually active? Did I know anything about her broken door? I was wary but cooperative until they asked if I used drugs. That was the red light that flashed "Danger." My ass got as tight as a Master Lock and I wanted to know what was going on.

Ruthie Lee was dead.

Sometime that morning she'd been beaten and strangled with a "sex toy." The dildo had been used first to bruise her face and then rammed down her throat. "It was a bloody mess" Petrocelli said and then studied my face. I was invited down to be fingerprinted and, stupidly, I did so without consulting a lawyer. I guess the idea that Ruthie Lee was murdered, and how it happened, so stunned me I'd have done anything they asked. Back from the station I laid in the bed where her scent lingered. Torn between burning the sheets immediately or never taking them off again, I just stared at the ceiling. They say tragedy makes an artist more creative. Well, actually, I have no proof. I was a zombie that day. Over and over I ran through my relationship with Ruthie Lee, trying to see what lust had blinded me to.

I hadn't loved her but I'd been affected by her. No, let me be real—I'd been rocked by her sexuality, her freedom. I hoped that hadn't been what had gotten her killed. Women shouldn't be judged for their aggression. They should be celebrated for the challenge they offer. Yet wasn't the instrument of my response to her challenge ultimately used to kill her? Somehow I was complicit in her death, but until I had more facts I wouldn't know how deeply guilty I was.

I realize that this doesn't sound like an appropriately emotional response. I didn't cry. I didn't pray. I didn't go screaming in agony. Death happens. My moms and pops had taught me that. They'd shown me that stoicism in the face of death was to be embraced like a lover. Of course I'd never before made love to someone who'd died. Died? Ruthie Lee had been murdered.

Yeah, that made things different, but it didn't alter the way in which I'd learned to accommodate death. What I did do was fondle my penis, looking at it, wondering if somehow it had now been cursed. Sex—dark, inky, black sex. That's what I'd had with Ruthie Lee and I'd never forget it.

I had a crazy dream that night. I was eight years old and down in the inner catacombs of the funeral home with my Pops. He was wearing black rubber gloves and a long smock, equally black and equally slick with fluids. He removed them slowly, carefully, and dumped them into a wide sink. With a big sweeping motion he poured disinfectant across them. He seemed to get some joy out of this action, as it was some private act of purification. The smell of disinfectants and the fluids was nasty like funk to the 14th power.

"Smells bad, don't it?" In the dream, Pops said it without looking my way. Guess he could feel my disgust. "But it's kind of sweet in its way. It's the smell of a job finished. A job well done."

That smell drove me out of the side room and into what Pops called "the Lab." The Lab was where the work was done—the sawing, the sewing, the injections, the dressing. In this particular dream, Mrs. Roberta C. Johnson lay on the main slab. She was dressed in her favorite pink and white Easter dress with white pearls, unbecoming beige stockings her eldest daughter had insisted she be buried in, and snow white patent leather shoes. I knew Mrs. Johnson had passed with a smile on her face and that Pops had straightened it out at the family's request.

"A lot of people die smiling, Derek." My pops, in a brown suit and a matching fedora, towered over me and Mrs. Johnson's body. "It scares the heck out of families when they see it. It's like that smile says they're happy to die and—I don't care how religious they are—the reality of that smiling face scares them. They say it just looks undignified. As if Mrs. Roberta C. Johnson cares about dignity in this world, anymore." The huge Pops of my dream put his hand on my shoulder and turned me toward him. "You gotta promise me something, Derek." His face was remarkably wistful—not an emotion that passed his face outside dreams.

I immediately said, "Sure," which irritated him.

"Wait, Derek. Don't promise anybody anything until you know what they want." Even in my dreams, Pops was stern and lecturing. This was the face I knew. Made me wonder if this had really happened. Maybe this dream was a memory and I was too confused to tell them apart. Then Pops transformed again. Wistful. Softer. Sure, this was a dream. "When I die," dream Pops said, "I'll be smiling just like Mrs. Roberta C. Johnson here. Don't be afraid when you see that, Derek. Don't let your mother be afraid, either. Now what do you say?"

"I promise."

"Don't forget that, Derek."

I found myself turning smoothly, as if I was a woman doing the hustle. Ruthie Lee was on the slab now. All dressed in Mrs. Roberta C. Johnson's finery but with that face and body I knew so well. And she was smiling so wide her pretty white teeth were reflecting the harsh overhead light. Then I heard a jingling sound and saw my dream Pops holding our house keys in his hand. "Time to go."

Awake I heard the jingling of keys in the main room accompanied by heavy male feet. Walter Gibbs at the bedroom doorway. "Now what the hell are you doing in my bed?" he scolded. "You know we have an agreement, fool. Now get up."

"I got a real serious problem."

He put his bag down, folded his arms and said, "How old is she?"

"The police think I might have killed a girl with a dildo."

"Damn, I've been on the road and I had some stories to tell you, but this doesn't seem like the right moment."

I shouted, "Real funny, motherfucker! This is probably your damn bad luck rubbing off on me. Everyone involved with you gets messed up."

"Did I buy the dildo?"

"No," I replied, "you didn't but I made love to her in this bed and I must have contacted some of your ground in whack juice."

"Derek," he said seriously, "you just screwed her, you didn't kill her, did you?"

"Come on, man."

"Good. I'll help you."

"I need it."

"By the way—"

"What?" I asked.

"What's a dildo?"

The next time I saw the object in question was on the desk of Officer Petrocelli. Also present was his partner Christie, my attorney, a ruddy-faced gent named Jack McCann, and my attorney's "advisor," Walter Gibbs, who told me he knew about precinct houses from bailing singers out on the road. The dildo had the rosy tint of dried blood. There were dents along the stem and, maybe, teeth marks near the tip. I shuttered looking at it. This instrument of pleasure had been used to slay Ruthie Lee. I felt pitiful and guilty.

The detectives were quite matter-of-fact in questioning me. They handled all the sordid information they gained with the dour professionalism of men hearing the perversions and degradations of Times Square. Gibbs, much to my dismay, sat in my sight line and smirked throughout the questioning, as if these were old war stories being told for his amusement. When McCann asked the million-dollar question, "Is my client a suspect in this homicide?" the detectives were evasive before settling on the oh-so-decisive "Not at this time." The answer was really "no," but they wanted to keep me jumpy because they thought I might know who did it.

They asked me about Ruthie Lee's door being kicked in the night we met. Did I remember any comments she'd made about her husband? Immediately I figured he was the killer. He'd gotten back inside Ruthie Lee's apartment, found the dildo, and just freaked out. As innocently as possible, I offered this theory and suggested, "Her husband did it, right?" That question ended the session. That the detectives didn't answer me only made me more convinced that I was right—right not just about the killer's identity but about my sick role in instigating his murderous actions.

Afterwards, McCann, Gibbs, and I went to dinner over on Forty-third Street, across from the Carter Hotel, a once-proud institution that was now a transient hotel, and just down the block from the *New York Times*. Amid the regular clientele of uniformed cops, hookers, pimps, and *Times* pressmen, we considered my situation.

"They know you're not the guy," McCann assured me.

"That's good."

"Yeah. But they think you might be holding back," McCann added. I wondered why I'd do that. "Well," he replied, "let's say the husband did the job. He's established in your industry, is he not?"

Gibbs cut in. "He's all right. He's not really large. He's just all right."

McCann acted as if Gibbs hadn't spoken. I told Gibbs to cool out. McCann continued. "The detectives think you may be blackmailing the husband into helping your career in exchange for your silence."

"That's crazy."

"Yeah," Gibbs agreed. Then he added, "But he could help you."

"My advice," McCann said, "is to keep a low profile in the music business for a while."

"Low profile!" Gibbs snorted. "My man's damn near invisible right now."

That was it for my attorney. "Look," he said, pushing away his plate and getting up. "Stay away from the business for a week or two. Visit your parents in Queens. The detectives likely won't make a move on this case until next week, at least." Then, with a dismissive glance at Gibbs, McCann exited out onto Forty-third Street.

"Grumpy redneck," Gibbs said after him.

"Your expert advice must have overwhelmed him."

"Probably."

"You're so damn cocky, Gibbs."

"Shit, man, a lot's been going on, but you've been so busy with this bitch shit, I couldn't really kick it to you right."

I ignored Gibbs' typically insensitive remark about Ruthie Lee and told him to get on with his rant. While on this last tour it seems Gibbs had been amazed at the response to the rap acts that opened the show. In different markets the tour had different opening rappers—Kurtis Blow, Grandmaster Flash, Joint-ski—but whoever the act was the result was the same—cheers, shouts, and an enthusiasm the big name r&b bands barely matched. While the regular concert continued on, these bands would leave the arena and do one or two more performances at clubs in the area. On occasion, Gibbs had tagged along and seen the intense response the rap acts generated. Most important, Gibbs noticed that the crowds at the rap club were younger than those at the arena gigs.

"You know what that means, don't you?" Gibbs asked.

"No. What?"

"It means that these kids will be growing up with these rappers. It means there's a lot more checks out there for these rappers and anyone who's down with them."

Personally, I figured Gibbs had just been on the road too long. Like a fighter who'd taken too many punches, my man was dazed. I didn't think he was totally crazy until he said, "I just bought out Joint-ski's management contract for this guy, Reggie Olds, who used to produce him. Mayo's producing him now, which means he should have some more hits. And I'll be managing the whole situation."

I hated to cut my man down but I had too. "Gibbs, it's too bad I'm so busy feeling sorry for myself, 'cause I'd like to spare some feeling for you."

"You don't understand, Derek. It's just a rapper, a deejay who cuts the records, and one or two homeslices to carry the crates, provide security, and pick up Buddahs. No instruments. No gang of beer-bellied roadies. Low overhead. If I pimp this right, Derek, I'm going to cold get paid."

I really wanted to be gung-ho about his new hustle, but my feelings about this hip-hop stuff were basically negative. I remembered how it helped ruin the Contemporaries. Sure, some of it was clever, like Joint-ski's "Break It Down" and Kurtis Blow's "The Breaks." But compared to r&b, all this hip-hop stuff struck me as a novelty, a one-trick pony like the one Paul Simon wrote about.

Besides, I had much weightier things to worry about. That evening I hopped an Amtrak train to D.C. and Candi Bailey. Hadn't seen her in two months. Hadn't been calling as regularly as I used to. Still, she'd been happy to hear I was coming. At Union Station, she treated me with the same sweetness as always, but my eyes saw many outward changes. She'd lightened her hair. A white and blue Acca Joe sweatshirt covered her perky body and Jordache jeans hugged her rounder than I'd remembered her hips. Her lips were sweet but not as hot as I remembered.

Candi had a cute little place just before the D.C. city line and the start of Silver Springs, Maryland. Between Howard classes she worked at a retirement home in the District. Compared to my cluttered living space, Candi had put together a nice place with soft earth tones, the smokey scent of incense fluttering in the air.

After she'd moved to Brooklyn, Candi had begun making a new life separate from the one we'd shared in Queens and molded by the realities of a tougher, less casual life. Still we were both high schoolers in New York though, so whatever differences in personal experiences we had were smoothed over by our past and the general commonalities of high school life.

Now, however, Candi was in a sorority, had lived in a new city for several years, and was studying for a career in health care, all of which was as far from my life in New York as things could be. I found myself struggling to keep the conversation going and to maintain my interest. D.C. was Candi's town now. She talked of the Florida Avenue Grill and hanging out in Georgetown and the pride she felt in attending a black college in a black city. I related, but not very deeply.

Plus, I was afraid to really open up to her. How could I tell Candi of my promiscuity, of my obsession with Ruthie Lee, and how I helped contribute to her death? I thought about finessing it by telling her of a friend's death, but I knew she'd know—know that I was sexing Ruthie Lee—she'd feel it in the tone of my voice. So I withheld Ruthie Lee's murder and, in so doing, withheld what was really going on in the foreground of my mind.

Candi was gonna treat me to a meal at the Florida Avenue Grill. It was near 10 o'clock and Candi's blue Pinto was parked right outside her front door. I was standing by the car when the first patrol car rolled up. Then a second and third. A white cop hopped out of the second car, his gun drawn and aimed squarely at my skull.

"Hands on top of the car! Now!"

Seemed like something I should do, so I did. As the police—all black except for the white cop in charge—cuffed me, it came to light that a nearby store had been robbed at gunpoint. Candi, now more frenzied than five rabbits in heat, wanted to know what that had to do with me. Turns out the robber's description—bearded black man in a brown leather jacket—kinda fit me. Next thing I knew one of the black cops was ushering me toward a squad car.

"Where are you taking him!" Candi screamed. "Where are you taking him!"

"Shut up!" said the white cop, but Candi was defiant.

"No! I want you to answer my question!"

"I'll be all right," I told her with surprising confidence. "I'll be all right." Knowing I hadn't done anything gave me a silly sense of security. As the patrol car rolled off and my cuffed hands rubbed against the back of the car's hard seats, I was convinced this was just an unexpected adventure. The black cop who drove me looked pleasantly bored and tried to act equally relaxed.

We stopped in front of a thrift shop only two blocks from Candi's. There was another patrol car out front and inside was a black cop behind the wheel and a black civilian, like myself, in the back. A white cop, this one with a walkie-talkie and the extra uniform ornamentation that signified higher rank, walked over to both cars and spoke briefly to the cops and then I was let out. The cop was very polite. "The people inside the store will take a look at you," he said in a soft, slightly Southern voice. "If you're not identified, we will let you go. We'll do this as quickly as possible."

The cops moved the other brother in front of the store at the edge of the sidewalk. Two men and a woman—apparently workers there, took a peek at him and shook their heads no.

So it was with complete confidence that I stepped over to be judged. That first man looked out at me, squinted his eyes and shook his head yes, a yes that indicated he recognized me, a yes that meant I had robbed him at gun point, a yes that meant I should be arrested.

The shiver that went through me was deeper than being naked in a Minnesota lake in late January. My bowels didn't move and I'm not sure why. My wrists began to ache from the cuffs. I felt a bit dizzy. I began babbling to the cop that I just came in to D.C. to see my girl, that I was a musician, not a stick-up kid, and that my leather jacket was as black as an Alabama night, not brown.

The bored black cop who'd driven me seemed to submerge deeper, as if I was talking to someone sinking into dark water. But I was the one sinking down into the depths of a "Couldn't-happen-to-an-honest-man-like-me" nightmare.

And, just as quickly as all this dread filled me, it was gone. The woman shook her head no. The second man shook his head no. Then the stupid fool who'd originally nodded yes took another look. He squinted again and, blankly, shook his head no. Within a minute my cuffs were off and the officer thanked me for my cooperation and I was turning down his invitation to ride back to Candi in the same car I'd just been cuffed in. I half walked, half ran the blocks to Candi's place. The police cars were pulling off and Candi was engaged in a shouting match with the white cop who'd pointed his gun my way.

"If you don't shut that mouth," he was announcing with finality, "I'm gonna lock you up."

She said, "I'm not afraid of you" like she was aching to be cuffed.

"Candi, I'm all right" I shouted and then she hugged me like I was a soldier just back from 'Nam. The white cop held out my wallet and I clutched it while looking dead into his blue eyes. A hint of embarrassment. A big dose of contempt. The glint of a hunter thwarted. Then he was gone and Candi was in my arms and I asked her if she still wanted to treat me to the Florida Avenue Grill and she said yes.

Over dinner I told her as much as I could about Ruthie Lee. That she was a singer I'd been working with who'd been murdered. As you might imagine, I didn't mention my little gift. I hated to lie but it would have been worse to say nothing. Candi had heart and cared about me. Had more fight in her than I had in me. Eating barbecued ribs, potato salad, corn bread, okra, macaroni and cheese, and two big hunks of sweet potato pie, we sat side by side, hugged up with each other, feeding each other, touching and laughing as she considered how close she came to spending the night in the District's nightly lock-up.

Candi told me she loved me. I told her the same. Then we went back to her apartment—looking both ways before we entered—and then made love like the world was about to end. I thought that was the end of the night, but then she woke me up and we began playing her tic-tac-toe game with the paper balanced on my chest. I won the first two games, but she rallied to take the next three. Then she rolled over and went to sleep, apparently finally satisfied.

Sunday afternoon I was back in Queens, in our dining room, eating at a new table, enjoying aromas as old as Moms' recipe for roast beef. It's the future, the one you dream about as a child, when you have your own world, different from that of your parents, and you sit at the table munching on biscuits, greens, and roast beef. You no longer just listen to them, but you tell them of your world, your life, your feelings. I always imagined it was an empowering confirmation of adulthood.

Maybe some other time it would be. But this time my return home was muted. Ruthie Lee's death was the most important thing that had happened in my life since I'd left home. Yet how could I tell my parents about it? I'd been telling my Moms I was suing an ex-collaborator for trying to steal a song we'd been working on. That's why I'd been having her make out checks to Chuck McCann, Esq. I'd also convinced her not to mention any of this to Pops. I argued it would just again confirm his disgust with my chosen profession. Moms understood that.

Still, she didn't like lying to him, especially about money. I felt guilty because she felt guilty, and guiltier still since I was making Moms lie to Pops even as I lied to her. Maybe the real evidence of my maturity was that I was so willful in deceiving those that have given me life. A sad maturity, but maturity nonetheless.

That should have been enough discomfort for one meal, but there was plenty more. Anna and Little Walt (all right, Wal-lee!) were at the table, too. They lived three blocks away from our house but clearly were as comfortable in my old homestead as I once had been. Anna had matured into a real beauty. It was like a light shined out of her eyes and lit you up when she smiled. There was still a harsh Brownsville edge to her voice, but the words that flowed out were about business. During the last few years Pops had managed to infect her with his deep love for business, an infection I'd always been immune to.

Pops was explaining to me how "All these business tax cuts and bank deregulation Reagan has put through have already helped me. I've been trying to expand for years. Now the Jamaica Savings bank says they're in a position to help me."

"That's right," Anna chimed in. "We want to fix up Mr. Walt's. Add some real chairs—"

"Not new chairs," I said. "You'll ruin the atmosphere."

"Sorry," she said, "new chairs and, I know this will hurt your feelings, but a new jukebox, too. And video games. The bank is gonna help us do it all."

"I'm gonna buy out O'Malley's. Finally." Pops and Anna were both looking pretty pleased with themselves, so I decided to stir things up a bit. "You really think these Republicans will be good for black people? Every time they cut a program it seems like it's something that's gonna hurt our people."

The response came from an unexpected source. "Sure," Little Walter, announced. "If more people are making dollars, it's a good thing." He glanced toward Pops for words of approval, or maybe just an affirmative nod.

"Truthfully, Reagan and his policies won't be good for most black folks initially," Pops replied. "Only people in a position to do business, people like me and Walter's father, will benefit immediately. All the cuts will hurt a lot of people until they realize white folks aren't looking to be extending themselves for us no more. They're going to have to do it for themselves 'cause the days of whites helping us because of moral suasion are gone." He nodded his head negatively for emphasis as he cut his chicken breast.

"Derek," Moms said, "you know the Franklins moved last week."

"Yeah, that's deep. They were the most Jack & Jill people around here."

"Of course," Pops said disdainfully, "they don't do the sensible thing. They took that beautiful house and they let this real estate agent talk them into subdividing it into a two-family rental."

"What's wrong with that, Uncle D?" Anna wondered. "There's always a shortage of good housing for black people. People can move out here into a good neighborhood. Compared to Brownsville, this is paradise."

I could tell by the look on his face Pops was in scolding mode. So I was gonna kick back and enjoy taking Anna to task when he looked over at me. He said, "Derek, tell your cousin what we've noticed about renters out here."

Damn, a surprise test. I knew the answer, but it irked me that he couldn't just tell Anna herself. "Well," I acted like I was pulling something out from deep in my memory, "well, you used to say Hollis and St. Albans would stay nice as long as the black folks who owned homes stayed in them."

"Owners keep the place up," Pops cut in, apparently peeved at my slow delivery. "It don't make renters bad people," Pops said, perhaps aware that his observation might offend his niece from the projects. "It's just that if you bought the property with your hard-earned money, then you take care of it better and you take care of your neighborhood better."

"Hmmm." Moms made us turn toward her. "I think it's got more to do with who you are than how much money you have. If you know how to keep something up, you will. It's about home training. It's not just about money. The Monroes over on 201st had plenty of money, but their house was always a mess." This show of independent thinking from Moms was cool. Wish she'd done it more when I was a kid. Maybe their relationship was changing?

"What about that, Pops?" I asked.

"Derek, you know how good-hearted your mother is," he began condescendingly. "But she knows I'm right about this. Sure there are exceptions. It's still about what you're used to. You could have been raised right, and if you're not used to dealing with the plumbing, the air vents, and the grass, it shows. Some of the blocks right off Hollis are becoming rentals, and you can tell which ones are rentals and which aren't. Garbage is put out sloppy. Places just look unkempt. That's how a neighborhood starts to slide."

Moms looked a little hurt by Pops' insistence on being right—I guess you never really get used to being corrected. I think Anna was peeved, too. Pops didn't mean it, but by implication at least, he was suggesting that people from the projects—black folks reared on renting—could never understand another kind of life. Anna was way too smart not to catch the spoiled, well-paid, Republican thinking Pops was buying into.

But she loved Pops too much to take him on. Or was she just too dependent? Like Moms and me, she owed the man a lot. The only person at the table who didn't was Walter, though I imagined Pops had been

lending this young couple more than moral support. ~~I~~
formidable man. Even now, though I was his height,
larger than life to me. I thought when you got to be a man
seemed smaller. Moms may have become life size n
seemed resistant to modification. A little grayer. A little
still the MAN.

"Golden Lady"

While I was at the house I kept waiting for him to interrogate me
about why I was suddenly back in Queens. I think Moms had already
intercepted him, telling him I was trying to save money to buy some
new equipment. Pops could always understand an economic argument. Also he was pretty busy. Angel dust was rolling through
Queens, knocking kids off their feet and getting others shot. Business
was booming and he was fixated on getting the O'Malley's spot on Jamaica Avenue.

McCann, when I could get the man on the phone, kept telling me I
was doing the right thing and to just stay cool, relax, etc., etc. But I
was missing gigs. Most of my old musician cronies were either in Manhattan or out in a Brooklyn neighborhood named Fort Greene (which
was close to the city) or on the road. Gibbs and Joint-ski were on a big
rap tour. Every time I talked to the guy he was signing up another rapper. He'd even found some kids named the Brothers Black from out
here in Hollis. He said he was making dollars and since he was paying
most of the rent on our place at the Chatworth, I suppose he was. So
being in Queens was making me antsy. Banging on my old piano in the
basement just made me realize that I hadn't traveled very far in my
career. I was still banging on those yellowed keys with no real significant checks on the horizon.

I started making calls. Timmons, who was clocking dollars as a session guitarist, told me about a demo session over at this studio on
Fifty-fourth Street next to Studio 54. I'd pick up a couple of hundred
dollars and make some good contacts. I was so anxious I didn't even
ask who it was for. An E train ride later and I was over at the studio.
Timmons was already there, playing his own sweet version of George

on's "Breezin." He introduced me to the players. No one major. A assist I'd seen around named K. J. and a drummer/programmer just out of Berklee School of Music.

Then the producer walked in and I damn near had a heart attack. It was Otis Clyburn, Ruthie Lee's estranged husband, the guy the police think I might be blackmailing. I was scared he was gonna hear my name, rear back, and coldcock me with a straight right. Instead he just smiled, gave me a nice hardy handshake and one of those "Relax-young-man-you're-in-good-hands" smiles that veteran producers specialize in aiming at youngsters like me. Obviously my name meant nothing to him. Of course that didn't mean I didn't wanna flee.

After all, wasn't this just the kind of confirmation the detectives would love? I thought about maybe acting like I had a stomachache or maybe the flu. I was even contemplating tripping over Timmons' amp and claiming a jammed forefinger when Clyburn played the melody line of this song he wanted us to cut on the Yamaha. It was Stevie Wonder's "Golden Lady," one of my favorite songs from *Innervisions*. He wanted us to redo it reggae style. I wasn't sure who he was show-casing the song for, but it didn't matter, the approach intrigued me. Next thing I knew there's a faux reggae beat programmed into the drum machine, Timmons is cranking up a riff on guitar and I'm sitting behind a Fender Rhodes next to Clyburn working my part.

Whatever else Clyburn may have been, the brother was a real good musician, who ran a tight, efficient session. Good ideas were spotted and elaborated on immediately. Bad ones discarded quickly. We did three versions of the reggae "Golden Lady" in about two hours—one fast, one mid-tempo, and one dub style. The whole time I kept waiting for the detectives to bust in, arrest Clyburn, and slap a subpoena on me. Afterwards Clyburn complimented me. "Thanks for coming in, Derek," he said. "You have a good song sense. Some young cats out here just wanna show out. You respect the song."

"How you gonna disrespect Stevie?"

Clyburn smiled. "And you know that's right. What you doing now?"

When I mumbled I didn't know, he invited me and Timmons over to Possible 20, a musicians' hangout I knew about but had never checked out. It was around the corner on Fifty-fifth Street between Seventh and Eighth. So there I was sharing a Heineken with Timmons, listening to stories of Marvin Gaye's grace and Norman Whitfield's bluster, and the last glorious gasps of Motown magic from a man whose late wife I'd had freaky sex with. Every now and then I'd imagine Clyburn on top of Ruthie Lee. He didn't seem capable of any of it. Clyburn was just amiable, even grandfatherly.

Once my eyes must have betrayed my search for seduction and murder in Clyburn's soul, because he stopped a story and said, "You're really into these stories, aren't you?" I'd said something polite like, "Who wouldn't be?" trying to camouflage the complexity of my feelings.

Then a tall figure walked over to the table. From above he bellowed, "Nigga, you still telling people about the time you jumped Diana Ross' skinny ass bones?" Edgecombe Lennox stood over us, with a big leer on his face and a long chestnut leather jacket shining like new money in the light from Possible 20's bar. A skinny guy with a scraggly beard, black Def Jam jacket, a Yankees cap, and a Heineken bottle in each hand walked up next to Edge. Written in script on the breast of his Def Jam jacket was "Dwayne."

"Thanks, Dwayne," Edge said. "Gentlemen, this Dwayne Robinson. He writes the Bass Line column for *Billboard*." Many times I'd read his column and looked at the names of the big shots of black music written in extra bold letters in his column. Nile Rodgers and Gladys Knight and Frank Beverly and Valerie Simpson and Don Cornelius and Evelyn "Champagne" King and all those other folks' coming and goings filled the Bass Line every week. Even Gibbs had made it once or twice. Not me. Not yet. But now I knew the man behind the words.

I shook his hand and that of Edge and, for a moment I felt, "Yeah, I'm in the game." When Clyburn asked them if they wanted to sit down and join us I got as excited as the morning Ruth Lee kissed me. This was a particularly embarrassing feeling considering her husband was sitting right there. Edge said, "I'd love to, but Dwayne and I need to have a little meeting. I'll roll by afterwards." They sat down two tables away, far enough to be out of ear shot but close enough to make eye contact every now and then.

The ridiculousness of me working with Ruthie Lee's husband had passed from my mind. I was just kicking back with my new main man Otis Clyburn, my old homie Timmons, and a bunch of brews after a session at a place music folks chilled. No trip home to Queens tonight. Nope, I was in the mix. Maybe the first time in my career. Be damned if I was going back to my room like I was a kid. Fuck the cops and forget Ruthie Lee's ghost. I wasn't being haunted anymore, I told myself as I sucked down my third or fourth Heineken. I'm sleeping in my apartment tonight. And so I did.

The phone woke me up. The clock radio read, 11:45 A.M. I picked it up, fumbled, then picked up the receiver again. "I thought you were staying in Queens," a white voice growled. It took me a second to figure out the voice belonged to my lawyer. I mumbled something resembling a greeting, but McCann cut through all that. "Meet me at the precinct at 12:30. The detectives want you to look at Ruthie Lee's murderer. Don't make them wait." Click.

Burgundy Adidas sweatsuit. Black shell toe Adidas. No socks. I'm running through the streets of Times Square. My head hurts. Sweat bullets fly off my forehead. I must look like a mugger. Don't care. Do they have Otis? My man Otis. Christie probably wants to know if I've been gigging. They've been talking to musicians. They saw me and Otis. Accomplice? Blackmailer! White justice + black man = bad news. These lightning bolts of fear had me sweating so much Detective Petrocelli asks, "Hey, you ready to confess?" Even McCann laughs. I must look that guilty.

Then Detective Christie starts asking about Ramon Hernandez.

"Who?" I ask.

"The Puerto Rican doorman. When did you first see him? How did he act? Did Ruthie Lee mention anything about threats or harassment? Did he ever say anything about her to you?"

"You telling me the doorman killed her?"

"Found the lingerie, a demo of your song 'Freaky Body Baby,' and some pictures of his place in the East Village."

"Why'd he do it?"

"Obsession. Sex. Crazy. Something along those lines."

Then I'm looking through the glass at Ramon Hernandez who stands quietly surrounded by four other Latins, who all look very unhappy to be there. None, however, looked as sad as Ramon. I remember him reading a magazine in Ruthie Lee's lobby and the night he told us about the door. Det. Petrocelli thinks he broke the door, just as they think he choked her with that thing I bought her. It doesn't seem possible that the doorman did it, because it doesn't seem possible it happened at all.

Leaving the room, Christie walks toward me with Otis Clyburn at his side. I want to die. Otis, however, forces a smile and gives me a hug. "They told me you gave Lee that song and you saw that bastard that night. Bless you for coming in, Derek. Life is funny, isn't it? Wait for me, man. OK?"

Every muscle in my body, every synapse in my skull, felt as tight as a well-miked snare drum. I just wanted to run back through Times Square, past the cops and the newsstands and the rumbling backed-up traffic and right back into the crevices of my sofabed. But I was an undertaker's son and now, with my fears abated, those old instincts came back.

At a Deli on Thirty-ninth Street we sat across from each other. I had a large O.J. and Clyburn had several sugar-laced cups of coffee as he told stories about how he met her, how she calmed him down, how he worked too hard, caressed her too little, and rarely praised her talents. It was revisionist history from the soul of the bereaved and, as my Pops had done so often, I listened, I nodded, I frowned.

"How well did you know her?" Clyburn asked. After his melancholy reminiscing, it surprised me, though it shouldn't have. I'd been lulled by his sorrow into thinking he suspected nothing about Ruthie Lee and me. But he knew what his true relationship had been with her when I met her, knew it better than me for sure, so all he was doing was trying to put me and her together.

"She was a beautiful woman," I said in answer. "So I first tried to hit on her." I watched his eyes. They were dark brown and narrow. A squint of jealousy passed through them, but so far I wasn't lying. Told him how I met her. About the broken door. He looked a little sheepish there. Maybe he'd broken it. I told Clyburn I'd watched over the night of the broken door by taking her to a dinner and a movie. By sprinkling the truth among my lies I hoped to keep his trust and obscure his reasoning.

My boldest move was to tell Clyburn, "I put her in a taxi and she stayed with some friend on the West Side."

"You think," he said quickly, "it was a man?"

"I don't know, man. She did hook up with me the next day. I played her some tunes. We kept in contact. Then my moms got sick and I went to spend some time with her in Queens. Ruthie Lee's death was a real shock, my man."

In Otis Clyburn's dark brown eyes I could see my reflection and in that reflection I saw my fabrications and suspected he could, too. But what was real and what was a lie? I knew and assumed he didn't. Who could he check with? Some guy she might have been sleeping with on the West Side? Everything else, like my visits, was my word against Ramon, the accused murderer, and my moms. After that Otis got the checked and hugged me when we parted, but I tried not to read anything deep into that, since music biz people hug at the drop of a needle.

I walked home now, fully aware of my spartan wardrobe and the way people avoided black men in track suits lined with sweat stains. Smelled like I looked, too. Found myself walking down Forty-fifth Street toward Eighth Avenue, toward Ruthie Lee's building, toward some damn complicated memories. Walked right by her building. Didn't break my stride and didn't peek. That was behind me now, literally, as I kept walking to the Chatworth and my sofa bed.

"Night Fever"

"There are only two things you need to know as a man, Derek. You need to know about women and you need to know how to make money. If you know about women, but not about money, you can still have a good life. If you know about money but not women, you'll find a few who'll still be by your side. But if you have no skills in either area, well son, you'll have a lot of time on your hands."

Edgecombe Lenox leaned back in his chair and laughed, a laugh that made heads turn at adjoining tables and that made me laugh. It was another night at a back table at Possible 20, another session of Jack Daniel's and storytelling, another jumble of questions and answers, slurred answers, in the hours after midnight.

"Well," I responded, "right now I'm not doing great at either."

"All you need is what the Army calls an 'attitude adjustment.'

That's all. Wait until I get back from the bathroom . . . Unless you wanna join me?"

I shook my head no, and told him, "Knock yourself out."

He said, "I intend to," and got up. So far I'd resisted the cool white temptations of cocaine, but Edge and many of Possible 20's other musical denizens found it as essential as water. Still, if my career continued on its current trajectory, I might be down for anything.

In the summer after Ruthie Lee I felt cursed. The Sweetwater's gigs were sporadic. I still hadn't placed a song, though everyone told me I had talent when they passed on my tunes. My old homeboy Timmons kept in contact with me, recommending me for jobs playing keyboards for remixers like Jellybean Benitez. You'd go in with the remixer, usually a club deejay, and put down grooves and rhythmic ideas that would be used to make a record more danceable. Eighties club music had remix after remix that, at least to me, seemed to defy the idea of songs, at least as I knew it. These remixers often scrapped the original tracks, brought in a guitarist like Timmons or a keyboardist like me, and abandoned the melody and harmonies the songwriters had crafted. They made it their own thing. Sometimes it was good, but mostly they struck me as bastardized creations. Philosophically it bothered me. But then, a job's a job, a check's a check. It was good money, and I needed it.

While I muddled along, my ex-roommate was blowing up. Gibbs had gotten a nice duplex in the Village, opened up an office on lower Broadway and, in all ways that mattered, was becoming established in the music industry. This rap thing that I'd been so disinterested in had become a real force. Joint-ski, the Brothers Black, the Fat Boys, Whodini, Grandmaster Flash & the Furious Five, and a number of others were enjoying gold singles and albums. Opening up to Dwayne Robinson's The Bass Line column you'd see Gibbs or Joint-ski or Run-D.M.C. or some other rappers' names there every week, as if they were as important as Berry Gordy or Morris Day or Millie Jackson.

In city after city the rappers were drawing capacity crowds, proving people would pay dollars to hear young black men tell rhymes on a microphone. Gibbs, because he'd gotten in early, knew everybody in hip hop and was becoming the man to see about making money in it.

All of which was driving me crazy with jealousy. My man's success,

S
E
D
U
C
E
D

coupled with my misadventures, had my stomach aching with envy. Not only was Gibbs doing well, he was doing well with a music I didn't respect! It was like he'd suddenly become Darth Vadar, and given into the dark side, while I was Luke Skywalker at the end of *The Empire Strikes Back*, laid up in an infirmary with one hand cut off.

The scary part was that I began to wonder if Gibbs was right. Gamble & Huff were over. Even Earth, Wind & Fire and P-Funk were starting to fall off. So was Smokey and Mayfield and so many of the people who'd made me want to write songs.

Maybe it was just me. Maybe nothing bad was happening to the music. But I felt it. I felt it deep and, if I was right, I didn't know where that left me. So I began to drink. Beers during the day. Usually Harvey's Bristol Cream at night. I drank while I listened to Miles and I drank while I was trying to seduce background singers I'd meet at sessions. As I said, I somehow had the will to avoid cocaine and stuck with liquid reality removers. And I began to hang out at Possible 20, which is how I ended up befriending my childhood idol.

For the record, Edge didn't remember me from Queens. He did recall Mr. Walt's and all the other places like it around New York and the country he'd plied his trade. "It's not about selling music," he told me when we first started talking at Possible 20's bar, "it's about selling plastic and vinyl. That's what you hold onto. That's what collects dust in the corner. I could be selling shoes or razor blades or booze. I mean, this is more fun, you know, but I never lose sight of that."

As a musician I hated Edge's view of the music world. There was no beauty in it and very little room for love. But the more I hung with Edge, the more I understood him and, I hoped, would understand this business my love of music had gotten me into. I promised myself I'd never get that cynical and then took a sip of Jack Daniel's and felt the top of my head flame up like a match.

And, speaking of flames, Edge's nostrils were red—I mean, we're talking Rudolph the Red Nosed Reindeer. As if the inner lining of his nostrils had been sheared by that snow blowing across his driveway. "I listened to some of your songs," he started. "I can tell you been listening, listening real hard, to sixties stuff, seventies stuff and I respect that. But let me ask you a question. Are you making music for the past or are you making music for now?"

"I'm trying to be commercial. I want a hit record as much as the next man. I just have a certain direction I wanna go in."

"Understandable. All recording artists got to have a direction, but don't you—a young man just getting out here—be so worried about them old Negroes that you ain't paying enough attention to the feelings going on out here now."

"I understand what you're saying but—"

"It's silly trying to sell the past to the present, unless the present asks for it. Understand what I'm saying?"

I countered, "White boys do it all the time."

"'Cause white people don't change as much as we do. How old are you? Can't be more than twenty-four or twenty-five."

"That's about right," I said.

"Well, since you been alive we've been colored, Negroes, Afro-American, and black. We've been r&b, soul, funk, disco, rap, and what have you. We ain't looked back yet. That's 'cause we ain't a looking-back people—not really. Look, somebody made February Black History month so we could 'reclaim our history.'" There was a little bit of Jack left in his glass so he paused to kill the drink. "But a lot of folks, they only remember the mess. They can tell you about all the laws that got passed and the barriers that were broken through. But I remember blood and dog bites and crazy white guys with eyes blue as hell."

As he talked, Edge pulled off his jacket, rolled up the sleeve on his right arm, and showed me a deep scar on his forearm. "They may say hell is full of fire, but I think it's blue, icy blue, and when they say cold as hell, it's about them crackers' eyes, cause the ones I remember were cold-blooded. So when they ask me to remember, I see those eyes, looking my way, as anxious to swing me from a tree as smile."

"You were in the civil rights movement?"

"I was a black man in the South," he said sourly. "That's all you needed to be."

"I've never been below Virginia."

"Virginia ain't the South," he snorted. "It's like a suburb of the South. What you doing next week?"

"Writing songs. Gigging. Paying the bills."

"Hustling," he said and I had to agree. "Okay, you gonna hustle with me next week. I'll give you three hundred dollars to drive me down to Jack the Rapper."

Jack the Rapper was the biggest black music conference in the business, though from what I heard "conference" was a euphemism for party. The "Jack" of the title was an old r&b deejay named Jack Gibson and he often referred to it "as a family affair," which apparently translated into wall-to-wall parties. Edge continued, "I got to drive a singer down to Jack and I need to get some sleep along the way."

"Seems simple."

"Uh huh," he agreed. "You heard of Cherri." Cherri had a bang-pop body, a husky voice, and three hit dance records around New York in the last year.

"This," I said, "sounds like fun."

"Uh huh," he agreed again. "A little money and a little pussy and a little driving." He smiled. "Couldn't be simpler."

"Edge." The shorter of two black men, my age but hard like the cells at Riker's Island, had spoken. They were Tony Tee and B. J., and within seconds of their arrival Edge's convivial mood had disappeared. It was after midnight. Possible 20 was nearly empty. Tony Tee and B. J. had faces made for nocturnal transactions. I wasn't in Queens anymore. Time to go. "Opportunity," Edge said when I got up, "is a door that opens twice—once to come in and once to go out. The door just opened."

Tony Tee and B. J. didn't smile when I left and I didn't mind. It was early August in Manhattan, and Eighth Avenue smelled like overheated garbage. Humidity filled my sinuses and cooked the alcohol in my head. Between B. Smith's and the porno twinplex, a cocoa-colored black man with woolly hair stood with a box in front of him. Nothing unusual about that unless you stopped to listen.

His trumpet was held together by two thick blue strings and shiny black electrician's tape. On this battered thing the old man played Ellington's "Take the A Train" slow and mournful like a dirge. Whatever sense of celebration the song contained, he squeezed out of it with dark, blue phrasing. The old man was playing old music. Maybe Edge was right about these sounds. Nobody was asking for it, and nobody but me paid attention. Still, as I stood on Eighth Avenue listening to the old man play, it struck me that I still hadn't written anything that good and, maybe, I never would.

"Got to Give It Up"

August in Manhattan. Late afternoon on a Friday. Gray hazy sky. An old Puerto Rican man selling ices on the corner. Somebody in a passing car has the Mets on the radio. A policeman barking his location in a walkie-talkie and attempting, unsuccessfully, to hoist his gunbelt over his gut. The nauseating aroma of hot-dog mustard, bus exhaust fumes, incense sold by Muslim brothers in white robes, shish-kebab peddlers with steamy carts, sun-hardened pizza sold in open-air shops, and layer upon layer of human funk filled my nostrils and boiled my psyche.

I stood outside a Hertz car rental place near the Hudson River in the Twenties with a tightly packed bag and a Coke that made me belch. Edge tapped me on the shoulder and we headed out to the back. My man rented a cream-colored Cadillac with tinted windows and whitewalls. "The only way to travel," he purred. I nodded in tacit agreement. My pops would love this car. I told Edge, and he replied, "A man of taste and breeding." Edge was wearing gray gabardine slacks, a gray silk shirt, and a white Kangol with a black nylon Jackson's Victory tour jacket under his arm.

Cherri lived up in Spanish Harlem over at 106th and Madison, which at rush hour can be a long, frustrating trek from midtown. As I guided the car up Eighth Avenue, Edge handed me a crisp $100 bill. "You get a third now. A third when we get to D.C. and the final third when we reach Atlanta. In between, I pick up all hotel bills and all meals. All you got to do is stay on the road and stay awake."

"And," I added, "do both at the same time."

"Yeah," he chuckled, "that's it."

Eighth Avenue right by the Port Authority on a hot August afternoon is about as congested and unpleasant as New York City gets. We were moving at the proverbial snail's pace, so I hooked a right on Forty-second Street, fooled by the illusion of movement east. But it was just as congested there as it had been on Eighth. Edge frowned.

"Youngblood, I hope that move wasn't representative of your driving instincts." I was gonna say something flip when my eyes got real wide and my grip on the wheel tightened.

My pops was walking out of a porno shop with a brown paper bag.

Our Caddy was jammed behind a *Daily News* delivery truck. I thrust my right arm damn near through the steering wheel and the blare of the horn filled the car. "Hey, Derek!" Edge looked at me like I was crazy. "Relax. That truck's not going anywhere fast."

My eyes were riveted to the sidewalk. I'd lost sight of Pops. The *Daily News* truck lurched up three car lengths and there he was again, standing in front of another sex shop in a dark blue suit and shades, his face impassive as he surveyed the sex tapes in the store's windows. And that brown bag was still in his hand. I inched the Caddy up until we were alongside him. Should I yell out his name? If I stared, would he feel my eyes on him—even through this traffic? I looked so hard I was sure my glare would cut his skin. But, if he felt my eyes, he didn't find it difficult to ignore them. My father, my mom's husband, my lifelong provider of food, shelter, and education, and undertaker to the dead black masses of Queens, put his free hand in his pocket and strolled into another Forty-second Street sex shop.

"You all right, Derek? Who'd you see just now? I saw you staring at somebody." Shrugging off his question I turned up the radio and Marvin Gaye's "Got to Give It Up" filled the space between us. All the way across Forty-second and up the Harlem River Drive, WBLS played the eight minutes plus of Gaye's jam, while I silently surveyed the traffic. Edge's complaining about BLS' unwillingness to program funk vaguely entered my mind, but it didn't stick.

Outside a housing project at 106th and Madison I mulled things over. So Pops liked peep shows. He was a grown man. I tried to be adult about it. Then the little boy in me popped up. Pops must jerk off. Just pull it out and look at the pictures. Just like the readers of *Playboy* magazine. Just like my friends, just like me. This revelation humanized Pops, but did I really want my Pops this human? I closed my eyes to the image of Pops leering at Vanessa del Rio and rubbing his groin. It was sick as hell, yet I kept watching Pops as he watched Vanessa. He was wearing one of his black funeral parlor suits. Pops looked somber and dignified and responsible as he started slowly unzipping his fly. While I kept watching he kept watching Vanessa the Undresser.

"Derek!" Edge rapped on the car window. "What's with you today!" I mumbled an apology and stumbled out to take Cherri's bag from him. Like I said, she had a "bang! pow!" body that her fake Gucci warmup suit with matching cap, unlaced Adidas, and jingling baby earrings covered but couldn't conceal. She had a long, mean mouth, a small nose, and slanted feline eyes. On every finger, including her thumbs, were little rings—some said "Luv," some said "Peace," and the biggest was a caricature of a couple kissing. Homegirl was real short. Couldn't be an inch over five feet, which somehow made her physical assets seem more extreme. Not that she cared what I thought. I'd barely introduced myself before Cherri was sprawled across the back seat, comfortable as she wanted to be with the latest issue of *Word Up!* magazine.

"You sure you ready, Derek?" My conduct this afternoon had Edge worried.

"No problem, my man." I put some bass and bravado in my voice. "First stop Atlantic City, right?"

"That's it."

On my first real road trip I would have preferred to have been the one in the backseat, chillin', getting ready to promote some record I'd written or produced. Instead I was a chauffeur, just some elementary driving skills away from being a straight-up flunkie.

The Garden State Parkway traffic was backed up with city folk fleeing concrete and gamblers in route to A.C. I was still mulling over Pops' sex life when Cherri, after scrutinizing *Word Up!* twice from cover to cover, began peppering Edge with questions. "Where we staying?" "Did Toni give you the backing tapes?" "When are we eating?" "You think my record's a hit?" "You know these deejays got bad breath, because they always be getting up in your face." And Edge answered her thusly: "The Atlantic City Motor Inn." "Yes, I do." "Ida's Soul Food restaurant as soon as we hit town." "No question about it. And if any of these stations don't think so they will before we leave their town." "Yeah, Magic Mike's breath is so foul it makes pigs run. But be nice to him 'cause he's gonna play the hell out of your record in A.C."

Cherri seemed satisfied with Edge's answers and pulled a Rubik's cube out of her travel bag. I was struck by her voice, which was constrained and small compared to the dark colors of her singing voice. I was also irritated that she hadn't addressed me yet. I mean, I was right there, too! Guess she figured I was a driver, so what did I know? And, to tell the truth, she was right in figuring that. Still it bruised my ego that this sexy little singer was paying so little attention to me.

This object of my desire was asleep by the time we reached A.C. and Edge made no effort to wake her. I could see why. A.C. was a battered old city with short, scrawny buildings and chintzy little stores. In the distance were the casino and hotels—tall, brightly lit structures, so new and formidable they seemed part of another city, one many miles removed from A.C.'s tawdry thoroughfares. "This used to be a fun town," Edge said, as we cruised past some ugly prefabricated housing. "Could take your kids to the beach, go to Steeplechase Park, eat cotton candy. But once the white folks moved out, Jersey left it to us. Until the casinos opened up, this town was just Newark with an ocean. Left at the light."

We stopped in front of Ida's, a diner as nondescript as a sewer drain, but Edge assured me the food was jammin'. Cherri woke up red eyed and cranky as if from a bad dream. Inside Ida's, the owner, a heavyset woman with short hair and mountainous breasts, welcomed Edge like a conquering hero and quickly lured him to a table in the back where she poured top-shelf whiskey and leaned over so that Edge's eyes wandered freely about her ample body.

That left me with Cherri and two very full plates of fried chicken, potato salad, greens and chitterlings. To break the ice I told Cherri I wrote songs. "Then why you driving the Caddy?" Money, baby and the chance to go to Jack the Rapper. "So you a wannabe, then?" That hurt. Really did. So she tried to show me a little mercy, I think. "Yo," she said. "I know how it is. Took me a while before I was successful myself." Bitch, didn't we just pick your poor ass up from the projects? No, I didn't say that. I thought it though. I thought it loud. But I knew better than to get into a dissing contest with my meal ticket at the first damn stop. Then it got worse. She started giving me advice on the record business, like she was Edge or somebody large.

Almost as irritating was that while Cherri schooled me, she started staring at some muscular construction worker type in a gray T-shirt and basketball shorts eating with his girl. I mean, she was just straight up macking this guy behind his girl's back. And he was looking back. Not only was she arrogant, she was disrespectful, too!

Edge strolled over from Ida's table and rescued me from her wisdom. "We'll check in at the Motor Inn, relax for a couple of hours, and then go over to the community center. You'll do two songs and then we'll go gamble, my treat, at Bally's."

"Wait," Cherri cut in. "Does that mean no sound check?"

Edge moved firmly to cut off any trouble. "It means," he said smoothly, "I'll check the levels while you perform, but otherwise this will be hit it and quit it, Cherri." She didn't like this but didn't challenge him. Instead she asked for a favor. When he agreed, Cherri gazed over at the guy, stared real hard, and then nodded toward the rest rooms. Ten seconds later he excused himself from his table and sauntered over to the men's room, trying to flex his muscles and look cock diesel. He stood by the door, apparently expecting Cherri to join him. Nope. She just smiled again and motioned with her hand for him to enter. Hadn't spoken to him yet, but she was already moving my man around the chess board. After he'd entered, Cherri told Edge, "Go into the men's room and invite him to the gig."

Edge let a smile cut his lips and then turned to me. "Derek, go in there and give him the message, okay." I slinked over into the men's room where Ray Ray—that was his name—was washing his hands and checking himself in the mirror. "Yo, I thought she was a singer," he said after I'd delivered the message. "Think I saw her on New York Hot Tracks. She's a healthy little thing. Shit, I was supposed to be putting up Deidra's shelves tonight." Ray Ray was talking more to himself than to me. He was scheming on his girl, just like Cherri hoped he would. Maybe she did have something to teach me.

"You know if she got a man?" No, I didn't. "You're not her man, are you? I only ask 'cause my cousin knows Rick James and he told me all you music industry folks are freaks." I assured him I was not her man nor was I a freak. On the question of her freakiness I could not vouch.

The A.C. Motor Inn was a block from Bally's and the boardwalk. The rooms weren't bad—they had pay T.V., clean bathtubs, and plenty of paper-covered glasses. It was a place hardcore gamblers stayed.

Less expensive than the casinos, yet close enough so that one lost no quality gambling time on transportation. For me the motel room was a dream machine. As soon as my head hit the pillow and my soul food bloated stomach got comfortable, the day kept playing and rewinding. Manhattan haze. Pops' porno. Cherri's Rubik's cube. "Got to Give It Up." Ray Ray and the unsuspecting Deidra and her sure to be unfinished shelves. My first day on the road and it wasn't over yet.

An hour and a half later I was awakened by Edge's knock on the door. In the hall, Edge, Cherri, and a chunky, dark brother in a white tank top and green sweatpants awaited. His name was Junior Bishop, head of promotions at WTTH. I noticed immediately that he and Edge shared that same nervous adrenaline vibe that I'd seen so often at Possible 20. If Cherri had taken a hit with them, I couldn't tell, because she was so relaxed and so damn sexy. With her makeup on and her hair pulled back Sade style, her face looked older and bolder. And the orange dress she wore had long slits that revealed an intense slice of thigh with her every stride.

The community center was a brick structure plopped down in the middle of a weedy field. The field was encircled by a score of ugly, two-story prefabricated houses and those houses bordered an empty flatland of weeds. The community center and the houses all looked like they'd been squished into the ground like a child pushes sticks in the mud.

Inside the community center a shaky metal platform was set up at one end of the basketball court, and on it a new rap duo, the Overweight Lovers, were doing a pretty lousy imitation of the Fat Boys. The group was composed of two overweight guys in matching burgundy sweatsuits and Cazelle sun-glasses worn fashionably without glass in the frames. The larger of the two was doing a human beat box and shooting out big drops of spit from his mouth. A healthy gathering of teens and young adults were scattered about the court and in the bleachers that lined both sides. Bishop guided us under the bleachers to the locker room where the air was heavily scented with mildew. Kids and adults in radio station T-shirts, shorts, and loose summer pants milled about, all of them gawking at Cherri as we walked by. We ended up in a back office with a glass window that looked out into the locker room. Warm Cokes, cold cuts, and plastic silverware were laid out for our use. "You'll be on in fifteen minutes," Bishop assured Cherri, then he and Edge disappeared back into the locker room in search of Magic Mike. I opened a Coke and asked Cherri if she wanted one.

"All it does is make you belch," she replied, though she did nibble on some of the baloney set out for us. "This reminds me of a club I played in Queens," she said. "It had been a supermarket before they made it a club. In the back it smelled like meat and they always had the best cold cuts 'cause the delivery trucks still came. You'd think they'd know it wasn't a supermarket anymore."

I told Cherri the story of my apartment at the Chatworth, which seemed to confirm her belief in life's basic ridiculousness. "People don't be paying attention. They just walk around and don't see what's going on." Now we actually seemed to be relating. Maybe I would get a chance to knock the boots. Then she wondered if the Walter Gibbs whom I'd mentioned as my ex-roommate is the same one managing all those rap groups. When I said he was, Cherri started asking me what kind of guy Gibbs was and what did he look like and was he nice and could I introduce her to him at Jack? Her sudden interest in Gibbs re-confirmed two things for me: I had no shot with this woman and that my man was really blowing up. Even a straight-up dance diva was feeling his vibe.

Edge entered shaking his head. "They're running late." Cherri was about to catch an attitude when Edge cut her off. "But I brought someone along to keep you occupied." Ray Ray, reeking of Polo, wearing a purple shirt, a black tank top, and three gold chains, appeared at the door with a grin that was crocodile wide. This seemed like my signal to split, but Cherri just told me to wait outside the door. Edge whispered, "Don't let her out of your sight," and then left.

So I stood sentry-like outside the door. Occasionally I'd peek in and see Cherri smoking a cigarette and appraising Ray Ray as if he were an item on display. That seemed appropriate since Ray Ray's body language was all sell. He was leaning forward, his hands moving smoothly, occasionally touching Cherri's arm with a light caress. Most of all he looked her in the eye. No matter what a man says, it's always the eyes that make the real statement. I remember somebody at Mr. Walt's saying how, "Even if you couldn't rap, you could look a woman right into bed," and Mr. Walt shaking his head yes, real hard, like my man had spoken the gospel truth. Ray Ray was talking with his eyes, but I couldn't tell if Cherri was buying. I got the feeling she'd seen this item before.

Edge appeared out of the lockers to get Cherri and, as quick as I turned my head, she was on stage and I was standing stage left with a beaming Ray Ray. "How'd it go?"

"That girl's da joint, man," he said with a boyish grin. If there was anything cool about Ray Ray, his conversation with Cherri had wiped it away. Homeboy was hyped. And I couldn't blame him, 'cause Cherri got me open, too. She began with one of her club hits, "Feel the Heat," and just started rolling those hips in that orange dress. Men and young boys crowded the stage as if drawn by the offer of free money. The clincher was the ballad that Edge was working, "Touch Me Good." It was an all right ballad—a little too soft and adult contemporary for my taste—but she sold it by literally reaching out to the men in the audience and touching them.

Edge was standing on the other side of the stage next to Bishop and a man in a white Fila jumpsuit I assumed was Magic Mike. Edge's mouth was moving a mile a minute and Magic Mike, who now had that hyper-antic look that seems to strike whomever Edge disappeared with, was nodding in agreement. Cherri closed with another up-tempo track, "Fill the Gap," that was in the nasty mold of "Freaky Body Baby." Cherri wasn't a great singer, but she did understand how to sell sex without being dirty, something she'd obviously learned working New York clubs. It was a skill to be respected.

If Ray Ray had been a puppy he'd have been panting. I mean, his tongue was damn near flapping out of his mouth. As Cherri came off stage Edge, Bishop, and Magic Mike whisked her past us. Ray Ray and I were right on their heels. At the door to the locker room, Edge told me to stay by the door and keep everybody out. Ray Ray was upset and his face showed it. I told him to relax. Cherri just needed to cool off. Besides, he and Cherri had bonded, right?

Apparently not. Bishop told me to go on in. When Ray Ray tried to go in with me, Bishop stopped in front of him. "Just him. No other guests."

"Yo!" Ray Ray was not having it. "What goes on?

"I was told that you weren't being allowed backstage—that's what's going on." Bishop's voice had a satisfied tone that suggested he enjoyed cock blocking Ray Ray. "Now move on!" he shouted. Several other folks—radio station personnel, fans, kids—who'd been milling around the door now turned to look at Ray Ray and started murmuring in that frenzied way that suggests a fight was about to start.

Trying to defuse the situation, I told Ray Ray to relax. I'd go in and find out what was up. Then there was this sudden wild look in his eye, like that of a child whose toy had been snatched away. However this child was too big to cry. Ray Ray moved toward the door again and this time Bishop pushed him away. Gallantly, and stupidly, I got in between them just as Ray Ray let go a hard left that caught me square in the nose. Blood spurted out into the air and I went down. Things got blurry after that. People scuffling over me. Shouts. The A.C. cops. A rather disjointed car ride. Things didn't come back into sharp focus until I was stretched out back at the Motor Inn with an ice pack against my nose and an aching in my skull.

Still woozy, I stumbled into the bathroom. There was a bandage over my left nostril and some puffiness around the side of my face. Overall, I didn't look as bad as I felt. I was gonna call Edge's room when I noticed a note on top of the receiver. It read: "We'll be in Bally's at the blackjack tables. Sorry about your nose. Welcome to the road. Edge."

A half hour later, showered, redressed, and sprinkled with my old Polo Cologne, I was walking through the streets of A.C. toward the Boardwalk. With each step the city got brighter and people, white people, began to appear all around me. The ocean rolled against the shore and a few tourists gazed at it. But most, like me, were moving toward one of the casinos that towered over the fast food joints, the small knickknack shops, and all us wannabe gamblers hell-bent on gaming.

Bally's was like the inside of a pinball machine—all the blink of lights, the clink of coins, and the feeling of being bounced around. Slot machines abounded. Voices laughed, cursed, and prayed. I was inside a temple of cash, yet the whispers of prayers, some occasionally answered, could be heard in the vast space. I wandered through the casino, my eyes embracing the faces of gamblers, more fascinated by the hunger in their eyes than the games themselves.

From across the floor I spotted Edge's Kangol bobbing up and down like a duck in dirty water. He was at the center of a crew of folks—Cherri, Magic Mike, Bishop, and good old Ida holding Edge's arm. They had a blackjack table at their disposal and a middle-aged black male dealer. "Hey, there you go!" Edge was in great high spirits. He flagged down a waitress and ordered me a Jack Daniel's.

"He drinks J.D.?" It was Cherri's incredulous voice.

"Yeah," I replied curtly.

"And," Edge added, "he takes a good punch too, young lady, which we all found out because of you."

"What happened?" My question cracked up every one at the table but the dealer, who was busy flipping over cards. Magic Mike beat the house and the dealer pushed a load of chips his way.

"Well," Cherri began, "I didn't feel like being bothered anymore. So you supposed to come inside the locker room and Bishop was supposed to tell him I had to go. I guess he got mad."

"Oh," I said, "it didn't happen like that. Ray Ray didn't swing until Bishop put his hands on him. I got hit just trying to stop anything from happening."

"Is that what went down?" Magic Mike asked.

Bishop, looking and sounding very defensive, cut in and said, "Something like that. You know, you can't reason with these 'Bamas down here." He clearly didn't appreciate me bringing up this old news, so he added, "Anyway, if your man here had just followed orders, he'd be looking a lot prettier."

"All right," Edge said cutting him off, "none of that matters now." He scooped up several chips from his pile and stuffed them in my hand. "You can join the game or start at another table or just cash in. You had a good day today. Relax now." He looked at his watch. "We leave for Philly at four-thirty." My drink arrived and the gang at the table turned their attention back to the game. Well, I wasn't tired and wasn't thirsty, so I just wandered around a bit and then cashed in the $50 worth of chips I'd just been given.

Not having been to a casino before I didn't know there were bands all around the betting marathons. Most of the bands were all white and played things like Morris Alpert's "Feelings" and Billy Joel's "It's Still Rock & Roll to Me." In a far corner was an integrated band with a black woman singing lead. Same crap as all the other bands, but she did it well and she was cute. I sat there for set after set, listening to pop song after pop song sung by this black woman with the straight, smooth sound of Top 40 radio. In fact, listening to her sing "Bette Davis Eyes" and "Hot Stuff" and "Never Too Much" and other contemporary pop made me flash back on those nights I listened to radio in my bed.

But now I heard all the flaws in these pop tunes—the sentimental emotion, the cheesy melodies, the fact that so many of the songs were like empty calories. At the same time, I also now knew that many of these songs had gotten on the radio because of people like Edge and the fact that he gambled with program directors and also had the ability to give radio people that hyper-antic look. The poor songwriters did the best they could with their talent, just like I was trying to do. It wasn't their fault that these songs were hits. I should be so unlucky. This was what I was thinking when Edge tapped me on the shoulder and said, "Let's hit it, youngblood."

"Sideshow"

Philadelphia had produced some of my favorite songwriters: Kenny Gamble and Leon Huff, Thom Bell, Linda Creed, McFadden and John Whitehead, Bunny Sigler. These were tunesmiths of soul and sophistication, gospel passion and classical strings. One of those great Philly songs, Gamble & Huff's "If Only You Knew," sung by Patti Labelle, filled the Caddy as we rolled down City Line Avenue toward WDAS. Though Philly is one of America's big cities, it never felt as congested or hectic as New York or even D.C. Most of the buildings in its busiest districts were relatively low and unimposing. Many of the side streets were narrow, less suitable for cars than the horse-drawn carriages of the WASP elite that helped shape the city.

WDAS was located in just off City Avenue, a strip bordered by Fairmount Park's tall, lush trees and thick bushes, which made you think you were traveling a country lane and not a major thoroughfare in a large Eastern city. The view outside my window was pastoral—all big, beautiful trees and summer breezes—but inside the Caddy the odor was of cigarettes, whiskey, donuts, and thick, dark coffee. Cherri, back in her Gucci gear, was curled up in the fetal position in the back-seat while Edge was next to me, sipping a cup of coffee so hot it was fogging his shades.

"You sure you can see where we're going?"

"Shit," he replied curtly, "I know this road like the back of my ass."

WDAS AM and FM was located in a flat, nondescript brick build-ing at the end of a woody road off City Line Avenue. As we drove up, Edge announced, "Welcome to the home of soul in Philly," then turned and shook Cherri awake. "Good morning star child. Time to sell some vinyl." Morning clearly wasn't Cherri's favorite time. As she slowly fought her way to consciousness, Edge gently prodded her to life. "We're gonna be on the second biggest morning show in Philly and you're gonna charm the hell out of the listeners with your smile and bubbly personality." Cherri grunted. "Then we're gonna go check in a nice hotel where you're gonna spend the rest of the day sleeping. Won't that be good." Edge shoved a cup of coffee in her hand and then spoke the magic words: "The photographer should be here any minute."

This made her open her eyes. "Nobody's gonna take my picture with me looking like this."

"Of course he won't," Edge assured her, "because a half hour from now, when he arrives, you'll be looking good enough to eat. Isn't that the truth, sugar."

Well, she didn't look that good, but Cherri was more than present-able when Edge ushered her into the studio with DAS' morning man Wayne Jolle for her on-air appearance. Cherri flirted, giving that same intoxicating look that felled Ray Ray, and he succumbed as well, pumping her up with great enthusiasm. Photos were taken with Jolle and Cherri locked in a sticky embrace. All the while, Edge was nowhere to be seen. As our half hour ended I went searching and found him in the hallway being dressed down by a heavyset white man.

"Don't try that 'you owe me' mess with me, Lennox." The white man was balding with a salt-and-pepper beard and one whale of a belly. "You know how we do things now. I may not like it. You may not like it. But that's how we do business now, okay? Today's not music day. If it gets around that I let you just pass through here and get a record added, I got the local reps all over me, maybe even going to owner-ship. I can't have that, Lennox."

Edge, my man of the hyper-antic powder and the old school cool, looked sheepish in the face of this barrage. His head was bowed and his body hunched over. Though the bearded white man was a good foot shorter, it was Edge who seemed to be cowering. The white man saw me gawking.

"May I help you?" he asked. When Edge spotted me, he pulled back his shoulders and tried to act as if everything was under control. He reached into his wallet and flipped me a Visa card.

"Register Cherri in the hotel and I'll meet you there later." Not that I knew where the hotel was or how to get there. Whether this was a sign of confidence or just a hasty dismissal, I couldn't tell. Still I got out of there, grabbing Cherri before the morning man, whose shift was ending, tried to take her to breakfast and make a meal of her. Armed with a map and the aid of a nice school crossing guard, we made it to the Sheraton in half an hour.

This may sound silly, but I was quite excited about the responsibility Edge had given me. Being trusted with his Visa card and Cherri's well-being made me feel good. Yeah, it was a little thing done under duress. Still, after my driving in New York and punch-out in Atlantic City, a vote of confidence was right on time.

I damn near had to carry Cherri to her room, the girl was so tired. Strangely, I felt very tired but could not sleep. My moms would have said I was overtired. "Too tired to even have the energy to sleep." As if sleeping was as exhausting an activity as walking or running. She'd told me that when I'd been practicing piano one day and it had always stuck with me. So I called her, hoping she'd say something so motherly and wise I'd curl up as if I was in her arms.

Instead, Pops picked up. The mad pornographer of Times Square was asking me where I was and was I all right. I provided the pertinent details, leaving out the punch-out since I didn't think he'd be as sympathetic as Moms. Then it dawned on me that my Pops was home in the middle of the day. "Pops, are you all right?" Silence was his reply. "Pops? What's up? Is something wrong?"

"Some guys robbed the funeral home." He spoke quickly as if the revelation embarrassed him. I asked again if he was all right. "Well," he finally admitted, "my left arm's in a sling." Reluctantly he filled in the rest. Near closing, two teenagers broke in a basement window, went right past two cadavers, and found their way into his office. He walked in after the last service that evening and one of the teenagers smashed his forearm with a baseball bat, before forcing him to open the safe. "Fools weren't real smart because I tripped the police alarm while they were watching. Those narcotics will do it to you so you can't even rob a man right." He forced a sad, bewildered laugh. Pops sounded old to me at that moment and I felt terrible for any mean thoughts I'd had at his expense.

"When did this happen?"

"Friday night. I'd just been in the city that day shopping for your mother. You know I never go into Manhattan. Must have been an omen of bad luck." Of course I let that comment pass. On the positive side, Pops hadn't been hurt other than the broken arm, and had given the police a thorough description of the robbers and everything, including the cash, was covered by insurance.

Less pleasing to me was the news that Anna was running the business while Pops recuperated. Here I was in a hotel room in Philly and my cousin—my little girl cousin—was picking up the slack for the family. As if reading my mind, Pops told me, "Don't worry and don't come back home. I know your mother will want you to, but you're out there learning your business. I think if you're gonna do something, then you better learn about it. That's just common sense. Besides, you didn't join the Army, so you never did get to travel any. Might as well do it when you're young. Now give me your number so your mother can worry you later."

When we'd hung up I was so happy. It was the best conversation I'd had with him in a long, long time. My rage at the robbers was cooled by his tacit approval of my career. It wasn't a ringing endorsement, but I'd take it.

My phone rang at 6 P.M. "Come on down and have some breakfast, youngblood." Edge was back to normal. Down in the hotel he sat with Cherri riffing on the rhythm and the blues. He was saying to Cherri, "Teddy was probably the last male singer I went out of my way to hear. He had guts in his voice. He made the women scream, but he made you proud to be a man, too. Then he got caught out there." Edge was referring to the car crash in which Teddy was crippled and the inescapable fact that a transvestite was his passenger that tragic night.

"That was a bad night, young brother. A bad night. Felt as bad that night as I did when Marvin's father shot him. His damn father used to dress up like a girl, too. That's probably what messed him up." After Marvin's death it came out that his father, once a Pentecostal preacher, had often worn women's clothes when Marvin was a kid. This intersection of cross-dressing and great male singers really rankled Edge.

"It's weird, huh?" I observed neutrally, hoping he'd elaborate on his feelings.

"Weird. Shit. Comics are weird. The Twilight Zone, that's weird. This stuff was sick. Nobody needed to know all that. The newspapers didn't have to know. And then they didn't have to tell. Teddy's still in a wheelchair; Marvin's still dead. Whether we know that stuff or not, those would be the facts of the case. It's probably why all these damn kids are grabbing their dicks now. They don't want no misunderstanding. Right?" Cherri smiled and nodded affirmatively.

Shifting the conversation, Edge asked, "So how you feeling, youngblood?" I told him I was cool and then wondered how he was feeling. Whenever I asked my Pops that question I usually got a brief, perfunctory reply. It even took him a minute to tell me about his broken arm. But whatever middle-aged restraints held back my Pops were not in Edge's make up. He looked at me sagely. He'd caught my meaning. More imporant, he'd felt my concern—he knew I was asking from the heart, not out of idle curiousity or meanness.

"When I came to Philly years back, you could see one man, a DJ named Georgie Woods. Georgie Woods, 'the man with the goods.' You hooked up with him and you were straight in this town. Airplay. A nice spot on the bill at the Uptown Theater. The record or artist would get a fair shot and the audience would decide if you had a hit or not. That's one reason the music down here got so good, 'cause it was made in an environment where you could grow.

"Now the power's spread out. Georgie's now a talk show host rather than a deejay. Now you got music directors and program directors and in-house promotion people and radio consultants who don't even live in town, and people walking around with market research talking about demographics. There have always been white owners involved in black radio, but now they have moved the stations into this format called 'urban contemporary' where what gets on the air or who's allowed to appear at station promotions is tied to financial commitments made between corporations, and not people who love the music. It's more political than Congress—in Philly now and everywhere else, too! So when you ask an old friend for a favor, it hurts to be turned down. And it hurts those that have to turn you down, too."

Edge had managed to admit weakness without seeming weak. All of this was related with little bitterness, but with a kind of amused fatalism. This man had fascinated me since I was a little boy in Mr. Walt's barbershop. This was the first time, however, he'd moved me.

Cherri didn't catch any of these sensitive undertones. As in the car on the Garden State Parkway, she suddenly unleashed a barrage of questions. "What time's the track date tonight? Does what you just said mean DAS isn't gonna put my record in rotation? Are you gonna pay for a hairdresser, 'cause I need one. When am I gonna get to sleep again?"

This time, though, Edge was slow in responding. He'd gotten her a chance to do two songs at half-time of a summer league all-star game on the Temple University campus, after which they were gonna stop by a spot called the Library Club to meet the club's deejay, a woman named Lady B who was becoming large in Philly playing dance and rap music. After that we'd hop on down to Wilmington, Delaware, check in, sleep a couple of hours, do a morning show at a small AM station there, go back to sleep, and head to Baltimore that afternoon.

And, yes, he'd pay for a hairdresser—in Baltimore. She did not like waiting to see a hairdresser, but Edge explained that her label would be sending him some cash halfway through the trip, which was Baltimore, so she had to accept that.

On the most important question, would DAS put Cherri's single in rotation, Edge was evasive. "They played it this morning," he started cautiously. "And between the response the record got and my conversation with the program director, I expect good things to happen." Not exactly a resounding yes.

With real ghetto attitude Cherri wondered, "Why am I on this trip if it doesn't mean my records are gonna get played. Otherwise I could—"

"Otherwise you could be the prettiest girl in your projects with two lovely kids and a great chance for more. Maybe you could get a job with the transit authority and get some benefits. That would be good for a Spanish black girl. Or you could be out here, doing what you're doing now—not sleeping good with your hair a mess and acting pissed as you try to become a millionaire before you're twenty-five. No guarantee of that happening of course, but no matter how good the TA treats you, they ain't making no millionaires."

I was sure Cherri was gonna go off, 'cause her face got beet red. But Edge must have made some sense to her. She looked away and said, "I hear you, Edge. I hear you." Then, like a scolded four-year-old, she looked up and said, "So, can we eat now?" Edge said, "I hope so" and started waving for a waiter. Me? I got the idea for this song.

"Knowledge of the Road"

Words come and go
But wisdom
Yeah wisdom
Keeps you from being low.
I listen closely
I try to hear
Because what I'm lacking
is knowledge of the road,
Cause what I'm lacking
is knowledge of the road.
People talk so much
Teaching nothing,
Yeah teaching nothing
About such and such
I don't pay attention.
Attention I don't pay
Because what I'm seeking
is knowledge of the road,
Cause what I'm seeking
is knowledge of the road.

"Derek, you wanna come in now?" I looked up dazed. Edge was on the other side of the glass. I was sitting in the parking lot outside the Library Club with a notebook in one hand and a tape recorder in another, sing-talking the melody. I was knee-deep into writing, the first time in a while I felt so inspired and nothing was gonna interrupt me now. Edge told me there was plenty of pussy inside, but none of it meant anything to me. Edge had never seen me like this and clearly didn't know what to make of it. As he walked back toward the club I began to wonder what Edge actually thought of me—mascot, joke, protégé. Probably not as an artist. But I was one, and tonight I was not being a bodyguard, gofer, and certainly not a punching bag. I'd written two verses and now I came up with a chorus.

K-N-O-W
L-E-D-G-E
E-E-EQUALS
Knowledge of the road.

K-N-O-W
L-E-D-G-E
E-E-EQUALS
Knowledge of the road.

When I looked up again Edge was back at the window with Cherri beside him, trailed by a big bouncer type. As they entered the car, I could hear that the bouncer was sweating Cherri and she was playing along. He gave Cherri his numbers and Cherri kissed him on the cheek, then we were off toward Delaware. Apparently the gig went well, 'cause Edge was praising her to the hilt. Me, I was whistling the melody to "Knowledge of the Road" to myself, feeling it, playing with it, filling myself with this new music I'd created in the car.

Then suddenly I was hearing harmony. Cherri was listening to me, even as she'd been talking to Edge. So while I whistled, she hummed. I started singing the words and she hummed along until she understood them and then joined in. Once she really knew it, Cherri began putting in little accents of her own. She was no Vernon Jackson, but Cherri understood what she could do, which is more than most singers do. Edge watched, looking quietly pleased. Then he closed his eyes and rested his Kangol against the window and fell asleep as we sang our way out of Philly.

After A.C. and Philly, Wilmington, Delaware, was nothing. We hit the morning show and since I was feeling energized by my bout of writing, we decided to get on the road to Baltimore. My eyes were itching but I made it into B-more by 11 A.M. A taxi took Cherri to a hairdresser Edge recommended, while he went to some crab place he liked. I stayed in my room and made a list of calls: Moms, Gibbs, and, most important, Candi.

I had been bad about keeping in contact with her lately. She'd been so supportive after my D.C. misadventure. The love had been true and she'd sent me a couple of games to work on and then mail back to her. You know, like long-distance chess. Between my nights with Edge at Possible 20 and hustling for gigs I'd been a little forgetful of my romantic responsibilities. Candi went to Howard in the mornings and in the evenings worked as a counselor at a retirement home. So the best time to reach her tended to be late at night. She wanted midnight love calls. But I was usually out playing or drinking or some combination of the two.

At first she'd call and was, if not happy, at least understanding about my nocturnal activities. She knew music was a night business and that if I was in, I probably wasn't getting paid. But my follow-through was piss poor. It wasn't like I was knocking boots all over town. Ever since Ruthie Lee's death I'd kept *Sketches of Spain* under wraps. Don't know why I didn't call her back quickly. One day, two days, sometimes four days later I'd call back. Usually I'd miss her because she wasn't home in the afternoons when I'd wake up. If I was honest with myself I'd have to admit that Ruthie Lee's passing had really shook me, shook me more than I knew how to express. Somewhere inside I didn't wanna connect with anybody, 'cause I was still feeling bad about my role in her death. This stop in D.C. would give me a chance to reconnect with Candi, to let her know I valued and needed her in my life. Of course when I woke up, around 1:30, she wasn't home, so I just left the relevant digits—hotel, time of arrival—on her answering machine.

That night, Cherri, Edge, and I sat at the Crab House restaurant in the newly renovated, user-friendly, heavily policed Inner Harbor area. Black folks were allowed in, but young black folks, people who looked suspiciously like me, were watched closely. Until I hooked up with Edge and Cherri in front of the Crab House, I had the distinct impression that two security guards had been shadowing me and my New York saunter. Despite that the dinner was great. Crabs from the Chesapeake Bay. Potatoes from Idaho. Steak from Missouri. Jack Daniel's from Kentucky. And stories, of course, stories. Told not by Edge but yours truly. Stories of funny funerals, condom misadventures, songwriting in the basement, and the first time I met Edgecombe Lennox.

Not that I had a deep catalog of tales. It's just that on this night I started talking and both my companions laid back and let me host. Edge had it in him, I knew from our many nights at Possible 20, but Cherri actually paid attention to me and seemed interested. Whether she genuinely thought I was interesting or was merely stroking me because she liked my song, I wasn't sure. And, as the Jack flowed and the laughter grew, I decided not to care. It was after midnight when we got back to our hotel and this message was waiting: "See you in D.C. I'll come by the hotel. Don't call tonight. Got a test in the morning and need my beauty sleep. Candi."

Baltimore proved hectic. The next morning we hit two stations, the AM WOL and the FM WWIN, before 8:30 A.M. Cherri was in good form, flirting with the deejays, while Edge was extra sharp, as if being quiet at dinner the night before had been a strategy to conserve energy. It was music day at WWIN, so other promotion men were in the house. Some had hard, predatory eyes. Others were loquacious handshakers with guile-filled smiles like Edge. He seemed quite content in their company, telling war stories, comparing notes, talking biz. I noticed the promotion men rarely discussed music.

Instead the talk was of indie budgets, expense accounts, PDs, MDs, and call letters. WWRL. WAMO. WOL. KACE. WBLS. V-103. WHUR. The four letter codes that identify stations flowed like rain. No cities. No geography. Just four-digit codes. If you didn't know they were talking about radio, you were lost. The only thing you could be sure of was that they savored their insiders' knowledge and had little patience for those seeking translation.

While I sat trying to decipher the call letters, Cherri sat in the lobby with two burly security guards hovering over her. No doubt about it, homegirl liked her men big with broad shoulders, thick necks, and thick foreheads. Men used to being hit. I was contemplating this when the two security guards started yelling at each other. "She didn't ask for all that!" announced the slightly smaller of the two.

"Hey, homes, get out ma face!" his larger partner suggested. Cherri sat underneath them, watching the immature chaos her looks had inspired, with bored eyes and amused lips. I moved over to this trio remembering my A.C. beat down, steeling myself for trouble. Cherri looked up at me with a huge, telegenic smile.

"Are you ready, Derek?" She looked at me sweetly. "I hope I didn't keep you waiting." The two security guards turned my way, as surprised by my sudden appearance as I was by her deference. "Let me introduce my friend. This is Derek Harper, one of the top songwriters in New York. He's gonna write me a song. Aren't you, Derek?"

"That's why I'm here."

One of the security guards was cowed by Cherri's hype. The other, obviously dumber brother, was giving me no respect. "Now," he said with an edge, "I know you ain't goin', baby. We ain't finished talking." If this was a Baltimore security guard, how were Baltimore thugs?

"Excuse me, son." It was Edge at his persuasive best. "But I understand that your woman is at the employees entrance wondering where last month's check was." The first security guard made one of those childish high school "Ooooch" sounds and covered his mouth. The meaner guard did a slow burn and then disappeared without a look back at me or Cherri.

"Where do you get your material? Edge?"

"Fear," he replied, "is a dark room where negatives are developed." I just busted out laughing. Didn't know what the hell my man was talking about, but it was funny and appropriate, too!

Another night, another radio station promo gig. A club halfway between D.C. and Baltimore that some local radio station deejay had a piece of. Before Cherri came on there was a dance contest. Contestants seemed pretty equally divided between Michael Jackson moon walkers and kids doing real awkward attempts at New York break

S
E
D
U
C
E
D

dancing. The farther South we'd go, the more jheri curls I'd see. Edge laughed and told me, "The grease is just gettin' ready to flow, young-blood. Black folks haven't been this moist since the glory days of the process."

Edge was in good spirits, but Cherri's mood was foul. Just as jheri curls proliferated as we rolled South, so Cherri's dance diva celebrity dwindled. Baltimore was about as far south as a New York 12-inch traveled. There were pockets of New York club music fans in places with lots of students and ex-residents from the city (e.g., Hampton, Virginia; Miami), but we were now entering the funk zone, where southern accents, slang, and sensibility ruled. Few in the audience seemed familiar with Cherri's music. Even the ballad that Edge later insisted was already being played by some local stations sparked little excitement.

Still Cherri did her thing. Big thighs, orange stage dress, and sensual steps will always generate some enthusiasm. She left the stage with a forced smile but once in the wings tears fell. I tried to console her. At first she pushed me away with her eyes. Then I came back with some burgundy wine and Cherri took both the glass and my hand, squeezing it tight as she sat silently and dabbed her tears with a paper towel.

When Edge finally walked over he was distant. No tall tales of r&b wisdom; no comforting stories of great entertainers who stumbled when young. Just looked at her and said, "Don't worry, Cherri. They'll know who you are soon. Count on it." His tone was half-hearted while the smell of Jack Daniel's floated in the air, more pungent than his brief words. As soon as Cherri was dressed we were off down I-95 for the short drive to D.C., all of us preoccupied and silent.

Edge had the heavy-eyed gaze of a Mississippi sharecropper after work on payday. I was beginning to realize I liked him better on coke than booze. Cherri had cracked a back window and twisted her body so that the fumes from her joint supposedly went out that crack. It struck me that marijuana smoke emanating from a rental Cadillac with New York plates on a major Eastern highway was not the smartest way to travel. No one stopped us on our way into D.C., but I was nervous all the way. Didn't know it then, but my anxiety wasn't about Cherri's drugs or Edge's moods. It was about going to D.C. again and Candi and sad things I couldn't anticipate but felt in my bones.

"Drop the Bomb"

Morning in the nation's capitol. Trucks drop off *The Washington Post* as limos with diplomatic plates glide past the Capitol Building and bureaucrats enter gray stone structures that house the "Department" of this and the "Agency" for that. A few blocks away from these clusters of government authority are row houses stuck tight together. Kids sporting Georgetown Hoya T-shirts and shorts troop around circular thoroughfares and old women wait patiently on the Metrobus, talking about last Sunday's service at Congressman Walter Fauntroy's church. Transvestite prostitutes are calling it a night down the block from the Convention Center as a Japanese businessman comes out jogging from the Capitol Hill Marriott. Hanging on a light post, right above two re-elect Mayor Marion Barry posters, is a sign advertising a gospel jamboree with twelve choirs and Shirley Caesar all scheduled to appear.

My eye is enjoying D.C. when I spy a battered marquee that reads "Howard." It was standing high on the side of a tired old building. I tapped Edge on the shoulder. "Wasn't that an old r&b theater, Edge?" Behind his shades, Edge cracked open one eye and then closed it again.

"Yeah," he said slowly, "that's the Howard."

"It was like the Apollo, right?"

"There was only one Apollo. But it was a sweet room, all right. Can't say it wasn't."

I slowed down. "I've been reading this book, *The Relentless Beat,* by that guy from *Billboard.*

"Dwayne Robinson." There was acid in Edge's voice.

"Yeah. I bought the book after I saw him with you. There's a lot about the Howard in it. He talks about how the groups on this old label—"

"Delux Records."

"Yeah, and how they'd get their haircut at this barbershop that used to be here."

Then Edge cut me off again. "Let's just get to the hotel. We got an in-store this afternoon and I need to make some calls."

"Sure," I said and I pulled off. I guess this was too much nostalgia for him, so I cruised over to where we were staying, the Howard Inn.

This hotel, located on a block between the Howard University Hospital and the campus, was owned by the school, and as such, was one of the few mid-sized black-owned hotels in the country. It made me feel good as a black person to be there. But the place was no palace. It wasn't smelly or nasty or anything like that. It was just not as well maintained or staffed as you'd like. The front desk people got an attitude quick if you pointed out a mistake. The bellmen, if you could find them, were lethargic. The room I was in had a view of the campus that was obscured by a heating duct. No pay T.V. Too few hangers. The bed, however, was fine and firm and even if it had been lumpy, I wouldn't have known 'cause I was so damn tired I fell out as soon as I went horizontal.

There was a knock at the door and I could hear Edge's voice, insistent and harsh, in the hallway. I stumbled over and opened up the door. "Youngblood, you look like dog pooh pooh." Couldn't say the same for him. He had a fresh new white Kangol and a navy blue shirt and slacks. His Bally shoes were as white and unscuffed as new-fallen snow. "I've been trying to ring you for fifteen minutes."

"I'm tired, Edge." I said as pitiful as a scolded child. "We've had one good night's sleep since we left New York."

"And does that mean the show is gonna stop?" Suddenly I knew how Cherri had felt in Philly. "You can read all the books you want about the road, but this is how it is. It can be better than this. Limos. Open bars. Four-star hotels. But mostly it's sleeping when you can, peeing when you can, and eating when you can." I yawned really loudly at this point, which led Edge to shake his head. "Everybody wants to go to heaven, but nobody wants to dig the grave. I'm gonna go wake up our star. I want you to meet me downstairs in ten minutes."

Thirty minutes later Edge strode into the lobby. I'd seen his face this red before but only after several glasses of whiskey. "Go upstairs!" Huh? "Go upstairs!" he repeated as heads turned all around the lobby. "Tell that little girl I've set things up for her! I got 'HUR! I got Kemp Mill doing an in-store! I got her stuff her cheap ass label could never afford!"

Clearly I was not the subject of Edge's rage, but since I was available I was the target. It was embarrassing to have him speak to me in such a scolding tone and I told him so. "Yo, Edge, chill out man. I'm not against you, baby."

"Okay. Okay, I hear you, youngblood." He plopped himself down in a cushy chair next to me and took off his Kangol like a king forsaking his crown, suddenly looking old. "Just go get her. I got some nice stuff going on at 'HUR, but we need to get there on time. Go talk to her. Get her to come down. Please."

When Cherri realized it was me knocking on her door, she opened it. She was wearing a white towel on her head, a Walkman on her ears, a blue satin bathrobe on her body with ten well-manicured red toes peeking out underneath it. We exchanged good mornings. Then a moment of silence. I really wasn't quite sure what to say. Guess I was a little surprised to see her like this. She invited me in.

Her room was the same as mine except that all of Cherri's belongings were either folded, stacked, or collected in a frighteningly organized manner. My self-conscious survey of Cherri's room was stopped by a familiar sound leaking out of her Walkman. "Are you listening to some of my songs?" She nodded yes and then walked into the bathroom and closed the door. I sat on the bed, taking in the sweet aroma of marijuana and holding up one of her orange stage heels. Her feet were small and dainty, like a little girl's. I took a sniff and then put the shoe down when she exited the bathroom.

She was wearing jeans, a low-cut pink blouse, and panty hose. Her makeup was done and her hair was again pulled back Sade style. She sat on the bed next to me, Walkman still on, sliding into some Loafers. "I decided I didn't like the way that girl in Baltimore did my hair," she explained before I could ask.

"Edge is waiting downstairs, you know."

"Whatever," she answered dismissively. "I've been rushing this whole trip."

"But the people at the station—"

"They'll wait for me, baby, if they really want to see me." Her shoes were on now. She lit a cigarette and gave me the once-over. Homegirl was oozing the kind of confidence I'd seen so often from her on stage. This time the target wasn't a bunch of horny men. The target was me. And she was hitting the bull's eye. "Derek. You know I like your

SEDUCED

songs." She touched my arm, as if to steady me. I flashed back to trying to seduce Pam Washington in my basement with my songs, and I flashed back to poor pitiful Ray Ray with his fruitless attempts. They were like wake-up calls to snap me out of my desire for Cherri. A little arrogance was called for here to get things back on track.

"If you want me to write you a song, it's no problem."

"All I said was that I liked your songs. Don't let it go to your head." Proximity had made me lust after Cherri, but I was not going to be messed with. She'd even gotten Edge down, so I was determined to stay in control. I could have given her orders, telling her to get her sweet ass downstairs. But all that would have gotten me was cursed out and probably fired. So again I bit my tongue and told her I'd see her in the lobby. She wanted me to sit down and put my ego in check.

"This is your party, baby," I said. "I'm just the driver in this situation, so don't fuck with my head. This ain't A.C." I didn't slam the door, but I didn't look back, either.

Back in the lobby Edge asked me, "How'd it go?"

"She's nasty and spoiled."

He frowned. "Oh, it went like that." He looked down at his watch. "My ex always nagged that I didn't really work for a living." Then he hissed "Shit" like an angry snake.

Fifteen minutes later Cherri came downstairs, all bright and chipper, and we drove the short drive over to 'HUR. I waited outside in the Caddy and found the station on the dial. Ray, Goodman & Brown's "Special Lady" was playing, which seemed to fit the M.O. of the tour. Then they played Cherri's record. When the record faded the deejay announced, "That was Cherri with the most requested song of the week." No wonder Edge had been so anxious—the song was happening in D.C.! When Cherri got back to the car, no matter what, I was gonna tell her off.

Soon Cherri, Edge, and a thirty-something white woman exited 'HUR. Everybody was smiling and Edge was yakking. He looked to be in full sales mode. He even took both ladies by the arm, like he was daddy and this was his family. They'd been inside about an hour, but judging by Edge and Cherri's faces, this was a new day. The white woman, Suzy Boscowitz, was a local concert promoter who went "way back" with Edge. The giddy way they were chatting in the backseat told me their relationship went "way deep" as well. I'd never seen Edge interact with white folks before and I certainly hadn't expected us running into any at 'HUR. Cherri sat up front with me. First time on the trip she'd been in the passenger seat and I often found myself glancing over at her. Everyone seemed to have mellowed, for now. Maybe all the traveling, the intermittent sleep, the stress of greeting strangers, of new surroundings and different foods had conspired to make us all bow and bend like reeds, even when situations made it seem like we'd snap. I mulled this over as we cruised around D.C. hawking Cherri's record at the Kemp Mill record store in Georgetown; WOL, a small station near the Capitol; an interview at the local black weekly, the *Afro-American*; and a little Mom & Pop retailer in the city's Adams Morgan neighborhood.

We got back to the Howard Inn at about 6 P.M. and the gig wasn't until 9:30. There was a message from my moms. Nothing from Gibbs. Nothing from Candi. Edge and Suzy were going over to Hogate's, a seafood spot on the banks of the Potomac, and Edge kind of invited Cherri and me to join them, but the offer was so half-hearted he could have saved his breath. In the elevator upstairs, Cherri inquired, "Do you wanna eat with me tonight?" Despite our little confrontation this morning she was still tempting and I was still drawn to her. But I surprised myself.

"No," I said, "my woman lives in D.C. and I'm gonna wait on her call." Cherri then slipped into interrogation mode: "How long have you known her?" "How serious is it?" "How old is she?" I mumbled my way through it and hustled off to my room before I weakened.

The phone back in Queens was busy, so I turned on the tube. I was watching George Jefferson do the funky chicken on a rerun when there was a knock on the door. Cherri stood in my doorway clutching a big McDonald's bag.

"Is that all for me?" I asked.

"Fries. Shake. The whole big brown bag." Full court press. Now I was tempted to turn the ball over.

Then Candi's voice says, "Hello, Derek," and she appears next to Cherri. Her hair was auburn and fried straight. She wore a white shirt with "AKA" written across it in blue letters, Jordache jeans, and white sneakers. A bulky handbag/book bag hung from one shoulder. Candi looked superbly collegiate, which either amused or threatened Cherri depending on how you read the expression on her face.

"Oh, you must be Derek's woman in D.C."

Immediately I tried to stop the bleeding. "No, Cherri," I said, "this is my woman, Candi."

Candi was chilly. All she said was, "Well, its been nice meeting you" and then sauntered right past Cherri and into my room. Cherri really wanted an excuse to be stank, so I assured her we'd meet in the lobby at 9 P.M. and tried to close the door.

But homegirl had to have the last word. "Don't be late," Cherri said, leaning into my room. "Hope to see you again, sugar." Cherri just flashed a totally fake smile and I happily shut the door.

"Can she sing?"

"She's got a decent voice."

"Well, it wouldn't matter, would it? I already know she can perform and I just met her."

Wanting to make Cherri a memory I moved to Candi and embraced her. Holding her, all my bottled-up enthusiasm came bubbling out and I babbled about how much I loved her. My joy was genuine and I needed her to feel it. I was so into my feelings, at first I didn't notice how cool her lips were. I wanted her to fall on the mattress and wrap around me like a blanket. Instead we sat on the bed with Candi's back upright and as rigid as an ironing board. Her control was unsettling me. I began apologizing for the missed phone calls, for not finishing the games she'd sent, and for the looseness that had weakened our bond. I was damn near on bended knee when Candi started crying.

"Don't cry, Candi." How bad did I feel now? "It makes me feel bad, baby. I know I can do better by us. I'll come down here more often. I'll call more. I've been seeing you since high school. Maybe I took you for granted, but that won't happen anymore."

Candi slowly wiped her tears, but didn't look me in the eye. Hadn't been looking my way the whole time I talked. It struck me maybe I was about to hear something I wouldn't like. She said my name and the hairs on my neck rose up. Her tone was so cold. "I have to tell you something." I didn't respond. I knew it was time for me to be quiet. "I'm moving in with someone."

Like a character in a sitcom I replied, "You're getting a roommate," as if she'd have been crying about telling me that.

"No. I'm moving in with someone. A man. Someone I've been seeing here. Isaac's been great to me," she said. "He's helped me in so many ways. Derek. Since my parents split up it's been hard. You know that. He's been here for me when I've needed someone here."

There was more. He was about thirty. Had a business. More of the kind of stuff a struggling twenty-three-year-old guy wants to hear from his high school sweetheart. I wish I was one of those guys who could just flip on a girl and put her in check. I wish I was cooler, shrewder, sharper. Suddenly my joy was now pain and every moment I breathed the same air Candi did made me sick. No screaming. No shouting. I just went to my door and opened it. She spoke words to me, but I couldn't hear her. When she kissed me I didn't feel it. I wasn't there. Not there at all. I was back in high school across the aisle from her and I was in the snow with her and I was in the balcony with Diana Ross and Billy Dee Williams and I was back in Queens, but I wasn't there. I wasn't alone in my room in D.C. even though my body, sadly, was.

What do you do in a situation like this? Yup. I called my moms and I spilled my guts. I told her what Candi said. I told her what I said and what I didn't say or didn't know how to. She listened quietly. I could hear her washing dishes as I rambled on. I kept saying, "I don't understand what I did wrong" as glasses clicked together in my family's sink so many miles away. I could tell when my moms sat down at the dining room table and that my pops was in the living room, kicked back watching the Mets or just asleep with the *Daily News* in his lap.

"You didn't do anything wrong," she assured me. "You and Candi just got older. You both have your own lives now. She's in another city. She's made new friends. So have you, Derek. Most high school sweethearts either get married after school or they break up after graduation. That you two have remained this close, considering the distance, is more surprising than Candi moving in with somebody there."

It made sense. It really did. "Don't blame yourself, son. And don't blame her, either. She's moved on and you've got to move on. You probably have already. You just hung on to her because you were used to her. It was comfortable. But you're young. You can be comfortable when you're thirty." That made sense, too. I guess that's what moms are supposed to do.

I asked about Pops. "He's doing fine now," she said, but there was something uncertain in her voice. "Business is booming. The negotiations with the O'Mally's are going well. And Anna has really been a big help." Funny what a difference a few days make—today I felt no jealousy. "But I'm worried about him working at the home late," she said.

"I don't think those guys will come back, Moms."

"It's not just them, it's all of them, all these young fools out here. This angel dust thing is getting out of hand around here. Over on Francis Lewis Boulevard and on Linden Boulevard young boys congregate selling this stuff. Your father thinks they're all from the 40 projects, but I notice faces I've seen coming from homes right around here. Walter says his father's been robbed twice this year." This was sad news. It was hard to believe all this was happening out in our section of Queens. Jamaica, sure. But somebody hitting Mr. Walt? Damn.

Then Moms added the kicker. "All these drugs have been bad for the area, but it's been good for our business. These angel dust kids get so out of hand that they either kill someone or have to be killed. This could be our biggest year ever." After that talk, I spread out on the bed and just wanted to be blank for a minute. I'd been thinking way too much.

Edge's call woke me up at a quarter to ten. When I got in the lobby, Edge, Suzy, and Cherri were ready and anxious to go. Whatever truce had been worked out between them was holding. Cherri, of course, tried to pry into my meeting with Candi, but I deflected her by mentioning that Walter Gibbs might be at the club tonight. Even Edge seemed energized by that prospect. Meanwhile I was still bruised inside. The most important romantic relationship of my young life had been shattered. All I wanted to do was get in the club and hear some good, loud music. In that, I would not be disappointed.

There were three acts on the bill. First up were the Brothers Black, a hip-hop trio from Hollis, who rapped over the groove to Cheryl Lynn's "Got To Be Real" and James Brown's "Funky Drummer." Dressed in black sweats and backwards baseball caps, they reminded me a bit of that other Hollis group, Run-D.M.C., with a bit of the Cold

Brothers in their delivery. The lead rapper, Attak, who couldn't have been more than sixteen, was rather shy. He barely made eye contact with Cherri when I introduced them backstage. But on the mike Attak was all New York b-boy swagger, which immediately made me homesick. No Gibbs. Attak said he was on his way to Atlanta, setting up some special presentation for Jack the Rapper. Cherri's voice was a little raw—maybe homegirl was too rested—but the D.C. boys enjoyed her, though some local girls snickered at her New York accent.

The Brothers Black and Cherri were just the prelude for Trouble Funk. I'd heard of go-go. Maybe I'd heard a record or two in the Apple. But when these eleven pieces hit the stage I was rocked by the rawest, darkest, deepest, most polyrhythmic dance music I'd heard since last seeing P-Funk. This funk was powered by four percussionists, not including the trap drummer, a three-piece horn section, and the fattest bass sound this side of Jamaica dub. Felt like I was back in Africa, that's how primal this stuff was. The interplay between the audience and the band was intense. The band and the crowd exchanged catch phrases, and I felt I was listening in on some special D.C. party code. Song wise, my critical nose for structure told me nothing was going on. But the funk was flowing back and forth between the musicians and the fans like water over a falls, so this was no time for me to be picking the experience apart. All I was obligated to do was feel it.

I was rubbing my pelvis up against this big chocolate-brown sister when Edge pulled my shirt. I mean, I was so drenched in sweat my underwear needed to be squeezed out. "A little bit longer, Edge! Please, man!" Edge didn't know about Candi, but maybe something in my desperation to party touched him and he disappeared back into the mass of undulating torsos that surrounded us. Fifteen minutes later, me and Tee Tee—my new friend's name—were pushed up against a wall trading saliva and dry humping quite obscenely. All around me was the moist aroma of black body heat and the acrid, acidy smell of angel dust. People were getting zooted all around me. The music filled me so that my chest cavity throbbed. In the Caddy, Tee Tee kept calling me "Daddy" as she clawed at my back.

Morning sun cracked through my window and my mouth was sandpaper. There was an arm across my chest and a mass of messed-up black woman's hair against my chest. Correct that. Black girl's hair. Tee Tee was maybe eighteen if I looked at her with one eye closed. I needed to get her home. I needed to find out from Edge when we were leaving. I needed to wash out my foul-tasting mouth. Instead, I reached over to the note pad on the table next to the bed and wrote this:

No, I wasn't looking for love
And I wasn't looking for pain
I was just looking for someone
(someone)
Who kinda felt the same.
But you done changed my mind, girl
You came and flipped my world.
But now that same door that you opened
(the same door you opened)
Yes, that same door you opened
You better exit through.

I called it "The Same Door You Opened." It was kind of bitter. Probably the most bitter thing I'd written to date. Its anger was real. Yet it didn't exorcise my pain. It didn't free me from Candi. It was just a song—words and melody, rhymes and chords. It wasn't Candi's love, it wasn't the love I lost.

"Endless Love"

In the car from D.C. to Atlanta I sang, whistled, hummed, and fixated on this tune and the woman who inspired it. Through Maryland, Virginia, the Carolinas, and across Georgia on Highway I-95, I barely spoke to my companions. And my companions barely spoke to each other. Whatever fellowship had existed in the Caddy before D.C. was history. Black radio circa 1984 filled the car. "Billie Jean." "Uptown." "The Second Time Around." "Sexual Healing." "Rock Me Tonight." "Hang On to Your Love." And every now and then "Touch Me Good" would float in and cover our silence with little smiles. Edge had done his job in every one of the Southern cities we passed through, generating airplay, doling out money or drinks or whatever to key radio personnel, and making sure Cherri was involved in any local promotional activities, be they an NAACP party fund-raiser in Norfolk or a wet T-shirt contest in Durham.

It was about 8 A.M. when we reached Atlanta's city limits. Edge had instructed me to wake him when we crossed that line and so I did. His waking eyes were cardinal red and his voice hoarse. "Atlanta? Good." He pulled six twenties out of his wallet and placed them in my right hand. "Derek, you did a good job."

"Thanks," I replied, "though I got less sleep and less pussy than I imagined. But I learned a lot. Even got some songs out of it."

"That's good," he said chuckling. "I'm glad of that. Sorry about the pussy, youngblood, but if you'd have gotten more, that would have been just a little more sleep you'd have missed.

"Okay, here's what happens next. You're gonna drop me off at the Omni hotel and then you take our lady friend over to the Sheraton and check you both in. You'll take my room. Sometime this afternoon, Hal Libby from her label will pick her up. You make sure they hook up and then you're free to party until your plane leaves Sunday night. The next three days are for you to meet and greet, my treat."

"You gonna introduce me to some folks, right?"

With some mild irritation he replied, "If we happen to be hanging in the same area, sure. But I've got to generate more work, so baby-sitting will be a real low priority."

That baby-sitting crack irritated me, but I understood. He'd get me in the game. Whether I hit my shots afterward was not his lobby. He wasn't my agent, he wasn't my coach.

Referring to Cherri, who was sound asleep in the back, I wondered if she'd talk to me once Jack the Rapper started. He chuckled again and said, "She's a few branches on the tree higher than you, youngblood. Once she gets rolling, she'll smile or nod or something like that. But don't expect much. That way she can only pleasantly surprise you."

"In other words, expect to get played."

He shook his head negatively. "It ain't even happened and you're already taking it personal. Look, you make sure you meet some new people. You already know her. Hang by the bar. Use that cash to buy some drinks. Act like you care about what people are saying—you're good at that already. You do that and you might end up playing me."

"Yeah, right."

"Stranger things have happened, youngblood. Believe that."

Everybody said Atlanta was becoming the new black Mecca. It had a black mayor in a growing, prosperous majority black city, and it had a solidly entrenched black middle class. The big companies in town, Coca Cola and Ted Turner's evolving media empire, weren't skipping town because Negroes were in charge. The city had history, tradition, and, if you liked light-skinned sisters with straight hair, some of the finest women in the country. Atlanta had many landmarks. There was a soul food restaurant called the Beautiful run by women in white Islamic robes. There was the A.U. Center where four African-American colleges (Morehouse, Spelman, Clark, Atlanta) were nestled next to each other. There was the Dr. Martin Luther King Center for Social Change and next to it the Ebeneezer Baptist Church where Dr. King and his legendary father Daddy King manned the pulpit. A few blocks from there was the original home of WERD, the first black-owned radio station in America. In my three days in the Peach City I saw all this and many other parts of town, from rich Buckhead and the Lenox Mall, from Underground Atlanta to the Omni Arena.

Yet the most important historical sights I encountered in Atlanta were in the lobby of the Sheraton, where several generations of black music were assembled. Billy Eckstine, Edgecombe Lennox, and Jack "The Rapper" Gibson sat in one corner talking. Across the room Gladys Knight, Patti LaBelle, and Dionne Warwick swapped stories of grand kids and nephews and ridiculed ex-husbands. There were other changing, evolving clusters of music biz types talking and drinking and, often, cursing all over this otherwise characterless, modern lobby.

The room had a distinctly Southern flavor. Most good soul music, even if it was recorded in Detroit or Manhattan, had that strong Southern flavor, 'cause it was at the root of our American experience. After all, soul music was the music of my parents' generation. It was the sound of a migrated people who lived in big cities, people who still savored pig's feet and corn bread.

My days and evenings were spent soaking up this soulful past and present. But my nights and mornings were filled with the future. At

Jack the Rapper there were special showcases held in the main ballroom that started at one or two and went on past the break of dawn. The old down-home delicacy of chicken wings and waffles were on the menu as act after act sought to impress the collected black music royalty. There were Michael Jackson imitators. There were Prince-influenced musicians. But there were no self-contained bands with live horns. Some didn't even have bass players. In their places were keyboards made either by Korg or Yamaha. Some acts didn't have drummers—or, if they did, they were augmented by the mechanical Linn drum, a sound that Prince had popularized.

Most telling to me were the two acts that got the biggest responses at the 1984 Jack the Rapper. The five kids in New Edition didn't sing that well, but on stage these guys were a magic blend of doo wop and hip hop. A couple of the kids, particularly Bobby Brown, could rap as well as sing. Moreover, he and his four cohorts could do Temptations/Jackson Five steps and then flip and perform eighties break dance moves. Even an old school fan like myself could see that this quintet was, to use the phrase of the moment, fresh.

And as fresh as New Edition was, the Brothers Black were fresher. Fueled by a forty-ounce bottle of Ole English 800 (I didn't know beer bottles came that big!) and a pep talk Gibbs gave in the wings before they went on, their lead, Attak, was pumped. He came on, threw his mike stand across the stage nearly decapitating Jack the Rapper, threw his Kangol into the crowd, and then began rapping his ass off. Attak had made an impression on me in D.C., but after tonight I knew he was a star in the making. Even the deejay, Donkey, seemed more skilled tonight.

Despite this real committed performance, the Brothers Black sent many an old-timer headed for the door. Others turned their backs and ordered another drink, while they waited for Z. Z. Hill to come on later. Younger folks crowded the front of the stage, chanting "Ho!" and waving their hands when Attak told them to. The Brothers Black left the stage at about four in the morning, but the party was far from over 'cause Gibbs invited a gang of us up to his suite on the twenty-third floor. Amid the bleary-eyed activity in the suite I found myself squished on a sofa next to my old roommate. He was wearing a Black Black T-shirt, Lee jeans, Adidas sneakers lacking laces, and three gold chains, the biggest of which dangled a medallion shaped into a "WG."

SEDUCED

"Well," he said, "this is that fresh, right?" This, of course, was a statement, not a question.

"Fresh," I agreed and then sipped on my Jack Daniel's and soda, and smiled wide, satisfied. I closed my eyes, fully prepared to go to sleep when Gibbs shook me back to consciousness.

"Yo, Derek!" Gibbs spoke with a boyishness that could only mean he'd spotted a woman. "Look at that freak in the orange dress and the Sade hair!" When I told him who she was and that I knew her, Gibbs dragged me to my feet and across the floor to where she stood. Thankfully she didn't play me.

"You said you wanted to meet Walter Gibbs." Then I pointed to my friend who was leaning back as if he was cool, when he really was as anxious as a boy with a new bike. Cherri laid that look on Gibbs, surveying his terrain with care. Finally she said, "So you're a mogul. You just look like any old brother to me."

Gibbs leaned forward and then responded to the challenge by saying, "I'm just me. I'm just what you see. If I'm a mogul it's only because you see me as one. This is my party. The Brothers Black is my group. So I can be any old brother or I could be more. You decide." Whether Gibbs was just inspired or just high, this line of conversation seemed to hold Cherri's interest but quickly bored me. After a moment or two I slid away back through the haze, the dancing bodies, and the talk and found my previous spot on the sofa.

The night was disappearing and there was a hint of sun creeping in through the window. Tomorrow, back to New York and my future. No Candi in it. No steady gig. My pops was robbed. Gibbs was large and likely to get busy with a woman I couldn't make up my mind about. And Edge? Last time I saw him was just before the Brothers Black hit the stage. Told me he was heading for L.A. Maybe because I was a little tipsy I asked him a stupid question. I said, "What should I do now Edge?" Maybe because he was a little tipsy he said, "Well, if I was you I'd write more songs. Figure out what was wrong with them and write some more, 'cause you ain't gonna make it as a chauffeur." If ever a conversation showed the dangers of a demon rum, this was it. After all this time with Edge I was still asking for advice and he was still giving me the same answer.

Slowly I rose from the sofa and headed toward the door. Time for

bed. Then a shower. Then the plane. Then New York and back to figuring out my life. A hand rubbed my shoulder. "You going to your
room?" she asked.

"Where's Gibbs?"

"Derek." Cherri looked at me like I should know better. "Niggas
like that bore me after a while. Anyway—" She leaned that hand on
my shoulder again and took off both her shoes. She held them out.
"Carry these to my room for me."

Maybe 'cause I was tipsy I asked her, "You think I write songs well
enough to get with you?"

She shrugged her shoulders. "Derek, not only do you write good
enough but you got a nice voice. But hey, that don't mean shit right
now. What's important is that I think your ass is cute, so let's go."

With her shoes in my right hand and my left hand around her waist
we moved out of Gibbs' suite over to the elevators. "If I sing so good,
promise me we can sing a duet together afterwards."

"Afterwards." She laughed me. "No. Afterwards I'm going to sleep.
Then I'm gonna wake up, probably do you again, and then have breakfast. If we haven't checked out by then, we can do a duet." The elevator door opened and we got on. As it began moving I sang the opening
verse of "Endless Love." Cherri rolled her eyes but joined in. I kept
singing. Reluctantly she joined in. We finished the song just as we got
into her bed and, while I'd like to tell you otherwise, our love wasn't
endless, though it was pretty damn good.

the road—1985

"Silly Pictures"

It is the summer of 1985, I am wearing my best (meaning only) summer suit, a blue linen number, a little short in the sleeves, and carrying my briefcase as I follow Danifa, a lanky, brown woman in a navy blue pants suits with gold buttons on the jacket, down a corridor laden with gold and platinum albums. I'd helped Celestial Funk's 1974 self-titled debut go platinum myself by buying two copies, one for the music, one for the Pam Grier look-a-like on the cover. Their hit, "Throw the Funk (Make a Move on My Mind)," was one of those essential summer jams, like Earth, Wind & Fire's "Serpentine Fire" and Parliament Funkadelic's "Tear the Roof Off the Sucka." As the guitarist, co-lead vocalist, chief songwriter, producer, and overall musical guru, Mayo was to Celestial Funk what Maurice White was to E, W & F and George Clinton was to P-Funk. Together, these three bands helped to define that era's black pop culture.

As the seventies wore on, Celestial Funk, like most of the legion of funk bands, began to shrink as synthesizers knocked out horn players, and keyboardists were able to replicate the sounds of the bass, guitar and, if you had the right instrument, even background singers. By 1982, Celestial Funk was more a brand name than a band, one that Mayo kept alive in lieu of doing solo albums. Mayo had once coached the team; with the new technology, he no longer needed the players.

As Danifa led me to the end of the corridor I saw Mayo's defining record of the eighties. In 1983, Mayo convinced a teenaged gospel singer named Melissa Klark (the "K" was his idea) to turn secular and created "Joy!" around her, a multi-platinum album that made funk sweet and processed gospel chops into cloying pop. It won him a slew of Grammys and made Mayo the producer of the moment. For the next two years he got big fees to produce three other female singers, each of whose voice was processed to a suffocating degree, in the Klark formula. Each of the three albums sold less than the other as radio, programmers, and the audiences grew tired of the regurgitated riffs.

Right outside Mayo's office the gold and platinum records stopped. Instead, opposite each other on facing walls, were testaments to the producer's recent artistic decline. On the wall was a framed poster of Marcus Silver, a Jersey-bred love man whom Walter Gibbs, back in his days as an r&b tunesmith, had nurtured and then lost to Mayo. Around him Mayo had created the most hyped black debut of 1984 and, as a result, it was also the biggest flop of the year. The producer had envisioned Silver as a vehicle for his music just as Celestial Funk and Klark had been. Instead with Michael Jackson, Prince, and Lionel Richie around, no one paid Silver any attention. Mayo was sounding burnt out and apparently he was the only one who didn't know.

To my right was a poster promoting the recent Joint-ski-Mayo 12-inch collaboration, "Deuce." It wasn't a bomb—the single went to number one on the black singles chart and *Rolling Stone,* who didn't know jack about hip hop, praised it. I didn't think it was a bad record, actually. Thought it was as much fun as any early Kurtis Blow record.

But the rap audience, the growing community of people who now defined themselves as hip-hop fans first and foremost, totally rejected it. While many in the industry felt Mayo's participation legitimized rap, the music's new true believers working with Mayo actually branded Joint-ski a "sell-out." The most scathing articulation of this position had just come in the *Village Voice* where Dwayne Robinson, *Billboard*'s black music editor, had written a critique of the single as a sign of rap's coming mainstream acceptance and of the mainstream's profound misunderstanding of the music.

As I sit across from Mayo he's just putting the paper down. My man's in the same gear he's worn, more or less, for years—dreds, a white naval captain's hat, a gray khaki shirt brightened by a Jimi Hendrix button. But his usually smug cocoa-colored face is red. "Did you read this?" I told him I had. "He really doesn't understand this business."

Since I was in no hurry to get to our business, I decided to play devil's advocate. "I don't know what you mean."

"He knows the dates," Mayo said. "He knows the historical context. He knows what cat came from what city. He's got that. But he doesn't know anything about how a commercial artist thinks and survives." I think Mayo expected me to play prompter and ask him another question. If he wanted to blow off steam, I'd listen, but I wasn't gonna interview him.

Picking up on my silence, Mayo continued. "A commercial artist is two things. One, he is a man with sensitivities, taste, and the will to express what is essential in evoking human emotion through art. Two, he is commercial because he responds and shapes the marketplace. He is excited by the challenge of capturing his share of the marketplace. When I was young I was in touch with everything." His voice, which had been fairly loud, now quieted a few decibels, as if even he was surprised at how angry he sounded. "The time comes in every artist's life when you are no longer in the moment, when you are no longer the state of the art. Just because I'm not twenty-three anymore doesn't mean my creative life is over. It sure doesn't mean the bills stop coming either."

Mayo's anger had ebbed into a kind of melancholy reflection. The subject was no longer Dwayne Robinson's piece but his own artistic mortality. I felt it was time for me to start the next argument. I was reaching into the battered briefcase my moms had bought me when I entered CCNY, but before I could start, Mayo looked back down at the *Voice* and unleashed one more volley. "You know what he really doesn't understand?" Of course, I did not, so Mayo filled me in. "He doesn't understand the key lesson. You'll learn it, too. The lesson is that my records—bad and good—will be remembered long after the critiques of that music—bad and good—will be recycled into prison toilet paper."

As he scanned the *Voice* again, his eyes narrowed at some particularly offensive words. Clearly Mayo was not at his most reasonable, but I'd been summoned and it was time we settled the issue. I placed the contracts on the desk and Mayo finally put the *Voice* aside and picked them up. He smiled. "Did you sign them all?" I told him I had not. His eyes narrowed again.

SEDUCED

"You understand that when you sign these papers I can get Warner-Chapell to cut you a check for twenty thousand. It'll be your first publishing deal. They'll shop your music for you. No more hustling. No more restroom stake-outs." Even in all my nervousness I had to laugh at that.

About six months before this meeting I'd been having Raisin Bran for dinner over at the Chatworth and listening to Elvis Costello's *My Aim Is True* album (I loved "Allison") when the idea for a song called "Silly Pictures" came to me. It wasn't precisely an r&b song since Costello's mean way with a metaphor was definitely an influence. I'd heard the guy wasn't too keen on black folks, but his writing was too smart to ignore. For syncopation I looked to Cameo's "Work Up." I inverted the bass line to give the song heart and, after an hour of messing around, came up with this:

"Silly Pictures"
When I'm out with my baby
On a sunny day
I pose for the camera
In a goofy way.
My baby just laughs
(She laughs at me)
Then takes silly pictures
Such silly pictures.
When I visit my baby
On a silky night
She poses for the camera
And I keep on the light.
My baby just laughs
(She laughs at me)
Then takes silly pictures
Such silly pictures.

When I followed my baby
As she drove to his place
I yanked out the camera
Held it up to my face

While my baby laughs
(She laughs at me).
Then takes silly pictures
Such silly pictures.

When it was finished I decided to focus on getting the piece to Mayo, the only guy in New York music progressive enough to understand the song's blend of rock and funk, and with the commercial skills to get it out. Dialed the usual numbers and knocked on the usual doors trying to get to him, and I got roadblocked all the usual ways. Then I got creative. I knew he block booked time at Sigma Sound on Fifty-third Street. I scammed my way into a session with this really off-key rock singer named Pantheon and then locked myself in the last stall in the men's room. I squatted in the stall for about two hours and then snuck around the studio, avoiding Pantheon's people and peeking into Mayo's session.

At about 12:30 that night I spied Mayo heading into the restroom. I had everything set up when I spotted his feet in the middle stall. Lucky for me Mayo was not only doing number two, but was snorting a line of coke off the toilet paper dispenser, so he was doubly preoccupied. So I cracked up my boom box and started singing along with the track. At first he was surprised—I could see his feet shifting uneasily when I began crooning. But Mayo was a real music man, so eventually he began listening and tapping his feet to the bass line.

I waited for him to flush before I came out of the stall. He was putting Visine in his eyes when I introduced myself. Despite my rude interruption, the hook up had been made. Over the course of the next few months, Mayo would praise "Silly Pictures" and tell me it was "a perfect song for the right singer." Every now and then Mayo would slip me a couple of hundred dollars and listen to my other songs. But about "Silly Pictures" he told me to be patient, that the song was a gold mine, that he would put me on the map, blah, blah, blah.

Then one night about 2 A.M. Mayo woke me up. BCR had a male singer named Jevon whom they thought "was going to be the new Teddy Pendergrass." This all sounded good. Then Mayo told me he'd just finished recording my song with this Jevon guy. This was strange. I asked all the obvious questions: Why wasn't I told? Why wasn't I invited down to the sessions? If that wasn't surprise enough, then Mayo added, "We made a few little changes, you know, we had to tailor it to Jevon's voice," which was a joke since Mayo was notorious for shaping singers to his sound. I'd never been married, but the call had that guilty I-just-screwed-someone-in-a-motel-room-so-let-me-call-my-mate-to-tell-them-I-love-them quality.

When I asked for a copy of the track, Mayo told me to call Danifa in the morning. Well, I called. And I called. And I called. I was about to go back to Sigma's men's room when Danifa hand-delivered contracts to the Chatworth. No copies of Jevon's version. Just stacks of paper. The bottom line—Mayo wanted co-writing credit and for me to sign with his publishing company, Mayonaise Music, through Warner-Chapell which would mean he'd get half the songwriting royalties and all the publishing money. He'd control 75 percent of my "perfect song."

Now I wasn't being totally screwed. I'd receive a $20,000 advance (which Gibbs assured me was okay for an unknown writer, but far from generous) and have the clout of Warner-Chapell behind my musings. But I felt the same way about this deal as my moms had the afternoon about the Vernon Jackson situation. I wanted the break. Hell, I needed the break. Yet the terms of the deal worried me. What was my artistic soul worth? Maybe $20,000 wasn't really a terrible price for a broke black songwriter.

But I valued myself a little more highly than that and made a proposal of my own. I'd agree to the share-writing credit with Mayo, but no future songs of mine would be administered through his publishing company—at least at this time. Nor would I accept the Warner-Chapell advance. "If I sign with them, I want it to be for me, not as a part of your deal."

If Mayo's eyes narrowed before, now they were as slender as the holes in a slot machine. "Now Derek Harper, why would I agree to that? I'm giving you your first payday. I'm linking my name with yours for the world to see. Even if Warner-Chapell doesn't sign you, someone will give you a deal after this. Why shouldn't I profit?"

"No reason," I admitted. "All I could do is prevent you from using the song. That's it. Maybe eating the sessions would cost you some money, but you'd live with it. For me, however, it's just a matter of maintaining my freedom until I can get in the game the right way."

Mayo shook his head. "This is the right way," he said. "You're just as bad with Mr. Robinson here. You don't understand either. This is how the world works. I piggyback on you. You piggyback on the next person. Didn't you used to hang with Edge Lennox at Possible 20? That should have been lesson number one."

He then flipped a switch on his reel to reel and the sound of his version of "Silly Pictures" boomed from his speakers. Maybe he thought this would impress me. Instead, it just made me stronger in my position. The rock flavor had been lost and in its place were candy-coated keyboards that undercut the song's deadpan desolation. What Mayo apparently had really loved about "Silly Pictures" was the hook which he'd underscored with girl singers. The verses that told a story of lost love had been obscured by Jevon's oversinging. When I told Mayo that the singer hadn't really understood the song, he replied, "You are really rather ungrateful, Derek Harper. What do you say to that?" I just looked down at my briefcase and resigned myself to the fact it wouldn't be getting replaced any time soon.

Back out on Seventh Avenue, I walked toward Times Square. I'd stood my ground, but so what? He'd given me a week to make up my mind. In the meantime, he'd warned me, "Things could change," meaning my song could not be the single and, in fact, could be thrown off the album. I stopped at a grocery store and bought a pack of Tums, wondering if I hadn't been pound wise but penny foolish.

"Felonious Assault"

"There's no time like now, my man." Walter Gibbs was talking as he stood backstage at Madison Square Garden. It was three days after my meeting with Mayo. Roadies were rolling by a large stage backdrop with the words "Overweight Lovers" written across it in huge Day-Glo letters. "I was a sorry ass r&b songwriter," he continued.

"I know," I interjected, but that hardly slowed my friend's roll.

"But now," Gibbs boasted, "I'm runnin' everything in sight."

Walter was going off again, but I couldn't totally blame him. My man was co-promoting a gig at Madison Square Garden where he managed all the groups on the bill. Tonight's headliners, the Overweight Lovers, were making $15,000 a night with Gibbs slicing off a promoter's override plus a 15 percent manager's commission. It was a hip-hop pyramid scheme.

I'm sure my eyes tended to glaze over when he rambled on about his "largeness." But it didn't matter to him one way or the other. This current presentation wasn't for me, but the two extremely cute girls with shrimp earrings, three gold chains each, and elaborately greasy do's highlighted by carefully curled "baby hair" on the sides. Tabitha and Sabrina, neither of whom could be over twenty-one, were hanging on Gibbs' every word.

"Now," Gibbs boasted, "I got you two choice seats on the side of the stage." Gibbs handed each a ticket. "After the Lovers come off-stage, you come back and ride to the party with me."

"You got backstage passes for us?" Sabrina asked with a strong Bed-Stuy inflection. "Don't be leavin' us hangin'."

"Of course, baby." Gibbs stuck bright red backstage passes on the breast of each woman. Tabitha, who had big doelike eyes and didn't say much, smiled broadly at Gibbs' flirtatious gesture, while Sabrina, the tougher looking of the two, sucked her teeth. As they walked off, Gibbs focused his eyes on their round young bodies. "Like I said, I'm running everything I see."

"That's cradle robbing, Walter."

"Man, girls aren't girls anymore," he retorted. "Girls are boys now. They think like boys. They talk like boys. They fuck as quick as boys do. Derek, you better get off of that old ass r&b bag and wake up and get fresh."

"I can't help it," I replied drolly. "I like women. You know, people with periods."

Just then the Brothers Black, who'd filled out into two rather intimidating roughnecks, suddenly approached us. Attak, so shy a year ago, now stepped to Gibbs like a trooper with Donkey, looking equally hostile, at his side. "Yo, man, why we gotta go on before Joint-ski!" He'd grown a good three inches since I'd last seen him and in his bright orange ski jacket, he seemed larger than life. The New York Yankee cap perched precariously on his head gyrated with every syllable from his powerful voice. "That nigga's garbage. Garbage. Shouldn't even be on the same stage with us."

"Look, guys," Gibbs explained, "Joint-ski has made his mark. He's got hits. He comes right out of the Dance Inferno—"

Attak sucked his teeth and cut in. "And he was worthless then! But I tell you what. Keep the line up like it is and watch him catch a critical beat down on his ass!" With that, Attak and Donkey stormed off toward the stage.

"I remember when that brother was reserved. Now he speaks in exclamation points!" I was hoping to get a chuckle out of Gibbs.

Instead Gibbs asked rhetorically, "You know why this rap shit is so much fun?"

"Because," I replied, "It's like basketball. Brothers constantly in the face of brothers."

"What? You a writer or something?"

"Yes, I am. And yes, you got that idea from me in the first place and you've been using it in every interview you do."

"What can I say, Derek? You come in handy."

"Listen," I said. "You know I turned down Mayo's original deal."

"That's fresh," he replied. "You can't let them do you."

"Yeah, that's true. But now I'm behind on my rent."

"Not for long, my man." Gibbs had that con-man look in his eye, the one I first noticed back in the CCNY cafeteria. It was scary to me, since whatever scam he had in mind obviously involved me.

"What have you got on your mind?"

"I'm not ready to tell you yet. Just enjoy the show. And don't worry. I'll take care of you, 'cause we go back."

From inside the arena there was cheering and lights and the intense, pounding bass line of Vangh Mason's "Bounce, Rock, Skate, Roll" being cut up by the Brothers Black's D.J. Donkey. I walked over toward the stage wings where I could see. Attak, now dressed all in black, stalked like a panther as he hyped the crowd. He was ripping into their 12-inch "Felonious Assault" like the mike was a fool he didn't like.

From the direction of the dressing rooms a ruddy-faced white man in a cheap brown suit, a uniformed NYPD lieutenant, and a burly black Madison Square Garden security guard rushed up to Gibbs and surrounded him. I moved toward them, but the security guard caught my eye so I stayed put. Gibbs frowned as the guy in the cheap suit

S
E
D
U
C
E
D

whispered hoarsely in his ear. Then the security guard led Gibbs and the others back past the dressing rooms.

Even as the sound of the Brothers Black echoed like canon shots through the Garden, I felt another vibration. I'd felt it at my first rap show. City College gym. Late seventies. DJ Hollywood on the mike. Love Bug Star-ski on the wheels of steel. In the middle of the show a fight broke out. Chairs went flying. Girls screamed. Boys cursed. Yet after the anger had played itself out, all the fans moved back to their seats. No Harlem kids were gonna let a fistfight or even a stabbing keep them from their music. It was too important for that.

Violence at hip-hop gigs, while momentarily chilling, had always been a staple of the uptown scene. It got so common that if nobody got stabbed, you questioned the validity of the rappers performing. This attitude sickened me, but as Gibbs always preached, this was a new culture and I was beginning to agree.

The Brothers Black's set went by uneventfully. Joint-ski hit the stage to a great ovation, but that vibe grew stronger. Two buxom groupies walked past me, speaking in rapid, fearful tones.

"Girl, it's time to go," the first said quickly. "These fools in here are going crazy."

"Look over there," the other replied. Two teenage males, blood flowing from unseen holes, were being led through the backstage area by medics. "I heard," the first continued, "there are gangs of kids snatching gold chains, pulling jackets and purses off women, and just running through the crowd stabbing."

Joint-ski was on now, but my eyes looked past him into the arena. In the vastness of the Garden people moved. Some danced. Some waved their hands in the air like they didn't care. Yet I could make out ugly, evil movements, too. Teenagers running. A girl leaping a seat in fear. A pack of fools stomping a guy as he rolled down some steps. Security guards were invisible in the dark.

As Joint-ski did his first hit, "Break It Down," the two women came rushing toward me. Sabrina, minus her gold chains, was crying. Tabitha wanted to know where Gibbs was, but I sure didn't know. "Niggas are goin' crazy up there," Tabitha shouted. "How come Walter didn't have no security?" Joint-ski came off-stage, looking dazed and confused. He was hustled past me by three roadies determined to knock over anything in their way. Instead of heading for the dressing rooms, the roadies veered toward the same corridor as Gibbs had disappeared down.

I took Sabrina in my arms and with Tabitha by my side followed Joint-ski and company. We went down the corridor and then made a left and another left where Joint-ski and his roadies were entering an elevator. One of Joint-ski's flunkies glared at me, but I held the door open and we jumped in.

"What's up?" Joint-ski's voice was flat, his face empty, and his spirit low. Before I could respond, the rapper volunteered, "It was ill, man. Right in front of the stage I saw a crew bum rush this kid. They yoked him, snatched his gold, and then stomped him. One fool took one of the kid's gold chains and had the nerve to throw it at me." The elevator doors opened and, without another word, Joint-ski's crew formed a triangle around him and sped the rapper out of the employees entrance. I guided Tabitha and Sabrina out behind them and the girls scooted of the building. I jumped back on the elevator and pressed Mezzanine. As the elevator moved up through the building, the Overweight Lovers' "Big and Fat" rumbled through the walls. When the doors opened, the music smacked me in the face.

Kids were on the move. Girls went to the bathroom. Guys waited on line for the phone. Normal enough. But the concession stands were all closed and I felt that vibration again. As I walked into the arena through Gate 60, the Overweight Lovers were grabbing their dicks on stage and shaking their hips to "Big and Fat" as people in the crowd mouthed the words or rocked in their seat to its tinny drum machine. In three different parts of the Garden I saw the mad swirl of bodies that meant bad news. It was random violence to the extent that their victims just happened to be in the wrong spot wearing the wrong gear (mostly gold chains, it seemed). At heart, these were organized wolf packs who came to the concert to prey on their own kind. In the dark, dressed like regular fans, they could roll on a kid and, before he'd even notice, beat him to the ground. It was weird, all this joy and pain in one building.

I felt that vibration on my back—I felt it strong. When I turned around I caught the appraising eye of a fifteen-year-old kid cold on my back. After a few seconds our eyes locked and my body braced for the

S
E
D
U
C
E
D

bum rush. But the kid moved on, in search perhaps for someone younger, shorter, maybe less aware. Time for me to go. With my eyes shifting left to right with every step, I slid back into the Garden elevator as the Overweight Lovers ordered, "All the ladies in the house say 'Aaaah!'"

"Scent of a Woman"

The Cellar's bar was, as usual, swarming with brothers and sisters in their thirties who resided on the West Side. The dining area, partitioned off from the bar, was half full with customers more interested in conversation than eating. The bar was for drinking and rapping, the old-fashioned romantic kind—more Isaac Hayes than Kurtis Blow. The Whispers' "It's a Love Thing" flowed from the jukebox as I stood at the bar looking over some notes for a song I'd been working on. I looked down at my watch—8:15 P.M.

I was supposed to meet Doris Gilliam at 9 down on Fourteenth Street in front of the Palladium for a listening party sponsored by BCR Records. Mayo had just signed a production deal with BCR, so if I wanted to stay in his good graces I needed to show up.

Doris was the kind of woman my moms wanted me with. In fact my moms had hooked us up. Doris' mother was a Link. So was my moms. And it was their idea for us to have dinner. (You believe that? Our mothers arranged a blind date.) Doris was one of those long-haired, light-skinned cuties that middle-class black families manufacture and then ship off to Spelman, Fisk, or Howard. A marketing executive for NBC with a condo in Chelsea and a calm, occasionally subdued, personality, Doris was "Q.P.," which meant either "quality people" or "quality pussy" depending on my mood.

Because of her job, personality, and age, twenty-eight, Doris was definitely wife material. Because of my life-style, personality, and age, twenty-six, I was certainly not ready to be a husband. The thing was, Doris said that was cool with her. I was "fun" and she said she needed some. Doris had just split from a Long Island real-estate broker. It had been serious. It had been long term, and had ended in disappointment. Doris wanted to change her life and, after our dinner, she apparently thought I could help her on this journey.

To be honest, Doris occasionally bored me. Interoffice politics consumed her sometimes. A conversation could get to be a big long series of "blah, blah, blahs." Still, she was attractive and I'd easily converted her from Grover Washington, Jr., to *Sketches of Spain*. Perhaps most important, unlike the singers I kept finding myself involved with, she was stable. Yet look where I was? At the Cellar thinking about checking out some other sister who sang who'd invited me to her gig. After another beer, I decided to get going.

By the time I'd flagged down a cab, been driven down Columbus Avenue and Broadway, to Fourteenth Street it was past 9:15 and a long line of people were being herded like cattle behind the Palladium's barricades. Standing in front of the barricade, with her arms folded and a substantial frown on her face, was Doris Gilliam.

"Doris," I said guiltily, "I'm not that late."

"Why do you say that?" she replied. Then she leaned up and kissed me lightly on the lips. "So you're a little late tonight. It's no biggie. I just had a long day today and I've got a little bit of a migraine."

I caressed her cheek and gave her my best comforting it'll-be-all-right-baby smile. "White boys messing with you again."

"No," she said, "just one particular white woman. One of the V.P.'s, but let's not talk about it."

"Cool," I said. "Let's go in and get you a drink."

I steered Doris past the barricades over to a burly white security man with a clipboard, drink coupons, and fashionably extra-pale skin. After a quick survey of the guest list we were handed two drink tickets and granted entry through a special door to the Mike Todd room. It was a cavernous space with its main wall decorated (or scarred depending on your taste) by a huge Jean Michel Basquiat mural.

I already felt restless even though I hadn't been inside the Palladium two minutes. Doris' face contained a mix of fascination and fear—her usual reaction to the flash and fakery of record industry functions. Like me she kind of enjoyed music biz types, but only in small doses. "Is that Luther Vandross?" she whispered. "Yup," I said, then I turned back to the bar, ordering her a piña colada.

"Think I could get his autograph? I know this is an industry party, but I love his music. Would that be tacky?"

Doris knew I hated this. She knew I didn't want my date acting like a fan. I was trying to be taken seriously in the industry. But Doris always brought up the autograph issue and it truly pissed me off. I was searching for a new way to say, "Yes, it would be tacky," when Mayo's assistant Danifa came through the crowd and kissed me on the cheek.

"Derek, how are you?" She seemed delighted to see me. "I love that song you wrote for Jevon. I hope you and Mayo work it out. It's really a good song." Embarrassed by Danifa's unexpected praise, I mumbled, "Jevon's talent deserved my best," and then introduced Danifa to Doris, forgetting they'd met before.

"Oh, I remember Doris," she said. "We had a great time at the Kashif party."

"Love your shoes, Danifa," Doris announced, and they were off, picking up on a conversation of clothes and careers they'd begun at a promotional affair three weeks before. Across the room I spotted Walter Gibbs and a statuesque sister sitting on cushioned banquettes underneath the Basquiat mural. I excused myself and headed over.

Gibbs was pouring champagne for his beautiful companion when I arrived at the table. We exchanged greetings, then he introduced me to Beth Ann, a model who was "exploring singing." I really wanted to crack a joke, but Gibbs cut me a "don't-act-stupid" look so I chilled.

"Have a seat, Derek," Gibbs said. "We haven't talked since that shit went down." Gibbs explained that he'd spent most of the evening of the Garden show in the building's security office, reviewing the crime situation and talking with the Garden's publicity people about damage control. With the exception of a couple of small pieces in the *Post* and the *News,* a longer *Billboard* article by Dwayne Robinson, the robberies hadn't gotten a lot of coverage. "That figures," I observed. "It was black kids robbing black kids, so nobody paid much attention."

In two weeks the same show was going national, fourteen cities over the course of two months, so suppressing the bad news was crucial in calming already nervous arena managers. "This tour has the potential to gross ten million and blow this whole rap game to another level," Gibbs asserted. "Or it could kill the whole thing. The booking agents, the record labels, the media will all look at this thing to see if it'll work. A lot of people want to be down, but I don't trust most of them."

"Believe me, my man," I replied, "I definitely understand how tricky this business can be."

Gibbs got that con-man look again and then, as if he was rapping to Beth Ann, he said to me. "The only way we can make it, really make it, is if we help each other. I want you to come work for me on this tour. I know you learned about moving bodies around from your pops." When I asked what I'd do, Gibbs said, "You'll be my extra set of eyes and ears. You could travel the country. You'll make up the twenty thousand that Mayo would have advanced you."

"You mean," I interjected, "I could make twenty-five thousand. Guaranteed. Then I might consider slowing down my artistic career." If I was gonna be macked, I wasn't gonna sell myself cheap.

He looked over at Beth Ann. "Baby, does my friend look worth it?" She surveyed me and sipped her champagne. She was enjoying being included in our conversation, so she milked the moment before answering. "It sounds like Walt needs you. And, if you're as good a friend as he says, there shouldn't be a problem."

"Damn," Gibbs said, "I guess we should meet tomorrow at noon at the crib to talk about the details."

"Derek." It was Doris. I got up so quickly I nearly knocked over the table. "I'm sorry Doris. I didn't mean to leave you for so long."

"It's all right, actually. I'm not feeling well. The day was so bad. All this smoke and noise is getting to me. I'm gonna go."

"You want me to take you home?"

"No. I see you're with friends. Just call me tomorrow, okay?"

We kissed weakly and then Doris disappeared into the crowd. I sat back down feeling I should have been more concerned, more attentive, but I was more interested in drinking champagne with Gibbs than taking Doris home. I felt bad about that, but probably not as bad as I should have. Gibbs disturbed my thoughts by pointing out Mayo, Danifa, and the writer Dwayne Robinson talking animatedly at another table.

"Have you gotten back to him?" Gibbs wanted to be there when I turned down his offer. He'd detested the record Mayo had made with Joint-ski, so he viewed getting me to work on the tour and pulling from Mayo's deal as some small form of payback. As I got up, Gibbs was right with me. Then Beth Ann placed her hand on his arm. "Stay with me," she said. "Let your friend handle his business and you sit here and handle yours."

Smooth. This Beth Ann wasn't another in a long line of wannabes that Gibbs had been knocking off since he'd blown up. It seemed like she had Gibbs under some control, an impressive work of manipulation considering his burgeoning ego.

As I arrived at the table, Robinson was in the process of getting up. "Look, I'm sorry you disagree with my *Voice* piece, Mayo." Robinson stood over Mayo. Though his tone was conciliatory, his posture was cocky. "I can't change my opinion, but you know whatever you're working on will have a home in my *Billboard* column. Danifa can get me anytime. She knows that, okay? Now excuse me while I go get a cranberry juice."

As Robinson exited, Mayo waved me over into his vacant seat. "Surprised to see me with him?" Mayo asked. "It's because life is long, Derek. That guy has a column in the world's biggest music magazine. That makes him useful to me. But watch, one day he won't be there and he'll need a favor. It'll happen. It always does. Remember, life is long. So, am I to understand you're not changing your position on the song?"

Danifa looked at me hopefully, as if surely I'd never pass up this opportunity. But Mayo already knew I wasn't budging. It was all in his body language. I just confirmed his suspicions and he confirmed mine. "All right, Derek. 'Silly Pictures' is now off Jevon's album." I'd expected this but, damn, it still hit me in the gut. It would have been my first major song placement. Danifa felt sorry for me. Hey, I felt sorry for me. From across the room Gibbs watched us with a wry smile on his face. How'd this happen? I'd passed up a chance to work with a major r&b producer to go on tour with rap groups instead. Maybe I didn't want what I said I wanted. Or maybe I was way too stubborn. Or maybe, in the simplest terms possible, I was a fool.

A BCR executive came over to the table and invited Mayo to take a photo with Cliff Clark, one of their new signees. I slid out of camera range, just past the frame of a photo I'd see in *Billboard* a few weeks later next to Dwayne Robinson's The Bass Line column. In a whisper, I asked Danifa if I could get a copy of Jevon's version of "Silly Pictures." At first, she looked at me like I was crazy and, finally, taking pity on me, she told me to call her at the office tomorrow.

I was back sitting with Gibbs and Beth Ann slurping champagne when "The Scent of a Woman," an up-tempo track from Jevon's album, flooded out of the speakers in the Mike Todd Room. Across the floor flashlights cut through the blue tinged darkness. "Listen to how fluffy that drum track is," Gibbs muttered. Jevon's voice filled the room. Surrounded by four women in sequins holding flashlights, Jevon came from the neon-lighted room and sang his way through the crowd. He shook hands with Luther Vandross. He winked at Melba Moore. When he reached Danifa, Jevon scooped her in one arm, bent her back as if they were dancing a tango, sang the lines "I so love the scent of a woman," and then stood her back up without smiling over a word.

"Oh, he's sexy," Beth Ann cooed, which led Gibbs to mutter, "He's not as corny as most r&b niggas, but he's still corny," which made me chuckle. This guy really worked the room, singing to women, stretching out notes, seducing the air with his voice. When he reached Gibbs' table, he shook my hand, nodded to Gibbs, and got right in Beth Ann's face. She stood up and Jevon, now repeating the tag, "Scent of a woman," began to bend his knees and lower his head as Beth Ann laughed at this bit of sexual showmanship. Jevon moaned "Scent of a woman" as his head reached Beth Ann's groin. Gibbs' yellow face was red with anger and, for a moment, I feared Gibbs would leap across the table and stuff the mike in Jevon's mouth.

The moment passed. Jevon ended the song by hugging Beth Ann and grunting. Out of the crowd Danifa and KRS morning man Ken Webb emerged. Danifa had a towel, with which she dabbed the sweat on Jevon's forehead, while Webb took the mike and spieled about how "tremendous a talent" Jevon was and how "Scent of a Woman" was "the number one request" among his Breakfast Club listeners.

All I could think of was that Jevon could have been singing "Silly Pictures" and how large I would have felt. It was as if this surprise performance had been choreographed to humiliate me. This led me to another unpleasant thought: Had Danifa dogged me out to Doris? Despite that kissy-kissy stuff at the bar, she had to be pissed about how I dissed her boss. Moreover, she could have confided in Doris that I was making bad business decisions, said it was a sign of immaturity or something equally acid. Maybe that's why Doris left so early.

Beth Ann must have noticed the haunted look on my face, because then she spoke with the serenity of a nurse. "We're going to Nell's," she announced. "Come on. We'll have a good time." Was it that apparent that I needed one?

"Axel F"

Walter Gibbs lived down on LaGuardia Place, just above Houston Street, where Greenwich Village turns into Soho. The building was blue with various barnyard animals (pigs, cows, etc.) painted between the windows. Inside, Gibbs' condo had a high ceiling, but was rather narrow. The walls were covered with mirrors. Everywhere you looked you saw yourself. Even the tables were glass. These mirrored walls, plus the many strategically placed subdued neon lights, gave the place a nocturnal atmosphere. I'd told him many times the place looked more like a disco than a home, an indictment of his taste that Gibbs took as a compliment. In fact, Gibbs molded it after the sinister apartment of the pimp played by Bill Duke in *American Gigolo,* a movie we used to watch religiously on cassette at the Chatworth.

The cleaning woman, who'd let me in, gestured up the stairs to the loft before resuming her polishing work of Gibbs' long, oval glass dining table. Looking down on it from the staircase, I observed her diligently scooping up grains of white powder that dotted the surface into her dirty rag. Thousands of dollars worth of adult recreation was evaporating into a filthy piece of cloth.

Up in the front there were two phones with multiple lines, a glass desk covered with papers and cassettes, a wide-screen T.V., and a stereo that was strategically placed next to a king-sized brass bed. Lying upon his bed was a comatose Walter Gibbs.

"Rap mogul," I said as I shook him. "Rap mogul. It is one of your loyal subjects answering your royal summons."

"Fuck you," he grumbled, "and the bitch you rode in on."

Over the course of the next fifteen minutes Gibbs rolled out of bed and into his hip-hop persona. Adidas, who was negotiating with him for a sponsorship deal, had supplied Gibbs with all a young man could need to start his day: sneakers in all colors, including yellow and green "for when it's time to get ill"; sweat suits; baseball caps; T-shirts; and even cologne that reminded me of that vintage blend, Old Spice. The only thing lacking from Gibbs' Adidas wardrobe was underwear, but my man was already stocked with BVDs, so he didn't beef.

The phones began ringing around 11:30 and didn't stop. Even as we were going down the staircase for a quick breakfast I could hear them echoing through his high ceiling. Over scrambled eggs, bacon, and croissants (when did my man start eating French?), Gibbs came to life. "Beth Ann wore you out, huh?"

Gibbs shook his head negatively. "I wish," he said regretfully. "She had a shoot this morning. She stayed at Nell's about an hour. Remember that girl Tabitha from the other night? Well, I called her and she came over."

"You better watch that blow," I suggested.

Which made Gibbs reply, "And you better watch that Jack. Your eyes get that liquor yellow in them and the shit never comes out." I looked at the mirror behind the counter. Looked tired. Looked stressed. But I couldn't let him win that easy. So I made an offer. "Bet you the more money I make, the less I drink. The more money you make, the more coke you do."

Gibbs snorted sarcastically. "That's a fool's bet. I'm not going for it." There was a moment of silence after that, as we both sipped our orange juice and contemplated our individual vices. Then Gibbs looked at his spanking-new Rolex and changed the tempo. "Let's grab a cab and roll." In the cab going uptown Gibbs started talking extra fast. Money was on his mind. He related that when he was a kid his father had always been afraid of running out of money, "that one day the bills would pile so high that they'd crush him. He used to say that the average working person was just four pay checks from homelessness." Gibbs wasn't sure if that was true, but he knew that his father's views had affected him. "Sometimes I get the feeling every check is like some salvation from God and every bill part of a plot to do me. Do you understand?"

The cab stopped in front of 1619 Broadway, a big old concrete Manhattan office building, the kind Hollywood once used for New York City shots when the rest of the flick had been done on a soundstage.

"Well," he said, as if bracing himself for something unpleasant, "it's time to act like Eddie Murphy in *Beverly Hills Cop*." I'd known Gibbs five years, but it was one of the rare times I'd glimpsed the insecurity and worry behind the hustler facade. This tour was Gibbs' biggest con ever and the pressure was building.

The booking agent, the tour co-promoter and his assistant, a travel agency rep, members of Gibbs' company GAP (Gibbs Artistic Productions), Gibbs, and myself sat in a conference room, around a table covered with contracts, maps, personal computers, rare roast beef and cold cuts, bottled water, Cokes, yellow legal pads, and blue ballpoint pens.

Gibbs spent most of the meeting at the head of the very long table, using a pad and pen to draw a very good likeness of Beth Ann in a variety of pornographic positions. The banter at the table concerned him—he'd nod his head from time to time—but he surely didn't seem consumed by it, though I knew he was.

All these folks had come to the table because, Gibbs reasoned, he did his job. Now they were doing theirs and he was getting paid. Fair enough. Every now and then Gibbs reached into the pocket of his Adidas sweatsuit and pulled out a bottle of Gin Sing Up, sucked down its bitter content, and waited for that rush of energy to fill his head. It wasn't coke, but it was legal.

I had been concerned that my presence would upset some of the other folks involved with the tour. But it turned out that the co-promoter, Don Schindler, well known in rock circles, was overjoyed that someone else, someone older, was helping Gibbs. That's because GAP was staffed entirely with young people, either just out of college or on leave from school. Because no one with experience had initially believed in Gibbs' vision, he hired anyone with enthusiasm, which meant the company was stocked with kids.

The best and brightest of his crew was a semiretired rapper named Eric Payne, a chubby, bespeckled guy who'd managed his father's tenements in Harlem between rocking microphones, and a wispy, cute redhead named Edith "E.D." Knowles, who had dropped out of New York University to run GAP's office. Neither was older than twenty-three, yet they were handling their gigs with energy, if not wisdom. The meeting went the rest of the day. It was tedious, but everyone seemed cool about the routing and the ability to get everyone where they needed to be on time. Gibbs seemed to be in good hands. I began to wonder whether his biggest problem wasn't the tour but himself.

"Your Body's Calling"

Doris Gilliam's apartment smelled good. It smelled like roses and roasted chicken and well-scrubbed floors. Though it was an apartment in a New York high-rise, Doris had made it feel as close to a home as one could. I felt comfortable there, sitting on her sofa, eating her food, watching television, and smelling her as she sat down next to me. I guess this was how it was supposed to be when you dated a woman. Since Candi had split for D.C., I hadn't been treated like this with regularity. Once we'd gotten back to New York, Cherri had talked about inviting me up to Spanish Harlem but hadn't, and even a one-night stand, this kinky girl named Victoria, had sort of offered a home-cooked meal. Doris, however, always delivered what she promised. I may not have been love with her, but I probably should have been.

When I told Doris about Gibbs' offer she'd been superficially supportive. "That's very generous of him," she'd said. But not far into our conversation she expressed her disappointment in me for not working with Mayo (she and Donifa were probably closer than I'd realized). Like many black adults, including myself, she had problems with rap as music (she wasn't sure it was), entertainment (why pay for school-boy rhymes?), and cultural influence (not enough about love; too much about the ghetto). I was sympathetic to her position, but I explained that Mayo, essentially, had tried to blackmail me. I wasn't having that, though it hurt to turn him down. And that Gibbs, no matter what you thought of the product, was a good friend trying to build something and he was willing to pay my price.

Things got a little out of hand when, after my food had digested, I began making those let's-get-busy-moves with my hands and lips. "Derek," she said softly, "I have something I have to tell you."

I was feeling extra arrogant at that moment, so I replied, "I already know you're gonna miss me." Then I tried to kiss her. She pushed my body away and told me, quite firmly, "You are a little too confident."

Not getting the hint I came back cocky. "I know I am Doris," I said. "But that's what you like."

"Listen to me."

"I'm listening to your body." My hands were all over her.

"I just started my period."

"Oh," I replied, "I didn't hear that."

Then Doris, out of the kindness of her sweet heart, picked it up for me. "You can be so silly sometimes." She kissed me then and slowly cradled me in her arms. "Let me hold you awhile, okay." I agreed. Then she said, "Don't worry. I have plenty of towels." If I didn't love Doris yet, then it was clear I really needed to try.

"Don't Look Back"

There's a smell your house has. It's the smell of your pop's clothes after work, of the apron your moms always wore, of your closet filled with shirts and slacks you'll never wear again, of the baseball glove so stiff and dry, of the backyard where Pops read the Sunday *Times,* of music books you once poured over so studiously, and of the dining room you eat in once again.

Pops sits a little cockeyed now, as if that left arm hasn't totally recovered from the robbery. Not that he'd admit it. Moms is still calm and nurturing, though she seems to be shrinking a bit. Maybe it's just that I stand taller now. Still, she seems smaller. When I ask, she just smiles and tells me how crazy that sounds.

Over a typically filling Sunday soul food dinner I tell my parents of my disappointment with Mayo and my new, albeit temporary job with Gibbs. To my surprise Pops was quite pleased with my decision. "It's nice to see a regular paycheck come your way, Derek." I assured him that once the tour ended I'd be back to songwriting full-time. This assertion seemed to amuse him. "Tell you what I think, son," he said. "You've done this free-float thing since you left school."

"You," I corrected him, "mean freelance, don't you?"

"Whatever you call not making steady money," he answered dismissively. "What I think is that you'll get used to a regular check. Most people do. I think you'll like getting one a great deal."

I wanted to argue with him about how much my creativity meant to me and how fulfilling writing music was, etc., etc. But I could see how the prospect of me having a *job* with a *company* made him extremely happy. So I just let it go. "Time will tell if you're right, Pops," which I knew he'd view as me agreeing.

Moms was pleased at this bit of communication between her two men and I always liked to see her smile. Moms' only request was that since I was visiting Indianapolis that I go see her brother, Uncle Zack. "I hear he's doing poorly and I know he'd love to see you." I had a vague memory of Uncle Zack from my childhood as a man with a round head in a red knit shirt. More concrete in my mind was that of his late wife. Emily Lee used to send us a rum cake every Christmas that would arrive along with a crisp $5 bill. I promised her I'd go see Uncle Zack, all the while knowing full well that I'd do my best to duck that commitment once I arrived in Indianapolis.

On my way home I drove my rented black BMW around St. Albans and Hollis, where the little homes and little lawns pretty much looked the same as when I'd grown up. The quiet, comfy dignity of the streets was intact. The cars signaled change. They were no longer big-finned Caddys or station wagons but BMWs and Suzuki jeeps.

It was the main shopping strips of Hollis—Linden and Francis Lewis Boulevards—that seemed harder, meaner, and cooler. This part of Queens wasn't Harlem or Brownsville, yet I could feel a change in the atmosphere and knew instinctively that the robbery at Pops' place wasn't an isolated incident. I slowed down as I neared Mr. Walt's. Since it was a Sunday the place was shuttered. Anna and Walter were on a weekend trip to Jamaica, and Mr. Walt, I imagined, was some-where nearby watching "60 Minutes" in his easy chair.

Hanging out at the pay phones outside the barbershop, lounging and looking both preoccupied and bored, were two teenagers, one in a white Fila sweatsuit and the other in black Lees, a Run-D.M.C. T-shirt, and a baseball cap turned backwards. They observed my car with cold, crooked eyes—eyes that marked me as prey and customer, payday and kindred spirit. I ignored them and looked at the vacant parking space a few feet from the phones, a space once occupied by Edgecombe Lennox's Caddy.

Time passes. Dreams are altered by circumstance. And St. Albans was clearly no longer the middle-class heaven of my memories.

"Some Pieces of Gold"

Is there a job more crucial yet unappreciated than getting an artist organized? No matter how intense, innovative, or inspired a creative person is, he or she must be funneled through a system. Without some order, some system, no artist can be properly showcased. Yet most artists have great contempt for order and its manifestations—control, procedure, tradition. Even artists who can control their drive toward chaos, still chafe under the regulations of order, especially budgetary constraints that place limits on their imagination. It's their right to rebel—they do it well. And it's part of why they strike such a chord with their fans—or those who can't, won't, and don't have a good reason to rebel but want to. Artists do it for them. That we often read into their creative rebellion a significance well beyond their abilities or intentions is not the artist's fault.

These rather portentous observations came to me the summer I was road manager for the Brothers Black. They fought me every step of the way, even to the point of hurting themselves. They were very hard working, as long as you made it seem like fun and not responsibility. Unlike my trip down South with Edge and Cherri, this tour—which spanned several months, four times zones and as many climates—comes back to me as jumbled as our itinerary. I recall it in impressions, and images like listening to a good hip-hop deejay catch wreck.

My overall memory is of weariness that often verged on exhaustion. There was the sense that you'd never get enough sleep to make a difference, so why try? You lived in a twilight where the everyday distinctions in time meant nothing.

It could be 6:50 eastern standard time or 4:41 mountain time or 5:45 central time or even 6:03 pacific time and it wouldn't mean a thing. They were worthless designations. What I needed to know, what I always had to know, was how long before the next show. Four hours or twenty minutes or two days. These numbers spoke to me. These digits gave definition to my life. These numbers meant the sound check was finished. That the backstage passes had been left at the box office. They meant that Attak had finished watching Jason slash open teenagers on Spectravision and that Joint-ski's dancers had, once again, lost their leotards in the hotel laundry. I was living on B.G.

time, which meant either "Before Gig" or "Between Gig" time, depending on my mood.

On a tour bus, the days are nights. The shades in the sleeping compartments are drawn as the bus roars down some nondescript American interstate toward the next gig. Like vampires, the musicians try to catch as much shut-eye as possible while the sun is high, because from dusk to way past midnight they punch a nocturnal time clock. In the later afternoon they'll hit a hotel, check in, and then roll over to the club-hall-arena for a sound check. Back to the hotel for some more rest. Maybe an interview. Certainly a meal. Often there's horizontal enrichment with a groupie who's laid in wait at the hotel lobby, though that could get as monotonous as listening to the wheels rumble on.

Of course it wasn't all doom and gloom. Nightly, for the three-plus hours of every concert, I got to witness the spread of codes from the underground, the growth of a culture literally by word of mouth. The black crowds were young, though there were exceptions. In D.C. a white mailman, fresh off work, sat with daughters, aged eleven and thirteen, waiting patiently for the Overweight Lovers to hit. When the Lovers appeared, the mailman's daughters squealed like these bulbous b-boys were David Cassidy, the Bay City Rollers, or some other white teen appeal concoction. More impressive, their father rocked to the Lovers' music as he chewed on his Milk Duds. And everywhere we went there was always a sprinkling of white hipsters, be they guys in spiked hair who looked like they'd gotten lost on their way to see the Clash, or suburban girls wearing the harsh, heavy black eye liner of Madonna, with crucifixes to match.

Still, the heart and soul of the tour was black on black rhymes. My Caddy tour with Edge suggested that there was an audience from outside New York for hip hop, but it wasn't until this tour that I saw how deeply it spoke to its listeners. There was a cultural and generational connection being made between the audience and the performers that was far removed from Edge's maneuvers at black radio and Mayo's gamesmanship with the major labels.

In so many of the cities we visited, black radio either played no rap or "day parted" the music, so it was aired at nights or on weekends. Joint-ski had enjoyed mainstream success with "Break It Down" and, to a lesser degree, with "Rap Is My Religion," so his name was well known to adults and he received the bulk of the interview requests at the start of the tour from black newspapers and radio stations. Yet, as I'd heard, those audiences that considered themselves truly down deeply resented his Mayo-produced album. They saw the record as a kind of cultural betrayal and they would not forgive him.

The Overweight Lovers were a joke, too, but they were a joke well told. Leon "Ikey" Barrett and Petey "Mikey" Rodriquez were a classic novelty act who marketed themselves beautifully to their young fans. Hip-Hop music had a sense of humor and the Overweight Lovers, by emphasizing their weight, hefty eating habits, and allegedly massive sexual appetites, tapped into its sense of fun. Where Joint-ski seemed to be suffering artistically as many of rap's fans grew more sophisticated, the Overweight Lovers' mildly ribald material ("Big and Fat," "A Fat Joint of Love," "Feed Me") played well with those attracted to the party-hardy aspects of hip hop.

But from day one to the end in Long Beach, the Brothers Black was the group that just kept growing. It was on this tour that the latest language in rap—one of aggression, assertion, and attitude; one that looked beyond praise of one's sexual skills and into the realm of politics, pain, and psychological horror—began to emerge. It was as if Joint-ski was the past, the Overweight Lovers were a temporal present, and the Brothers black gatekeepers for a grim future. Right after the tour ended the Brothers Black would record *The Demon Inside*, which I believe was one of the great albums of the eighties. That I, a hard-core r&b head, would place a rap album up there with *Thriller, Dirty Mind, The Night I Fell in Love*, etc., was inconceivable to me at the start of the tour. The catalyst for such change, both in hip hop and my attitude to what it meant artistically, was Attak, who turned eighteen while we were on the road. I contend he was at least thirty the day he was born.

In background, Attak and I weren't different—he was raised in Roosevelt, Long Island, three blocks from where Eddie Murphy grew up, both parents had stable gigs (his father was a bus dispatcher, his mother a Board of Ed bureaucrat, and his uncle a famous and controversial judge), and he'd come of age in an upper working class groove.

But while a similar milieu had soothed my soul, Attak (christened

Lawrence Peters) rebelled like some precocious white boy. After a lengthy flirtation with Led Zeppelin, heavy metal, and satanic T-shirts, Attak discovered Schooly D's "PSK (What the Hell Does that Mean?)" one night while listening to a rap show broadcast on WBAU, Long Island's Adelphi University radio station. The song showed him the possibilities of rap for the kind of ill, horrific images that filled his head and, strangely, gave him comfort. At a roller-skating rink in Jamaica, Attak hooked up with DJ Donkey aka Anthony McNeil, a real technician on the turntables, and together they began cutting 12-inches for indie labels using cash Attak made assistant-managing at the McDonald's in Roosevelt Field mall.

To call Attak a fan of horror flicks would be as big an understatement as saying Indiana Jones was white. For him, Jason Vorhees of the *Friday the 13th* series was some kind of personal savior. He had respect for Freddie Kruger and would have a shout-out to the undying Michael Meyers of the *Halloween* flicks. But for Attak, Jason was a special kind of evil, one that preyed on young white kids and liberated their souls from boredom. This may seem a scary way to view a hockey mask–wearing mass murderer, but that was Attak's vision and it informed his writing.

This first real conversation we had, Attak told me, "The evil of America locks the black man into poverty and the white man in psychic pain for perpetuating these ill conditions. That's why I write what I write." In Attak's mind, the original horror story wasn't written by Poe or Mary Shelley. It was taken down the day the first tribal chieftain sold Africans captured in war to white traders from Europe. To him the brothers who did that cursed the African continent and set the stage for African self-genocide here and there. For every African who was tossed overboard during the Middle Passage, part of that dead soul haunted Africa and part of that soul haunted America, so that both lands were infested with their ghosts. In this context, Jason Vorhees was not simply some horror movie mad man but was a seed of death blossoming to seek vengeance against the off-spring of slave owners.

When Attak spoke this way you felt real uneasy. Was home piss a wannabe killer? Behind his stern young face was there a confusion that, one day, would turn to murder? I'm still not sure. Yet when he funneled this vision into rhymes, the results could be amazing. The Brothers Black's breakout single had been "Critical Beat Down," which was about a street fight and the state of race relations. It was a hard-core urban drama in the tradition of Melle Mel. But the song that made them the critics' darlings and opened my eyes to his abilities dropped just before the tour started. "Pieces of Gold" was written from the point of view of a Yoruba chief who'd sold captured Ashanti warriors to Europeans for a golden bowl, which he later discovered was gold-plated. Part of the rhyme went: "I didn't know/what the white man wanted with me/I didn't know/how he desired to destroy me/I didn't know about the holocaust awaiting me/I didn't know/So I sold my people for some pieces of gold/Yeah I gave up my soul/ for some pieces of gold."

It's a risky thing to narrate a song from the perspective of stupidity. Ballsy writers like Elvis Costello and Randy Newman did it often, but it was a rarity for black songwriters to do it outside of a love song. This was a fairly sophisticated technique and this kid brought it off with flair.

Considering we were both songwriters, though clearly coming from different places, I'd hoped we'd hit it off right away. It didn't happen that way. At first Attak saw me not as a fellow artist but as simply a new employee of Walter Gibbs, which made me, if not a villain, at least a stooge. It took awhile for us to see eye to eye. Partly because of Attak's suspicion, partly because of all the craziness that went on around us.

"The Way You Do the Things You Do"

Detroit—In the Detroit of my dreams, David Ruffin drives a cream-white Caddy convertible with a leopard interior. The Temptation is wearing a blazing blue sharkskin suit and dark green shades. As my mother used to say about him, Ruffin looks as cool as a cucumber. In the Detroit of my dreams, Little Stevie Wonder sits on the steps of Motown's West Grand Boulevard offices playing harmonica as Diana Ross walks by, pats the kid on the head, and strolls out to her limo where an impatient Berry Gordy sits waiting. In the Detroit of my dreams, Marvin Gaye stands, lanky and choirboy-charming, on the sidewalk signing autographs for giggling schoolgirls.

Detroit 1985, the city we rolled through on our way from the airport, was as sad as the faces of the bereaved at my father's funeral home. It felt weighed down by a sorrow that seeped up from the streets and filled its lungs. My giddiness at being in the home of Motown dissipated with every dispirited street.

"Ain't much, is it?" Gibbs sat next to me, studying my reaction to the city. "For anybody like you, a student of this game, this is Mecca and shit," he continued. "But for real, this is the murder capital. Get your cap peeled quick here."

Downtown Detroit was dominated by Hudson's, a big brick building from the days of smoke-stack industry. A place where the high school–aged Diane (later Diana) Ross worked was now battered and empty. There were sundry municipal buildings—none very memorable. Finally, at the river, a place where Detroit ended and Canada began, was the Renaissance Hotel; two huge black glass towers which can best be described as Darth Vadar's home.

"Nice, huh?" Gibbs knew this joint was creepy but they gave him a great group rate and it was a ten-minute ride from the Joe Louis Arena. Gibbs, being smart and being the boss, wasn't staying at the Renaissance. He was staying at the Ponchartrain, a vintage hotel right across the street from Joe Louis and considerably more user friendly.

The main gig was at the Joe Louis the next night, Friday. This evening each of the three acts had solo shows of their own: the Overweight Lovers were playing out past Eight Mile Line (the demarcation line between black Detroit and the vanilla suburbs); Joint-ski was out at the University of Michigan in Ann Arbor for a frat house party; and the Brothers Black were staying in the Motor City for a show at a local club.

Each act was assigned a van, a burly black Detroit driver, a bodyguard from New York, and a GAP representative. Gibbs was rolling with the Lovers and I was hanging with the Brothers Black. The plan was very calculated on Gibbs' part: there were rumors that the Overweight Lovers were being romanced by Russell Simmons, so Gibbs wanted to supply the personal touch, while Gibbs hoped Attak would warm up to me, since Attak was still very irritated about having to open for Joint-ski.

On the way to the club for the sound check, Attak felt me out on Joint-ski. "Didn't I think he was wack?" "Wasn't his last album some sellout do-do shit?" I tried to be diplomatic, being fearful that if I agreed too enthusiastically, it would come back to haunt me. This early in the tour I wanted to stay as neutral as possible. Attak, however, was seeking some definitive sign of allegiance to the Brothers Black or, at least, a show of contempt for Joint-ski.

"Either you down or you not," he challenged me at one point. DJ Donkey shared his partner's disdain for Joint-ski ("yeah, that nigga's booty," he said at one point), but his focus was elsewhere. "I hear the girlies in this town are freaks," which he mumbled again and again. Their homey bodyguard, a beefy Puerto Rican kid they called Dirt Bike, seconded that emotion.

The club was a dump. It was called the Pipeline. It reeked of mildew and alcohol, and its manager, Chucky Rockowski, was equally aromatic. He had the look of a boxer who'd gone one round too many. Back in the day, his body might have been powerful, but now he just looked plump in overalls, a blue T-shirt, and a mop of dirty blond hair.

Immediately I sensed we'd have trouble getting paid. While Attak and Donkey were on stage, Chucky wore out my ear talking about how the gig at Joe Louis Arena hurt his gate and that GAP should cut him some slack, that he was the first person in town to back rap, how the police were always harassing him because he booked it, blah, blah, blah. Chucky was shocked when I passed up a line of coke in his office, which may have been the first time he really looked at me, as if I was some strange new species of road manager. I wanted to tell him to offer me some Jack Daniel's, but this was not a guy to get too familiar with.

Back at the Ponchartrain I fulfilled my duties, telling Gibbs both about Attak's sour mood and Chucky's whining. He seemed somewhat pleased at my thorough report, though mostly he was preoccupied with the two rather nubile young girls who were sitting on his bed, smoking cigarettes and watching "All My Children" on T.V. When I asked what I should do if Chucky tried to jerk me later, he reached under his bed, pulled out an Adidas travel bag, and unzipped it. Inside were several quite frightening-looking hand guns.

"What? Are you crazy?"

"No," he replied, holding up a .45 for the inspection of his two playmates and me. "These are a few local purchases that'll help us avoid financial problems later."

"I'm not gonna shoot anybody for you, Gibbs."

"Please, Derek. You just go to Chucky after the gig and ask for our money. And, if there's any beef, just know Dirt Bike is taking no shorts." Then my ex-roommate, my road-seasoned friend, slapped a clip into the .45, a sound that made his two female friends shudder. For Gibbs, the guns were toys. Clearly he didn't plan on using them himself. But for these two Detroit teens, guns were no joke, and when they threatened to leave if he didn't put them away, I was kind of impressed that somebody in the room had common sense.

It was 5:30 when I left the Ponchartrain and, feeling adventurous, I decided to walk to the Renaissance through downtown Detroit. This was rush hour and in other big-time American city the streets would have been teeming with outgoing commuters. Here, the streets were eerily empty. Counting myself, I spotted only two other people on foot and even the traffic in the Motor City was like water dripping from a faucet. It was one thing to read articles or hear news reports about how the sixty-eight riot, the Japanese auto industry, and racism had gutted Detroit. It was quite another to walk through such a storied city and see your most innocent fantasies ground down by how beat down the town felt.

I thought New York was hardcore, but there was really a tough edge to these Detroiters. I'd heard that Prince's most fanatical fans were here and Ready for the World was a local band, so I was prepared for the greasy hair and the Morris Day styling. But I couldn't dismiss these folks as soft. There was tenseness in them, a blend of anxiety and anticipation that made them a perfect audience for Attak. That night he fed off their energy and gave a really intense, focused show. He ended the set, like he would every night I saw him afterwards, by saying, "As long as a mind is open, you better pour something in it!" and then he'd drop the mike at his feet.

There was a local television crew backstage. One of those black-

S
E
D
U
C
E
D

themed public affairs shows that every big city puts on Sunday mornings. The reporter, Ms. Bernice Joseph, was a tall ebony sister with a beauty-pageant smile and purple everywhere—her pants, blouse, shoes, even the little turbanlike wrap that covered most of her black hair. She looked both attractive and extremely out of place. Apparently somebody at GAP's New York office called about interviewing the Brothers Black. I knew nothing about this arrangement and told her so.

Donkey, after giving Ms. Joseph the once over, walked up to her and said, "Yo, there's no problem, Derek. We'll give this fine-ass reporter some of our valuable time. Why don't you come into the dressing room with us, brown sugar." I hated leaving the lanky Ms. Joseph in Donkey's horny care, but Chucky had walked by without a word, and it was time to do some business. An unsmiling Dirt Bike, Heineken in his beefy paws, came up and said to me, "Dollar bill, Derek. Dollar. Dollar bill."

A moment later we were in Chucky's office. Stickers were everywhere. Punk bands. Rock bands. Radio stations. Corny sayings. My awe at this paper-and-glue pop history was ended by Chucky's hoarse elocution. "Your guy damaged my best mike. I've had that mike since Edgar Winter's first tour and now it's broken." From underneath his desk he pulled out a mangled tan microphone. "This mike's state of the art, so I'm docking you guys four hundred for it."

Considering that the Brothers Black were only guaranteed $1,500, minus GAP's 15 percent, Dirt Bike's $100 per night, and expenses (van rental, gas, beers, herb), Chucky was talking about a lot of money. Since I was GAP's designated representative, it was up to me to either agree to this deduction or fight it.

"That ain't the mike." Dirt Bike pointed his Heineken at Chucky's desk. "The mike Attak rocked was an old piece of shit back in the day Shure. What you got there is a Star Maker Shure with a tan matte coat. The one Attak rocked was jet black and wack."

"Are you sure?" I asked him.

"Word. I always check Attak's mike before a show. He hates using them old Shures. Says they make his sound weak. That's why he dropped it."

Chucky said, "That's bullshit," and I said, "No, the only animal odor in here is coming from you. We want all our cash. Plus we're gonna sit here and go through all the money to see if our bonus is in order."

Well, not only was that not the microphone, but when we tabulated all the money, the Brothers Black were actually owed an additional $300. Dirt Bike was now my new best friend and, as we exited Chucky's sticker museum, I promised him a 40-ounce on me. Chucky, sagely, was not in a celebratory mood. "We better get out of here. Word. That white boy wasn't too happy. There's a lot of ways to get back your cash in Detroit, you know what I'm sayin'?"

Back in the dressing room Attak was talking on camera to Ms. Joseph. He was deep in some explanation about why rappers wear so many gold chains. "Where's Donkey?" I asked the driver. He grinned real nasty and nodded toward the restroom. I didn't see him when I stuck my head in though I did hear a strange breathing pattern. Sticking my head into a stall I saw Donkey and how he'd gotten his nickname. A teenaged girl, her brown face partially obscured by jheri-curls, was on her knees with Donkey's massive member moving in and out of her little mouth. It was long and yellow and this lady was either choking or having a real good time.

Donkey looked up. "You got the money?" he asked. I was quite impressed by his ability to split his concentration and told him, yeah, I had the money. "Bet," he replied, "I should be finished in a minute."

Back in the dressing room, Attak and Ms. Joseph had finished yakking. "Now," she announced, "I'd like to talk with you. I understand you're their manager."

"Yeah. Yeah." It was Attak. This must have been his idea. "He handles all our business. You know, black on black. Our money flowing in a circle of black, and Derek's the pivot."

Another test by Attak. Wanted to see how I'd handle myself. I wasn't sure how he wanted me to act, but I wasn't gonna front. "Sorry," I told her. "I'm not their manager. That's Walter Gibbs. I'm just the road manager. Besides, we gotta go!"

Ms. Joseph seemed quite surprised that I didn't want to talk to her, but my fear of robbery was stronger than my interest in her show, or her. Donkey emerged from the restroom and announced, "Damn, that bitch bit me!" On that happy note I ushered the Brothers Black out to the van, while Attak teased at me for not pushing up on Ms. Joseph. A gang of kids hung by the van. Some were fans. Some were wannabes with tapes squeezed tight in their hands. A few were looking hard and scheming, as if they were measuring our capacity for self-defense. Dirt Bike nodded their way and my neck muscles got very tense. Donkey was shouting his room number out the van window as we drove off.

From out of the club's parking lot a jeep came rolling up way too close to our bumper. Attak was still talking about Ms. Joseph when Dirt Bike pulled his gun out of his pants. The driver opened his glove compartment, sliding out a nasty-looking silver-plated weapon and Attak mumbled, "What goes on?"

"Nothing yet, my man," I said. I was trying to sound nonchalant, as if you could be relaxed in a car full of guns driving through the murder capital of America.

"Yo," Dirt Bike told the driver. "Don't stop at any lights."

The driver snorted out a laugh. "Shit, man, I ain't new to this."

Over the next twenty blocks our van careened, skidded, and slid toward the Renaissance, either running red lights or splitting right through the heart of yellow ones. About three quarters of the way downtown, the jeep behind us got cut off by a *Detroit Daily News* truck. Still our driver kept his foot on the accelerator. "Man," the driver announced, "people are struggling here. Detroit is a cold-blooded town right now. Money's too tight, you know. People around here no worse than anywhere. Life around here just pulls you out of shape and you can only figure on a few ways to get right."

Inside the relative safety of the hotel's shadowy lobby a party had started without us. The oily aroma of hair-curling juice, various cheap colognes and perfumes and, from somewhere out of sight, the sweet aroma of marijuana wafted into my nose. Security guards in cheap suits whispered into walkie-talkies. It was a scene I'd witness often over the next few months. In a town like Detroit, one short on fun and long on frustrated black folks, any tour, and certainly our tour, was a movable feast that unleashed what everyday life kept in lockdown.

I recognized a few women from the club, which made me nervous, since if these honeys were here, could the bad guys be far behind? As if reading my mind, Attak and Donkey, along with bodyguards, drug dealers, groupies, and wannabe rappers began piling into elevators.

With Dirt Bike watching my back, I went over to the front desk and was taken back to the manager's office where, with very sweaty palms, I pulled out the money belt I had strapped to my waist and laid it in the safe.

With that done I thanked Dirt Bike and he cracked an embarrassed smile that told me he wasn't used to gratitude. I hadn't had a drink all night and now was feeling quite thirsty. I invited him to join me, but he was anxious to join the Brothers Black and maybe grab one of Donkey's spare groupies.

Not too long afterwards I was sitting in a revolving bar at the very top of the Renaissance watching Detroit, Canada, and the river that separated them turn slowly. I was on my third Jack Daniel's when Ms. Joseph appeared by my side. "Persistent, aren't you?" I said sarcastically. "Well, just let me state for the record that Detroit is a lovely town and I think Berry Gordy should sell his Beverly Hills estate and move back immediately."

Ms. Joseph crossed her legs and lit up a Virginia Slims. Then she asked, "Why do all you music business guys try to act so obnoxious? Or is it just leaving New York and Los Angeles that does this to you?"

Man, I felt small. I apologized profusely, bought her a piña colada, and then told her the story of my ride from the gig, even adding a couple of gunshots for dramatic effect. That smoothed things out between us and we moved on to relating our life stories. You know mine. Hers was a rather straightforward narrative: Reared in a working-class neighborhood in a Chicago suburb. Attended the University of Michigan at Ann Arbor. Journalism major. Post-grad gig at an Ann Arbor T.V. station. Down the road to Detroit. On air doing local news. Co-black public affairs host. Single. Ambitious. Aggressive. Once dated a Detroit Piston who shall remain nameless. Plays piano. Can't wait to visit New York.

These facts were related over the course of a couple of hours before we arrived at the moment all traveling men come to. Was this lady looking for sex with an interesting man who'd be leaving tomorrow—namely me? Was she seeking sex with one of my stars—who'd also be leaving tomorrow, but who would be nice to have on her sexual résumé? Was she seeking a hook-up with someone in the glamour business of music? Was she just looking for some free drinks—which she'd already acquired? Maybe all of the above or none of them—maybe she just happened to come by this place for a night cap.

Then it hit me. I really didn't know what to do next. I had backstage passes around my neck. I had an expense account. I guess within the realm of this particular tour I was kind of important. And I was uncomfortable trying to woo Ms. Joseph as this guy I apparently was. Now I'd picked up girls on the road. That girl in D.C., for example. The thing was that I felt honest there. We'd danced. We'd dry-humped in the corner. I was the driver and we'd gotten busy in the Caddy. That all made sense to me.

This was a new role. I'd get used to it. I just hadn't gotten used to it yet. So I started yawning. Yawning real loud. "You must be tired," she said finally and I agreed. "Well, I'll see you tomorrow. I'll be shooting at the show." That meant I'd have another shot at her tomorrow and by that time maybe I'll be feeling more comfortable. She stayed at the bar and kissed me good bye on the cheek. Soft lips. On the elevator I did get an urge to sing "Endless Love," which made me smile.

My floor was a mad house. People in the hall moving in and out of the hallway shadows. Beat boxes blasting hip hop from behind half-opened doors. Dirt Bike tapped me on the shoulder. "Yo, Gibbs told me to tell you that the tour buses arrive at 10:30 at the arena and he wants you to meet him there."

"Word," I said. Then I asked. "When do you think it'll get quiet?"

"After the 5-0 comes." He spoke very matter-of-factly. "That usually clears out the hall."

"The other guests complain and call, huh?"

"Yeah and I usually do, too. Donkey will go all night if you let him."

"What about Attak?"

"He said that T.V. interviewer had talked about coming by."

"Really."

"Yeah. But if she don't show soon, he'll go fishing for whatever cute girlie walks by. Donkey's got the equipment, you know, but Attak's the man. He talks that angry shit and they all fall down."

Long night for me. The first of many. Despite the noise I was asleep in minutes. For some reason I dreamed of Edgecombe Lennox. He was tall and blue and floating in the air with a Kangol cap perched on his forehead and shading his eyes as he rambled on about the road, telling me the first rule was to count the money, the second rule was to count the house, the third rule was to wear a condom, and the fourth rule was to fill it with water when you were finished. Couldn't remember if he'd actually said this stuff. I wanted to make a note to track him down in Cali the next day, but dreams are very bad places to try to take notes.

The phone woke me at 9:30. Gibbs, a nocturnal creature if ever I'd known one, was up and way too awake for me. His first gleeful words were, "Heard some stick-up kids tried to take you off last night?"

I answered, "I thought this was just a baby-sitting job."

Gibbs laughed and told me he was down in the lobby. Would I like some breakfast? His eyes were cocaine red, although his manner wasn't jumpy, but wry. Instead of three lines, he'd probably started the day with one. Over eggs and bacon he said, "There's no cash without sweat, my man," he said. "Dirt Bike's a good guy, right?"

"No argument from me. You always up this early on the road?"

"Basically yeah. I meet the day head on. Deal with the nine-to-five people at the venue and then sleep in the afternoon 'til sound check. So how the women treating you?"

I related my Ms. Joseph tale, including Dirt Bike's closing comments, and he shook his head. "You put too much pressure on yourself, Derek. We're only in these towns one or two nights. There are always girls, women, freaks, whatever. The pressure's not on you. The pressure's on them. They've got to prove they're worth your time. Remember that.

"The other thing is, you gotta get over them wanting to hang with the artists. Unless you look like Billy Dee Williams or somebody like that, when you're on tour the artist always gets first choice. I don't care who the woman is—your mother, your aunt, Nancy Reagan—the man whose name's on the ticket is the center of attention. He's filling an arena and you're working with him—big difference, my man."

"This is still true even for you?"

"Maybe some industry women might jock me first, but that's it. So don't trip on the T.V. lady. Anyway, if Attak got with her, it probably was only to talk. You know the kid's got herpes."

Herpes was the sexual disease of the moment. *Newsweek* had it on the cover. "60 Minutes" had spotted it. I had working knowledge of how you got it and what it did to you. You could still get busy when not in crisis. Still it was no way to go through life. Attak was barely twenty-one. Damn.

"Yeah," Gibbs continued. "Got it on the road his first tour. He can still have sex, of course. But the shit has fucked up his head. He'd rather look at them and jerk off than actually get in there." Then, with a voice more resigned than sad, added, "I'm real careful out here. I seen niggas' dicks damn near fall off from being ridiculous with these girlies. I get mine, but I fly in women from time to time, so I kinda know what I'm getting."

"Please," I said sarcastically. "She could have been fucking half of New York while you're away."

"Yo, Derek, what can you do? It's all a risk. This music game is not guaranteed. You finally make money and some 'bama from Detroit tries to rip you off. The women got diseases. You got to keep on going. At the end of the day, it's kinda fun, right?" Right then I wanted to hop on the first plane back to New York.

Of course I didn't. Instead we drove over to the parking lot next to the Joe Louis Arena. It had been around forty-five degrees when we got in yesterday. Now the temperature had fallen to about thirty and the sky had that soft cloudy look that meant snow was coming. Gibbs was a little concerned. The arena was only half full and snow could hurt his day-of-show walk-up sales, which was a problem since black folks are notorious for waiting until the last minute to purchase tickets.

Unlike white fans who'll sell out a show months in advance, black folks usually can't afford to tip up cash for that long. After work on Fridays, when the check was cashed, is when the major weekend entertainment decisions were made. The choice of buying herb or rap show tickets could be determined when it started snowing.

From the outside, the two buses looked only slightly more impressive than the kind a community center would rent for a day trip to Atlantic City. Inside they were cream-colored minihomes with a living room area right behind the driver with a color T.V., a VCR, a sofa, and tables. In the back were several bunk beds, a restroom, a refrigerator, and shelves stocked with coffee, tea bags, crackers, and other easy-to-prepare items. Van Halen had been the previous occupant of one; the Temptations of the other.

Dirt Bike and a couple of other GAP staffers met us at the buses. We talked a bit, got our stories straight, and then went into the arena to meet with the building's assistant manager and the head of security. After what happened in the Garden, Gibbs had decided to go out of his way to make the arena managers comfortable. This was a meeting we'd take in every city, either the day of or the day before a concert. Gibbs knew many of these guys from previous r&b tours and he bantered with them with the familiarity of old soldiers exchanging war stories. It was at these meetings that Gibbs got his money's worth out of me.

I had what Gibbs called "a crossover voice." There was no ghetto in my tone. No harshness. No unnecessary cockiness. I used slang sparingly, like spice in a good soup, not like it constituted the whole meal. In the past, Gibbs had commented that this "smoothed out" articulation was holding back my songwriting, but for talking to white men he found it an asset. After the meeting, which ended in hearty handshakes and dirty jokes, Gibbs patted me on the back and told Dirt Bike I was the tour's Lionel Riche, which made him laugh and embarrassed me. It was a compliment that felt a bit disdainful. Even worse, it felt like it might have been true.

Back at the Renaissance there was a message from Ms. Joseph. What was I doing for lunch? The rappers wouldn't be heading over for sound checks until 3:30, so I had plenty of time and I was feeling pretty cocky after the meeting. Didn't ask Attak or Dirt Bike about her. Seemed wise not to. She picked me up at noon in a red Mazda and was intent on taking me to Greektown, whatever that was.

But I desperately wanted to go to Motown's Hitsville home on West Grand. Ms. Joseph rolled her eyes, as if this was a pilgrimage she could do without. Still she was pleasant about it. The building looked just as it had in the countless pictures I'd seen of Gordy and his musicians. It was a cute little home, emphasis on little. The stairway to the second floor didn't seem wide enough for two people, much less the gang of young talent that flowed up and down it for over a decade. Memorabilia filled the walls. Clippings. Photos. Framed *Billboards* and *Cashbox* charts. BMI awards. The stuff of record business royalty.

The basement studio seemed like a larger version of my family's basement in Queens. A drum kit, old and with yellowed skins, sat in the center of the room amid music stands, sound baffles, and miscellaneous stools and chairs. I sat on the steps for a long time with a great goofy smile, hoping that some whiff of greatness would flow into my lungs. In the car I was as giddy as a well-fed baby and Ms. Joseph, after her initial disapproval, seemed to enjoy my enthusiasm. Unlike last night, this was Derek Harper, unguarded and joyous. Even if she didn't really like me, at least at this moment I liked myself.

Greektown was a cute little strip of restaurants and shops that were the last echoes of a once prosperous Mediterranean neighborhood in this chocolate city, and it was a welcome respite from the rest of Detroit's grayness. And our conversation was different, too. Deeper. More fun, more like friends.

She didn't mention Attak, but I felt obligated to. With a smile and a shake of the head, I told her, "He's a sweet, confused little boy."

"How's that?"

"He's got a lot of good ideas. He's very observant and all that. But where he ends up with them. He told you his views on *Friday the 13th?*"

"Yeah." She rolled her eyes. "So tell me more about your music."

I thought I'd kicked all this to her last night, but Ms. Joseph seemed to crave more details and I gave them to her. Time passed. I began to think of her as Bernice, not Ms. Joseph. We sat closer. So close I smelled the onions on her breath and saw my reflection in her iris. So close that when I realized it was 3:30 I said, "Let's just sit awhile longer" and it was 4:15 when I realized I'd fucked up."

Gibbs' anger was somewhat abated by my bringing Bernice along to sound check. Her presence was the best explanation I could offer. Dirt Bike gave me a high-five and Attak, who'd just finished his sound check, greeted us both with affection.

"Yo," he whispered into my ear as we watched the Overweight Lovers at work. "You gonna get with her, man? She's real nice, you know." Forget his apocalyptic visions—Attak was still a kid when it came to women and a nice one at that. Donkey, whom I was growing to truly dislike, seemed pissed that Bernice and I were hanging.

Showtime. A near sell-out. The snow held off, though it was a mean sub-thirty degrees outside. I guess if you grew up in the Motor City, this was light stuff. Detroit crowds reputedly partied hardy and 15,000 plus gave everybody a strong reception. For a first show, things went fairly smoothly—a few lighting cues were off. There was a little feedback during Joint-ski's set, etc. Little things, really. Gibbs and I alternated between the sound board and backstage, troubleshooting, looking at women, and in general basking in the largeness of ourselves. If the night before I'd felt out of place, on this evening I was right in the center of everything and getting an incredible buzz from that fact.

Ms. Joseph appeared backstage near the end of Joint-ski's set and grabbed hold of my hand. "You all right?" I asked because she was shaking.

"Some boys out there are snatching gold chains." Her cultured voice had an edge of fear.

"It'll be okay. The show's almost over."

"I left my car in the parking lot. And I—"

Of course I was flashing back like crazy on the Garden show. I'd be damned if this fine-ass lady wasn't gonna be taken care of.

"Don't worry. Just stay with me."

We'd been shuttling buses between the Renaissance and the arena, moving the acts and our other people in case those brothers from last night were trying to clock us. Bernice vanned it back to the hotel with me and, holding my hand the whole time, came up to my room.

Two days of foreplay isn't a lot by normal standards. By touring standards, that's a lengthy courtship. The irony was that sex with Bernice was horrible. I mean, the worse sex I'd ever had in my life. She was still a good woman, of course. But we didn't click. To top if off, she fell dead asleep right as I slipped off my condom. The clock said 12:30. I looked down at the snoring Bernice Joseph and wondered if the sex would be better now that she was asleep. Sorry, but that's what I was thinking.

So then, I did what I should have done the minute we reached Detroit. I punched in Doris' number after pulling the phone into the bathroom. She was glad to hear from me. She figured I'd been out partying. "Nothing I wanna do in this town but talk to you." That's what I told her. Then I peeked out at Bernice to make sure she was still out cold.

I pleaded with Doris to come meet me out on the road. Tomorrow in

Chicago was out of the question. By next weekend we'd be somewhere down South where it'd be warmer. Doris talked about her continuing unhappiness on her job and how she was interviewing for another position. I told her that was great news. She wouldn't say what it was—didn't wanna jinx it. At the end of the conversation, I told her I missed her, feeling "I love you" was, under the circumstances, way too strong.

Afterwards I took a shower, put in for an 8 A.M. wake-up call and lay as far from Bernice Joseph's slumbering body as I could.

"Keep On Pushing"

Chicago—Lake Michigan was ice for as far as my bleary eyes could see. A mangy dog tiptoed across the mass of frozen water. When I pointed the dog out to Attak, he stared out at it with a kind of cockeyed glee, like the sight of it just confirmed his already dark view of life. I didn't wanna know how cold it was outside and when our driver told us that, after factoring in wind chill, it was twenty degrees below, I shivered.

But believe me, that little involuntary nervous shutter was nothing, nothing at all compared to how my body felt when that first nasty blast of Chi-town wind ripped through me. We had some interviews lined up, an in-store on the West Side and, of course, a gig that night. A busy day. But once we'd gotten the gang ensconced in the hotel, getting them out required major door banging and an emergency trip to the Water Tower department store for triple goose-down winter parkas, more thermal underwear, and ski masks before the brothers would budge.

The wind was blistering and no amount of Tanqueray gin at the hotel bar thawed my charges out. They were stiff as boards as Earl Calloway interviewed them at the *Chicago Defender* offices. Even the presence of a particularly busty intern named Chanya failed to rouse Attak, though Donkey saw this as just the motivation he needed to defrost. In fact, because of Chanya, Donkey was actually rather lively, droppin' science (as he called it) on the origins of rap, how much he hated the break-dance moves, and how to cut a record hip-hop style without scratching it. Attak, still shivering slightly, just leafed through the *Chicago Defender*, every now and then stopping to read a crime story and nodding.

Snow canceled our in-store, so we went over to a soul food spot on the South Side. Joint-ski was already there, along with Gibbs. We commandeered a big table—a gang of hungry, cold New Yorkers amid a restaurant teeming with grandly dressed families fresh from the morning service. Donkey had brought Chanya with him and was knee-deep into a conversation with her. Attak, still looking icicle-stiff, sat down next to me. He watched me squeeze the corn bread in my hands and decided, why not? So we're both sitting at the table holding this corn bread like it was a hot water bottle. It was so ridiculous that we both laughed at each other. We started to talk. Stories of being cold going to school, or playing football. Easy, relaxed male bonding type stuff. We flowed into a talk about songwriting, though all the while I was reflecting on Attak's sex life. If it was true he had herpes—and why would Gibbs make that up?—then his world view was profoundly, irrevocably altered. Even as he told me his story of loving heavy metal and his taste for horror films, I saw it all now as an expression of his dark sexual reality. To be all around all this sex yet to have been scarred by that freedom, well that would make you change your actions.

But then what about me? Had Ruthie Lee's murder changed me? I could say so, but my actions spoke so much louder. Even after her death I still chased after Cherri and many others. I could have gotten herpes, the clap, or maybe even this AIDS mess that Haitians and gays were getting around New York. All this should have had a sobering effect on me. But even as I talked to Attak, rap writer to song writer, I knew that my life hadn't really been altered—I was still a horny fool. I mean, even bad sex in Detroit wasn't gonna stop me.

Just like me, Donkey wasn't gonna let life interfere with his desire. If Attak's homie, Donkey, knew of his partner's malady, it hadn't made him a bit more cautious. He'd led Chanya from the table toward the restrooms not long after the corn bread arrived. When he returned, alone, they were clearing our plates and asking if we wanted peach cobbler or sweet potato pie. His face was flush and his manner surly. "What? You niggas ate without me?" Remember this was a real family spot in the years before "nigga" replaced "brother" and "bitch" "sister" in hip hop's everyday lexicon.

So Gibbs came over and told Donkey to chill on the cursing. Donkey's back curled up like an angry cat and he damn near hissed an obscenity at his manager. His defensiveness made me suspicious. "Yo, man," I asked, "where's that girl from the *Defender?* You send her home?"

"That ain't none of your fucking business!" Now heads were turning around the restaurant. Something was up. Perhaps to cover, Donkey tried to goad me into a fight. "You got something to say?!" he challenged me.

Then Attak said, "Yo, stop showing your ass and answer that man's question." This surprised Donkey and made him angry at Attak. I felt an evil vibration that reminded me of that night at the Garden. I headed toward the men's room. "Where are you going?" Donkey asked. There was worry in his words. Dirt Bike followed me. "Your man is bugged," I told Dirt Bike, who had no reply.

In a stall at the men's room we found Chanya. She was crying. Her clothes were ripped. There was some coke residue atop a roll of toilet paper. It was ugly. "Get Gibbs," I told Dirt Bike. He came back with Gibbs and one of the winter coats we'd purchased. I saw headlines, policemen, and lawsuits in his future. He ordered Dirt Bike to secure the restroom, while I paid the bill and got everybody out of the restaurant. I shot daggers at Donkey who, realizing that I knew what he'd done, was suddenly sheepish, even timid. Everybody wanted to know what was up, but with Attak's help we got the rest of the group out to the cars.

Back at the restroom, Dirt Bike was assuring the restaurant's manager that "one of the musicians just got sick. We just want him to have a little privacy before we bring him out." Inside Gibbs was bent down in front of Chanya. With some of the coke-soiled toilet paper, he wiped her tears and spoke softly, calmly to her. I couldn't really make out the words since he was real close to her. I have no idea what you say to a girl after a man has molested her in a restaurant men's room, but whatever it was, Gibbs was saying it.

He laid the winter parka around her and, almost fatherly, he moved her through the restaurant, past the gaze of curious diners, and into our remaining car. He took Chanya up to his suite and, with steel in his voice, told Donkey "to get his ass up here." When the fool arrived, Dirt Bike and I stepped out. Two hours later everybody was in the lobby, about to roll out to the Rosemont Horizon for sound check. Dirt Bike was next to Donkey, like he had a dog on a leash and Gibbs was a few feet behind. "It's handled." That's all Gibbs said to me.

"Are you sure?"

He sighed. "For now it is. She's up in my room asleep. She's going to be my guest at the show. She and a girlfriend. I think she'll be cool tonight. But when she gets home, talks to her parents, talks to someone at the *Defender*—" He let his words trail off.

"Donkey's a worthless piece of shit." That was me talking.

"But he's a good deejay," Gibbs replied. "I got his back for now, I have to. If this gets out, it could mess up everything."

"Don't you feel bad about it?"

"You don't feel bad about that money in your pocket, do you? Look, I can't let one monkey stop this damn show. Time comes when I need to cut Donkey—he'll be cut. Until then, Derek, we keep our mouths shut. You down?"

"I'll do it, Gibbs, but believe me, I ain't down."

Technically, the show was tighter than in Detroit. Lights, sound, set changes, etc., all went smoothly. And to my surprise in this frigid weather, we had another near sell-out. Backstage, however, the events of the afternoon were not forgotten.

The Overweight Lovers were defending Donkey, arguing that Chanya was "nothing but a skeezer" who shouldn't have gone into the men's room if she didn't wanna get busy. Dee Nasty, the group's human beat box, was particularly hard on her. "Yo, she was down to sniff his coke but not to suck his dick? Yo, the two go hand in hand."

Joint-ski felt Donkey was simply a fool. "He just met the girl. Hadn't had no time to feel her out. Instead of taking her back to the hotel for some privacy, he tries to do her in a public spot. Anybody could have walked in there." This wasn't a full out condemnation of Donkey or a defense of Chanya. For Joint-ski it was all a matter of strategy. Donkey wasn't handling his game right.

Attak stayed out of it. Didn't say a thing. It was like he didn't wanna acknowledge it had happened. In the van back to the hotel, he said nothing to Donkey, Donkey said nothing to him or me. After all that action in Detroit, the van ride after this gig was as quiet as a tomb. We didn't even have the radio on.

Cars were waiting at the hotel to take us to Schnick Rick's, a popular black club where the official after-party was being held. When we gathered in the lobby, Attak was no place to be found, though Donkey, unrepentant, was trying to get the hotel's cute blond night manager to join us.

"You coming?" I'd called Attak's room on the house phone.

"No, man. I'm staying in. Gonna write. Got to get something out. you know how that is." I told him I did, hung up, and realized, sadly, I hadn't felt that way since the tour had begun. So I followed Attak's lead and skipped the pleasures of Schnick Rick's for a night with my notebook and tape recorder. Don't know how it went for Attak, but I didn't get much. For some reason the phrase "To the one who sees" came into my mind.

I built on that by adding "To the one who sees/to the one who listens." And then nothing. Not a thing. Other than the image of Chanya crying in the men's room and, for financial reasons, me not in a position to do anything about it. "To the one who sees/To the one who listens." Well, if God saw and heard me and my comrades today, I'm sure he didn't smile.

"Royal Garden Blues"

Indianapolis—There was a message from my moms at the front desk when we checked into the Indianapolis Sheraton. I'd forgotten about Uncle Zack. She, of course, hadn't. "I've got things to do, Ma," I told her over the phone. "There can't be a thing more important than seeing your family," she retorted from Queens. I was going to see Uncle Zack. Luckily there wasn't a lot of media in old 'Naptown, so I didn't have to do anything with the Brothers Black after an 11 o'clock stop at a local black AM.

Since I was being paid, I felt obligated to communicate with Donkey. Donkey, however, wasn't talking to Attak because earlier Attak hadn't been talking to him. So somehow I ended up as the intermediary between my two charges. Dirt Bike, who was also talking to both, thought this was all real funny and was making book on how long it would take before a) a fight broke out and b) they made up after the fight. Betting was hot and heavy with Gibbs, drawing upon his vast experience in such matters, predicting it would all happen in the dressing room before they hit the stage. I put down $25, betting the fight would start in the van on the way to the gig and the reconciliation occurring in the dressing room. The pot was up to $500 when I got in the cab to Uncle Zack's.

Uncle Zack lived in an area that reminded me of St. Albans. A commercial strip on the main drag and neat, quiet residential streets a quick turn around the corner. A few of the homes looked well preserved. Most were weathered frame houses that surely had seen better days. Uncle Zack's had. The yard looked a little weedy. The white paint was chipping. And the front porch creaked loudly under the weight of my Adidas.

I'd forgotten how much Uncle Zack favored my moms and, as a result, favored me as well. He had sort of a bald, peanut head, and was a stooped-over, dark-brown version of Moms and me. It was almost like seeing myself as an old man, which I found as unsettling as the stale air that filled his dark living room. You could tell no woman had lived here in quite a while. Things were as disorderly as the inside of a man's top desk drawer.

I felt like I owed Uncle Zack at least a half hour for all the fruit cakes Aunt Emily Lee used to send me, so I used my most respectful demeanor and tried to make conversation. It was painful, at least for me. These rather inscrutable expressions passed over Uncle Zack's face. Sometimes I thought he was bored. I even suspected he might have been asleep with his eyes open.

Then the day took a sweetly unexpected turn. I glanced over at the knickknacks on one of the living room's dusty tables and saw this framed picture of a young Uncle Zack in a suit and tie—so young really that he could have been me—and a famous face, one I'd spied in some Black History Month presentation. When I asked about it, Uncle Zack had me bring the photo over to him and he smiled deeply.

"That's A. Philip Randolph and myself."

He spoke with great pride, as if by saying the name I would automatically understand how important this association was.

"A. Philip Randolph was an activist who organized the first black labor union."

"The Pullman porters?"

"Yup. You see I was a porter. I was supposed to be a senior in college the year that photo was taken. Nineteen hundred thirty-two. Chicago, Illinois. The Savoy Ballroom over on the South Side. The Brotherhood of Sleepingcar Porters was gathered to discuss strategy, and from the floor I spoke to the collected membership. Afterwards, A. Philip Randolph came over to praise me. He was one hell of an orator himself, Derek, so it was a high honor for me. I wish my father had heard me speak, but he never did.

"I loved him. Deep down, he loved me, too. I disappointed him and he never forgave me in this life. Your mother ever tell you about your great uncle?"

"Not much" I said. "Just that he ran a black newspaper and was very famous among black folks at one time."

"Yup. He kicked up a lot of sand for the race. Many of our people moved North because of his editorials. Wanted me to take over his newspaper one day." Uncle Zack got quiet. I waited for him to continue. His face got wistful as his pause grew into a silence. This could have been my cue to leave, but the old man had intrigued me.

"Uncle Zack. Uncle Zack." I was trying to be loud, but I didn't wanna holler at him. "What did you say that impressed A. Philip Randolph?"

Slowly he came back to me. "I talked about my father and why, despite his opposition, I stayed with the Brotherhood." Another break. A tiny smile. A bit of brightness in the eyes. He began again. "When I was small I fell in love with trains. It's not like now with American Airlines and Greyhound buses and such. The train was the only way to travel great distances. We lived outside of Richmond in a town called Bracey, Virginia. Every Tuesday evening at eight-fifteen, the Colonial rolled close by. My father would carry a bundle of newspapers down to Blake's Ridge. It was a low cliff that overlooked the tracks.

"My father would drop the bundle down on the roof of the caboose, cause that's where we were made to ride. A porter by the name of E. L. Mathias would stand on the back of the platform and drop off another bundle that consisted of colored newspapers from up North. *The Chicago Defender. The Pittsburgh Courier.* It was a barter system that helped spread word of the race's works around the country. My father would take them home and by the fireplace he'd read me the news."

Another pause. A glint of joy came into his eyes. "You see, I loved trains. The newspapers were powerful all right, but the idea of traveling. That's what filled my dreams. I wanted to roam around the country. I wanted to see the big towns—Chicago, Memphis, New York. I admired my father and the life he made for our family. But, Derek, at night I saw myself as E. L. Mathias wearing that uniform and traveling as far from Bracey as those rails would take me."

"But Uncle Zack, no disrespect intended, weren't the porters just sort of glorified waiters?" Why did I say that condescending shit? Uncle Zack's eyes got as narrow as mail slots. I saw the hard edges of a fighter under his wrinkles. This sudden intensity made him appear years younger.

"Derek, don't you know that being a Pullman porter was one of the best jobs a colored man could have! Most of the race did some kind of service work. Maid. Cook. Gardener. Chauffeur. That's what most of us did. Being a porter wasn't like being any of that 'cause being a Porter meant you were a man of the world. One night, Chicago. One night, Memphis. You drank from the Mississippi. You could see Louis Armstrong when most of the race only heard him on the radio. You could buy silk suits from the finest tailor on Beale Street. You could call on the tenderest, sweetest-smelling ladies at a house in Brooklyn, Illinois."

Uncle Zack looked a bit embarrassed that he'd admitted visiting a bordello to me, so in a very calm tone he explained, "For most colored folks then, the world was just a closed door. You could stay in your place, meaning where you lived was your place in life. Being a porter opened a lot of life's doors for you. Among colored folks you were a damn prince. I know you don't know nothing about that, but God bless my soul, that was the truth Ruth."

"So," I asked cautiously, "Uncle Zack, how'd you end up with this great gig when your pops was against it?"

A sigh. A bittersweet smile. A deep, enduring memory. "Well," he began, "I was supposed to attend Hampton Institute over in the Tidewater area of the state. Between his newspaper and printing business, my father could have paid my tuition. However, my father believed the race always had to be ready for labor. He'd say, 'You're only two generations removed from the field. I don't ever want you to forget the dignity of hard labor.'

"So in one bundle of papers he sent Mathias a letter asking if there was any kind of summer employment available. A week later he dropped a note back. Said he would be honored to have me apprentice for the months of June, July, and August.

"Well, my father drove me to Richmond on June first. It was a rainy day. The roads were muddy. I thought I'd miss the train. My father never worried. It wasn't in his nature. 'If the Lord wants you on the train today, he'll make a way.' That was basically what he said about everything. Still—" Uncle Zack stopped his narrative for a chuckle. "Still my father worked like the devil to get us there on time."

The spirit of his younger self filled his face and I recognized that face, and the childish wandering spirit, as my own. It was eerie and intensely pleasing. I touched his hard wrinkled hand and stared into his eyes, seeing myself. "Uncle Zack," I said softly, "tell me what happened next?" Time was traveling across his face, going back twice as many years as I'd lived. Now I was gone from his face and he was old again and filled with the perspective that life granted him.

"My father got me to the station on time. We marched through ankle deep mud back to the porters' quarters behind the station. As we got there, Mathias was standing in the doorway. He'd always been a small figure that stood in the back of a moving train. Up close, Mathias was as big as a summer moon and just as yellow. He was holding a canvas bag and a silver pocket watch. When Mathias saw us, he checked that pocket watch and smiled moonbeam bright.

"My father and Mathias were both race men. That probably means nothing to you since no one teaches you children about yourselves. To be a race man was to be ready to stand up for the race, to help move it forward in everything you did. I was being entrusted in Mathias' care by my father. From race man to race man. I didn't know, what none of us knew, that I wasn't just being passed on for the summer. That day in the Richmond mud, I was being passed on for life."

I was hooked. I needed this story. The hint of familial tension made me see that there was something in this tale for me. Maybe my future could be found in Uncle Zack's tale. He began again.

"I don't think I really knew what white hate was about until that summer. I'd grown up in a loving place, Derek, where the race took care of its own and white folks stayed in their place. I'd known of lynchings—it was always written about in the colored press—but hadn't seen any. Well, that summer I saw that the white race's problems came from expecting to be served. He needed someone to shine his boots, serve his drinks, and smile at him even when he was disrespectful. I didn't hate them, but I sure didn't respect them worth a damn, either. Still don't. My father had always told me labor defined a man's worth. If that was the case, then the porters were some of the worthiest of God's creations.

"You know what really burned me up? They called us all 'George.' Whether you were black blue from the Delta or banana yellow from Savannah or a brown boy from Virginia like me, it didn't make a piss bucket's worth of difference to them. You were just another old polywog that did their bidding.

"It was hard, Derek. My pampered little boy hands grew hard that summer. But, and I know this is hard to believe, I ended up loving it. I saw a world I'd never thought I could. It was like the dispatches in my father's papers had come to life. There were places in Philadelphia, New York, and Boston where the race had stores, grand churches, and ballrooms where people dressed fine and the women smiled as pretty as Mama's garden in May. And the race was moving, Derek. People were talking about going back to Africa. The race was building banks and insurance companies. The porters were organizing a union, a union just like the white man had, just like the ones the Pollacks and the Irish had.

"I wanted the Brotherhood to exist. I got to admit though, I probably wouldn't have taken the path I did if it wasn't for your aunt, Emily Lee. The train was just outside Indianapolis when I saw her. The day was hot. I'd been asleep in the porters' room. Between the heat and my sleeping hard, I was kinda groggy. Didn't know whether I was awake or dreaming. Work them long hours and it feels that way, Derek. The car for our race was crowded. People going to see relatives and friends. Big bags with preservatives in mason jars. Sweat poured off people. Smelled like a barnyard with all that food and people mashed together.

"Standing in the space between that car and the last white car was Emily Lee. It was dusty out there. Smoke was thick as cotton, Still, she looked to me like I was sitting in a meadow reading her Bible. I had things to do—I'd been sleeping as I said—but I just stood there and talked to her like we were in her mother's parlor. She was a fine-looking woman. But she was more than that; your aunt was an unusual woman for her time."

"Yeah." I spoke sheepishly, afraid to cut in, but he had finally paused. Then I added, "I remember Moms was saying her aunt worked for the lady who invented the hot comb."

"Madame C. J. Walker," he answered proudly. "Because of her, black girls have been burning hair on Saturday afternoons ever since." Uncle Zack was glowing now. His smile revealed yellow teeth full of gaps and spaces. Yet in that smile I saw my mother's smile, my smile, my family's smile. "Walker was out of Indianapolis and had used this hot comb contraption to make millions of dollars. Made more money than any other woman of the race and quite a bit more than most men. Emily Lee was one of her workers. She traveled throughout the Midwest and sold hot combs to women in little black towns near the Mississippi."

"Did women have that much freedom back then?" I asked. "I didn't think they had it like that."

"Well," he said softly in reply, "that's what we talking about. I was telling her she shouldn't have been out there by herself. Not just between the cars but out on the road by herself. We argued, but we argued in a nice way." A big smile and a wistful, sweet laugh. "Of course I almost got fired that day. Mathias hollered at me. I was just a whipping boy the rest of that ride. Did I care? Not a whit. She got here to good old 'Naptown. I was doubly blessed because we had a stopover there.

"The next day, I saw 'Naptown through her eyes. Now normally a woman in that time would never have gone anywhere with a man she just met. She would have sat in her family's living room and talked all day. But Emily Lee was ahead of her time. While we clashed about it sometimes, I gotta admit I'd never met a woman like her."

"That evening we went over to this ballroom where a local big band was playing. She danced much better than I did. You know, I was really just a well-read country boy and she was real worldly by comparison. I was stumbling around on that damn floor, but Emily Lee didn't comment. She kept me moving along and smiling. Then the band played an Ellington tune. The 'Royal Garden Blues' it was. And well, we came together on that. It was just fine. We moved along with the clarinet and it was fine, fine, fine."

Uncle Zack was me and I was Uncle Zack—young men out on the road listening to our hearts and loins on some sweet American night. There was a rapidity in his speech that sounded like me at my most hyperbolic.

Then that strange silence re-entered the room. The long pause. The hesitation. The feeling of harsh memory. Time—hard, disappointing time—began an ugly creep across my Uncle Zack's face. "This all happened in June," he began again. "By late July, I decided I didn't want to go to Hampton. I'd found something I wanted to do. I'd found the world. I'd found my love. Seemed like it was all set. And in a way it was. Those decisions made me a man, my own man, and my father, well he never understood that."

"I don't think my pops understands me." I didn't mean to say that. Uncle Zack might tell Moms and she'd freak if she thought I was snapping on Pops to a relative.

"I believe that," he replied. "The Harpers were always rigid folks. Hard working and all that, but stiff and clannish. There's a streak of the wandering soul in your mother's side. Not all of us feel it. Your mother has stayed close to home with your pops. That was a good thing, too. But, Derek, you got that wandering soul in you, just like me and your aunt, bless her beautiful soul. Eventually you'll land somewhere. You can't know where it'll be yet. But when you do, it'll feel like you belong there." Gesturing toward the kitchen he said, "Now go in the kitchen. There's something up on the stove for you."

In the cab back from Uncle Zack's I sat stuffing hunks of fruitcake in my mouth. He'd remembered how much I'd liked Aunt Emily Lee's fruitcake when I was child and he'd made me one in celebration of my visit. It wasn't quite as good as she'd made it, but I was not complaining. It made me wonder when I'd find my own Emily Lee. I'd already disappointed my pops. Had that part down. But my Emily Lee had proved as elusive as the fruitcake was sweet. Maybe I had to land at home first. History does repeat itself, I figured, but not always in the same way.

When I walked into the lobby, I saw Dirt Bike by the elevator with two enormous McDonald's bags tucked under each arm. "For the Overweight Lovers?"

Dirt Bike smiled. "For Attak and Donkey."

"So," I said as we moved in the elevator, "who won the bet?"

"Nobody, homes. Wasn't no fight."

"So Gibbs was wrong?"

"Word."

The doors opened onto our floor and the loud thump of a drum machine filled the hall. "Damn," I said, expressing my surprise at the noise.

"Yeah," Dirt Bike said, expressing his pleasure. I followed him down the corridor to the source of the sound, a suite down at the far end of the hallway with one of its double doors wide open. In the living room of the suite all the furniture had been pushed back against the walls and a clump of technology, including a four-track board, two mixers, a drum machine, a Casio keyboard, two turntables, and a bevy of microphones, was haphazardly arranged.

Behind the turntables, Donkey was cutting up Herman Kelly's "Dance to the Drummer's Beat" in time with a fresh drum pattern. Attak was right next to him with a black and white composition book in his hand. Scattered around the room were the Overweight Lovers, some roadies, and a very cute college-aged white girl who was damn near sitting at Attak's feet. As Dirt Bike distributed the Mickey D's, I walked over to Gibbs, who sat curled in a loveseat with an unlaced Adidas dangling from a outstretched foot.

"Why didn't you just rent a local studio?"

"Well," he said quietly, "there's been a lot of bootleg demos floating around. Engineers at some studios are being paid off to make dubs. So until we get some place we're comfortable recording in like Miami, we're gonna chill like this."

I was gonna ask what had gone on while I was away, but the mood in the room explained it all. Must be the music. Somewhere during the day someone had an idea for a track. Could have been anyone—Donkey, Attak, the Overnight Lovers. No matter who came up with the spark, it lit everybody up. The suite was filled with music minus ego, attitude, ill vibrations, or bad thoughts. Donkey was creating thick beats that you felt sticking to your ribs, while Attak and the Overweight Lovers rhymed with rapid freestyle elocutions.

As soon as he was finished working, Donkey'd be that guy again who so blithely molested the young woman in the men's room. However that wasn't this moment, that wasn't now. Now Donkey was in touch with something better than his nasty personality or the smelly feet I'd had to endure in the tour bus. I liked Donkey now, or more precisely, I liked what was coming through his fingers.

That night, after the concert, after I'd gone to sleep with images of Uncle Zack and Donkey and Attak and the white girl at his feet filling my mental screen, I woke up and scribbled these words on the back of my tour itinerary.

"The One Who Sees"

To the one who sees, to the one who listens
There is no reason, there is no passion.
There is only you and him and me
And the ways we have to be.
To the one who sees, to the one who listens
There is no confusion, there is no fear
There is only good and bad and different
And the spirit that guides all three.

I needed more. I needed a bridge, another verse. But I liked it. Somehow it made me feel good in that intangible way creating something always did. I should have called my moms. I should have talked with Pops. It would have been nice if I rang Doris. But I spent the next couple of days thinking about these words, obsessing about a melody, and staring into space when Dirt Bike, Gibbs, or anyone else spoke to me. It was like I was lost inside this song. This feeling had been my way of traveling when I was a kid, and with all that I was experiencing and seeing now, remained my favorite mode of transportation.

St. Louis—I had the best steak and the biggest baked potato I've ever had at this restaurant near the great arch. I mean, the potato was damn near as long as my foot but much tastier. And one of the stage hands at Keil Auditorium, an old black man with the red undertones of an Indian, told me that the pyramids were only in three places in the world—Egypt, Mexico, and across the river in East St. Louis, which is now one of the blackest cities in America. "Centuries ago a flood submerged them, but that energy is still there," he instructed. "That's why Chuck Berry and Miles Davis are from the same area. They are children of that energy." Yeah, I would have thought he was a crackpot, too, but he's the one who directed me to that great steak house, so homie definitely had some knowledge.

Memphis—Memphis is a town that borders the mighty Mississippi and is saturated with overflow from the great myth of Elvis. Graceland is a shrine, the city is a ghost town, and the spirit of this white-trash icon haunts the land, filling strip malls, souvenir shops, and the hurly-burly of daily commerce. The town just stinks of the infinitely recy-clable visage of Elvis. The Sun Records studio, where he and sundry other white boys lost in the blues cut their first records, is immacu-lately maintained. Beale Street, an avenue once as important to black America's soul as Harlem's 125th Street or Los Angeles' Central Av-enue, has been gentrified as a yuppie theme park where the blues is viewed not as the deep root of all American music but in relation to Elvis. ("He learned this listening to B. B. King." "He bought his first suit from this tailor on Beale Street who sold stuff to black pimps." Blah. Blah. Blah.)

Driving this town alone in a rented BMW and holding my nose from the stench of Elvis, I went in search of my musical heritage in Mem-phis and found it on a forlorn corner of the city. Shuttered, dilapi-dated, forgotten was a converted movie theater that had once housed Stax Records—the rawer, country-inflected, Southern soul label that was ying to Motown's Northern yang. This is where Otis Redding recorded "Try a Little Tenderness" and Booker T & the MG's grooved on "Green Onions" and Isaac Hayes reinterpreted "By the Time I Get to Phoenix" as a meditation on infidelity. It was a place where white and black musicians made a truly soulful blend of country, blues, and gospel that was as satisfying as my moms' greens, yams, and fried chicken. It was the real thing, not that American nightmare of a dream where black innovation exists to fuel white fantasies of fun.

The area surrounding Stax was filled with nondescript weedy homes and quiet decay. It wasn't a ghetto, but it looked as forgotten as a date-less teen on a Friday night. I'd always been more a Motown and Philly International man than a Stax fan, but I knew how much people who'd toiled in this old building had given the world, even if Memphis didn't really seem to care.

Behind the theater, Attak, Charlene (the white girl he'd met in Indy), and Dirt Bike were sitting on the tour bus steps, eating craw-fish. Beers were being consumed. The sun was shining. It was 60-something and, from the other side of a fence, a few fans screamed out for autographs. I imagined that in the old days, when I was still in elementary school and my moms and pops were young, the Stax musicians stood outside under the marquee after a session and ate crawfish plucked out of the Mississippi, just as we did now.

Dallas—There were two messages at the front desk for me when we checked into the hotel. One was from Doris. Not unexpected, since we'd talked about her joining me once the tour had rolled down to warmer climates. The other one, however, had me scratching my head. It was from Mayo's assistant Danifa. That was strange enough, but then under her name was the listing Warner-Chappel Music, the big music publishing company.

Curiosity got the better of romance so I called Danifa first. A very officious young white woman answered and inquired if Ms. White knew why I was calling. After I was put on hold it occurred to me that I'd never known Danifa's last name. She'd always been just Mayo's assistant to me.

"Hello, Derek Harper!"

"Hey, Danifa." Her energy surprised me. "I take it you don't work for Mayo anymore."

"That's right." Danifa White was now an employee of Warner-Chappel Music, one with the expressed mission of signing a crop of new r&b songwriters. And, yeah, she wanted to sign me. "You're talented, Derek," she said. "And you're strong willed. Very few young writers would have turned down Mayo's deal. Believe me, I know." I sat on my hotel room bed, making no sound except an occasional grunt to let her know I was still listening. "So I want to sign you to a publishing deal. We'll negotiate an advance for you. Get your catalogue of songs put in a nice package so they can be presented to a&r people as well as artists' managers. I'll arrange for you to write with some of our other writers, which often increases the chances of getting your song covered. Are you there, Derek?"

Finally, I said, "Yeah," and then she wanted to know if I was interested. Interested? I was so interested I wanted to roll over on my back, stick my legs in the air, and pant like a dog getting its belly rubbed. I'd been waiting for a moment like this since I'd graduated from college. So here it was, coming to me deep in the heart of Texas.

This could have easily been the greatest phone call of my life—right up there with Candi saying she still wanted to go to the movies with me that wintry Queens Sunday—except for how it ended. "This must be an exciting time for you and Doris." I didn't know what Danifa meant by that and told her so. "You don't know about the job?" Now it was her turn to pause and mine to plead for a response. After some prodding, Danifa stammered, "This really should be coming from Doris. I really don't want to get in the middle of any miscommunication."

"Look," I cut in impatiently, "she called me this morning. We just missed each other. I'm sure she was calling to tell me the news. Now don't torture me. What's the job?"

"Well, she got my old job. She's working for Mayo."

You leave New York for a month or so and the world changes around you. I hadn't been paying as much attention to Doris as I should have, but this was so bugged, so unexpected. Doris knew how my business relationship with Mayo had ended. Now she was on his payroll. Danifa tried to play down Doris' move, telling me "I'm sure she wasn't hiding this from you. You've been so busy traveling it probably slipped her mind." That was weak. She knew it, too. What made it worse was that Danifa had clearly choreographed the whole thing. She was making a power move and she put Doris down with Mayo. No question that that was the play. This publishing offer was, on some level, her way of placating me for using my girlfriend as a pawn. Remember, Danifa had learned slickness at the knee of Mayo.

As if she could read my mind, Danifa assured me, "Your talent is why I'm making this offer. I know you can be a hit songwriter. You have the drive—just look at how you sat in that toilet to meet Mayo.

What you need is to be showcased, and I can do that for you." How mad could I be at a woman who'd say that? So I bit my tongue, told her to give me a day or two to think about the offer, and sat on the bed, lost in thought.

The rest of the day, thankfully, didn't give me much time for reflection. Dallas is a big, sprawling metropolis—I mean a Texas mile is at least three times as long as a New York mile—so we spent a lot of the day shuttling across Big D to radio stations, an in-store appearance in East Dallas, and an interview at the *Dallas Morning News.* The Brothers Black were blowing up at the same time the effects of Joint-ski's wack Mayo album were being felt. At the concerts, the intensity of the cheers for the Brothers Black seemed to build in every city, while kids were starting to stream out during Joint-ski's closing set. Even the press were now asking to talk to Attak, not Joint-ski. Though I'd known Joint-ski for years I kept my distance, figuring he now associated me with the Brothers Black.

The shifting balance of power should have excited Attak and Donkey, and to some degree, it did. Onstage they were extremely tight, with Attak and his mercurial D.J. radiating a kind of manic energy that Joint-ski simply couldn't match. On this tour, the torch was definitely being passed from old school to new.

The blemish on this otherwise pretty picture was that the Brothers Black weren't the only new kids on the block. This group from Hollis, Run-D.M.C., was generating amazing news coverage and their current album, *King of Rock,* while not as good as their debut, had solidified their place as rap's first act to sell albums and not just 12-inches. At all of our stops in Dallas, Attak was asked his thoughts on Run. Did he feel competitive with him? Was he a better rapper? Was Run the new king of rap?

As irritating as this line of questioning was for Attak, I knew the business implications were worse for Gibbs. Russell Simmons, Run's brother, had a rival tour on the road and, according to attendance charts in *Billboard,* it was out-grossing us. In Dwayne Robinson's Bass Line column, Rush, as Simmons and his management company were called, seemed to be getting mentioned every week.

Then there was the Donkey problem. Though Attak and Gibbs had on the surface patched things up, there was a surly edge to Donkey that only softened on stage, or during impromptu demo sessions. Otherwise he was still a threat to any young woman under eighteen who came within spitting distance. In short, Donkey was a living, breathing, touring potential lawsuit. And he was jealous-hearted to boot! Whenever Run-D.M.C. came up, he'd make a nasty joke. And whenever he felt Attak was answering too many questions—which was at least twice an interview—he'd suck his teeth loudly and slump down into his seat like a reluctant eight-year-old at Sunday service.

With all this going on, I didn't cheer my sudden good fortune or chew over Doris' mysterious career move. I waited until after the sound check before calling her. "Oh, I'm so glad you called me back," she said.

"Why wouldn't I?" I was already mad and we hadn't even gotten into it yet. I tried to chill and let her explain herself. She talked about how frustrating her old job was, about how great an opportunity working for Mayo was, how much better she'd understand me now that she'd be in my business, and with a touch of humor, how nice it was to be in an industry that encouraged parties and sleeping late.

All the while I felt my face getting red and my neck stiffening. I was listening but I wasn't hearing. "All that's fine Doris," I said heatedly, "but I just had the biggest beef of my professional life with your new boss. The reason I'm out on this damn tour is because my deal with Mayo fell through. Now if I wanna call you during the day I gotta call his office. You're gonna be helping make money for a guy who tried to rip me off. Now what's that about?"

To my surprise, Doris wasn't fazed by my anger. As well prepared as a lobbyist giving Congressional testimony, Doris came back with quite a strong argument. "Do your problems automatically become mine, Derek?" she asked. "I care about you. I care a great deal. You've helped me through a rough time after my breakup. But we're not married or even engaged. I knew this would upset you. In fact, I turned the position down at first. Even Mayo knew it had the potential to be awkward."

"I'm sure he did."

"But," she came quickly, "he said I came highly recommended."

"By Danifa."

"Of course. And that in the record business relationships can be so transitory that it doesn't make sense for me to turn down a job over a relationship—"

"—that might not last."

"Well," she replied rather plaintively, "he made sense, Derek. You're out on the road. I'm in New York. I needed a new job and Mayo made a fine offer." Then she added, "Don't worry about calling me. I'm getting a beeper, so you'll be able to reach me at the job without calling Mayo's office."

Doris' argument was totally rational and, thus, totally disappointing. Whatever passion she had for me—and there was still some there—Doris had put aside. Long-term thinking on her part. Long-term thinking that factored me out. It hit me that by taking this job, Doris was, in fact, putting me on notice. I could be gone soon.

There was a banging at my door. Loud teenaged banging. I told Doris to hold. Attak, Dirt Bike, Donkey, and a couple of roadies were outside. The latest *Friday the 13th* had just opened and since our hotel was right next to Reunion Arena they felt comfortable sneaking over to catch a screening that would end at 6:15, which would be cutting it close. They knew that but figured if I went along, Gibbs wouldn't get too upset. When I got back to the phone, Doris had me on hold. Now I had a room full of anxious b-boys awaiting me, and my "woman" had me in long-distance discomfort. "Come on, homie," Attak pleaded. I waited another minute and then hung up, quietly relieved that I had an excuse to end that conversation.

Friday the 13th was all right if you loved dismemberment, screaming, and nubile white girls running scared. Traffic going back to the hotel and Reunion Arena was horrible. Around 7:15, a half hour before the Brothers Black were due on stage, we moved slowly through Daley Plaza where JFK was gunned down. I pointed out the school book repository, but the brothers weren't too impressed. The general attitude was that people got capped all the time. That was just part of life.

What got everyone excited was Donkey's question, "Wasn't Kennedy hittin' Marilyn Monroe?" I told him "Yeah." Then Attak offered, "That was a fine-looking white girl." Which led Donkey to say sarcastically, "You should know about white girls." Which led Attak to turn in his seat and throw a punch at Donkey, which led to general chaos in the van. Apparently Donkey, a young man with deep respect for women, wasn't happy about his partner's affection for Charlene. I guess I had missed that dispute.

So while they wrestled and shouted in front of the site of a great national tragedy, my mind wandered back to the day's phone calls and the question of how much they had changed my life. One day real soon I was gonna be a songwriter—a real one who actually made money. But right now I was still just a baby-sitter and, judging by my charges' behavior, not a real good one.

Houston—There were three things I'll always remember about H-Town. One is me getting sick from Mexican food and spending much of the day sitting on the toilet of my very spacious Hyatt Summit Hotel room. Two is me on the toilet and on the phone with Doris: "You mean so much to me, baby. Maybe I don't show it as much as I should. But I want you to be happy and if taking this job achieves that, then I totally support you. I just wanted to make that clear to you, Doris, so you don't think I resent you or have bad feelings or whatever." Doris seemed relieved by my words, and I was relieved that she was relieved.

The third and final thing I remember about Houston is how deep into hip hop the crowd was. After the gig at the Summit, we all rolled over to this a huge barn of a club where they played rap and funk records over booming speakers. It was like a hip-hop Gilley's, which was quite unexpected and totally dope.

Ah, there's a fourth thing I remember about Houston. Everybody scooped up one of these big, healthy Texas girls. Everybody. Yeah. Even after my talk with Doris I got with a groupie that night. What can I say?

New Orleans—Walter Gibbs was wearing a bib, a very crisp beige blazer, and a smile as vibrant as the Mississippi River which rumbled right down the street. He reached into the clear glass bowl in front of him, pulled out a succulent barbecued shrimp, and turned to his right. Beth Ann opened her lovely, wide-lipped copper mouth and took the shrimp from his happy fingers. She'd flown in from a photo shoot in Jamaica and had a deep, reddish tan that elevated her from merely beautiful to drop-dead gorgeous.

Gibbs had arranged the schedule so we'd have two days off in New Orleans. Originally, I thought I'd head back to the Apple just as the rappers had. I'd planned to see Moms, Pops, Doris, and do a little business with Danifa. Instead, Gibbs and I ended up checking into this cool little hotel in the French Quarter that had terraces, canopied beds, and basically looked like a *A Streetcar Named Desire* set. I slept late. I sat by the Mississippi River with my note pad writing whatever came to mind. I spent a lot of friendly energy flirting with cleaning women, waitresses, and cute Creole passersby.

In the afternoon, Gibbs and Beth Ann would roll out of bed and we'd ride streetcars, like any good tourist, and at night drink our way through the music bars along Bourbon Street and environs. Mostly we ate. Barbecued shrimp. French pastries. Pop corn shrimp. Gumbo 'til it filled my mouth like saliva. After hotel grub and fast food stops across the Midwest, New Orleans' cuisine was like being in tastebud heaven.

If I didn't know my man better, I'd have sworn Gibbs was falling in love. Wine, a great woman, and song all night long, all at a very high level, would have knocked out most men. And Beth Ann was no ordinary G. Very confident. Had her own money. Had a life of her own. Still, my ex-roomie had too much game, or so I believed, to be that open. Not now. Not when he had so much money to make, so much to prove to the industry.

The New Orleans shows were as saucy as the local food. We played two nights at The Saeger Theater where Maze, featuring Frankie Beverly, had recorded a great live album a few years before. Just as on that record, the Crescent City crowd was crazy alive. They had this chant, "Go head! Go head! Go head!" that they shouted spontaneously when they felt the groove. They were much nicer to Jointski than Texas had been, though the Overweight Lovers were the real favorites.

Attak and Donkey were talking again. Dirt Bike, in a rare use of metaphor, started calling them "the rap Abbott & Costello," which amused everybody but them.

On our last day in New Orleans I received a gang of legal papers from Danifa. All fired up by my possession of these papers I went down to the Mississippi and scribbled these words down:

Your love is hotter than summer
Softer than cotton
And deeper than the craters of the moon.
All I can say is that when I slumber
I sleep with no bottom.
Your face comes to me soon
So soon.

But ever soon enough. There was a song in there somewhere and eventually I'd find it.

"Papa Was a Rolling Stone"

Miami—As you know, Donkey was far from my favorite person on the tour. He didn't give a damn about anyone's daughter or anyone's time. But on our way into Miami he said something that actually made me appreciate my upbringing. Of course, this wasn't his intention. It just worked out that way. We were both sitting in the center section of the tour bus, eating McDonald's and sipping Cokes, when I started talking about how sheltered my life had been.

I grew up in a house with a basement, a piano to pound on, with both my parents and never any shortage of spending cash for albums, movies, and dates. My pops had his own business and my moms was always home after school to check my homework. This wasn't so unusual, but for a black child in New York City I was living a charmed life. Even my trips to Brownsville were relatively sheltered, since Anna always hovered around and rarely let me out of her sight. The murder of Uncle Teddy was my introduction to the world that Donkey took for granted. He didn't grow up that far from me geographically— Jamaica was a long summer's day walk from my house. Yet in so many ways, I lived on another planet. Still I wasn't going for that you're-not-black-because-you-didn't-come-from-the-ghetto-mess. Fuck that. I had my own angle on black reality.

I told Donkey about how Pops sat at Sunday dinners and talked about undertaking and how boring that was. Then he told me he'd never spoken to his father, had never seen him and, at this point, didn't care to. "Fuck my biological!" he said. "That nigga don't mean shit to me!" Then he went back to his burger and waved his hand, as if I'd engaged him in a stupid conversation. Right at that moment I realized the price he'd paid for his anger. Whatever was wrong between me and my pops, I did have him. For that I should be grateful.

When I tried to explain this to Donkey, he got mad at me for bringing this father mess up again. "Nigga," he said, "you better wake up. Getting involved in this crazy conversation. You been living your whole life in a black child's heaven and don't even know it." Then Attak stuck his head out of the back and started doing a human beat box and reciting the phrase, "Living in a black child's heaven," finding the cadence in the words, finding its flavor, writing a rap right before me about my life. It was strangely flattering. I threw in a rhyme or two, each time speaking very sheepishly, but Attak seemed open to my idea. Donkey just looked at us both, eating his burger, obviously still agitated by all this father talk.

Most of the brothers were excited about being in Miami. This was in the glory days of *Miami Vice* when scruffy beards, white linen suits, and no socks were the height of a certain kind of cool. Nobody on our tour was trying to rock that style, but the idea of being in the center of all this hype was still exciting. For the tour's more gangster-oriented element, namely Dirt Bike and Donkey, Miami was home turf for Tony Montana, the anti-hero of *Scarface* and a violent, nihilistic coke dealer who was damn near every rap star's favorite movie hero.

Though critics trashed the flick when it first came out, there was something about Montana's crude, ballsy drive for power and respect that reached right into the heart of the age and voiced its desires. Even Attak, who was more into the metaphorical evil of Freddie and Jason, shared an affection for Montana. It was one of the few points on which both Attak and Donkey seemed to agree these days.

Considering everyone's anticipation at visiting Miami, our time there was relatively uneventful. Temperatures peaked at 80 degrees and a few souls dived in the somewhat chilly Atlantic. Most of us laid by the pool or on the beach soaking up sun and talking about how the temperatures up in New York were already below 40 degrees. Some of the old white retirees cut the brothers some funny looks around the hotel, but on the surface everything was fine. At both shows they did in Miami, the Overweight Lovers rocked and brought in a lot more white fans than I'd expected. After both gigs I saw Gibbs talking with a balding thirtyish white man sporting a satin baseball jacket and a rather arrogant smile.

The night of the big concert, a local hip-hop collective known as the Ghetto Style Deejays held an after-party in our honor over at a spot in Liberty City, which was the center of Miami's black community. The spot was modest but the champagne flowed and the local deejay was playing "Planet Rock" like it was coke and he needed a hit. I was sweating it up on the dance floor with two local girls when I spotted a late-arriving Gibbs and Beth Ann hugged up in a booth off the dance floor.

From a distance, they looked quite content. However the closer I got, the more sour my friend looked. "What's up, my man? You look beat down." Instead of answering, Gibbs rolled his head back and looked up at the ceiling. "Come on, Walter. What's going on?"

"It's the Overweight Lovers," Beth Ann answered as Gibbs laid his head on her shoulder. "Walter isn't managing them anymore."

Gibbs lifted his head—his eyes flared with anger. "Some mother-fucker got them a television commercial promoting bubble gum. Some shit called 'Oversized Sticks.' And promised them a movie deal and a lot of other stuff he can't deliver."

"Russell Simmons did this?"

"I wish," he said. "At least then it would be a fair fight. But it was some slick white dude. He's been hanging around the last couple of days. Name's Lawson. He got them one thing and promised them a lot of other stuff that he said I couldn't do. When a white man offers candy to a black kid, it's like he's never seen no candy before. It's like my candy isn't as sweet as his, though they been eating it for years. It's as simple as that. They'll stay on the tour through this leg, but they won't go to the Coast with us. They'll be in New York eating that man's candy."

"They aren't the only fat rappers in New York." Beth Ann's voice was as soothing as a mother's is to a new born baby. She poured Gibbs a glass of Dom P and he sipped from it, then rested his head back on her shoulder. I smiled at her, she nodded, and then I headed back to the dance floor and went looking for those two girls.

"Slippery When Wet"

Atlanta—"Buck wild" is the only way to describe my second road trip here. Donkey dominated this visit, which I guess is fair warning. He set the tone in the tour bus on our way into town. About five in the morning, Donkey rolled out of his bunk in the back, staggered past the toilet, and peed up against a wall behind the refrigerator. Asked later why he didn't use the toilet Donkey replied, "I didn't feel like aiming."

When I'd visited Atlanta before, school was out and the cluster of black colleges that form the A.U. center (Morehouse, Spelman, Morris Brown, Clark, Atlanta) were empty. Now it was early November, the schools were in session, and Donkey's hormones were in overdrive. We'd scheduled an interview at the Clark College radio station for Joint-ski. But, for the first time on tour, everyone volunteered to show up to "promote" the gig. Well, Donkey and company had a novel promotional strategy.

Donkey cruised our van through the all-girl campus of Spelman with his stereo blasting Brothers Black 12-inches and a fist full of papers in his hand. Donkey's general rule was plain girls got flyers, cute girls got tickets, and fly girls got backstage passes. It was all pretty predatory, though there was something beguilingly juvenile about it. And, if that was as far as it went, I'd still be smiling about that wacky Donkey kid.

After the gig—a near sell-out at the Omni—the Atlanta Marriott was overrun with fans. It wasn't Jack the Rapper, but it was close. Guys were hawking demo tapes. For example, one scrawny kid saw my backstage pass and announced, "I got a dope track."

"What's it called?" I wondered.

"Vish-Ass!"

"You mean 'Vicious.'"

"No," he corrected me. "It's about a girl with a 'Vish-Ass.'"

Another guy was pulling on Gibbs' ear by the bar. Apparently he was a wannabe Eddie Murphy. Sample joke: "I'm a handicapped pimp. What do I do? I pimp the handicapped. You seen one of my girls roll by?"

Attak came up behind me holding the hand of a plain-looking girl with baby's hair. Couldn't be more than seventeen. He whispered, "Derek, listen to this." He turned to her. "Beatrice. That's it, right?" She nodded. "You want me to kiss you, right?" She nodded again. "Okay, tell Derek here why."

Beatrice opened her mouth, exposing more heavy metal than "Stairway to Heaven," and said, "You just don't know what a girl with braces can do." Then she stuck a big old pink tongue out from between her teeth and her braces and I just about fell out. I think I hurt her feelings with my laughter, but I couldn't help myself. Attak took her by the hand and went to display Beatrice's charms to someone else.

The whole scene was well in hand—until Mr. John Bishop started asking about his wife. Mr. Bishop was a cocoa-colored brother, six foot two or so, a chunky 250 pounds of country ass department of public works employee. Apparently he'd gotten separated from his wife at the Omni and had come over to the hotel on a hunch. Obviously any man whose hunch takes him to a hotel full of musicians knows more about his wife than he's telling.

I was standing at the bar with Attak when Mr. Bishop came over. "You seen my wife?" In his hand was a wallet-sized photo of a smiling, hershey-brown sista with bright, dancing eyes. Hadn't seen her and told him so. Attak blinked noticeably when he saw the picture and then told her husband the same thing.

"Ain't you in that group, the Black Brothers?"

"Brother Black, my man," he corrected Mr. Bishop. "The Brothers Black. My name's Attak."

"Yeah." Mr. Bishop surveyed Attak closely and then peered at me. "You ain't that guy Donkey, are you?" I explained to him who I was. He got that and then said something scary. "My wife loves the Black Brothers. She got pictures of your group up in our basement and at her job. Like that Donkey. He 'round here?"

I took another glance at Mrs. Bishop's picture and got a sinking feeling. While I hadn't seen her at the Omni, she did look vaguely familiar. Then it hit me. Mrs. Bishop looked an awful lot like Chanya, that unfortunate intern at the *Chicago Defender*. I cut Attak a look and realized what his blink had signified.

Suddenly Dirt Bike, looking flush and uncharacteristically excited, stepped to us. "Yo, yo," he said." You niggas need to come upstairs. Shit is being set off."

Mr. Bishop stuck that lovely picture in Dirt Bike's face, asked if he'd seen her, and my man's face got beet red. His "No, my man" was as convincing as Nixon's "I am not a crook."

Well. What we had here was a serious situation. I decided to buy Mr. Bishop a drink. "How about a Jack Daniel's?" Quickly Attak and Dirt Bike escaped the bar while I stood drinking with Mr. Bishop, listening to his wife story.

"My wife loves music," he told me quite innocently. "It makes her happy."

All the while he's talking members of the tour—roadies, drivers, you name it—are all whispering to each other, laughing, and then disappearing from the bar. I'm feeling real bad for Mr. Bishop right now, but silence at this moment definitely appears golden.

"I'm sure she's home by now, John." By now we were on a first-name basis.

"Maybe you right." Still he looked reluctant to leave.

"I've got the drinks."

"Can't let you do that, partner," he said pulling out a $20. "Jack ain't cheap."

I insisted, telling him these rap groups would pay for it, which made it all right with him. We shook hands and Mr. Bishop moved toward the front of the Marriott. Quickly I got into one of those glass elevators that provides a panoramic view of the lobby. As I slowly elevated, I noticed Mr. Bishop showing his wife's photo to Beatrice with the braces. Apparently Attak hadn't kissed her and she held a grudge, because I saw Beatrice point up, at which point my eye balls started to hurt.

Once on the floor I sprinted to Donkey's room. The Do Not Disturb sign was on the knob, but there was noise aplenty coming from inside. It took a minute or so. Finally a bare-chested Overweight Lover, blubber rolling before him like ocean waves, cracked opened the door. "Full house, Derek," he said, but I just pushed his fat ass aside and entered the tour's first full-blown orgy.

Me personally, I've never been big on being in a room full of a lot of exposed dicks. Obviously my feelings weren't shared by many of my peers. Attak was sitting in a chair, drinking a Heineken and photographing everything with his brand-new camcorder.

"Where's Donkey?"

"Oh," he said as he taped my face. "He's in the bed room with the freak of the week."

"Mrs. Bishop?"

"Oh," Attak replied, "she didn't give her last name, but she did favor that lady in Mr. Bishop's picture."

"Mr. Bishop's coming."

Attak, calm as could be, observed, "This could get criminal minded," and suggested we go outside from some air.

We were in the hallway when Mr. Bishop, three uniformed security guards, and the hotel's black woman night manager exited the elevator. "Excuse me!" Attak announced. "Mr. Bishop, I do believe I saw your wife enter that room, not ten minutes ago."

In a loud comic whisper I asked Attak if he was crazy. He just laughed and reloaded his camcorder. Got some classic stuff. An angry husband screaming at his wife. Embarrassed coeds scrambling for their bras. Out-of-shape rap stars fighting over whose bikini briefs were whose. Donkey, defiant to the last, displaying his ample wares in the hallway by refusing to get dressed until he could speak to an attorney. There's even footage of Gibbs, rap mogul and lover of a beautiful model, arranging bail over the phone even as he zipped his Lee jeans and searched for his red Adidas sneakers under a sofa.

The next day I found out it had all started with Mrs. Bishop sitting in the same chair Attak had occupied, throwing out double entendres but refusing any action. So Donkey, as he was quick to do, unzipped his pants and dropped his dick on Mrs. Bishop's shoulder. After the initial surprise, things proceeded from there. Due to various legal and logistical problems, the next night's show in South Carolina was canceled.

About a year later, Mr. Bishop sent me a postcard announcing the birth of a bouncing baby girl. His wife had named her Jeanie Black Bishop. Well, Mr. Bishop, he was a better man than me.

"Traveling the Highway to Heaven (Part 2)"

Charlotte—The White Rock Baptist Church of Charlotte was founded by freed slaves during Reconstruction. A white wooden building with ancient stained glass, it was built with the sweat of deeply devoted African Americans. It had withstood Jim Crow, the Depression, two world wars, a KKK bombing in sixty-two, the Vietnam War, and the rise of Reaganism, while managing to give comfort to the black citizens of this growing city.

I stood outside White Rock's brick steps in a dark blue Sunday suit, gathering myself before I entered. The junior pastor, Reverend Vernon Jackson, was preaching today and the thought of seeing him made me quite nervous. It had been years since we'd spoken. I know my life had changed and I had no idea what had happened to the best singer I'd ever heard.

"Sin is only a temporary distraction from the everyday values of life," he pronounced looking out over a sea of grunting, fanning parishioners. "Only the Lord's loving goodness can truly fill your day. You get drunk. It's good for a minute. Maybe two. Then you wake up with a hangover and the rest of the day is misery."

He wore a gold and burgundy robe, the gold in the fabric matched that of the big watch on his wrist and the shimmer of the large cross dangling from his neck. "You have sex out of wedlock! Lust fills your loins! When it ends, you can be scarred for life with the burden of an unloved bastard child and the sure death of this new demon, AIDS, that is stalking the streets."

His face still looked adolescent, though a thin mustache curled across his upper lip. His hair was quite moist and elaborately styled into something Little Richard or maybe Prince would have envied. His face answered one of the great questions of the era: What would Michael Jackson have looked like if he'd have stayed brown? The answer: Reverend Vernon Jackson.

"Heroin! PCP! Freebase!—they are all sinful substances designed to separate you from you senses, melt down your mind, and give you escape through sin from worldly pain. Once the high ends and, sisters and brothers, the high always ends, you are back on the Lord's plane!

S
E
D
U
C
E
D

215

On the Lord's ground! The Lord's consciousness! You will face judgment! No amount of alcohol! No amount of fornication! No ingestion of cooked cocaine is gonna prevent his judgment! Let the church say Amen!"

A man in the White Rock congregation stood up, clapping and praising and signifying. The faces in the large choir behind him beamed at his back. The camera man, who'd been shooting Reverend Jackson from the center aisle, moved in closer. Another camera was aimed toward him from the edge of the balcony.

His voice quieter now, Reverend Jackson intoned, "There is but one path to the Lord, one road right up to the doorstep of heaven." The members of the White Rock band, neatly groomed unsmiling young men, began shifting as if getting ready to play. The choir director, a dark brother dressed like Reverend Jackson's twin save the expensive watch, rose from his seat.

"You can't drive upon it as if riding in a sports car, because you'd be going too fast and surely miss a signpost or two along the way. You can't ride a bike on it because while you'd see the signpost, you'd still be going too fast for reflection and without reflection how could you savor the Lord's message, how could you let it become one with you?" Now his passion rose and again, his voice hoarse and strident, filled the White Rock with his intensity.

"NO! NO! NO! The only way to heavenly salvation! The only way to true understanding of His revelation is to take it step by step!" The choir director flicked his wrists and the choir began to hum slowly, along with the low buzz of a Hammond B3 underscoring Vernon's words. "That's right! The only way is by taking the time to know, step by godly step, to travel that highway to heaven, as Jesus did. I've traveled it that way and, praise the Lord, it brought me here!"

Suddenly the words that I'd composed in my Queens basement some seven years ago were coming out of Reverend Jackson's mouth. It was a slow, stately version of "Traveling the Highway to Heaven." Not since I had facial hair had I heard this song and it was so satisfying. Reverend Jackson savored the message, savored the journey as the White Rock choir cradled the chorus like a baby in its arms. About halfway through I was crying. Had the Lord touched me? Maybe. I'm not sure. I do know the tears came from deep inside me, reminding me of how great it had felt to write that song and how nothing since had been as good.

I don't remember much else about the service. I guess that was enough. Afterwards, there was food in the basement, and I felt so strange being in a crowd of black people who were neither young nor anxious nor vaguely dangerous. I'd been living in the bubble of the entertainment business for so long I'd forgotten how real people lived. Families and nine-to-fives and Sunday service—that whole world I'd grown up in. I'd totally fallen out of contact with the rhythms of the ordinary and I felt a little bad about it.

I tried not to get too sentimental. After all, this was the mid-eighties and the White Rock wasn't just some back woods Negro church. Services were taped for broadcast in their entirety on a local cable channel, and a half-hour edited version played on the local independent station. Walking past a table I heard a deacon bragging to his wife about a possible BET deal for the show. I thought getting a quiet moment with the Reverend Jackson would be difficult. Then, to my surprise, he sent for me.

"Brother Harper?" A chubby woman in a sky blue dress, matching hat, and a courtly Southern manner was smiling at me. "My name is Minnie Rogers-Jackson. I'm Vernon's wife. Vernon saw you from the pulpit and wanted me to come get you." I followed her out of the dining area into a narrow hallway lined with photos of the choir and various church bulletins, then down some steps to a subbasement with several offices.

As we took this curious journey, Minnie explained that the church had been constructed in the wake of the Civil War by ex-slaves worried about retribution form their angry white trash neighbors. "The church elders knew that one day the North would leave us at the South's mercy, so they built this subbasement to house people, food, and even guns. During the days of the civil rights movement, workers from the North were put up here in secret. You see, this has always been a progressive church."

Evidence of that fact was all around me. One room contained an off-line video editing facility. Another featured a Universal gym, a Stairmaster, and two stationary bikes "for those in the congregation who can't afford a health club." In the last room was an old sixteen-track board, a drum machine, miscellaneous keyboards, a smiling, gap-toothed five-year-old girl looking adorable in a tot-sized version of her mother's blue dress, and her father, who sat at an electric piano absently fingering the keyboard. "Hello Reverend Jackson."

He looked and said, quite theatrically, "Don't even try it!" Then he rose up and embraced me like the long-lost brother I kinda, sorta, was. "Kenya," he said to his daughter, "this is Derek Harper. Remember I told you about him?" Kenya surveyed me with a penetrating mix of intensity and precociousness unique to little children. She asked. "Do you make rap records?"

"No Kenya," I said earnestly. "I don't make them. I'm working right now with some rappers, that's all." I felt awkward contradicting what her father apparently had told her, but I sure didn't want any confusion over my role with the tour. If I was uncomfortable with my answer, Kenya's next question really had me going.

"So if you don't make rap records, does that mean you accept Jesus Christ as your personal savior?"

I looked at Vernon, not sure what to say, and then blurted out a firm, "Sure, I believe in God." He seemed to savor my discomfort and then, apparently deciding I'd squirmed enough, picked up Kenya. "That's enough questions for now, darling. Why don't you go with your mother and make sure the afternoon Bible study is going well. Okay?" Reluctantly, Kenya consented. Minnie took her daughter by the hand and, after receiving a light peck on the cheek from her husband, disappeared into the hallway.

"You've come a long way from Queens, Vernon." My tone was appreciative and respectful.

"We both have." There was a cutting quality to his voice, as if he felt superior to me. Considering the surroundings and his current job, as well as mine, I couldn't blame him for being a little condescending.

"You," I told him, "seem to be keeping up with me."

"Derek, you probably don't know this, but I've always kept up my correspondence with your mother. A truly wonderful woman. She keeps me plugged into what everyone's doing back home."

"I hear that."

"I was sorry to hear that financial pressures forced you to work with these rappers, but I'm sure the Lord has a higher purpose for you in all this."

Now I felt like I had to justify my life, not to my old collaborator Vernon but to the suddenly very formidable Reverend Jackson. Then something welled up inside me. Likely it was the same impulse that led me to reject Pops' choice of college and Mayo's songwriting deal. I decided I wasn't justifying a damn thing. Very off-handedly I told him I was about to sign a publishing deal with Warner-Chappel and that basically, "I'm doing fine. As you know, Vernon, life is long. You never know where it's gonna take you. Look at you. Thought you were going to be a big gospel star in New York. Like it was destined to be. Instead you're the junior pastor of a big historic church in North Carolina and you're not even thirty."

"No question. I've been blessed." This shift into a discussion of his good fortune brought out a flash of the ambitious, self-centered artist side of Vernon. "When Reverend Benjamin died of a heart attack, there was talk of bringing in an older pastor. But my wife, God bless her soul, made the case for me with the church deacons. I mean, I didn't campaign for the job. Her family's been coming to White Rock for years and she felt it needed me. Minnie's a lot like your mother in that way, always looking to do the Lord's work. Just as she did when she brought us together."

There was something incredibly false about Vernon now. Maybe it was just that the time he'd spent in the pulpit had smoothed out his delivery so much that he felt slick to me. When he sang I had definitely felt that old honesty, that honesty that the Lord had invested in his lungs when Vernon was still in the womb. But the Reverend Jackson was somebody I didn't know I didn't really like.

"I got something I want to play for you." He said this in his Rev. Jackson voice, so immediately I was on the defensive. The song had a traditional gospel acoustic piano at its heart, but the rhythm track would have been fine for Freddie Jackson. "I don't have the words, Derek," he explained. "And just this bit of melody." He closed his eyes and began humming. What he had was a thin bit of major chords, a little old school black church flavor, and the silky grandeur of his tone. Just as when we were teens, my chair trembled at his power.

And then I sang the words of the verses I had of "The one who sees, the one who listens." They weren't a perfect fit. I had to finesse the ends of a couple of lines. But it was close enough to sound like something. After the track ended, I told him to play it again.

"Your voice has gotten stronger." This observation came with his first genuine smile during our time together. The music kicked in again. I listened to the intro. Started singing. Started singing with a cocky vigor inspired by Vernon's praise. And then Vernon joined in. Not Reverend Jackson. Vernon, the kid with the tenor I'd sell my soul to the devil to possess. Now he sang my paltry lyrics and gave them a feeling I could grasp for but never ever reach. I sang with him a minute and then fell into silence and closed my eyes. When he was finished we sat there. No words. Just silence.

"Well," I said finally, "if you want to use it, you can. It's been in my head for a while, but I never could finish it. You pretty much just did."

"No," he corrected me. "Derek, God finished it. God gave it to you and you delivered it to me. You see, that's your purpose. You see that, don't you?" I actually did and I told him so.

"Derek, you have a gift, a divine gift. It you gave your life to the Lord, you could be one of the greatest writers ever, creating music that would bring glory to His name and convert the souls that cry out in need. You could do that, Derek. You could be as great as Thomas Dorsey." I must have been grinning in embarrassment because then he added, "Don't laugh, Derek. I'm serious. You need to get serious, too!"

"Excuse me." It was that rather flamboyant choir director. Vernon invited in Tyrone Baxter and, after shaking my hand with exceeding politeness, he sat down on a bench in front of the drum machine and to the right of Reverend Jackson. Not Vernon. He'd already started reverting during his little lecture and now with the pious Tyrone in the room, Reverend Jackson launched into a lengthy sermon comparing me to the prodigal son "who needs to come home." As flattered as I'd been, that's how turned off I became. I nodded more than I listened.

Not that I necessarily thought he was wrong. I believe in God. I believed that my talent was God-given. I even believed this song was intended for him and that I was just the conduit. At the same time when I looked at Vernon's setup, I didn't see some innocent serving the Lord. I saw a man building an empire. I saw a bit of Edge and a lot of Gibbs. His conversation about my songwriting reminded me a great deal of Danifa's recruitment speech.

Not long afterward, I was gone. Back to the hotel, back to Attak and

Donkey and Gibbs, back to hip hop and, hopefully real soon, to writing commercial r&b songs. This isn't what Reverend Jackson wanted to hear, but at that moment that was the truth or, at least, my truth. That night I tried to avoid the substance of Reverend Jackson's words and remember Vernon's voice, so beautiful, so rich, so much the voice I craved but could only borrow.

"Call Me"

Hampton, VA—"I love you."

"I know that, son. So does your father. Don't you ever question that. Wherever you are, our prayers go with you and we know yours go with us. Don't worry. Now it's late and I'm tired. Your father took me to see *Sarafina,* that South African play, and all that dancing tired me out."

I hung up and looked around the room. Adidas sweatsuits. Sneakers. Two duffel bags. Portable cassette player. Cassettes. The *Hampton Journal Jet. Rolling Stone.* The national edition of the *New York Times.* Underwear, clean and unclean. Socks. T-shirts. TV. TV remote. Hotel copy of Gideon's Bible. A half-written letter to Doris that I crumpled and banked into the trash off the side of the TV. A towel with which I dried my eyes.

The day had started well. Aunt Alma lived over in Newport News and I'd gone over with T-shirts, tickets, and backstage passes for Alla and Alice, who'd grown into adorable, adolescent, rap-loving girls. They greeted me with fat buttery biscuits and awe as I told tales of my travels with Joint-ski, the Overweight Lovers, and the Brothers Black. Aunt Alma had gotten her nursing degree and purchased a lovely three-bedroom home for her girls. A big portrait of Uncle Teddy hung in the living room. In it he sat surrounded by his wife and daughters back in that Brooklyn apartment I used to love visiting.

Like any good Southern family they had a piano and we sang along to old Motown (Aunt Alma wanted to hear the Four Tops' "Baby I Need Your Loving") and recent Michael Jackson (the girls did harmonies on "She's Out of My Life"). I knew Aunt Alma had been dating, but it felt like I was the first man to come over in some time. They were pouring so much love on me I felt like sugar.

I was half-watching a "Good Times" rerun and half-reading Toni Morrison's *Zula* while completely devouring a huge hunk of sweet potato pie when Aunt Alma picked up the kitchen phone and announced that Anna was on the line. One by one, Aunt Alma, Alla, and Alice took their turns reporting to their older sis.

"Derek!" Aunt Alma shouted. "Anna wants to say hello." Well, she did and she didn't. "Hello" was the first word out of her mouth and if the talk had ended there, Aunt Alma would have been right. But Anna had more on her mind than that simple greeting. "When was the last time your called your parents?"

Pissed and surprised by the attitude in her voice, I replied, "And how are you doing? How's Little Walt? Are there any Little Walt's on the way?"

"Stop acting a fool, Derek."

"And you stop scolding me like I was one of your little sisters." Aunt Alma, who'd moved into the living room with the girls, heard that. I lowered my voice and began speaking in a mean whisper. "It's none of your business when, how, or how often I talk to my parents."

"It's my business when it affects Pops."

This caught me off guard. "He said something to you about me not calling?"

"You know how Pops is. He doesn't just come out and tell you all his feelings. But I'm around him every day and I know he feels he's lost touch with you."

That struck a chord. I told her, "Anna, to be truthful, we were never close. That's just the truth. I love him and all that, but that's how it is." There's probably no one else, not even Moms, that I would have admitted that to. Anna wasn't sympathetic.

"Like you tried," she said, pissing me off again.

"What?" I said.

"You heard me. Like you tried. Ever since you refused to go to St. John's you've been rebelling against him. It's like you've gone through some delayed adolescence. Running around the country playing at being an adult."

"Don't make me break on you, Anna."

That was an empty threat. I really didn't have any information to break on her with. It was just something to say. Still, it seemed to sting her. Her voice softened. "Listen, Derek, I'm not trying to make you feel bad."

"You haven't."

"But it hurts me to see our family getting so loose."

I was still feeling defensive and overreacted to her words. "Loose? What are you saying? That I'm a ho?" Aunt Alma had moved within ear shot and I felt disrespectful for talking so loud on her phone to her daughter.

"No. That may be your guilty conscience talking. What I was talking about was that we used to be close. Your parents, my parents. You and me. It's not like that anymore."

Trying to sound sage, I replied, "We're adults now, Anna. Everybody's got their own life now."

"I know." Then I heard Anna quietly begin to sob and the whole conversation took on another tone.

"Hey. What's going on? Is this about Little Walt—"

"Walter," she corrected.

"Walter. This is about Walter, right?"

I could hear her gathering herself. I didn't want to push it. Didn't want to tip off Aunt Alma, who'd moved back into the living room with the girls. I looked her way with a smile as phoney as a two-dollar bill.

"Remember when Richard Pryor got all burned up?" I did. "Well, Walter's been doing that stuff that made Richard Pryor catch on fire." Freebasing. Hadn't seen anybody on tour doing it, though there were rumors that Joint-ski had graduated to it from cocaine. "Somebody gave him some in exchange for a haircut." She laughed, a ghostly sound that put an ache in my heart more than her tears. "That's what somebody told me. His father says money's been missing from the cash drawer. It's been going on since the summer. The shop's changed, Derek. I don't know if it's because of Walter's habit or just that the area's changing. I don't go over there anymore."

"Is there anything I can do?"

"Call your parents, Derek. Talk to them. Walter's father and I will handle it. I'm not gonna let what happened to my father happen to my husband."

After that call, taking the girls to the concert wasn't easy. Even the show itself was lackluster. Probably the weakest of the entire tour. But Alice and Alla couldn't tell, which I guess was more important. Backstage, Donkey cut a look at fourteen-year-old All and budding Alice and I hit him with an eyeball. Attak video-taped the girls and me in front of the tour bus before Aunt Alma came to pick them up.

I woke Moms up when I called. Pops, whom I desperately wanted to speak with, was sleeping, and Moms, being Moms, didn't wanna disturb him. She heard the upset in my voice and tried to calm my nerves. She knew things weren't right between Anna and Walter but, thank God, didn't know how deep it had gotten.

Pops was busy preparing for his takeover of O'Mally's funeral home. The loan had gone through and business, sadly, was booming in Queen's black community. Crime was up. Jamaica was becoming as bad as Brooklyn. The dead kept getting younger and younger. It was the irony of my pops' profession that the worse people acted, the better his business was. I told her I was glad things were going well. Then for the sixth or seventh time, Moms said she loved me and then she was gone and I was alone again in the latest hotel room, surveying my possessions and waiting impatiently for sleep.

"Don't Look Back"

Washington, DC—We played the old Olympic Auditorium, a place that the Beatles performed in on their first U.S. tour, which would have been cool if the building wasn't as old and crusty as a grandfather's big toe. A big-time pol stopped by—Joint-ski had done a fund-raiser for him—and the two disappeared into the dressing room and emerged as jumpy as two frogs on a very moist log.

But DC wasn't about the tour. It was about Candi. Not that I saw her. Or even talked to her. It was about me remembering her, remembering I hadn't spoken to her since the Howard Inn, remembering how I'd basically thrown her out of my room, remembering my stupidity at throwing her out of my life that evening.

So I called. The first time a man picked up. "Hello?" he said. I hung up. The second time I called I listened to him say "Hello?" and "Who is this?" and analyzed his voice. Probably older than me. Probably fat and probably four-eyed. Ugly, too. Yup, old, fat, four-eyed, and ugly. That's what he sounded like to me. That's what he had to be.

The third time I called, the tape machine was on and Candi's voice flowed out of the receiver. She said, "Candi and Albert aren't home right now. Leave a message and we'll call you back as soon as we get home." The key word was "home." She and this fat, old, four-eyed, ugly old man had made a "home" where they shared an answering machine, an apartment, a bed, and a life. I'd made great love in that bed. I'd played Candi's tic-tac-toe in that bed. I'd held her in that same place after my adventure with the DC police.

I'd spent most of my time after college in a shitty Times Square apartment while she was yearning for a "home." Maybe not yearning, but I guess it was on her mind. Now, instead of having a songwriting career and Candi, I just had cash. I was seeing America by bus and plane, and I was baby-sitting a bunch of brothers who were, right now, fucking everything that moved in DC while I sat in a dark hotel room listening to Candi say "home," knowing that that word had nothing to do with the life we'd had together, and it could have.

I think I called three more times, each time listening to her voice and letting her message time run on. The seventh time I called Candi, I acted like I was ringing for the first time. "I'm in town with the rap tour," I said brightly. "I'm acting as road manager. You believe that? If you want free tickets, you got them. I'd love to see you." Then I added, "Bring a friend," and left the hotel number.

She didn't call back.

"For the Love of Money"

Just off the Metroliner at Penn Station, I crowd into the Uptown #1 local. It's my first time in New York in months and as Chuck Dee says, "I'm hyped 'cause I'm amped." I'm looking around and I'm stimulated by what I see. Two raincoated yuppies scanning *The Wall Street Journal* and talking investment banking while standing over a Puerto Rican woman and her bright-eyed, frisky daughter and a black security guard shaking his head to the sounds on his Walkman. That's just in one corner to my right. In no other city we'd visited had I seen such a diverse group of people in the same space. Maybe I just didn't look hard enough in cold-ass Chicago. But in Indianapolis, Houston, etc., it's rare that this set of people would ever be this close or so comfortable, so matter-of-fact about that proximity.

At Fiftieth Street and Seventh Avenue, I exit into a late fall New York morning. A McDonald's cup spills out of an overflowing basket. The same breeze that lifts the cup sends bits of dirt into my eye. A panhandler shakes his cup at me, as his fetid smell overwhelms my nose. A white woman hits me with her swinging purse and then clutches it as if I was responsible for our fleeting contact. The exhaust from a crosstown bus sullies my clothes.

To many, this would have been quite disgusting, ample grounds for hopping back on the subway and Amtrak home. For me, it's like the embrace of a beautiful lady. Here in New York you feel life right up against your skin, pawing at you, rubbing against you, slapping you awake by going upside your head. It's not for everybody, but it suits me fine.

Warner-Chappel offices were located on Sixth Avenue, in a skyscraper nestled on a block between Radio City Music Hall on Fiftieth and CBS' "Black Rock" corporate headquarters on Fifty-second Street. Walking up to it as the wind whipped down from Central Park, I felt chilled and empowered. I was about to have my first meeting as an (almost) signee to a major music publishing company.

Danifa was sitting behind a glass desk looking chic in a charcoal blue pant suit, her hair cut in a severe, boyish trim that accentuated her angular eyebrows. She'd never made much of an impression on me before, always in Mayo's shadow, talking bags with Doris. Now she looked quite formidable. And considering a lot of my dreams were in her hands, she had a lot of power over me.

"Right now," she said, "I really want to sign you to a development deal which would only be worth maybe fifteen thousand in total." I expressed my dismay and she sighed. "I know," she said, "I talked about twenty thousand or more. But without any pipeline income it may be hard to get you any kind of deal at all. I believe in you, but you have walked away from money before."

What could I say to that? It was true.

Danifa kept bringing up "pipeline income" and the resistance she was getting from some insiders to signing me. "Pipeline income" refs to the money coming in from songs already recorded or that are about to come out. I'd placed a few songs, but none with high profile artists, and being on the tour these last couple of months had really taken me out of the mix.

"Derek. The name of this game is to get songs on records. Songwriting is a business. It is not a test of artistic purity. In a way it's a pyramid. You start at the bottom, you share publishing with better-known writers, you get placements. Later, once you're established, you do the same to younger writers."

It sounded like Gibbs' describing the hip-hop concert game. On some level it irritated me. All of it sounded like Amway and my songs were not toiletries. At the same time, I knew spiritually, artistically, and financially I needed this deal. On her office walls were gold and platinum records produced by Mayo—testaments to his success and power. A thought passed through my mind. A chilling thought. A pragmatic thought. Then I voiced it. "You think May would still be interested in 'Silly Pictures'?"

"Are you seeing Doris today?" was her answer. When I replied affirmatively, Danifa told me to have her bring it up to Mayo first and then she'd follow up. "He likes her," Danifa said. "She's working out well. If she approaches him with it, it'll smooth over his ruffled feathers. Sounds like you're growing up, Derek."

I forced a smile, gave her some demos (including a copy of Vernon's "The One Who Sees"), and left to meet Doris at her apartment. For lunch we had take-out Chinese, cranberry juice, and each other spread out all over her bed like newly purchased sheets. Afterwards we dressed quickly, she grabbed her overnight bag, and we hopped on the 3:50 Metroliner to Philadelphia.

It was on the hour ride down that we actually talked business. Things with Mayo were going well. Almost too well. Through him she'd met Quincy Jones and Al Teller and Whitney Houston and Bob Krasnow and Lionel Richie and Clive Davis—the high and mighty of American pop, producers, singers, and record moguls—everyone I wanted to know but hadn't met. There was a deep swell of jealousy in me. I changed the subject and ask her about resubmitting "Silly Pictures" to Mayo, which she thought was a great idea. In fact, Doris was generally excited by everything.

This career change was having an amazing effect on her. Doris' skin

SEDUCED

227

glowed. She dressed more casually yet better. That dour, lockstep quality Doris used to have still reared its head, but it no longer dominated her. I liked her better, though I was a little worried that when she was through evolving she wouldn't want me.

Entering the Sheraton we ran into Gibbs, Dirt Bike, Attak, and Charlene, that white girl from Indianapolis. While Doris began chatting up Gibbs with her new-found industry insight, I checked out Attak and a woman who was clearly becoming significant in his life. They'd just seen the latest Freddie Krueger flick, which Attak thought was "stoopid fresh." She'd driven to Philly from Indianapolis to see him, which either meant real commitment or she was catching vapors from his fame, and I didn't know her well enough to tell which. I wondered what Donkey would make of this but figured it was best to keep my mouth shut and my hands ready, 'cause there was surely a fight somewhere over the horizon.

Donkey rolled into the lobby with three rough-looking Queens homies—Leroi, Head, and Vickie Vic. In his hand were two cassettes. One was a copy of the Brothers Black debut LP and the other a compilation of tracks from artists on the tour. Both were bootlegs. The deejay was too angry to focus on Attak's love life.

"Yo!" he shouted at Gibbs. "Niggas is plannin' on selling this bootleg shit outside the concert tonight. Motherfuckers coming in from New York with boxes of this mess. We got to let them know what time it is!"

Gibbs reached into his pocket and peeled off three $100 bills. One was given to each of Donkey's boys. For this fee they were now employees of GAP under the supervision of Dirt Bike. Their job would be to confiscate bootleg tapes. Donkey was very pleased at how quickly his manager had moved to address the situation. I, in contrast, was appalled. After Donkey and posse left, I told Gibbs, "You know if those knuckleheads really hurt anybody you could be liable."

"Did you see a contract or any other kind of papers?" he replied. "That money won't last two hours. If they bust the heads of some bootleggers, fine. If they buy buddas and bug out backstage, fine. Donkey seemed happy and that was what it was about, anyway."

Ever since he lost management of the Overweight Lovers, Gibbs was kissing the ass of his rappers so hard his breath was turning black. In a way, I couldn't blame him. Russell Simmons was getting bigger and deffer every day. Other promoters were starting to book rap groups. The hip-hop gravy train was starting to roll and, despite the tour's success, Gibbs was increasingly nervous about missing any stops. In the van going over to the Spectrum, he revealed to Doris and me that he'd managed to keep the Overweight Lovers on the tour by calling in their new manager on his promotional slice of the dates. The new manager, whom my friend characterized as a "walking, talking piece of shit," would be commissioning the Lovers' fees plus getting a share of the door along with Gibbs. He wasn't too happy about this deal, but he needed them for the West Coast concerts. Joint-ski's star had already fallen out west and the Brothers Black were just building a name out there, so the Overweight Lovers were crucial to ticket sales.

Doris and I told him about our meeting with Warner-Chappel music. Gibbs seemed legitimately happy for me, though he still thought it was a mistake to deal with Mayo. By the time we got backstage, Doris had shifted the conversation from that point of contention to Gibbs' love affair with the beautiful Beth Ann. As he rhapsodized about his leggy lady love, I walked to the side of the stage and surveyed the crowd.

Philly fans had a bad reputation in sports. They were noted for boorishness, nastiness, and being down-right evil. However in hip-hop circles, Philly fans were considered the best around. They were close enough to New York to really understand the music yet far enough away to be less hostile. For that reason everyone had been looking forward to this gig before we headed for Seattle the next morning.

Inside everything was chill. Still, I had a bad feeling about Vickie Vic and his two thuggish pals. I left Doris in Gibbs' care and then walked up the Spectrum's long back ramp, through the security gate, and into the gathering crowd of young Philadelphians. Adidas had been the hottest sportswear of hip hop's early years, but now Fila sweatsuits, Nike sneakers, and Starter sports gear were making an impact. Lots of New York Yankee caps, worn forward, backward, and sideways, dotted the crowd. Crimson Philly 76er jackets were everywhere.

Several T-shirt vendors standing just outside the box office were draped in the kelly green jackets and caps of the NFL's Philadelphia Eagles. I wouldn't have paid them any attention if I hadn't spotted Dirt Bike and Donkey's boys rolling up on them with bad intentions. Vickie Vic reached into a bag of T-shirts, threw them on the ground, and then pulled out a handful of cassettes which he, Head, and Leroi began stomping with gusto. And after one of the Philly Eagles protested, more than tapes began getting stomped.

Vickie Vic threw this guy quickly to the ground and, with the kind assistance of Head and Leroi, put his sneaker in the young salesman's mouth. And his neck. And lastly but hardly least, in his stomach. For a generation that was turning its back on old-style, one-on-one slap boxing in exchange for multi-member brawling, the tactic of throwing an opponent down and then doing a collective dance on his torso was a prime example of the age's cruel logic.

Then it was over. Dirt Bike assumed control of his young charges and pulled them away. Wisely, Dirt Bike himself hadn't touched the bootlegger. While his flunkies pummeled the kid, Dirt Bike had busied himself stomping cassettes and grabbing the bags they'd been transported in. A crowd of concert goers hovered around the groaning body. The kid couldn't have been more than sixteen. A few fans scooped up T-shirts and the odd cassettes that escaped destruction. Others shouted for the police in vain.

Inside the Spectrum the house was rocking. I'd missed the Brothers Black, but the Overweight Lovers were doing that whole "Throw your hands in the air! Now wave them like you just don't care" riff that was as important to this culture as two turntables. Hands all over the Spectrum were swinging. People danced in their seats. After the fight outside it was essential for me to remember why we were all gathered here. This was supposed to be a party. It was supposed to be about rhythm and wit and earthly delights. Black music has always been about that, I guess, and through hip hop this generation had found its own way to party.

This night at the Spectrum and so often during the tour, I'd watch the crowds and wonder if I'd been born at the wrong time. Too late to be a real soul man and too early to be reared with hip hop in my blood. It's not that I felt cheated; it's just that I'm not completely fulfilled.

Somebody put their hands around my waist. Lucky for Doris I have the reflexes of a writer, not a fighter, otherwise I'd have jabbed her in the ribs. "You having a good time, baby?"

"Oh, Derek," she said in my ear, "this is dope."

"Dope?"

"Or is it fresh?"

I turned and faced her. "Doris, this is any damn thing you want it to be."

"We'll see" she said. And she was right. We'd see.

"Smells Like Teen Spirit"

Seattle—The phone rang at 9:30 A.M. Seven hours or so from when we'd hit. Too early for any of the usual tour-related foolishness. I was right. This was some new shit. "Derek, come to my room." It was Gibbs. he sounded as tense as I was tired.

"What's up?"

"Just come, man. We'll talk when you get here. Suite 1919."

In a navy blue Georgetown sweatsuit and matching blue and white Nike's I rolled up to Gibbs' room. We'd only gotten in about 9:30 P.M. last night so for Gibbs to interrupt his beauty sleep for a morning meeting, it must have been serious. They were on the sofa. Gibbs was having coffee. Dirt Bike was sipping on Heineken. I grabbed some O.J. from the mini-bar and slumped into an end chair.

"So, who got arrested now?" I asked.

"Don't look at me, man," Dirt Bike said testily. "I don't know what this shit is about." We both looked at Gibbs, who poured himself another cup of coffee.

"What I'm about to say is between us. No one else on the tour is gonna know about this until they have to, if they have to. If it gets out, no insurance company will underwrite us and I'll be back working as a road manager for Patti LaBelle."

This made me laugh. "C'mon, home piss. I didn't get out of bed for no movie speech. Kick it or let me and Dirt Bike get our ugly sleep."

"After we checked in two niggas showed up at my door. Straight 'Bamas in jheri-curls, locs, and lots of blue."

"Crips, huh?" Dirt Bike asked.

"Yeah," Gibbs said, "gang-banging, drug-slanging fools from Tacoma by way of Compton. Anyway I didn't let them in—"

"Smart move," I said.

As grim as a deacon, Gibbs replied, "But they didn't expect me to, Derek. They knocked on the door, got my attention, and then the phone rang. Nikko was the nigga's name. I'd heard of him. He's from Cali. Used to manage this band the Funknauts to launder his loot. Told me either go down to the bar and talk to him or they were gonna bring me down."

"You called Dirt Bike?"

Gibbs turned and cut Dirt Bike a nasty look. "Yeah, but our head of security had a block put on his calls."

"I was tired, man."

Gibbs snorted dismissively and continued on. "Anyway, these niggas were at my door. I knew if I called the hotel detectives, that would be like declaring war with these fools. So I went down to the bar where Nikko was waiting. I'm not writing a detective book or nothing so I'm just gonna cut to the end. The nigga says if I don't give him half of our take from the Long Beach date next Saturday, he says the shit that happened in New York will be nothing."

"Fuck that nigga!" It was Dirt Bike. "Let's bring in some heads from Brooklyn and put a cap in these matte head motherfuckers!"

I ignored Dirt Bike and asked Gibbs what he did next. The con man in Gibbs emerged from underneath his fear and his voice took on that smooth quality that was probably his best asset. "I told him, 'You're gonna have to prove it.' I told him, 'I know you Crips got respect and all out West. I definitely heard of you. With the crew you got right here, you could do me right now.' I told him, 'But you saying you can disrupt my show and disrupting my show are two different things. Before I could even consider doing what you want, you got to show and prove.' That's what I told him."

For the first time this morning Dirt Bike relaxed. "You something, man. You know he got your dick on the table and the blade by the tip, but you still frontin'."

"So," I wondered, "what did Nikko do? You don't look maimed so obviously he didn't hurt you."

"Naugh," Gibbs said. "He acted like Dirt Bike. He laughed with me, not at me. Told me I had heart and shit. He said watch the area in front of the stage tonight and we'll talk again."

"So," I asked, "what do we do now?"

Dirt Bike said, "We bring in some New York help."

"Yo," Gibbs said, "they can't get here tonight. We'll fly some home-boys into Sacramento and for the rest of the dates. Meanwhile, I'm gonna call L.A. and see what the situation is down there for real. Out here where there's Crips, there's Bloods."

"Who?" I said.

"That's a rival Los Angeles gang. Maybe we can make a deal with them. In fact, I'm probably gonna leave this afternoon. I'm not feeling too safe right now."

For the next hour we planned out the day. Dirt Bike would accompany Gibbs to Sea-Tac airport while I made arrangements for private security guards to watch our vans, the hotel, and backstage. Everyone would check out before the gig and we'd take off right after the show. We wouldn't leave from Sea-Tac. It was right between Seattle and Tacoma, and while Seattle had a small black population, Tacoma had quite a few brothers and sisters increasing the potential for an ambush. Instead, we'd drive all night to Portland and grab a plane to Sacramento from there. Only Gibbs, Dirt Bike, and I knew the full story, though the other GAP staffers on the tour were brought in later and told about the change in plans.

In theory, this should have been one of the tensest days of my life. Blackmail. Gangsterism. Intimidation. Instead, and I know this sounds bugged, I ended up falling in love with Seattle. From my window I could see out to Mount Rainer, a white peak atop a chocolate pyramid, surrounded by gray clouds and a bright blue sky. On any day that sight would have enchanted me, but after such a sinister wake-up call and the brooding night to come, Mount Rainer seemed like the promise of peace of mind.

After Gibbs was gone and the security arrangements made, I grabbed a Seattle tourist guide, ordered a sedan, and drove down the city's hilly streets to Puget Sound and Pike's Market. At Pike's, big, shimmering salmon were flung across stalls by men in leather smocks, their hands covered with gills. Alongside the fish stalls were vegetables and fruits, notably lovely red apples and local tourist knickknacks like miniatures of the Space Needle, Supersonics and Seahawks T-shirts and more faux Native-American gear than in a John Wayne Western.

From inside a funky little restaurant called the Athenian (in which years later Tom Hanks and Rob Reiner would discuss tiramisu), I sat by the window that looked out over the Sound. I had clam chowder and coffee and, in a half hour, counted four different kinds of rain: hard and pounding; steady and dark, drizzly and light; misty and partly cloudy. I'd never seen rain change its nature and intensity so quickly. It was like emotions running across a person's face.

Afterwards, I walked to a pier overlooking Puget Sound. The water was remarkably clean, compared to the look and smell of big city bays back East. A ferry cruised past me out toward one of the mysterious islands that dotted the Sound. Then from somewhere in the water I heard a weird animal noise. Looking down I saw two sea lions swimming through Puget Sound, their heads up and their voices meshed into some honking harmony. I felt far away from hip hop and gangsters and anonymous hotel rooms and faceless, cheering crowds. But I wasn't. Not at all.

"Yo, Derek Harper! Yo, motherfucker, you better stop looking at them swimming dogs and wake the fuck up!" It was Attak, wearing a big grin—he really enjoyed upsetting my solitude—accompanied by Dirt Bike and a couple of middle-aged white men in casual off-duty cop wear. It was a curious sight—an interracial quartet of entertainment and authority intruding on my meditative afternoon. But then I reminded myself, with Gibbs gone, I was kinda, sorta in charge.

After that loud initial greeting, Attak quieted down and enjoyed watching sea lions before asking me, "Why, all of a sudden do we need all this extra security? We in Seattle, holmes, not Newark. And I hear that Gibbs is outta here. Add to that, Dirt Bike tells me Donkey's crew from Queens is meeting us in Sacramento. Sounds to me like somebody's under pressure, you know what I'm sayin'?" I glanced over at Dirt Bike and knew he hadn't told Attak jack, which is why he'd hunted me down.

Like a character in *Kojak,* I insisted, "You know as much as I do. Gibbs made all these moves this morning and then broke out for

Sacramento. Obviously something's up, my man, but I'm not exactly sure of anything else except that we should be watching our backs."

"So," Attak wondered facetiously, "this is how you stay secure? We could have run up on you and flipped you down into the water and the seals would have been munching on you for lunch."

"They're not seals. They're sea lions, I think."

"Whatever."

"I heard Seattle was a beautiful city and I plan on seeing some of it."

"Okay, tourist, where you going next?"

Next was Old Town, a section of Seattle lined with vintage brick buildings that housed bars, art galleries, restaurants, and the biggest, most imposing bookstore I'd ever seen. Elliott Bay was the name. It was nearly a block long with row upon row of well-stocked shelves and a basement cafe where quiche, teas, and sandwiches were available. Attak was intent on buying Stephen King's latest. One of the store managers suggested that if he liked fantasy he should give Octavia Butler, a black sci-fi writer a try. Attak, who actually favored gore over speculation, bought Butler's *Kindred,* but hedged his bet by scooping up King's *Christine* as backup.

We drove around some more, going down a strip of restaurants and stores called Broadway, which Sir Mix-a-Lot had immortalized in "Posse on Broadway," before getting back to the hotel. The crew was tense. The presence of all these security men, mostly white, mostly off-duty cops, was freaking folks out. Rumors were floating all over the place. Stuff like someone was gonna shoot Joint-ski from the crowd and these cops were assigned to us to plant drugs on us. Truth be told, I had no idea what was gonna happen. It all could have been true.

Well, nothing violent happened. And the off-duty cops didn't set anybody up for a bust. It was scarier than that. Midway through the Brothers Black's set, just as they went into "Felonious Assault," a group of blue-clad brothers moved through the crowd. Each man had his hand on the other man's shoulder, creating a long chain of bodies that marched up the center aisle, past the venue's security, past the standing customers in the orchestra, and right to the front of the stage. Attak, to his credit, kept his cool and keep on rhyming, though all of us backstage were in a state of panic.

The blue-clad brothers fanned out until they were two or three deep in front of the stage. They didn't bumrush the stage. Instead they began making these signs with their hands. "It's gang signs," one of the off-duty cops told me. "Crips by the look of it." Its organization was very impressive, if you consider intimidation impressive. Attak kept flowing, but all eyes in the building were on the Crips. I remembered New York and Detroit and all the ill moments of the tour.

This, however, was just a warning. Nothing more. Just as they'd rolled up to the front of the stage, the Crips, hand on shoulder followed by hand on shoulder, moved back down the center aisle and, once in the darkness of the concert hall, dispersed swiftly. They were nowhere now, and they were everywhere.

Not long afterwards, Dirt Bike was on the phone in the arena manager's office talking with Gibbs. I asked if Gibbs wanted to speak to me. Dirt Bike shook his head no and listened more than he talked. After the Brother's Black's set, the house lights came up. I figured the Crips would take off their colors to avoid detection. I was wrong. From around the arena, young men in Dodge caps and jackets flicked signs in the air, unafraid and proud. Joint-ski didn't want to go on, but Gibbs told him—no show, no cash—and so he did. It was a pitiful fifteen-minute set, during which Joint-ski damn near did his entire show from behind the turntables.

There were no incidents. No one threw anything. Or phoned. Or in any way disturbed us as we drove out of Seattle. They didn't have to. They'd already sold their wolf tickets and we surely had blinked. The silence on our tour bus was deafening. Donkey seemed really scared. He just sat with his ear-phones on looking out the window. Attak was giving his book a chance though he seemed distracted. Me, I got a melody in my head. No words yet. Just a tune.

"California Dreamin"

Sacramento—Was there a concert? Probably, but I don't really remember. What sticks in my mind about our visit to California's capitol is a scene in Dirt Bike's room. I'm on the phone next to his commode, Dirt Bike's on the phone in the bedroom, and a couple of GAP employees are crowded around a phone in the living room. Gibbs is on the other end. He's in Paris. That's right, Paris as in France.

After his unscheduled meeting with Nikko, Gibbs made a lot more calls than Dirt Bike and I were aware of. Beth Ann was on her way to Paris for the fall collections and Gibbs, of course, feeling the need to escape, decided this was a prime opportunity for further bonding and boning. The usually taciturn Dirt Bike went ballistic, calling his employer all manner of obscenity with "punk," "pussy," and "sucka" among the lighter accusations.

In exchange for Dirt Bike's continued loyalty, Gibbs offered him a part of the tour, a title position with GAP, and sundry other deal sweeteners. Dirt Bike took them but was stung by Gibbs' escape and would never quite forgive him. I shared Dirt Bike's disdain. I mean, my ex-roomie had booked for Europe with a fly-ass model while we were left holding a very dangerous bag.

After Gibbs had hung up—he'd been anxious to catch Beth Ann at Isaac Mizrahi's show—we all sat in Dirt Bike's room talking about Gibbs' plan, wondering if it was the right thing to do. For GAP's younger employees, it was a no brainer. They had no choice. They needed the job. Dirt Bike had just been given a good deal and was gonna take it. Me, I still had no publishing deal and thus no guaranteed income. I hadn't heard whether Mayo was gonna take "Silly Pictures" or not. Danifa told me my deal likely depended on it. So, as much as I wanted to flee, I couldn't afford to and Gibbs knew it and he was taking advantage of it. When Edge had flipped on me, it was no surprise. He'd warned me. It still hurt, but he'd been brutally honest about it and I could respect that. Gibbs was supposed to be down for me. Instead I was about to do his dirty work so he could be safe and sound. I guess that's what moguldom is all about.

On the bus to L.A., I played Dirt Bike a tape of my voice accompanied by piano as I worked on the words to the song that had come my way in Seattle. Dirt Bike had never heard my music before and he told me, "Yo, man, you got it going on, holmes." He actually praised my voice, comparing it to Alexander O'Neal and Freddie Jackson, which was nice, except that neither sounded like the other and I certainly wasn't as good as either one. Still, I took the compliment graciously. At that point, it was nice to have something to smile about.

"Batter Ram"

"My rock house on Central got hit by the bulls last week, cuz. Pushed a battering ram through the front door at one broad daylight. By one thirty the place was empty—rocks, my crew, my fiends all on the way to county. By noon the next day, my crew was out, the fiends were back sucking glass dicks, and I'd moved a new supply over there," K-Dee said with a smirk and "I'd even got a lot of my rocks back from the local precinct. This is how we do it. This ain't New York but we all right." Then K-Dee filled his "mothership" (a big old red refurbished 1975 Coup De Ville) with his hardy Texas-meets-South-Central accent. We were cruising on Ladiera Heights, the main drag in Fox Hills, an integrated, predominantly buppie section of Los Angeles that abuts the bourgie home–owning neighborhood of Baldwin Hills and the working-class ghetto known as the Crenshaw district.

K-Dee continued to ramble on about the largeness of his criminal domain as Dirt Bike and I listened impassively, occasionally nodding our heads to suggest ongoing interest. I suppose one of us should have been chatting him up, but Dirt Bike was too quiet and I was too damn scared to do the proper ass kissing. This was a job for Gibbs, except that he was at the shows in Paris and I was having a meeting with a known dope dealer in L.A. Clearly one of us wasn't living right.

In the backseat next to me was K-Dee's main man, Doo Doo, a rough-looking brother in locs, a tank top covering a massive chest, and an Army surplus camouflage hat. When he wasn't nodding at his boss, Doo Doo slicked off and on the safety on his nine-millimeter Glock. This activity was freaking me out, but later Dirt Bike said the gesture reassured him. "When you about to propose something ill," he explained later, "it was right to have a violent type nigga at hand. If they like what they do, you can always jew them down on the price, because they wanna do something ill. You're just giving them the opportunity."

K-Dee turned into a garage beneath one of those stucco constructions that pass for buildings in southern California. As we went up in the elevator to the third floor, our host kept up his spiel. "Lots of lawyers and straight business types in here. Lots of families and shit."

I blinked when I entered the apartment. Everything was gold. The rug. The sofa. The lamp shades. The walls. Not yellow. Bright gold. This was some nasty ghetto decor I thought, while Dirt Bike, uncharacteristically, complimented him on it.

We sunk into K-Dee's fluffy gold sofa as he, still rambling about his condo and his rock houses, rolled two joints on his glass coffee table. Doo Doo sat back on the other end of the sofa. He was still clicking his safety on and off.

"So," K-Dee goes, "I try to act as a middle man between the Bloods and Crips." A gray haze floated out of his nostrils. "Even though my car is red, this whole color doesn't matter much to me. Only one color I like you know—what I'm talkin' about." He offered the joint to us and Dirt and I both took a light hit before handing it to Doo Doo. "I got relatives on both sides of the colorline, cuz."

"Yo," Dirt Bike interrupted, "that's why we're here."

"Well, cuz, I was wondering when you'd get down to it." Doo Doo clicked the safety on and put down the joint.

Dirt Bike started the show but knew it was on me to do the singing. "Are you coming to our show out at Long Beach this Friday?" I asked.

K-Dee said, "Brothers Black. Overweight Lovers. I wasn't gonna miss that, cuz. And now that we met I'm sure I'm gettin' some free tickets."

He laughed but I didn't crack a smile. I just followed up with, "We're gonna take it for granted that you know all about Nikko and his Crips threatening to flex at the gig. I know Gibbs told you some of it, but I figure you've heard the rest by now." I paused and K-Dee just took another hit off the joint as if to say, "You got the floor." I continued, "We got arena security. We got regular security. But we know that ain't gonna be enough. We want to prevent it from happening, or at least minimize the damage by cutting them off early. Gibbs sent us here to find out if you'll work with us on this."

"Well," K-Dee said slowly, his red eyes glistening, "I know something about it. Nikko's been making lots of power moves. Steppin' on toes. Messin' where he shouldn't. For a price I might—and I say might—be able to cut this off at the pass, cuz. Now what is your man Gibbs talkin' about for this?"

I quoted $75,000, which made both K-Dee and Doo Doo chuckle.

"My rock houses turn that over in one day with less risk, cuz," King Dee replied, sounding profoundly unimpressed.

Now I leaned forward on the sofa, looked K-Dee dead in his grill, and did my best imitation of Gibbs. "That money is a down payment on a bigger, long-term deal, my man. I know you've financed a few 12-inches out here in L.A. that Macola Records distributed. You got cash to turn over and the record business is an easy way to wash it. Gibbs is prepared to help you go national. He's negotiating a deal with BCR for a GAP label. For helping us with Nikko and squashing any trouble, he's prepared to create a West Coast label—you could call it K-Dee records or Doo Doo records or whatever. The point is you could expand out of L.A., go national. Build your own empire. Gibbs thinks that's why Nikko went after us. If he could pimp our tour this one time, he'd be doing it all over at the next. It could make him very powerful. Better you than him, right?"

Then I sat back on the gold sofa. I was kinda exhausted by my effort to sound sage and street. I was worried that they'd see the middle-class boy in me and wouldn't take my words seriously. Then, just like that, I knew I'd won.

"Can you get that kid Donkey to produce some of the tracks?" It was Doo Doo. "Yo, that kid makes dope tracks."

"He's all right," I said suavely. "He's all right."

A couple of hours later Dirt Bike and I were in a converted railroad car on Sunset Boulevard. The joint was called Carney's and we were chowing down on its specialty—huge, tasty burgers made of gristle and grease. I was still kinda jumpy from our negotiating session. We'd left our offer on the table and it was up to them to deliver. I kept going over our talk, trying to dissect it for some hidden deception, but Dirt Bike was more wired than I'd ever seen, if you don't count the Atlanta orgy.

"When this bitch is over," he said with great conviction, "I'm gonna take my cash and all my contacts and build my own thing. I know Gibbs is your boy and all that, but shit is getting critical out here. This rock thing is throwing up dead presidents like they was pennies.

"There'll be niggas like K-Dee and that fool Doo Doo all over the place, young paid gangstas looking to get paid in the rap game. It's time to build before this shit goes multinational. It's the same game you know. You establish a territory. Find some new jacks to do the leg work. Protect that turf awhile. You don't have to advertise rock cocaine; niggas come looking for it. Rap is like that, too!"

"But," I countered, "drug dealers either end up dead or in jail. Rap is not like that, Dirt Bike."

"Not now, Derek. But this is like insider trading. White boys weren't getting arrested on Wall Street before, but you hear about it now. In this day and time it's all about gettin' paid, from white boys in suits to niggas in Nikes. None of the people I met in this game are smarter than me and that includes Gibbs. Plus I got more heart than most of them. I been doing the dirty work. That shit is almost over."

This was the single longest conversation I'd ever had with Dirt Bike. It was as if the negotiations had hot-wired my man into some new consciousness. More likely it had been growing for a while, and the deal Gibbs offered K-Dee finally drove him to verbalize it.

After Long Beach, there were three more scheduled dates—San Diego, Phoenix, and Denver. There was already talk of more cities— Cincinnati, Minneapolis, San Antonio had all been mentioned. For Dirt Bike and me, however, handling this mess had made it clear we needed to leave soon. I'd listened to his dreams and now suddenly felt obligated to tell him mine. I bought us each another large burger and told him my tale of rhythm & blues.

Dirt Bike listened, first politely and then intensely, and then surprised me. "You," he said gravely, "are gonna be more than a songwriter, holmes. You gonna have your own thing."

"What do you mean?"

"I been around a lot of niggas trying to get paid in full. They all think they know the deal. But the ones that really blow up, they allow themselves to be surprised. Not scared but surprised. This whole tour was a shock to your system. But you came through like a trooper, holmes. Today them country-ass L.A. niggas could have stuck us up and no one in South Central would have gave a fuck. You handled it. Just like you do with those redneck arena managers we deal with. That skill's about more than just songwriting. I don't know what it'll bring you, but it'll bring you something, holmes."

Dirt Bike's words echoed in my head for the next few furiously busy days. Between radio promos, in-stores, interviews, and parties our tour was the talk of L.A. Gorgeous, high-quality L.A. groupies filled the lobby at the Sunset Hyatt. Dope men were hawking cocaine like candy, and both women and men were offering head for backstage passes. In the background, buzzing like white noise all week, were rumors about a planned riot by the Crips at Long Beach Arena.

Gibbs kept threatening to come back to L.A. in time for the gig, but I told him to stay in Paris. "Why come back?" I asked him. "You'd just be a walking target."

"Word," Dirt Bike chimed in from the other extension. "All they really need to do to get paid is to kidnap you. They could have done it in Seattle, so they damn well could snatch you down here."

"It sounds right," he said with a sigh from across the Atlantic. "I guess I'll meet the tour down in San Diego. You heard anything from K-Dee or Doo Doo?"

Dirt Bike and I replied negatively. Then there was a knock at the door. It was Attak with an adorable strawberry blonde he identified as Faith Dawson. At first Dirt Bike, not feeling too charitable, told him, "We on a conference call with Gibbs, so we got no time to be entertaining girlies," which made Attak laugh. Then he told us Faith was a reporter from the *L.A. Weekly,* doing a story on rap, which made Dirt Bike even more anxious to get her out of the room. But Attak insisted, "You all better take time out to listen to my friend."

For the next fifteen minutes Faith (who looked remarkably like Attak's girlfriend Charlene from Indianapolis) told this story: while doing a piece on South Central's mobile DJ scene she learned about a conflict between sects of the Bloods and Crips that involved music. A drug dealer who'd been financing demo sessions for a Compton rapper took the rapper's tracks, dubbed his own voice on them, and pressed up a couple of tracks on a 12-inch single. Turns out the drug dealer was a Blood and the older brother of the rapper was what they called an O.G. out here—an Original Gangsta, one of the founders of the Crips. One drive-by led to another and now, by some strange L.A. logic, word had spread that our Long Beach concert would be the venue for some loosely organized gang-bang.

To me, this was a totally fantastic tale. It sounded like some musical "West Coast Story." I mean, I was laughing as Faith related it. "Why would they go to a concert to settle a beef? That's silly."

"Yo," Dirt Bike said, "it's no sillier than shooting niggas over the color cap they be wearing."

"Gentlemen." It was Gibbs, who'd been listening in on the speaker phone and running up an incredible long-distance phone bill. "If Attak's friend is right, it means several things."

"Faith is my name," she interjected.

"Excuse me. If Faith is right we should consider canceling the concert. No amount of security is gonna stop that kind of bumrush. Nikko probably knew this was going down and so decided to scam some cash out of us."

"And," I cut in, "it means K-Dee couldn't help but know about this and was just stringing our sorry New York asses along."

All the confidence that had built up handling that negotiation seeped away.

Gibbs broke up my thoughts. "Before we really consider canceling the show, I want you guys to check Faith's story."

"It's true, guys," Faith said with pride boarding on vanity. "And if I was you, I'd stop the gig."

Ignoring her, Gibbs said, "I'll call back in six hours. Find out whatever you can and we'll go for that."

Roscoe's Chicken & Waffles, located on Gower Street just off Sunset, was one of the few hangout spots black Angelinos had up in West Hollywood. It was a small, dark space with little leg room at the tables and chintzy wood paneling on the walls. Its specialty was a potent combination of sugar and grease, which generated long and patient lines of casually clad locals and celebrities. Wolfing down chicken wings you might find boxer Mike Tyson or members of New Edition or black film producer Suzanne DePasse.

If you were in the black Hollywood mix, Roscoe's was a regular haunt. Which is why we met Doo Doo here. It was the kind of spot L.A. tourists like us would want to visit. Moreover, we could have Vicky Vic and company with us, and no one would think that we were paranoid or suspicious. Dirt Bike was prepared to pull Doo Doo out of Roscoe's, stuff him in our rental van, and "convince" him to tell us the truth if he had to.

Thankfully it didn't go down that way. Donkey, who we'd been trying to keep as far out of the loop as possible on all this, rolled with Vicky Vic over to Roscoe's. He knew something was up—how could he not, with us springing for Vicky Vic and his crew to come on tour, as stupid as they'd acted in Philly? So, with the kind of bravado only a New York rap star could muster, he just pulled up a seat next to our tight little table with Doo Doo. Dirt Bike was upset since he was all ready to move into gangster mode and didn't want Donkey involved.

In fact, it was Donkey's presence that made that unnecessary. While to our New York eyes Doo Doo looked to be just another blue-wearing, country-ass, L.A. 'Bama, he saw himself as a connoisseur of New York hip hop. Turns out he'd been born back East, in Newark to be exact. A big part of Doo Doo still identified with the East Coast.

So once Donkey showed up, Doo Doo just melted. No Glock cocking today. Instead he smiled excitedly at Donkey's stories of the road (he loved hearing about Atlanta) and slowly began telling us the truth. Not only did he confirm Faith's story but added an important wrinkle. "Yeah, Bloods and Crips will be at y'all's concert," he agreed, "but the way I hear it, most of the banging's supposed to happen in the parking lot. No one bought no tickets or nothing like that. Might be none of them even really be checking for the show."

So the concert wasn't really a target. It was just a place. The same mess could have been planned for a movie theater, a club, school, wherever young people were coming together. Like the robberies at the Garden, the audience of concert goers would serve as camouflage. As far as I was concerned, it didn't change anything. Ticket holders would still be in danger. And there was no question in my mind that the music, not the gangs, would take the weight.

Dirt Bike wasn't so sure. He though this might change Gibbs' mind. As long as it happened outside the arena, we were not responsible. "What they do to each other outside the arena is not our problem, Derek," he said. "If we weren't coming to town, then they'd be beefing somewhere else."

I'd come to really respect Dirt Bike for his instincts, but I totally disagreed. Neither one of us had the find word. It was Gibbs' show and Gibbs' call. Literally it was Gibbs' call. And we waited in vain for it early into Thursday morning. Finally, Dirt Bike dug around and unearthed a number for him in France. We had no idea what time it was in Paris. Beth Ann answered. When I asked for Gibbs she slammed the receiver down. Just figured we were calling real early. Maybe she and Gibbs were getting busy. I tried again. Same result. I tried one more time. As soon as she picked up, I pleaded for an answer.

"Your friend is gone!"

"Gone where?"

"Back to New York with his trifling ass!"

"What happened?"

"Just tell him don't call back!"

It wasn't hard to figure out. My man Gibbs had been a kid in the model candy store. Must have eaten too much. Never been good at math but by my imprecise calculations, it suggested that if he'd left Paris within the last six hours, Gibbs would still be in the air headed to New York. He'd likely call when he changed planes for L.A. Unless he got on the Concorde, which meant he'd have landed in the Apple by now. Either way it meant I could do nothing.

Sixty percent of all tickets had been sold for Long Beach. We knew, in general, that blacks were walk-up, day-of-concert ticket buyers. But because rap's audiences tended to be younger blacks, people on even tighter budgets, people who loved movies and video arcade games as much as arena shows, day-of-concert sales were even more crucial. That worried me. If things got too hectic outside the Long Beach Arena, many fans, especially white ones, would drive off.

All this uncertainty gave me a fitful sleep. But turmoil, while bad for peace of mind, was good for art. On Friday afternoon I finally came up with a verse to fit my melody.

This journey it seems
Just like the places that I've seen
Are just pieces of a dream
That I've been building.
Now I'm saying to you, my man
That it's time to take a stand
To stand up and fight on for your dreams.

This lyric struck me as a lot more "we-shall-overcome" than I was actually feeling. Still it flowed and it had backbone. Sounded like the narrator had come out of some painful period and was rising above it to take control of his life. If it was wishful thinking, then I had to thank my subconscious for articulating it. I felt a chorus would be coming soon.

"You Know How We Do It"

Gibbs looked like shit. I hate to be so harsh, but my man was haggard, red-eyed, and fuzzy-minded. His exotic, purchased-in-Paris shades couldn't disguise his befuddlement. As he listened to Dirt Bike and me run down all Saturday's possible scenarios, he methodically ate a huge salad, as if every piece of arugula had to be carefully weighed before being committed to his mouth.

We sat at the Source, an outdoor vegetarian restaurant just down Sunset from the Hyatt and Carney's. The customers had that disgustingly robust look I'd learned to hate and envy in well-paid Angelinos. It seemed strange to be discussing rap music, its fans, and its problems in a health food restaurant. It felt like we should at least be back at Roscoe's.

"What are we gonna do?" I inquired. "Cancel the concert?"

"We aren't gonna do anything."

"Excuse me, boss," I said sarcastically. "I made the mistake of thinking since Dirt Bike and I handled everything during your vacation that we were part of the team. My bad."

My response seemed to wake him up. "Look, Derek, don't act like I don't appreciate what you guys have done. I do. But it's still all on my head. My name's on every contract. If things get fucked up, I take the weight." He paused a minute, letting it sink in and making me feel like a chump.

"You didn't answer his question though, holmes." Dirt Bike clearly wasn't impressed by Gibbs' sudden acceptance of responsibility. "What are you gonna do?'"

Gibbs chewed on another leaf of arugula and said quietly, "Nothing."

"Because?" I asked.

"Because," he replied, "to cancel the concert at this point is worse than having something happen."

"Oh, man," I said as I slumped in my seat. "I know this one's gonna be good."

"Listen, Derek." He'd finally stopped picking at his arugula and focused on us. "The tour survived the Garden. That shit went down in the biggest media town in the world. These L.A. gang guys talk all this mess. Nikko. Kay Dee. Doo Doo. All of them. But we don't know if anything's gonna happen."

"What about what that girl Faith told us?"

"Hey," Gibbs shot back, "she's just another one of Attak's white girls. Maybe she half heard something. The truth is we know fans will be there. They always come. The truth is we know somebody will get ripped off by some stick-up kid. That always happens. We know we'll be there. We know it will start. We know if we have the show—even if something happens—that it'll make money. If we get sued, well we'll just sue the arena and the local police and tie the whole damn thing up in court while the money earns interest. When you get down to it, that's all we know."

There was a long, uneasy silence. His argument was compelling. At least that's how it struck Dirt Bike and me. This was prime-time Gibbs, the man who had helped spread rap, the man who was building an empire of music without musicians. He was giving us that look, the same one that got international models to drop their drawers overlooking the Seine.

"Okay," I said glumly. "I hear you. I don't agree. I hear you, though." It was time to change the subject. "So it's time to tell your boys how you fucked up in Paris."

Now Gibbs' energy sagged again and his con-man glow evaporated. The confident I'm-in-charge look disappeared. "You know what happened, Derek. I've never been around that many tall, bad bitches. I can't front, man; it was intimidating at first. Beth Ann did all my talking for me. Rap this. Concert that. Eventually I started getting the vapors."

"How were the skins?" Dirt Bike asked.

"No. That's what's really fucked up about the whole thing. I hit this six-foot-two Swedish girl. She had long, long blonde hair. Seventeen or something. Didn't know shit, couldn't do shit. Laid on top of me like a blanket."

"Damn," I said. "Don't tell me. Afterwards she told all her friends and it got back to Beth Ann."

"Word. And you know what the worst thing is?"

"What?"

"I love her."

Dirt Bike laughed. "Nigga, please." He just found the whole situation funny. Me? I could feel that Gibbs really meant it. His dick had got the best of him and he truly regretted it. I just hoped he wasn't feeling the same way Saturday night.

"Black Steel in the Hour of Chaos"

A door. Just one door. Steel reinforced. Painted black. Obscure. Back near where the vendors stored popcorn. Afterwards a weary arena manager told me, "We've been talking about cementing that door over for years. For years." Maybe they've done it since that night. Too late for us, though. Way too late. The Long Beach police reported many of the Insane Crips they'd arrested came through that obscure steel reinforced door. Of course it was open at the time. It's amazing to note that one entrance can have national impact.

"Angry, disillusioned, unloved kids unite behind heavy metal or rap music, because the music says it's okay to beat up people." That's what was Tipper Gore, wife of then Senator Al Gore and co-founder of the Parents Music Resource Center, told *USA Today*. I guess it was a sign of rap's growing strength that politicians' wives were going after it. She wasn't alone, either. After Long Beach, the phrase "Rap Riot!" entered the headline writer's lexicon.

I keep going back to that door. Crips must have been rolling in as early as 6:30. By the time the Brothers Black hit at 7:35, there were fights everywhere. Only later would we discover that the head of security—who was already on thin ice for previous violence at Long Beach—would call back and report that everything was under control and we, the GAP staffers, were overacting.

Meanwhile kids were driven onto the stage to avoid the craziness. The First Aid station was filling up. Bruised and slashed and stomped and dazed, these brown and vanilla children moved in for help. Despite their injuries many wanted autographs. Latisha Barnes wanted one from Attak. Latisha, sixteen, skinny and now missing two front teeth courtesy of some fool who'd snatched her gold name plate, very much wanted Attak's autograph and I very much wanted to get it for her. Gibbs, whom I was doing my best not to look in the eye, had passed me in the arena's gray corridor, too.

My man said he was too busy to be bothered. I told him I didn't like his attitude. He looked at me like I was crazy, so I reared back and sucker-punched him. Got him right on the bridge of the nose. Latisha Barnes still didn't get her autograph.

About 10:30, the LAPD arrived and Latisha Barnes and all the other attendees began their journey home or to the hospital or even jail. We rolled our tour bus back to L.A. as helicopters and cops wearing sunglasses at night swirled around us. Attak, his new friend Faith, Donkey, and his Queens crew sat around drinking sodas and Olde English. The air was thick with cigarettes and marijuana. Stories were flowing about how "niggas back East" were more civilized than their West Coast cousins.

Attak made every one extra uneasy by comparing the evening to a horror film. "It was like watching a bunch of Freddies out there." His eyes were wide and wired. "It was as if we were cursed with some evil wound, you know, and all the backed-up puss poured out. This was all puss tonight. It had to come out. We bandaged it up and we'll be all right. You know what I'm sayin', right?" To be honest I really didn't. But I thought Attak was a true artist and figured he understood it on its own terms. Like I said, the album Attak made after the tour was a masterpiece.

We got back to the Hyatt around midnight. Within ten minutes I'd packed my bags and was checking out when Gibbs rolled up, ice pack on his nose and that con man look in his eye. I tired to ignore him. He was saying something about stress and pressure as I read the message that had been waiting at the front desk. I didn't say a thing. When he put out his hand I just shoved the message in it and walked out of the Hyatt.

The message was from Danifa. It was simple: "Mayo will take 'Silly Pictures' for Melissa Klark's new album! The deal will be done soon! Congratulations!"

I walked across Sunset, then past a cowboy bootery, a tattoo parlor, and across a side street into the Mondrian Hotel. After checking in, I went down to the bar, ordered a double Jack Daniel's, and squatted down behind its poorly tuned Baldwin. A white barfly yelled out, "Play 'Wind Beneath My Wings.'" I just sipped some Jack and played this.

This journey it seems
Just like the places that I've seen
Are just pieces of a dream that I've been building.
Now I'm saying to you, man
That its time to take a stand
And stand up and fight on for your dreams.

Fight on/ Give it all you got
Fight on/ Make it your best shot
No matter the consequences
Or the defeats that penetrate your defenses.
You must fight on to win your dreams
Fight on/ You may not feel strong enough
Fight on/ But it's impossible to stop.

The struggles that we've won
Just like the pain that we've endured
Are just what gives me the strength that I've been building.
Now I'm reaching out my hand
Cause it's time to take a stand
And stand up and fight on for your dreams.

Why this song? Why now? The truth was I'd just officially given in on my principles in order to make a deal. Truth was my ex-roommate had, out of some combination of ego and greed, facilitated some brutal violence and by not walking away sooner I'd played a role in it. The truth was this song was "positive" while there was mounting evidence that I wasn't really a positive kinda guy.

I decided to take this song's appearance as an omen. I was supposed to fight on here. In Hollywood, in this new hotel, in this strange world of real anger and unreal possibilities. It actually didn't make a lot of sense. But if I'd given Attak the benefit of the doubt on the tour bus, I figured I needed to be that understanding of myself.

About two weeks later I became a demi-celebrity in L.A. My picture, comforting a bleeding young woman, was on the cover of the *L.A. Weekly.* Equally prominent in the picture was my Brothers Black T-shirt. The headline was "Black Rhymes" and Faith Dawson's story focused on Attak's lyrics, his middle classness, and the debate over rap's impact on the young. It was well written, though I didn't finish it. I was trying to put that behind me, which I did by throwing my copy of the paper in the trash right after Faith quoted Gibbs saying, "It's not about money, its about self-expression, art, and all that good shit. Why else would I be involved?" At that point it was time for me to take a dip in the pool.

los angeles—philly

"The Sweetest Taboo"

Smog sat perched on the shoulders of Los Angeles just like it did every morning. From the terrace of the Mondrian Hotel I could see for miles or, more accurately, I could see the smog for miles. The tour was long gone—it was in Cincinnati by now and soon headed for Europe. There was $10,000 in my bank account, the most I've had in my life, and I'm living off a Warner-Chappel expense account while I work with Larry Lawrence, a hot white songwriter with an r&b feel, on some tunes being submitted for Michael Jackson's first post-*Thriller* album.

Word on the street is that Michael wants some material with a "street" feel and Danifa thinks that my New York sensibility and Lawrence's L.A. style could result in something good. Cool with me. This guy writes poppy r&b influenced by Thom Bell & Linda Creed, and after being immersed in rap for all those months, I'm happy to be around soothing music. The irony, of course, is that because of my involvement with the tour I'm now perceived as a "cutting edge" writer who's "in touch with the street."

It had been six months since I signed with Warner-Chappel and things were going all right. I'd sold a song to Melissa Klark—she was no longer working with Mayo—that went top five r&b and did very well on the "churban" stations that combined urban contemporary and pop hits. The song, "That Moment After That," temporarily revived Klark's career and made Danifa look good for signing me. And, I'm proud to say, it was my best work up to that point. I wrote it with a sweet funk groove and a syncopated melody that, if I do say so myself, was slammin'.

"The Moment After That"

The moment after that
(3X)

First verse:

It's right after
lips part sweetly.
It's right after
hot sweat turns chilly dry.
It's right after
your body moves from me.
It's right after
my body moves from you.

Chorus:

Will I want you?
(the moment after that)
Will you need me?
(the moment after that)
Can you feel me?
(the moment after that).
All these questions
(the moment after that).

Second verse:

There are many
tender moments
Softer than
your softest kiss.
Times when we hug
We hung in satin bliss.
But all that
All that makes me wonder
'Bout the moment
the moment after that.

Will you hurt me?
(the moment after that)
Will I change you?
(the moment after that)
Will we stay together?
(the moment after that).
All these questions
(the moment)
(the moment after that).

That morning I ran into Jevon on the Mondrian Hotel patio. Since "The Scent of a Woman," his career had, like many other male r&b singers of the period, settled into a rut of mediocrity. While Luther Vandross was the dominant balladeer and Michael Jackson was the ultimate dance pop star, the middle ground was cluttered with decent singers struggling to find an identity.

Jevon was one of those unfortunate guys. In an effort to change his fortunes he'd moved to L.A. and signed with two white managers known for handling rock stars. They were having a breakfast meeting when I walked over. Said they were on their way to a press conference for some black charity. Wanting to seem down and angling to get a song on his next album, I tagged along. I never did get a song placed with Jevon, but going to that press conference changed my life for quite some time.

We went over to the Universal Hilton where the event was already underway. I'm not sure if the conference was on how to save black folks from extinction or on how to save extinction from black folks, but I am positive folks on the dais wanted to organize a commission and otherwise "monitor the situation."

Anyway, while all this race saving was going on, I first saw Lydia Manson's legs. She was standing on the side of the dais in one of those cute corporate outfits. Cream-colored jacket and skirt arranged tastefully and quietly expensive. Down below were two thick, shapely legs in black panty hose and black suede heels. Best of all she had on these adorable little Oliver Peoples spectacles. As she squinted from behind them across the room, our eyes met and, despite the presence of these very august ministers, Congress members, and other dignified types, I hit her with my biggest, widest I-must-get-with-you grin. Damned if she didn't blush. Adorable.

Turned out she toiled for one of the event's corporate underwriters, Crown Burger, a fast food chain willing to put a little cash into this effort to save blacks from extinction (or was that to save extinction from blacks?) just so we'd be available to eat their next generation of fatty beef patties. Our conversation opened with her rationale for the company's press release, which advocated selling a useless product in our neighborhoods, when it claimed to have our people's best interest at heart. (I mean, their ghetto billboards had a thick-lipped brother with gold teeth eating a burger. The tag line read: "For the taste that puts gold in your mouth.") She articulated her defense with gusto, while her eyes danced across my face, shoulders, and regions down below. Every time she said words like "responsibility," "commitment," or "understanding," the light flowed through her glasses and lit up her baby browns.

I had just asked for her business card, but after the conference Lydia ended up depositing me in her black BMW. I told her that as an artist I was concerned with the state of our people. I attended the press conference looking for artistic inspiration. This was communicated with all due earnestness, though in retrospect it's doubtful she swallowed it whole. As a corporate woman, Lydia made her living listening to smiling men tell lies.

Impulsively she asked if we could have dinner that night, an offer which seemed to surprise her as much as me. I didn't get that groupie vibe you feel from some women who've never been around the music business. She seemed way too poised for that. Lydia had taken off her shoes and moved the pedals with her lovely panty-hosed feet. I mean, Lydia's feet looked delicious and her legs succulent. I guess I was staring real hard because she asked me what I was looking at. I told her. Then I told her why. She just said, "Hmmmm" and spread her legs a little farther open.

We were jammed up on the freeway on our way back to West Hollywood. Cars were stacked up as far as the smog would let you see. Sade's "The Sweetest Taboo" seeped out of her CD player and the image of Sade, with no shoes, singing to me at Radio City flashed on my mental screen. During the third verse my left hand found Lydia's savory right leg. During the tag my hand slid slowly down her inner thigh. I was way out of line, yet Lydia didn't look my way. Being a good driver she kept her eyes on the road. My left hand now went on a torturous journey—inside her dress, inside her panty hose, and finally inside my lovely new friend.

Lydia slumped down in the driver's seat and rested her head back. A low moan issued from the back of her throat. She kept her eyes on the road, though as we progressed, they occasionally fluttered. This had been going on quite a while—Sade's *Promise* CD was on its second play—when I took one of Lydia's red-nailed hands off the wheel and put it on me. Lydia had slid open the sunroof and the sun and her movements and my hands inside her and her hands around me and the voice of sweet Sade all conspired to stop reality. I moaned now, too. All praise the L.A. freeways! Sade seemed to play all day. Four. Five. Six times we heard "Is It a Crime" and "Jezebel" and "Never As Good As the First Time" and "The Sweetest Taboo." Usually the music fades when I'm having sex, but this was an unusual act so I guess my reaction was, too.

By the time we'd snaked off the freeway exit, Lydia was wet and I was bubbling over. She instructed me to reach inside her glove compartment where I fished out tissues for both of us. In front of the Mondrian she kissed me hotly. Then I ran upstairs and masturbated with visions of corporate pussy in my head.

The rest of the day was strange. At Larry's house in the hills I wrote lecherous lyrics to a pop ballad he wanted to pitch to Michael Jackson. He wasn't too happy about my approach. Meanwhile Lydia didn't beep or call. It wasn't until that night that I realized she hadn't given me her home number. It had felt great in Lydia's car. Now I wanted more, and I clearly wasn't getting any that night.

The next day the *L.A. Times* had a piece in the Metro section on the press conference. A photo of a local political leader and a gang member filled the center of the page. On the edge of the frame Lydia's shoulder could be seen. My mind filled in the rest. I dialed her office and was told, quite politely, she was in a meeting. This occurred four more times that afternoon. Lydia's assistant's name was Bev and her politeness was unflagging, though mine wore down. The next morning

I got a package from Crown Burger. Inside was a lovely brown leather notebook case with a legal pad and an expensive pen inside. Written on the top sheet was a restaurant name, a time, and Lydia's signature next to the outline of her red lips. I said, "Ah, shit" out loud and then began rearranging my schedule to accommodate hers.

I met her at this cool little bistro on Third Avenue near the Beverly Center. The walls were all white, with subdued lighting and original oil paintings hung along the walls. Lydia was already there in a red pant suit combo set off by a white blouse. Her nails and hair were immaculate, as if she'd just walked out of a cognac VSOP ad and into my life. I had a hard time keeping my hands off her during the appetizers, but by the entrees I was caressing her knees.

"You never gave me your home number," I said. "Am I to assume that you live with someone?"

Lydia blushed. "You could say that."

Now, as far as I was concerned, the ball was in her court. If what happened in the car was just a freaky situation, you know, just a fling, then fine. Don't send me gifts and invite me to dinner. Inviting me to dinner makes me think that you want me again. I told her this as she carefully cut her roast chicken and avoided my eyes.

"I have never done anything like that before," she said. "I was ashamed of myself later."

"But you enjoyed it," I said. "Didn't you?"

"Whether I enjoyed it or not—"

"But," I insisted, "you did enjoy it."

"Whether I did or not," she said with intensity, "I live with someone who I care deeply about. Someone I would never ever want to hurt. You understand that, don't you?"

Yes, I did. Still, what were we doing here tonight? Becoming friends? I understood where Lydia was trying to go, but I couldn't follow her. I could still feel her on my fingers. I thought I could smell her right now, wet and juicy, beneath her nice outfit and fabulous hair. Little pecks on the cheek and friendship dinners were not gonna make me happy. I said all this. I knew my passion touched Lydia, but she kept her guard up and then flipped the script on me.

"I hear you're a very talented songwriter."

"Some people think so."

"And some people don't."

"And," I said, wondering where this was going.

"I checked up on you," she said proudly.

A little defensively I replied, "And you found that I was doing all right."

"That's it. All right is what people said. I know how you could do better."

"Keep going."

"Crown Burger is about to start a campaign introducing a new burger," she said. "It's called the King Burger. It'll be ready for Black History month. Instead of going to the same jingle house we always use, I want to develop the campaign inside. I want to guide and control it. I understand the product—I understand the consumer. I need a songwriter to help me."

"That's cool. But what's that got to do with us enjoying mutual masturbation in your B-mer listening to Sade?" I asked this question in all earnestness, though the implications of the offer were obvious. You could really get paid writing jingles. I would work with and for her, leaving open the door for clandestine activities of all variety.

Lydia's reply was sharp. "Do you always have to speak so bluntly? It's probably why your reputation is so shaky. Anyway, I may be wrong, but there's something about you I really like."

"My hands, maybe."

Now she blushed again. It seemed a good time to get some questions answered. I wanted to know about her man. Rebuffed on that front, I then asked about her background. Aside from being an L.A. native and earning an MBA from UCLA, Lydia didn't give up much info.

After dinner we stood outside, saying nothing as the valet delivered her BMW. I let her get in first. Then I opened the door and stuck my head in.

"I'm not getting in until I establish something," I said with equal amounts of conviction and guile. "I wanna make love to you tonight and many nights after that. Is that okay with you? If it isn't, you can keep your burger and your jingles and all that other shit. Are we clear?"

Lydia looked to see if the valet or anyone else was listening. After deciding I wasn't overheard, she replied, "Don't you think you're a little too dramatic?"

"I'm an artist, you know. I'm allowed to get away with saying stuff like this."

"Is that right?"

"That's what it says in the handbook."

"Okay. I heard you. Get in."

She refused to go back to the Mondrian—she knew too many people who stayed there. Likewise I refused to be satisfied with more hand sex—no matter how expert. Maybe if she'd called sooner or hadn't offered to turn me into her musical mistress I would have been more opened-minded, more flexible. But, as we drove around West Hollywood debating, I remained determined to have my way.

Somehow we ended up parking on a dark street in lower Beverly Hills. She put the seats in recline, programmed Sade again, and clutched me tight like a fleeting dream. Somehow she ended up on top with her legs locked across my thighs. Before, we'd made love cool and mellow—lovemaking that could be washed away with a tissue. This night, whatever veiled hostility was apparent at dinner was now unleashed with demonic power. Against Lydia's protest I marked her with my teeth and licked her wherever I could. She'd have to shower for days to get my flavor washed off her body.

Sweat and passion had sucked off Lydia's professional sheen and I saw a woman, lusty and loving, whom, I suspected, usually kept her passion in check. Something about the chemistry between us had us acting like teenagers. I knew this kind of desire couldn't last. It was too hot and already moving toward complications. I wanted to write a song about us, but I sat up all night in the hotel and could scribble nothing worthy of Lydia.

That night was the beginning of a two-and-a-half-year stint in the luxurious purgatory of jingle writing, a place where money was ample, residuals divine, and my naked creativity was defiled by the products it sold. With Lydia smartly negotiating the corporate waters, I was forced down the throats of several black advertising agencies. In exchange for Lydia steering them contracts, I got first crack at writing and, on occasion, performing in the companies' campaigns. Lucky for all involved, I was good at writing "minority" jingles. Incorporating the company's original slogan in the ditty, I penned the following:

Chorus:
Feel the pride/
Feel the pride inside/
With King Burger.
You feel real proud
You can taste the flavor
You can savor the crown.
Man, you can really get
The taste of gold in your mouth.
Feel the pride
Feel the pride inside.

Well, Lydia loved it. Her bosses loved it. So I smiled and listened as that song played across America all that summer. It was the most exposure I'd had in any of my work. That fact sort of made me sick, but that wasn't the least of it.

After years of knocking my head up against walls, through Lydia I was finally working with some of black music's best voices. On one gospel version of the King Burger spot, Luther Vandross, Dionne Warwick and Whitney Houston's mom Cissy were in the studio. Jeffrey Osborne, Howard Hewitt, and Johnny Gill put their voices together to make a joyous noise on another version. Quiet as it's kept, Prince did one spot which everybody thought was a Prince imitator. I mean, Prince sang my words! Of course that's Prince singing my words in praise of a Crown Burger.

The Crown Burger company, a subdivision of a larger beverage company, was so impressed with the jingle that they, at Lydia's suggestion of course, commissioned me to craft a tune that would launch a new malt liquor called Big Mouth. Their research showed that the consumers of malt and rap music came from the same urban demographic. Years later, St. Ides would capitalize on this connection, but I was the first to exploit it. I mean, it's not quite like being Jackie Robinson, but a "first" is still better than a second. I even had Donkey come in and work on the track. Though he was a disgusting individual, there was no question that Donkey was the kind of guy Big Mouth was targeting.

I remember the day we cut the spot. I wondered to Lydia if, just maybe, we were helping her bosses exploit the weaknesses of the

SEDUCED

black community. Her reply was to note how much cash her employers had contributed to community centers and scholarship funds. In other words, yes we were partly exploiting the black community, but as long as hush money was paid regularly we wouldn't get caught. Unlike Gibbs, who was in the business of giving the rap audience what they wanted—their own music their way—Lydia (and now me) were using black America's innovations to sell them something they didn't need while making it seem integral to their culture.

If I had been living in New York full-time, doing this might have really bothered me. I'd have seen the ads on the subway. Seen the 40-ounce bottles piling high. But I was mostly in L.A., either in trendy hotels or artist hangouts like the Oakwood Inn out in Burbank. I wasn't near "real" black L.A. and didn't know anyone in Watts or Compton. I was living in the creative vacuum better known as Hollywood, so it was so easy to take that check and then kick back and scheme on how to get my next one.

"Money"

During this time, roughly 1985 to 1987, all my dreams had dollar signs. Every rhyme, every melodic idea, every piece of juvenile poetry I'd invented on the D train had a price tag. And those prices were, through Lydia, being met. Maybe it was not the best thing, though at the time I didn't know what the hell could replace getting paid except not getting paid, and I'd already been through that.

When your dreams have a price tag nothing can be discarded, nothing thrown away. Every scribble on a napkin, each sentence in my notebook became a dollar bill or $20,000 if it was particularly deft. I found myself recycling bad rhymes and repackaging them with other bad ones as if two negatives could become a positive by sheer force of will. During this period there was no other reality for me. I could have gone to church every Sunday and sung in the choir. A lot of people in my position did that. They prayed to God and then checked their watches during the sermon.

But when your dreams have a price tag, that kind of spiritual con game gains you nothing. After all, didn't God create the concept of value? That X is worth Y. That this melody can be translated into this amount of dollars? So why go to church when I already understood the rules and I lived them everyday, not just on Sundays? I rationalized that, in fact, I was spiritually whole then, because I knew my value was determined by how many times my commercials were played on the radio and how many burgers, beers, cupcakes, and how much cognac I got black folks to consume.

When your dreams have a price tag there is no time for those silly lifelong dreams of self-expression for art's sake. At least that's what I told myself when I knew—and I knew often—that working for Lydia may not have been selling my talent short, but it certainly wasn't fulfilling my dreams.

"L.A. Woman"

Over this period my love life became as dysfunctional as my creative life was lucrative. Though I didn't admit it to myself at the time, Lydia had me pussy whipped. I'd redirected my career to accommodate her agenda. Yet I wasn't in love, not because I didn't want to be but because she wouldn't let me. She gave me enough to keep me strung out, but never enough to endanger her central relationship. She'd make love to me on the spur of the moment in a sound booth on Thursday night. Then I wouldn't hear from her all weekend. The following Monday I'd find out that she and her man had gone skiing with friends. In short, I was her piece on the side and, strangely, I didn't fight it.

My relationship with Doris, of course, continued to suffer. Since we were both bicoastal now, we saw each other fairly regularly, but we both seemed comfortable with our relationship's lack of depth. I think we stayed together just so we could tell people we were in a relationship. It made us seem stable in a business where everyone was unstable. Obviously, any words of commitment I mouthed to her were lies. Lydia was my main obsession. And it was likely Doris was lying, too. I was sure she had another man (maybe men) in New York. Perhaps even Mayo.

If I'd just been wrestling with my relationships with Lydia and

Doris, my days would have been full. But there was more than that going on. Lots more. I was spending most of my time in Los Angeles during what, in retrospect, I see as a kind of sexual golden age, before rape charges and AIDS put an evil spin on all of it. It was the era of straight black male pop stars—Eddie Murphy, Prince, Mike Tyson, Magic Johnson, Arsenio Hall—who hung out at places like Carlos & Charlie's on Sunset Boulevard and were magnets for the young and nubile starlets of Tinseltown. The best-looking girls from all over the country gravitated to L.A. Some had actual talent. But too many simply had their beauty as currency. Though I wasn't a celebrity, I had access to celebrity circles, and like a saucer under a cup, I caught some of the overflow. So when Lydia wasn't available and Doris was in New York, I wet my beak. But these activites only made me want Lydia more.

Sex with these L.A. women was good, but it was never great, never transcendent. I was never drained, never dizzy, never elated. Sex without love was one thing. I could deal with that, even revel in it. Sex without satisfaction? Well, that'll drive a person crazy. Maybe this was some mad metaphor for my lack of creative fulfillment, but there were times I felt better when I didn't come than when I did. I just couldn't get satisfied. I changed women. I changed condoms. I changed sex manuals. And I changed sheets.

I couldn't remember who all these people I was sleeping with were. I couldn't remember one woman's background from another. Was it Laura whose baby-sitter had been an infamous feminist poet? Or was that Tasha? The fact that I knew a woman had split her childhood between Pittsburgh and London was interesting only if I could recall whether it was Andrea or Alla. If I couldn't determine whose story it was, then it was just clutter. One more thing I didn't need to know, but that I did.

So many life stories. Stories related over dinner, stories told in taxicabs, during long-distance phone calls and in bed. All of them, so important to the teller and vaguely heard by me. They filled my mind, overflowing like water on a dirty plate in the sink. Days, months, even years later these stories would appear randomly on my mental screen while I frantically pressed the delete button.

"Same Old Song"

Damn, I don't want it to seem like L.A. was like being in purgatory. I spent one very pleasurable afternoon reading and re-reading a *Musician* piece by that *Billboard* guy Dwayne Robinson on my old "friend" Mayo. In essence, Robinson argued that hip hop was running the Mayos of the world out of the black music business. Within the last two years, hip hop's ascendance had made Mayo's music seem dated almost overnight. BCR hadn't renewed his contract and Mayo, apparently in an effort to keep up his cash flow, had revived the Celestial Funk name, hired a crew of young musicians, and was touring Asia where the band's records were still big. According to what I read in *Musician*, Celestial Funk would play outdoor stadiums with other older bands (the Lionel Richie-less Commodores, K.C. & the Sunshine Band) as well as Army bases.

There was this one long quote in the piece that really struck a nerve, both because it was perceptive of Mayo, while still communicating that arrogance that was hurting him and non-rap r&b.

"Funk is food for the freak. It's the thing my people—by that I mean my generation—were weaned on, so I've got to keep feeding them. Some people want to take my crown and give it to George (Clinton). He may have been out there before me, but I hear funk my way and nobody else hears it like me. That's what I do and that's what my people desire.

"My audience is being fooled now by people using tricks. This stuff here, all this technology we have now, can produce gold and it can produce shit and if the record companies aren't careful with these tools—and you and I know both know they won't be—one day we'll look up and my people won't be able to tell the difference. Remember when everybody started using this Linn drum? Turned the clueless into geniuses overnight. This Fairlight thing did the same. You give someone an 808 keyboard and one good idea and some a&r man who couldn't hum 'Mary Had a Little Lamb' without a song book is hyping him as the new Stevie.

"I can say all this because Celestial Funk was the best funk band there was. We played with George, with Maurice, with Lionel Richie and the other college boys from Tuskeegee and blew them all the fuck away. We were the baddest-big-Afroed-horn-playing-flair-pants-wearing niggas since Sly. And, if you caught us on the right night, smoking the right shit, in the right town, and anxious to get with the big-assed Creole sisters in New Orleans or Lake Charles, well we would have fucked with Sly too.

"But we had to give it when the tricknology started taking over. Ray Parker & Raydio originally had four pieces. Then he had him and a bunch of toys. Instead of splitting the money Ray kept it all. It costs to feed a real band. Our fees stayed the same while everybody else was getting smaller. Earth, Wind & Fire. Cameo. Con Funk Shun. Kool. George even cut back here and there. If people hadn't gone for the tricks, things might have been different.

"You see, I eventually ended up replacing the entire band, all of Celestial Funk, with lots and lots of toys. Even now, as I prepare to go back out, I don't need horns or a bass player and barely need a drummer. I don't really want to do this but, like Jerry Butler said, 'Only the Strong survive.' And I am a survivor."

As much as I disliked Mayo, I knew he was right. If I was disappointed by not having had a chance to be a part of the real soul era, he was equally bitter about what had happened to the musical landscape around him. I hadn't liked how he treated me initially, but that was the pragmatic side of him, the one that had fired his band, made Xerox copies of his hits, and was trying to stay current even as the tide changed. On that level I sympathized with him. But the fact that I was now making more money than he made it much easier to enjoy the piece. In the music game, you see the same people on the way up as you do on the way down. Me and Mayo were going in opposite directions on that elevator.

"Black Magic Woman"

Speaking of different directions, remember Cherri? The Puerto Rican dance diva Edge and I drove down to Atlanta with? Well, I ran into her in L.A. Hadn't spoken to her much since that road trip. We'd often talked about hanging out, but it had never really happened. She swung with a Latin hip-hop clique that made fast-paced dance tracks and hung in the Bronx, Spanish Harlem, and other Latino strong holds where there was some intersection with Gibbs' rap world, but not a lot.

Anyway, when I ran into her, all that history was moot. Like untold ambitious visitors before her, Cherri had come to Cali to create a new life, one wholly manufactured by her dreamy projections of herself. No doubt about it, people run the same game back in New York, but there was a kind of flamboyant fabrication at work in Cali that was as charming as it was dishonest. Gone were the four little rings on each hand, the extra thick eye liner, and the big jingling baby ear rings. They had been replaced by a Bulgari watch, a short, chic designer hair cut, and very smart looking onyx ear rings. Her accent was now a warring mix of New York barrio, L.A. slang, and her own unique approximation of Castilian Spanish. Her name, well, that was history too, but I'll get to that in a minute.

I ran into this new woman at the Forum Club, a bar-restaurant in the home arena of the Lakers. During the "Show time" era, years when the team led by Magic Johnson and Kareem Abdul-Jabbar won five NBA titles, the Forum Club was one of the hottest spots in a city that prides itself on hotness. As Hollywood hang-outs go, the Forum Club was rather low rent—wood paneling, Lakers pennants, and stale air that stank of cigarettes and beer, spiced by pricey perfumes. Jack Nicholson, Dyan Cannon, and members of the whole courtside crew did roll through, but the Forum Club was really a hustlers' convention—guys with business cards that read "Producer" who'd never produced, girls with head shots that read "Actress" but had never acted, and plenty of other people who said they were "in the business," though one was never sure what that meant. Heidi Fleish, madam to the stars, rolled through. Ola Ray, the cute girl in Michael Jackson's *Thriller* video, was often in the house. Then Laker girl Paula Abdul, along with her dance mates, stepped in for an after-work drink and some conversation. It was in this environment of fun, fly-girl flair, and flakery that I spotted a similar face across the bar during one half-time. As I said, her style was radically different but that sexy Latin face was the same.

"Cherri!" I yelled across the bar. "Cherri!" She stared at me anxiously. Then that look melted into an amused smirk.

"Do you know me?" she yelled back, clearly deciding to mess with me before she did anything else.

"Cherrie. Come on. Derek Harper." Even as I spoke, I was winding my way around the bar toward her. A big black man with a Miami Vice–styled white ice cream suit stepped over to help her carry her drinks. He looked like a snowman with a big charcoal lump of a head. "Cherri," I pleaded, "don't play me like this."

The snowman grunted at me and wanted to know if I was bothering her. "No, baby" she said, slowing his roll and quieting my heart. "I'll be over in a minute." After the snowman moved away, she looked me dead in the eye. "My name's Carman Montez. Not Cherri. Carman Montez."

"Carman Montez," I repeated dumbly.

She continued: "If you're ever asked, you met me in New York at a recording session a few years ago. You got that?"

"Recording session in New York. Carman, right?"

"Carman Montez."

"Carman Montez. Recording session in New York."

"Yes."

"So am I to take it you and I never got busy in the Atlanta Marriott?"

"My friend is a tackle for the Raiders. He's really very sweet and very protective."

"I'm sorry to have mistaken you, Carman."

She excused herself and strolled confidently toward a corner table where an amazing-looking collection of friends awaited. The snowman sat next to another huge brother, this one in an olive green swath of fabric fashioned into a suit. Scattered around the table were four blonds in tight-fitting outfits, homogenized by their enormous bosoms. Never seen anything like it outside a porno magazine. And sitting amid this group of huge pecks and gigantic breasts was Cherri/Carman looking well paid, relaxed, and at home.

I was prepared to let Cherri/Carman go on about her business. No need to slow her roll with embarrassing reminiscences of New Yorican accents and 12-inches. It's just that life intervened. It happened at Carlos & Charlies, a Sunset Boulevard spot that in the mid-eighties was one home base of the NFL aka Niggas Fucking Large. Eddie Murphy, Arsenio Hall, Prince, the Lakers and, when he was in town, Mike Tyson and any New York rapper on tour were leading members of

NFL; representatives of a new, high-rolling, high-profile black pop culture. Rich, promiscuous, and famous, like flies to shit, these brothers drew hustlers of every imaginable type—coke heads, crack dealers, agents, hookers, groupies, macks, managers, and wannabe everythings.

I was at Carlos & Charlies, too, and, just like everybody else, I was basking in the NFL heat. Like all the men, I was waiting for the league leaders to make their selections before making mine. If this sounds like roach behavior, I've already admitted that this was a pretty roach time in my life.

Anyway, I'm standing at the front bar at Carlos & Charlies when this white guy in a gray silk shirt, black jacket, and a gold chain introduces himself. Dr. Bernard Weisman, he said. He'd read about me in the *L.A. Weekly* and said he'd recognized my picture. Said he was a plastic surgeon. "My specialty is breasts," he explained with neither lechery or lust. "In L.A. it's like having your tonsils taken out," he said. "Routine, you know?" I wasn't sure I did.

"But I do more than plastic surgery, Derek. In my business you come in contact with many talented young women."

"I'd imagine you would."

"There's a young woman from Spain who works as my bookkeeper. She has a wonderful singing voice. Quite a striking Spanish woman. She's looking for songs. When I saw you I wondered if you'd be available to work with her."

"Well," I replied, "I'd have to hear her voice and see what direction she wanted to go in."

"Well, Carman's here tonight. Why don't you come downstairs and meet her."

Downstairs, situated in a booth and having a late dinner, were two of the big-breasted blonds from the Forum Club and Cherri/Carman.

She frowned, but I smiled broad as a billboard and said brightly, "It's a pleasure to meet you, Carman. Dr. Weisman told me you have a great voice. I'd love to hear you sometime."

At first she was giving me no rhythm. It was like I was a piece of spinach stuck between two back molars that was irritating the hell out of her. But as I began regaling Dr. Weisman and company with tales of hip-hop touring and the jingle game, she slowly defrosted. I gave my professional history as if the Jack the Rapper drive had never happened.

S
E
D
U
C
E
D

She still didn't love me being at the table, but Cherri/Carman at least knew I wasn't going to poke holes in her facade. Before heading back upstairs I exchanged numbers with Dr. Weisman. Well, I sure wasn't going to call him. Me, I was very happy with my breasts.

The next day Cherri/Carman left a message with my L.A. answering service to call after six which, with some trepidation, I did. "Where are you staying?" she asked harshly when she picked up. I was then staying out at the Oakwood Towers in Burbank, a complex of short-stay furnished apartments that catered to traveling entertainment industry types. An hour later the "C" lady was at my door. I'd anticipated some belligerence. I already knew the lady had a tart tongue. But she didn't seem to have the energy. She flopped down on the apartment's nondescript sofa and wondered if I had a joint. I did have some Jack Daniel's.

"Yeah," she smiled at the memory. "I remember you didn't have much respect for your liver. Give me some. Unlike you I'd like some water in mine."

After I filled the glasses and handed one to her I asked, "Can I call you Cherri tonight?"

"My name's Carman."

"What if I called you Cee? I'm more likely not to slip if I do that." She went along with this compromise and motioned for me to sit next to her. "You know," I said quite matter-of-factly, "the plane from L.A. to N.Y. still runs daily. I can't be the first person you've run into who remembers Cherri, the Puerto Rican club Queen."

"Well," she said between sips, "you'd be surprised how little people out here know about Puerto Ricans. Mostly I just take things one day at a time. Doc W is very smart about a few things and naive about most everything else. The resemblance has been mentioned from other New Yorkers in the biz, but I tell him it's just that. Besides it's not that important to him. He trusts me. In L.A. that's more than enough."

She wanted to know my post-Jack the Rapper life, including the stuff I'd censored out at Carlos & Charlies. I ran down the facts in an incredibly honest manner. Don't know why actually. Something about talking to Cee, someone who'd known me when (and had sexed me then) made me very relaxed. To my dismay she found my relationship with Lydia amusingly typical: "This is a pimp-ho town, Derek. Everybody is offering up that ass to the highest bidder. It's straight up here. You got to be able to negotiate. Cherri didn't have much to offer. A few East Coast Latin records and some ghetto sex appeal. Carman is exotic Euro-trash who's lived in New York and the continent. Either way, I'm still ass-out poor, but I'm a bit less common."

"You really think you're fooling anybody with that accent?"

"In a town where everybody's either acting or an actor, who's gonna bust me?" By now she was finished with my Jack and looking restless. "So what you doing tonight?" With that question Cee began a spicy side chapter to my L.A. story. I became her new bodyguard. Doc W was all right for a white boy, but he was a bit too clumsy to be cool in every set Cee was hanging in. Being a musician and from New York I could be her escort, talk about the biz, and be sensitive to her moods.

If there was a guy she wanted to get with, say the shooting guard for a visiting NBA team, I gave her space to run her game. If some knucklehead was playing her too close, say a full-of-himself television agent from William Morris, Cee could grab my arm and use me to cock block. In exchange, Cee hooked me up with sitcom stars, actress-waitresses, and some of those enormously endowed Raider cheerleaders for more sessions of the empty sex I told you about earlier.

That first night set the tone for our new relationship. I followed her in my car up Crescent Heights to some big house where a twilight pool party was in full swing. Many of the Detroit Pistons, who were playing the Lakers the next night, were engaged in nonrigorous training with beer bottles. Several legendary members of the famed "Bad Boys" were kicked back on deck chairs, talking shop, even as booties and bras passed dangerously close to their noses.

Carman immediately got engaged in a conversation of low murmurings with one of the lesser Jackson brothers, while I found myself discussing mike technique with Rick James' wardrobe lady and later did the wop dance with an extra from "A Different World." We had a lot of fun that night and we would many times during my two-and-a-half-year L.A. sojourn. We never did work together. We rarely saw each other during the day—like vampires we only hunted after sun down. And, no, we never did get busy again. We joked about it and sometimes we touched each other in places buddies never do.

Since I was busy getting paid, I was largely distracted from the fact that I was a long way from being Gamble or Huff. I'm really not sure what Cee was trying to accomplish. Doc W paid for her demos and she knew much of black pop L.A. But the ambition she had on our trip to Atlanta had either disappeared completely or had subsided into a satisfied complacency that L.A. sometimes produced in folks.

A couple of times Edgecombe Lennox came up. Each time I expressed my feeling of abandonment, as if his ignoring us back at Jack the Rapper was some kind of betrayal. "Derek," Cee said one night at somebody's party up on Laurel Canyon, "you got to get off that. We were just something to do until his next big job. I ran into that old nigga at a listening party for the Deele at Bar One and I didn't need to tell the motherfucker my real name 'cause he didn't remember me, anyway."

I laughed, but Cee wasn't amused by this memory. Then with an evil smile she added, "He's back in New York at BCR Records. Head of promotion. But I heard last night that his ass is on the way out. He married some white woman."

"Remember, he had one with him in DC."

"Whatever. Anyway, he was kicking her some business—she a weak ass concert promoter—and somebody up in there reported it to the white boys and now they're using it to throw him out."

"Everybody in this business is corrupt. He shouldn't get fired for that."

"Hey," she countered, "he's black and that means white boys can do whatever. It's their company. That's why I'm Spanish, baby." Whatever had happened to Cee had certainly made her lose all illusions. I watched her move gracefully back into the heart of the party, a place where her past was less than a memory and her present much more important than her future.

"A Jazz Thing"

Just as Lydia had changed my life with her belief in my talent (and my desire for her sex), she'd be the catalyst for another important twist in my life. Her domain now included all "special markets" (aka black folks) advertising at all the parent company's subsidiaries. The account she was proudest of was Rimbert Cognac, which she considered the corporation's classiest product. It was a potent beverage that had long been a favorite of those either aspiring to a veneer of sophistication or who'd already acquired the real thing. Quiet as it's kept, black folks constitute over 50 percent of all cognac purchases. If malt liquor signifies a sense of ghettocentric community for homies, then cognac bestows a warm feeling of arrival on the wantonly upwardly mobile. Pops drank it religiously. Need I say more? Anyway, being involved with Rimbert was for Lydia some prayerful form of validation, a secular benediction of success. For me it meant easy access to a Christmas gift I knew Pops would savor.

Lydia had a marvelous idea for the campaign. We'd get great jazz musicians to appear in Rimbert ads and play a jingle I'd compose. This concept excited and terrified me. Like many folks committed to r&b, I was slightly intimidated by jazz musicians, particularly those who'd paid dues through bebop, the cool school, or might have jammed with 'Trane. Many key figures had passed, but we went after all the surviving greats we could find. Sonny Rollins, the world's greatest living saxophonist, was still around and he was down. So was the rhythm section from Miles' greatest combos, drummer Tony Williams and bassist Ron Carter. The obvious choice for piano would have been that band's pianist Herbie Hancock, but sadly Herbie had made the unfortunate decision to endorse VSOP cognac, Rimbert's chief competitor. Besides, Lydia wanted a woman involved, and Lydia, being a truly progressive lady, wanted it to be an instrumentalist and not "just another singer who was manipulated by some male band leader." I decided to call Uncle Mike in D.C., who knew more about jazz than anyone I knew.

"Madam Walker is who you want," he said over the phone. "She played keys with 'Trane before McCoy Tyner. Did a few years with Rollins back when he had the mohawk haircut. Later she gigged for a while with Fathead Newman. Liked sax men. Didn't give a damn about trumpet players though. Hated Miles."

"I thought all women loved him, Uncle Mike."

He chuckled and said, "Not Madam Walker. He hit on her one night at the Five Spot—she was an elegant brown thing with legs for days and eyes dark as chocolate cake. Anyway, she didn't like his cocky attitude or the way he tried to whisper in her ear, so she sassed him in front of his band and he cursed her. Called her a bitch and so forth. Well, she didn't play that. She went on back behind the bar, got a roll of quarters from the cash register, came back around that bar, tapped him on the shoulder, and smacked him upside his little greasy ass head."

"Making sure not to damage his lips?"

"That's right. That's right. She wasn't mean or nothing. She just wasn't having it. But the bad part was that her right forefinger got squashed between the quarters and Miles' head and it messed up her playing for a long time. She dropped off the scene. Opened a music school in Philly and cuts the odd album every year or so. She was death on a ballad, boy."

Lydia loved the idea. Loved it. She made the contact herself and set up the meeting. We flew in on the red eye, had a morning meeting in New York, and took the Metroliner down to Philly. Lydia suggested that we make love. By now, some two years into our arrangement, I was tiring of her demands for sexercise. Slowly, Lydia was beginning to blend in with all the other L.A. women.

And after all this time, she still never wanted me in bed, never wanted it regularly scheduled, never previously arranged. Lydia's unconventionality had in fact become conventional. Not to mention inconvenient and irritating (though I do mention it here).

Still, there I was, in one of Amtrak's rather roomy phone booths. I shut the door behind us. She slid up on the counter. I helped her lift her dress and slid down her panty hose. Then I was on my knees with Lydia's legs on my shoulders and her head thrown back as the train rolled on underneath us. Right then I decided I couldn't do this anymore. Which is what I said. Probably not great timing.

But Lydia didn't hear me. She was on automatic pilot. It was the setting, the surroundings, the risk that was getting her off anyway. So I just got up and looked her dead in her quivering eyes. "I don't wanna do this, Lydia." Then I turned and left her on the counter. I went back to my seat and pulled out my copy of Ishmael Reed's *Mumbo Jumbo*. When Lydia finally came back to the seat she looked as prim and pulled together as an *Essence* makeover.

"Are you all right?" I said.

"I'm fine," she said, while looking straight ahead. "You're crazy, but I'm fine."

I tried to explain my position. Lydia just raised her hand, signaling me to stop. "There's nothing more to say. You said it and you live with it. And," she spoke with great finality, "you'll regret it." We continued on to Philly in silence.

"Embraceable You"

I tried to take my eyes off of Madam Walker's legs, but I couldn't. We were sitting in her living room—Lydia and I on her soft embroidered sofa and Madam on her piano bench facing us. She lived in Gladwynne, a prosperous Philly suburb where Teddy Pendergrass and Kenny Gamble, among others, resided. But that wasn't important. Her legs were.

I knew she was fifty-plus years old, but her legs, supported by black suede high heels, covered by black pantyhose, and left uncovered by a short, classy black dress, would certainly shame a younger woman. Her face wasn't bad, either. She was light brown with a sophisticated, knowing smile and salt-and-pepper hair that reminded me of Bill Cosby's wife Camille. The only thing unadorned on her body were her hands. They were unusually large for a woman. No nail polish and the nails themselves were cut short. I tried to keep my focus on them, instead of her legs.

"So," she said after our introductory small talk, "do you have a tape of the music?" Her voice was hoarse and smokey with a real kick to it, like sipping JD on a late January night. Reluctantly I handed her a cassette which she popped into an antique stereo system. I'd cut three sixty-second versions of the spot—each had the same melody but differed in how the piano and saxophones were arranged. "Very cute," she observed afterwards. My fear had been that she'd laugh at it, so even that mild approval was fine by me.

Madam Walker proposed cutting the spot at Sigma Sound, the legendary Philadelphia recording studio. "The place could use the business," she said. "Over the years, Philly lost its jazz standing and then its r&b standing, too. Anything you could bring to the city would be appreciated." Lydia was polite but noncommittal. For her it was an unnecessary hassle and, potentially, more expensive since she'd have to put the other musicians up in a Philly hotel. So many of the players we wanted either lived in New York or had residences there.

However, to me this suggestion bordered on genius. Sigma Sound was where "TSOP" (the Sound of Philadelphia) was created: the Spinners, O'Jays, MFSB, Teddy Pendergrass, the Stylistics, the Delfonics: all of the soul music of my adolescence was made in that building. David Bowie even cut "Fame" there. I argued passionately for Sigma Sound, but, after turning her down on Amtrak, Lydia didn't seem at all enthusiastic about accommodating my desires.

Ultimately, practicality won out. We called the studio and got its rates. Since it was eager to get a chance at a national spot, we even got a nice discount.

A couple of days later I was in the control room of Sigma, sitting at the same board Kenny Gamble, Thom Bell, Linda Creed, and all the living legends of Philly soul had made magic behind. In the studio proper, Madam Walker and a collection of the world's finest living jazzmen sat reminiscing. A photographer had placed lights around the room and was furiously snapping photos of the gathered immortals. My lead sheets lay atop the Steinway. The musicians had glanced at it, displayed some mild interest, and then fell deep into conversation.

It was Madam Walker who turned the focus to my music. "Soon as we finish here, you're all invited to my home for dinner. My cook can burn, so let's not waste any time." With those words the session kicked in and revelation ensued. The pitiful sounds of my jingle were muffled by the majesty of their blues. I'd composed sixty seconds of faux bebop, which the fingers of Madam Walker and company transformed into a swinging meditation. Nothing I'd composed, with the exception of Vernon Jackson's voice, had been quite so elevated in interpretation. I felt ridiculous employing these geniuses to peddle cognac. They didn't seem to mind, though. For them, it was great money for a few hours of work. For me, it was watching my limited skills being exposed by watching how, quite off-handedly, they made this meager melody seem vibrant, even profound.

Later at Madam Walker's home I drank Rimbert with the jazzmen and tried to feel like I was a peer. They were indulging me until I made a rather glib comment about how hip hop and bebop were "so connected." This was the wrong audience for that kind of dialogue. Suddenly I was challenged to prove my statement musically when, realistically, what I really had done was make a sociological connection between forties jazz rebels and eighties rap upstarts. While there definitely were parallels in slant, style, and attitude, these were musicians and that was their frame of reference. Moreover, they really were not interested in hearing this from some young, well-paid jingle writer. It was like I'd passed wind at a perfume counter. Right then, in the middle of that bebop–hip hop debate, I could feel the jazzmen revoking my peer card.

Lydia, who'd continued to be professionally supportive but personally distant, sat next to the son of one of the jazzmen. He was a Wynton Marsalis clone in demeanor and dress who worked as road manager for his father. His name was Donald, but that's all I ever got out of him. I could tell he thought of me as some kind of r&b/hip hop roach, and I was beginning to wonder if he wasn't right. Lydia and Donald both seemed amused by my excommunication from the good graces of the jazzmen, so there was no use walking over there. I left them to their smoothed-out conversation and corralled the Jack Daniel's bottle from Madam Walker's bar before heading for the door.

Back at the Philly Hilton I helped myself to the JD before climbing into bed. The next morning, there was an envelope for me at the front desk. It was from Lydia. It was short and sour, saying something about unsatisfactory performance which, from her point of view, was quite true. I was dismissed.

I had a ticket back to L.A. in my jacket pocket, which I took with me to the steam room in the hotel's health club. I watched it slowly disintegrate in the heavy wetness. It was a long, slow process but I had nowhere to be so I took my time. Afterwards, I packed up and went to check out.

Downstairs, a very respectful doorman was hailing me a cab when a dark blue BMW pulled up and Lydia got out of the passenger side, looking as she always did after she'd had an unexpected nice time. Inside the car was one of the jazzmen who glanced at me and, like a shark, showed his teeth before driving off.

"Hello," she said.

"Good bye," I said.

"Nothing personal, Derek," she said.

"I can't touch that," I said with the small ounce of flippancy at my command. But I was too beat down and disappointed for anything more. She walked by me, the taxi came, and I directed it to Thirtieth Street station where, on the train to New York, I hoped to pick up the melody to a song I never seemed able to finish.

brooklyn—1987, 1988

"A Change of Mind"

Entertainers are the articulators of our sexual fantasies. In public, they repeat our closed door dreams to us. All our horny, nasty, embarrassing, and often most romantic selves are spoken for by people with microphones on large stages and in hidden little rooms around the world. And for a time I was one of them. No longer a songwriter. No longer a musician for hire or hip-hop road manager or jingle scribe supreme, but an entertainer who helped America pass time more pleasantly. During the spring and summer of 1988 there was no African-American artist bigger than me, Derek Harper or, as I was known to millions of radio listeners, D. Harper.

It all began on September 1, 1987, my thirtieth birthday, which I celebrated with the purchase of a pair of Gucci Loafers. They were brown suede with that classic gold bit across the top. My hands caressed the suede as I held them to my nose, savoring their classy aroma. I rarely purchased any designer gear and any time I did, it freaked me out. It was a sign of success and, I worried, self-satisfaction. I'd purchased the Loafers two weeks before but hadn't had the nerve to wear them until my thirtieth birthday, thinking it was the perfect symbol for crossing that numerical barrier into deep adulthood.

It was a pretty late summer day. A really nice, high blue sky. But most of my energy was focused on navigating Manhattan's treacherous streets. I avoided piss rivers from homeless men. I stepped around two half-empty McDonald's ketchup packages. I stepped over countless candy wrappers, discarded gum, and broken bottles that dotted the top layers of so much New York pavement. None of it was going to soil my Guccis, at least not on day one. They felt as snug as my Air Jordan's and, I may be blaspheming here, they were actually more comfortable and only slightly more expensive.

Still, because the soles were still relatively unscuffed, I should have been a little more careful crossing the intersection of Union Square West and Sixteenth Street. But my eyes looked across to the Coffee Shop, a trendy bistro popular because of its Brazilian menu and fly model-waitresses. Michelle, a five-foot-ten honey brown beauty just off the plane from Denver, was the hostess of the Coffee Shop's outdoor sidewalk section and I, quite smitten with her wide, toothy smile and lanky legs, spotted her, menu in one hand, cranberry juice in the other, standing by the door. She was a vision of cocoa-brown loveliness and I had on my suede Guccis. What could be better than that?

Then my left foot hit the edge of the curb and didn't land squarely. Instead, my unscuffed sole slid, throwing my balance off and my body forward. My right knee buckled, my head pointed down, and my body followed suit. My hands and arms hit the ground first, blunting much of the impact. Still I landed in the middle of a New York street at lunch time, in the sight line of an amazon sister from the West. This would merely have been embarrassing if it was the extent of my misfortune. But when I looked up and saw a yellow taxi barreling toward me under the direction of a Nigerian who, just two days before had been selling fake Rolexes on Seventh Avenue, well I knew I had a problem.

I can report my life didn't pass before me. It was just that everything seemed to be happening in slow motion. The fall. The taxi. The surprised faces of passersby. It all happened in seconds, but it felt like an hour. The Nigerian pulled up two feet short of my face, so close that I could smell rubber as he screeched the tires against Sixteenth Street. As I staggered to my feet, the taxi driver cursed me and Michelle ran to see if I was all right. At first all I could think of was how dirty the sides of my Guccis were and how typical it was that my beautiful new shoes were as soiled as the city's streets. I guess I was a little delirious.

Then it hit me how close I'd come to being flat as day-old beer. If I'd been killed, my obituary would have been sad: "Thirty-year-old wannabe r&b tunesmith. A few song placements on commercially released albums. Wrote his most popular song, a gospel composition, "Traveling the Highway to Heaven," when he was a teen and coasted thereafter. Took odd jobs as a caddie and caretaker for touring r&b and rap performers. Wrote obnoxious jingles for beer and burger makes. Got paid. String of dead-end relationships, including one with a murdered singer. Drank too much Jack Daniel's. His liver will not be donated to science."

If those thoughts weren't sobering enough, then there was the prospect of a birthday dinner Doris was having for me later. She'd mostly invited people in the business since, at this point, those were all she knew. It was to be as much a promotional party as a birthday celebration and, at this moment, that didn't seem to be what I needed. When I'd left Gibbs' tour in L.A., I appeared to be on the verge of getting my creative life together. Instead I met Lydia and took a rather lucrative detour. Now I had my rap-tour money and my jingle money. I was, by single black male standards, paid. But, as my pops would say, I hadn't put down any roots. I owned nothing significant—I was renting back at the Chatworth, had a car out in Cali and, if *Billboard* was right, had a collection of vinyl that was about to be made obsolete by something called compact disc.

More important, I hadn't really done anything. I had a wealth of experience, but I hadn't turned it into anything powerful, passionate, or enduring. I liked what I'd been writing, but to date the outside world hadn't embraced my best work and I hadn't, to my mind, demanded enough of myself. So I had no home, no woman, and shaky self-confidence. I did have the cash, but what could I buy that would address my dissatisfaction?

Michelle came over to my table and gave me a damp cloth to wipe off my Guccis. Trying not to stare at her legs I asked her something stupid like, "Have you done anything exciting lately?" She told me about this great house party she'd gone to out in an area of Brooklyn called Fort Greene. It was at this beautiful brownstone near a park, that same park that *She's Gotta Have It* had been shot in. Everybody was there, she said. Branford and Wynton Marsalis. The actor Larry Fishburne. Even Spike himself.

Ever since that movie had come out last summer, people had been buzzing about Fort Greene. That it was some kind of black artist

Mecca, full of young black folks starting to bust out. Outside of visiting my cousins in Brownsville, I'd never spent any time in Brooklyn. Queens and then Manhattan had been my New York. But maybe, at the scary dawn of my thirtieth year, it was time to expand my horizons.

"Nola's Theme"

I'd forgotten that the D train went over the Manhattan Bridge, so when it emerged out of Chinatown into the sky I smiled, an action usually frowned upon on New York City subways. From my windowseat I spied lower Manhattan—the South Street Seaport jutting out into the East River, Wall Street skyscrapers reflecting the fading afternoon sun, the aging, majestic Brooklyn Bridge, and visible just between the bridge's girders, the Statue of Liberty in the harbor.

After descending past cluttered old industrial buildings and the Brooklyn Bridge's entry ramp, the D went underground, and I looked at the piece of paper in my hand. DeKalb Avenue next stop. Upstairs, on the corner of DeKalb and the Flatbush Avenue Extension, I scanned the scene of downtown Brooklyn for my landmark, Junior's restaurant. I walked over to the deli and then made a right across Flatbush, past Long Island University, and directly, so the paper tells me, to Fort Greene.

First there wasn't much to look at. Some converted factory buildings. An ancient garage. A bunch of tenements with storefronts. At the corner of DeKalb and Fort Greene Place, things picked up. Across DeKalb was a converted firehouse that I'd read was home base to Spike Lee's 40 Acres & a Mule Productions. On my side of the street the sprawling brick building that housed Brooklyn Hospital was replaced by a long, hilly expanse of nature known variously as Fort Greene or Washington Park, depending on who you asked or which sign you read. The park was boarded by a high cobblestone brick wall with large, leafy oak trees providing shade as I strolled down DeKalb. Across the street there was Brooklyn Tech, one of New York's premiere egg-head high schools, along with a series of beautiful brownstone-filled streets.

At the corner of the park I made a left and crossed the street. I walked past grand-looking four-story buildings made of bronze, brown, and gray brick. Peeking in the windows I spied chandeliers dangling from high, grandiose ceilings and half-painted rooms in the process of elegant transformation. At Willoughby Avenue, a street that disappeared into the park, I turned right and began checking numbers. On the far corner was a four-story red stone building with black bars on all the lower windows. I walked up its stoop and checked the address—number 19, my destination.

The owner, Morris Bradshaw, greeted me at the door. He wore a dark gray charcoal suit and brown business shoes. His deeply furrowed brow and receding hair line made him look like a man in need of a massage. The previous tenants had just moved out, so the place was empty, which made it seem immense. The living room ceiling was twenty feet high and the room was three times as long as my place at the Chatworth. It had two marble fireplaces—one in the front, one in the back. Wood floors. Kitchen with exposed brick. The bedroom was downstairs. It had windows shrouded by bushes and a bathroom bigger than my Chatworth bedroom that included a washer and dryer (lovely!). A backroom with more exposed brick and yet another fireplace opened up onto an unkempt backyard. There was also a very nasty basement full of mildewed, rotting furniture, and the bracing aroma of mice feces. All in all, it was more raw space than my parents' house in Queens and that didn't count the upstairs duplex I'd look at next.

It was a lot of house, but my accountant said I needed an investment and my soul definitely needed a home.

In the living room we talked price ($275,000 with $40,000 down) and life. Morris had planned diligently for marriage. He'd bought property cheaply using his contacts as a member of the city bureaucracy and, most important, he'd found a smart suburban girl with a Columbia J school degree to marry. That was his one miscalculation.

"You're in the music business, so you must have heard of Dwayne Robinson."

"Sure," I replied, "he writes for *Billboard*. He's the black music man."

"She left me for him."

"Oh, that's rough, man."

"I know that's true."

"But," I added, "if you still want her back, it could happen."

"Why do you say that?"

"He's a music guy. And music guys are as flaky as they come. He's got her now, but he may not have her always. Believe me, I know." I don't know why I went into that speech. I mean, I'd just met the guy. He just looked hurt in a way that men rarely admit to. Maybe he was honest because he didn't know me. Besides, Dwayne Robinson hadn't done a thing for me. In the back of my mind, maybe, I thought Morris would cut his price. Well, that didn't happen, but Morris was touched by my concern and the slim branch of hope I'd offered his way. If nothing else, I'd not only bought a house, I'd made a friend.

"Music of My Mind"

I saw the house in the first week of September. The closing was in October. By the second week of November I was almost all moved in. I did Thanksgiving with Moms, Pops, and Anna in Queens. A melancholy affair. Much talk of crack and Little Walt and the shame of all the homeless people on Jamaica Avenue. Even Pops had to admit this Reagan thing, while good for his taxes, hadn't done black folks any justice. Still, he held out hope for Bush, while somehow hoping David Dinkins would run for mayor. I didn't tease Pops about that contradiction, though he deserved some harassment for it.

I guess my mind was elsewhere. The Saturday after Thanksgiving, a truck full of recording equipment rolled up to 19 Willoughby and, after much hauling, grunting, and consultation with an engineer pal, a candy store of pop music delights was stacked in the backroom. I had a CAD board with Yamaha NS-10 monitors, a Maxcon mixing system, and an old Mini-Moog synth that gave stuff that early seventies flavor. I won't bother you with more tech talk other than to say I spent my money well.

It snowed early that year. Sometime in early December. It piled up outside my windows. It iced up my stoop. I didn't care. I was wrapped inside a womb of my own making, one my moms, with all her love, couldn't have created for me. I conceived it by pulling together wires, reading manuals, scribbling in notebooks, obsessing over dreams, and making music at a furious rate. And I was singing. I mean, I'd been singing on demos for years—putting down guide vocals for others to mimic. But in my womb I put a degree of seriousness into it that I'd been afraid to before. With all my gadgets, I felt I could do anything.

The collected technology liberated me from dependence on others, which was great, but it also isolated me. No longer did I need any interaction with other musicians to make my music full. I could be Dillon, my high school tormentor, and create my own pumpin' bass lines. I could be Timmons, my high school comrade and session contractor, and approximate his precise runs. Most certainly I could be a drummer, using the Syndrum, the Linn drum, and a beat box much like the one employed by hip-hop deejays. Like those geniuses Stevie Wonder and Prince, I was now a one-man band.

That winter I rarely went out. When I was hungry I'd order take out from the local Italian restaurant, Cino's, or grab a home-cooked meal from the small black-owned spot, Christina's, or order cold cuts from Perry's grocery store. When I sought human interaction, I'd go over to Junior's for cheesecake or Two Steps Down, a black bar-restaurant, to gaze at people and eavesdrop, listening for any slang I might have missed. Most days I'd roll out of bed between 11 or 2 P.M., eat leftovers, and then climb back into my womb, playing with knobs, plugging in wires, and making up melodies as time first stopped and then evaporated around me.

Creating had always made me horny, but I didn't do much about it that winter. After all, I'd had my share of empty sex. I suspected one reason I had been relatively unfulfilled artistically was that my libido had been too wild, too frivolous, too flighty. Perhaps that kind of energy worked for other musicians, but it hadn't enhanced my music, so it was time, as Smokey had written, to try something new.

I wasn't celibate, but I was pretty damn close. The strange time was that whenever I did masturbate, which wasn't that often, I found myself fixating on Candi. I'd try other faces on my mental T.V. screen. I'd pick up the latest *Players* or ogle this week's *Jet* centerfold, but Candi haunted my erections like a ghost. I knew she was married and lived in DC. Unobtainable. Yet, of all the women I've known, it was Candi, only Candi, I was thinking of the night I wrote a song called "Black Sex."

The song's verses were sung-talked. It wasn't quite hip hop, but it wasn't open-throated r&b, either. In some ways, my vocal approach on the verses was influenced by Slick Rick, a Bronx rapper with a faux British accent and quite melodious voice. The keyboard-laden track was, if not a loyal son, at least a close cousin of Marvin Gaye's "Sexual Healing" and other records I thought were influenced by it (e.g., Freddie Jackson's "Rock With Me Tonight," Eugene Wilde's "Gotta Get You Home With Me Tonight").

The choruses were a blend of "Black Sex" chanted in my technology-manufactured bass voice, and pleading interjections by way of Michael Jackson's "woo!" on "Don't Stop Until You Get Enough" except softer, like a caress. There was one sustained note I went for near the end that, with a lot of vibrato added, sold the song's passion. I attempted to model the intensity of Vernon Jackson, hoping to manufacture with my toys what God had given him. These were the words:

"Black Sex"
Your love is sweet
Like the day we met.
Your love is bitter
Like the day you left.
And I will always, always, taste you
In my heart.
It's always black sex
(with you)
It's always black sex.

Your body is dark
Like the night we touched.
Your body is rough
Like the times we fought.
But I can always, always, feel you
In my hands.
It's always black sex
(with you)
It's always black sex.

Bridge:

Sex (Black Sex)
Yeah, baby, it's always gonna be
Black Sex
(repeat once).

Your soul is warm
Like your pumping heart.
Your soul is cold
Like the pain I felt.
Still I will always, always, know you.
In my mind
It's always black sex
(with you)
It's always black sex.

Though I'd made a great track, it still needed a little magic. I reached out to Timmons to double a guitar riff I'd concocted on synthesizer. I wanted something more enchanting, like the guitars on "Billie Jean." The brother was so busy he couldn't come over until on one frigid midnight in January, and that's only because I'd promised him an entire Junior's cheesecake in lieu of cash. Timmons had put on a lot of weight in the last few years. But the same hands that grasped slices of Junior's best also laid down a slinky, smooth doodle of a guitar that contrasted nicely with the bass line.

"This is nice, Derek," he said when he was finished. "Sounds like you're growing up."

"I just turned thirty."

"So did I. But you know what? I know fifty-year-old kids in this game, man. I ran into that guy who always used to be at Possible 20."

"Edgecombe Lennox?"

"Yeah, that's him. Saw him at a listening party for Luther's last album. Still talking like he was all in the mix when everybody knows he just got thrown out at BCR."

"Damn," I said back. "I haven't spoken to him in years. Think he still hangs out at Possible 20?"

Timmons sucked his teeth. "Don't know and don't care really. Did you hear who got his job? Otis Clyburn."

S
E
D
U
C
E
D

291

"Who?" I said stupidly.

"You remember Ruthie Lee, don't you, chief? Well, the old man got remarried. Took some time off to get himself together. When Lennox was big up at BCR he put Otis down, but when the shit hit the fan, Otis didn't miss a beat."

"He's not a bad guy," I said of Otis, all the while hoping I didn't ever have to do business with him. "Wonder how I could get in touch with Edge?"

Timmons sucked his teeth again dismissively and changed the subject. "So what you gonna do with this track? I think it's a hit and I've played on a lot of them."

To be quite honest, I didn't have an answer. After buying the house and stocking up with equipment, I'd avoided the "b" in r&b—that is the business in the rhythm. Bringing Timmons into my home I'd opened myself to all the things I'd avoided all that creative winter—industry gossip, corporate strategy, and bitter memories.

On a cold February evening Spike Lee's *School Daze* premiered at the Criterion on Broadway. I'd run into a staff member of his 40 Acres & a Mule team at Cino's, and she put me down for two tickets. Danifa went with me in hopes of smoozing Spike into including some of her writers on his next soundtrack. After the movie we swung down to the Roxy rollerrink for the party. The Roxy had been one of the first lower Manhattan venues to showcase rap music, a place where break dancers in particular came to the media's attention. So it was quite appropriate I ran into Attak there with a few homeboys I didn't recognize. He embraced me like I'd just come back from upstate. We sat up in the upstairs VIP section and, over multiple champagne bottles, discussed the state of hip hop. I praised him over the platinum success of the last Brothers Black album, but he was surprisingly modest. "Yeah, yeah, yeah," he said dismissively, "but yo, did you hear 'Bring the Noise'? Did you hear 'My Philosophy'? And 'Raw' by that nigga Kane? New jacks are blowin' up all around me, Derek. New York is rough right about now."

"But you are still ahead of the game."

"I have been," he agreed, "but the game is changing. I can feel it. Look at what happened to Gibbs."

"Huh," I replied stupidly. "I been out the mix this winter. What's up?"

"Russell Simmons bought him out last week, Paid him off. GAP doesn't exist anymore. Rush owns it all."

"Well, where's Gibbs?"

Attak and his crew started laughing. "That nigga flew off to Tahiti or some shit like that after that skinny Beth Ann."

"Get the hell out of here!"

"Man, that nigga is so open, it's ridiculous."

Then Attak looked over my shoulder, waved his hand, and shouted, "Yo, my man, what goes on?" I turned and there was Edgecombe Lennox in a blue double-breasted suit, white shirt with no tie, and a matching blue Kangol. He looked less robust than when I'd last seen him and much thinner in the face. His mouth smiled, but his eyes displayed more curiosity than delight.

"Long time, no see, youngblood." Edge held out his hand—he was a lefty—and I noticed a wedding ring.

"You got married? Congratulations."

"A horse," Edge replied, "can only run the track for so long before you got to shut the stable door behind him."

We all laughed at that, though it was hard to tell whether Edge meant it as a joke or not. Still, there was something rascally about him that responded to all these young brothers. Attak reached into his pocket, pulled out a cassette, and handed it to Edge. "That's the remix, Edge," Attak explained, "I wanna get it in the street before the bootleggers get it."

"What," I wondered, "you guys in business?"

"Oh, yes." It was Edge. "Got an independent label. Edgey records. Run it out of my house in Englewood and an office on Broadway."

"Yeah, Edge is doing work for me," Attak said. "I have this group, Masters of Liberation, that Edge put in the street for me. All ready sold forty thousand 12-inches."

Edge handed me his card and, for a moment, I was a kid again outside Mr. Walt's and Edge was driving a Caddy that matched his clothes. "So," he said, "I hear you been writing jingles. That's some real good money."

"That's true, but I've been focusing on real songwriting again. That's all I'm doing right now."

"Well," Edge said with undue deliberation, "that's what you wanted to do, right?"

Edge's tone irked me. It hit me that maybe he'd never really taken me seriously. Maybe it was just as simple as that. It was childish of me, but the idea of Edge and Attak being in business together and their easy camaraderie made me jealous. Suddenly I was squeezing the card so hard the words could have been imprinted on my finger tips.

"Respect"

People think the major constant in an artist's life is creativity. But to me the one inescapable fact of the artist's life is judgment. At some point you must submit your endeavors to someone for approval, support, and, often quite painfully, criticism. It comes from the audience. It comes from the critics. But first, and perhaps most crucially, it comes from the middlemen, the people who take an artist's private fantasies, the fruit of their creative womb, and decide whether it gets exposed or not. Whether they make their judgments based on personal taste, market research, or by flipping cards, it doesn't really matter. They have the power. Without them the artist is just another person whose mother thinks they are special.

On this late winter day, in a converted loft where gold records vie with steam pipes, Edgecombe Lennox sits with his arms folded and eyes closed listening to music made in the backroom with snow piled against my door. I find myself pining away for something I've wanted since I was thirteen—Edge's approval.

He's been respectful—nodding his head to the beat, smiling on occasion—but he seems too professional, too mannered to soothe my anxiety. Then the last song on my tape comes on and the mood in the room alters. I can feel the molecules shifting around me. The receptionist, a sister who could have been the L.L.'s "'Round the Way Girl," turned her head and yelled, "Oh, that's stoopid!" which was the then current hip-hop designation for excellence, having replaced "da joint" and "fresh" while I was working inside 19 Willoughby.

Edge listened to it all the way through, rewound it, and played it again. A bike messenger came in looking like Mars Blackmon's body double and started body popping to the track like he was a member of the Dynamic Breakers. I know it sounds like a scene from "Beat Street," but that's how it went down. I started laughing 'cause this was real funny to me. Edge was serious as a heart attack. He leaned over the desk, his lips straight as a 12-inch single and his eyes as black as vinyl.

"What are you doing with this?" Edge asked.

I replied, "What do you have in mind?"

At one point, the Red Parrot, a long, faux posh club with a real red parrot housed in a glided cage, was as synonymous with New York young black culture as Technics turntables. Located on Fifty-seventh Street between Tenth and Eleventh avenues, it was both a showcase for young rap and dance performers, an essential mating ground for the twenty-five and under black and Latino party people, and a haven for drug traffickers, both those small fry peddling nickel bags and new jacks making millionaires by crack cocaine. Shootings, both in and outside the club, would eventually consign it to memory. But in 1988 the Red Parrot was still the place to be on a Manhattan Saturday night.

It felt a little strange to be rolling in the Red Parrot with a guy who'd all ready seen the dark side of forty. Still, Edge was never out of place anywhere black folks and music converged. He was truly a nocturnal man. To him the unlaced sneakers, gaggles of gold chains, and dangling ear rings of those in attendance didn't faze him. Just new beats to an old song.

Near the Red Parrot's back bar were some sofas and on one of these sofas sat three burly young black men drinking Möet from the bottle. Two of them were hard-eyed and barrel-chested, and reminded me of my old comrade Dirt Bike. The man in the middle had a face I recalled from rap shows, *Right On!* magazine, and the cover of Joint-ski's debut album. His name was Rahiem and he'd been Joint-ski's deejay back when the rapper had cut the classics "Break It Down" and "Rap Is My Religion." Then, as I vaguely recalled, he'd been implicated in some shooting at the Dance Inferno, ended up upstate for several years and, as far as I knew, hadn't gotten back in the game. I was mistaken.

"As you know," he began, "I was deeply involved with this music before it blew up."

"Yeah, man," I responded with a fan's enthusiasm, "I saw you guys rock the Apollo one night before an Ohio Players' concert."

He smiled. He was much heavier than I remembered. His face was fleshy and furrowed in a way a man thirty or so shouldn't be. Rahiem looked like a man who's neck was slowly disappearing under the weight of his head. "Yeah," he responded, "back in the day Joint-ski and me opened a lot of doors for these young boys out here. Then I had to step back for a while." That last sentence hung there for a minute and then he continued. "Now I'm moving back into the music business. I'm not deejaying anymore, but I'm supporting my man Edge in building his label. I know you go back with him, so you know how dope he is."

"Derek"—it was Edge again—"we want to put out 'Black Sex' on my label independently."

"It's dope, my man," Rahiem chimed in. "You did work."

"Derek," Edge interjected. "I can work that record. I can build it down South, get support out of the Northeast, and spread that bad boy until it's number one r&b in *Billboard*."

I wondered, "Who's gonna sing it?" which made Rahiem chuckle. When he asked, "That's your voice, right?" I confirmed that fact.

Then Edge took the floor again. "Well, we want you to keep on singing it. That record feels right. You go in, wipe the vocals, and put somebody else on it and I guarantee you the magic will be squeezed out. At BCR all we did was squeeze the magic out of records. All the imperfections, all the dirt—this feels good. Wherever you made that record, it gave it something special. I wanna go with it, as raw as it is."

Rahiem reached over and touched my leg. It was a firm yet comforting touch. "Yo, my brother," he said, "don't be scared to win."

"I'm not scared."

"Okay," he said smoothly, "I hear you. But whatever your words say, your face is telling me this idea fucks with you. Listen. Being scared is part of life. When I first went in the joint, I was scared. When I first got on stage, I was scared. But I'm still here. I'm doing all right. What's that thing they say? 'Whatever don't kill you makes you strong.' Well, I'm real strong right now. Put this out with us, with your voice on it, hit, miss, whatever, and I promise you two things—you'll make a little cash and you'll be a better man afterwards. Believe that."

It is the sense of things hidden that gives some events such resonance. The subtext of the Red Parrot meeting was that Rahiem was now a drug king pin and was laundering his money through Edge's little label. Moreover, because they were starting out, they'd give me a chance that no major label would, and they'd drop a lot of money to run "Black Sex" up the chart. And, on the most fulfilling level for my ego, they believed in the record.

"Tell Me Something Good"

"Right now the record business is still a hustler's game. You got some money. You got a kid who can rhyme or a really hot dance record and you're in business. You press up a few records. Work the clubs, the black retailers, and then a few record programmers who owe you a favor, and good things can happen."

Edge paused to drain his glass of Jack Daniel's. "But it used to be that anybody could compete at the highest level. You could go from your basement to top ten. That's why there were so many independent labels. That's why I did business with so many people. Well, it's not like that anymore. Hasn't really been like that since the seventies. I remember when Warner Bros. rented out the Beacon Theater for about three days to show off their new black music roster. Called it "California Soul." Think it was in seventy-six. George Benson, Ashford & Simpson, Al Jarreau, Graham Central Station, the Impressions, First Choice, Curtis Mayfield—every last one of them had been on an indie label. CBS. MCA. BCR. Polydor. They all made the same move."

Edge poured himself another hit and poured some in my glass, too. "The more serious big houses took the money black music could make, the more space they took up in the marketplace. The space available for labels like mine gets smaller every day. Pretty soon there won't be but enough room for you to slide your pinky through. I got fucked over at BCR, so before the door closes I just want to shove one more gold record through the damn crack."

We were back at Possible 20. Back at the table in the back. Back drinking JD. But I wasn't a mere student anymore. Which is why I asked, "If my record is good, wouldn't it make more sense for me to sell it to Freddie Jackson or Luther Vandross or somebody like that. That's guaranteed money."

"Derek," he replied smugly, "you act like we just met. I remember you and that girl singing them damn songs on the way to Georgia. The way you watched people when they performed. You want it. The money, the bitches—"

"Yo, man," I interrupted, "I've done all right in both areas. I'm not a kid anymore."

"—And the fame. You want your name written up in all the history books. I don't know why. It's all bullshit. But, hey, let a man's desires rule his motherfucking heart and he's a happy man. Come on, Derek, let me make you happy."

Sunday afternoon. Pops has the Mets versus the Dodgers on in the living room, but Moms has the stereo on playing Vernon Jackson's gospel album, the one that has "The One Who Sees" as the third cut on side two. Moms is beaming. The presence of that song on Vernon's record is, she hopes, a harbinger of a future where I use my gifts in praise of He who sees. As time passes, Moms is getting increasingly devout, which I take as a subconscious commentary on her life, though she seems quite content today.

Pops, sad to say, looks awful, just awful. When I asked him, "So how's business?" he said "Fine" with such gravity it sounded as if he were going bankrupt. I looked over at Moms and she acted like Pops was fine. She went into a story about how there'd been a fire over at First Baptist of St. Albans, Vernon's home church, and that there was talk of him coming up to do a benefit.

I told them about Edge's offer and anxiously awaited their responses. Moms was vaguely disappointed. "I've always thought you had a sweet voice, baby," she said with the diplomacy of a U.N. delegate, "but is getting on stage really want you want to do?" Yes and no, I replied, which didn't satisfy her. Nor did the fact I hadn't brought a tape of the song with me. "Is this one of them nasty songs they make now?"

I tried to avoid eye contact. "Moms, it's like a Marvin Gaye song."

"A Marvin Gaye song?" She wasn't gonna fall for that dodge. "Hmmm, is it more like 'Pride & Joy' or 'Let's Get It On'?"

"I don't know what you mean." My moms rarely got angry at me. After all I was her only child. Her baby boy and all. But she was steamed now. "Derek, don't play with me! You know what I was asking."

"Sorry, Moms."

"What's the name of this song, Derek Harper?" This was no time to be cute or even a bit disrespectful. When I told her it was called "Black Sex," she shook her head and made some wordless but deeply disapproving sounds.

Then, from the living room, Pops spoke. "How's that house working out?"

Thankful for the change of subject, I told him everything was good and that I even had tenants upstairs, which pleased him. But Moms wasn't through.

"Did you hear what your son's doing? 'Black Sex'! With all the stuff going on out here, he's putting his name next to something called 'Black Sex.'"

Pops' reply was patient, with just a hint of irritation. "Derek's a man now. He's got bills to pay. Once a man starts investing in property, he's got to keep some income coming in. And, you know I know about this."

"Is something wrong, Pops?" I asked. "Wrong at the business?"

Pops sighed, which I don't remember ever seeing him do before, and Moms, who had a legitimate reason for being mad at me, pulled back. It was as if some shadow had suddenly entered the room, cloaking everything in pain. "Business is great. In dollars and cents terms, this will probably be the biggest year I've ever had." He sighed again. "It's just that I used to deal with old folks, people with diseases and unfortunate car and household accidents. It was all sad, you know, but I dealt with it. That's what I do. But now it's just a stream of kids."

"Overdoses are bad," I agreed.

"I wish it was just that. Kids are shooting each other all over Queens. Never seen anything like it. They stand on corners and pop each other like clay pigeons."

"How," my moms asked, "can you be so cold?"

But Pops continued, as if she hadn't spoken. "I saw this little boy the other day. You wouldn't know him, Derek. You'd been long gone from here when he was born. But I'd see him around with his little basketball. Had a head shaped like yours. Round, it was. Kind of sloped in the front."

"Just like yours," I said.

"I guess. Every now and then I'd grab his head and rub it."

"You never did that to me." I don't know why I went there, but it just popped out.

"What?" he replied. "Sure I did. Sure I did, Derek." I let that go. He was opening up a bit and I needed to let him. "Anyway, he was walking past Mr. Walt's, going to get a hair cut. Went right past that pay phone. Some fool dealer was talking on it. All we know for sure is that somebody shot at the dealer and blew a big old hole in that little boy's head."

Moms got up and went into the kitchen. "I did my best to make that boy's head slope again. It was a real challenge because the parents wanted an open casket service. Now I've done a lot of work, seen a lot of evil things done to and by people. But, son, this is the first time I've ever cried while I worked."

My moms was sobbing from inside the kitchen. Pops stood up and looked in that direction as he spoke to me. "So if you wanna put that record out, go on. You got bills to pay. Go pay them." He walked into the kitchen and I heard my moms' sobs subside. I sat down in my pops' chair and leaned back. The Mets and the Dodgers were still playing and damned if "The One Who Sees" wasn't coming from the stereo.

B. Smith's, a nouvelle cuisine spot on Eighth Avenue near the theater district named after a retired black model, was the site of my dinner with the D's—Danifa and Doris. Danifa arrived on time, which meant she was sitting at B. Smith's long metallic bar when I got there fifteen minutes later. She seemed a touch tense but still self-possessed as always. "I'm leaving Warner-Chappel," she told me after we'd been seated. "I'm starting a company, along with a couple of partners, that'll focus on developing young songwriters."

"What does that mean for me? Can I leave with you?"

"You sure you want to? I know you loved being associated with Warner-Chappel. I remember how excited you were when I signed you."

"I needed that then, Danifa. I needed that kind of acceptance. Now, well, I feel more confident. And you believed in me as a talent. I won't forget that. One question, though—is Mayo one of your partners?"

"No." Looking very uncomfortable she continued, "In fact, we don't talk very much any more. Ever since his situation with BCR ended, he's been very hostile toward me, as if my moving on was some sign of disloyalty. It hurts me, since he'd encouraged me before."

"It's time for you to get your own thing."

"That's right. I've got to pursue my own desires."

"Desires. Funny you used that word. Edge used it when he was pitching me the deal. I guess when you really get down to it, decisions come down to what you desire, more than anything else."

"Amen," she said.

A slightly out of breath and very apologetic Doris came rushing up to our table. Immediately she started babbling about some conference call with BCR's vice president of pop promotion about crossing over Jevon's current single. Doris had survived Mayo's fall and Otis Clyburn's rise at the label to become its top black product manager, a position that made her a liaison between promotion, publicity, and marketing.

This was the first time I'd been with these two together in years and the evolution of both was amazing. Danifa had become a very precise, ambitious, focused lady. She reminded me of the edge of a diamond—sharp, elegant, and, if not handled correctly, capable of cutting you. Meanwhile, Doris had traded her awkwardness for enthusiasm. She positively buzzed with joy about being in the record industry mix. She was so giddy, in fact, that it was off-putting, as if her life was simply more important than yours. This was probably especially irritating to Danifa and myself since, in different ways, we'd put her on this road.

A reflection of the change in our relationships was that Danifa knew more about my deal with Edge than Doris, a situation I could never have imagined a few years back. So when I told Doris I was accepting Edge's offer, she seemed outraged that Danifa knew this before her.

S
E
D
U
C
E
D

"How long have you known this?" she asked Danifa. When she was told at least a week, Doris' face grew flush.

"As far back as I go with both of you, I can't believe no one told me before tonight." She cut me a steely glare. "How come you didn't go directly to BCR or CBS or some other major label? I could have walked this in myself!"

"Number one," I said through clenched teeth, "lower your voice."

"Don't tell me to shut up!"

"I didn't tell you to shut up."

"Excuse me," she exclaimed, "but yes, you did. I see you still can't see me as an equal in this business. You should both have told me about this deal. But no, you don't see me as a real music person."

The rest of the meal, while spoken in slightly softer tones, was equally contentious. You'd have thought Danifa and I were sleeping together the way Doris reacted. Whatever bond Doris and I had shared—and I admit it was never that strong—was totally splintered by her bad attitude.

In contrast, Danifa, who had laid back and refused to engage Doris' anger, seemed more important to me than ever. Perhaps because she was about to risk her career when she could have stayed put in corporate America, there was a kinship between us.

The next day I signed a deal memo that contracted me to Edgey Records for a 12-inch deal with an album option. The one concession I made to my moms' feeling was to release "Black Sex" not as Derek Harper, my mother's son, but D. Harper, the mysterious, sensual singer-songwriter. She still didn't much like the idea of the record—she refused to listen to it—but it made her feel better that I'd been somewhat sensitive to her feelings.

While the long form contract was being hammered out we mastered "Black Sex," and the acetate was shipped off to a pressing plant in Pennsylvania. A few days later I brought the completed record back to Brooklyn. It was packaged in a crimson cover and had a red label with a glistening white razor blade on it that was Edgey's logo. The label read "Black Sex," produced, written, and performed by D. Harper. Curtis Mayfield, Marvin Gaye, Stevie Wonder, Prince—they'd all experienced the same rush of musical authorship.

I mean, it was a deep feeling that really overwhelmed me. I didn't play it at first. I just flopped down on my sofa and heard the record inside my head and then closed my eyes. I had a vision: myself on national T.V. about to sing. The music filled my head. I swayed my body to the groove. I opened my mouth and tried to look as sexy as my song, but my voice! No sound! No sound came out of my mouth. It was as if the volume knob had been turned off on my throat, and millions and millions of people, all gathered around the tube to see me, came to the same collective conclusion—the boy can't sing!

I blinked my eyes. I shuddered. But I couldn't shake that evil vision in my mind.

"Burn Rubber"

The Stairmaster is one of those contraptions, much like the compact disk and the personal computer, which will be forever linked with the eighties. I walked the Stairmaster, bored as a man could be, as a bunch of guys played a spirited game of three-on-three on the court before me. Sure looked like fun.

Every time I slowed down on the Stairmaster, with my eye on the St. George Health & Racquet Club court, my trainer smacked my butt, and not affectionately. "That hurt."

"Then," Jacksina Jones-Peters scolded, "don't slow down." She was a beauty. Tall, brown, incredibly toned, and had gone to law school, too! She lived down in DC now, but Jacksina was from Jersey and used to work out at the St. George when she was a student. Now she and her husband, a retired New York City judge, were opening up a couple of health clubs in DC and, apparently, Edge was an investor. As part of the deal, Jacksina was helping Edge by getting his artist in shape.

When I first saw Jacksina, I thought "Yeah." Quickly she made it clear no extra-curricular training was gonna jump off. "Listen Mr. Black Sex," she told me after a couple of suggestive comments, "I'm gonna make you look good for the ladies—real good. But the only man who looks good to me is my husband. Now get back on the Stairmaster." Apparently, her husband was a fifty-something stud—an Ed Bradley with rippled stomach muscles. Actually, it was real reassuring to hear a wife, a fine wife at that, who was so loyal to her man. There was some real love in the world.

While I worked out, Edge worked the phones at his Broadway loft. Every time I rolled by, there seemed to be more people and the buzz of committed activity. One day at Edgey's offices I saw Edge with his arm over the shoulder of a short, balding, bearded white man. Then it hit me: this was the same man who had the shouting match with Edge at WDAS. Later I asked Edge who that was. "He used to work at 'DAS," he answered. "Now he's gonna work the Philly market for us. He knows everyone in that cheese steak town. You're gonna be fine there, believe that."

It was like Edge was an old general rounding up his troops for one more charge up the hill. They wanted to plant their flag up at the top of my song. Well, my song was as fine a flag as any. Every time the Stairmaster grew tedious and Jacksina's studied disinterest bruised my ego, I thought of Edge rounding up old soldiers and stepped a little stronger.

Throughout March and early April the momentum for "Black Sex" built. Positive previews of the single began appearing in the trades— *Cash Box, Black Radio Exclusive,* the *Gavin Report, Jack the Rapper,* and *Billboard.* Dwayne Robinson mentioned the record favorably in his *Billboard* column, The Bass Line, and the week after that he wrote a piece on Edgey Records that featured the record. Radio began adding it throughout the Southeast and the Deep South. I kept waiting for it to debut on *Billboard*'s black singles chart, but Edge told me to stay patient: "I want to debut as high on the chart as I can get. We're going all the way, Derek, but I want to keep the ride short."

Edge hired the hippest young music publicity firm in town, Set To Run, to handle the press. In conjunction with Set To Run, we decided to emphasize the lusty nature of the song and position me as the post-Teddy (as in Pendergrass) Teddy. Tactically, it made sense. I agreed that the spot was open. Personally the idea scared me to death. Sure, I was decent looking, tall, and, because of Jacksina's butt kicking, as cut as a health club recruiting poster.

But to be a love song–crooning soul man, even one using new jack beats, is to make yourself part of a tradition rich in style, machismo, and vocal genius. Sam. Otis. Marvin. Smokey. David. Teddy. Some kid from the projects, a guy just in touch with his dick and his voice, wouldn't feel this burden. He'd just get on his knees and beg for the pussy until his throat was raw. Me, I was worrying about things that had nothing to do with selling records in 1988. I wasn't being arrogant enough and, for a man to present himself to the world as a sex object, it takes balls as big as bowling balls.

First we had to study the competition. Al B. Sure! had wavy hair, a lemon-shaped head, and jeans with holes in the knees. Keith Sweat had dark brown skin, a sly smile, and great sweaters. Freddie Jackson had suits that screamed Baptist church by way of Vegas. After much discussion it was decided I could keep my beard—precisely because no one else singing had one, though it had to be kept close. I'd wear collarless shirts, expensive slacks or specially tailored jeans. Most important, at least to me, was that everyone agreed I could wear my Gucci Loafers. It was the only piece of clothing we all agreed on that didn't feel like a costume to me. And since my favorite shoes would remain on my feet, I felt grounded, no matter how much hype I participated in.

This look wasn't as youthful as Edge wanted but, after testing me in everything from Michael Jackson–styled faux military regalia and imitation Luther Vandross–sequined jackets, this was the look that worked best. Danifa made the final judgment, symbolic of my continuing confidence in her. Although she was never that warm or showed even the vaguest interest in me, Danifa was one of the more stable people I'd encountered in the music business. I could tell Edge didn't like her much, but it was also clear he respected her. I remember him commenting approvingly that Danifa wasn't "serving poontang up in the obvious places," which was his way of saying she hadn't fucked any men in the industry, particularly Mayo. (The implication was that Doris may have sexed up Mayo, an image that made me more sick than jealous.)

In April 1988, with "Black Sex" at #25 with a bullet on *Billboard*'s black singles chart, I embarked on the third tour of my musical career. Only now I was the one sitting in the backseat. Rahiem must have been clocking amazing sums of money, because everything on the

"Black Sex" promo tour was first class. I mean, we stayed in Four Seasons hotels most of the time, traveled first class on every flight, and when we rolled it was always in the limo Sinatra, Streisand, or even Barry Manilow had just been in. Edge was spending money like water, like it didn't mean anything to him, like it was a game and no longer his life.

Edge was different now. Number one he was married and he spent a lot of time using his calling card. He also did a lot of time talking about a house he and his wife were building in Columbia, Maryland. Edge was bitter, but nostalgic, too. "You heard of the kid in the candy store?" he once said about his BCR years. "Well, over there I was both the kid and the candy store. I was selling it and I was eating it." I figured it was that appetite that got him fired.

During the "Black Sex" tour I got the feeling that some kind of scam was underway. Every now and then Rahiem or one of his stoney associates would show up and Edge spoke to them, not like members of the same team but with the glib charm he aimed at radio programmers. Unlike many of the young brothers I knew, men who tried to assert a sullen masculinity most of the time, Edge had several faces—wise man, con man, joker man. After all these years, he still fascinated me.

Of course it didn't hurt that his strategy was working. We sold about 270,000 singles in three months—amazing numbers for a single from an unknown artist on a newly inaugurated indie label. You don't sell that many records that quickly without reaching white folks. Using the excitement at black radio as a base and a considerable amount of Rahiem's cash for "independent promotion" (aka payola), Edge was making serious inroads at progressive pop stations.

To them the record was something of a novelty, like the Timex Social Club's "Rumors" or Frankie Smith's never to be forgotten "Double Dutch Bus." This aspect of the record was enhanced by promotional T-shirts that asked the musical question: "Tired? Run down? Depressed? Let me prescribe some 'Black Sex.'" Morning jocks ate this up. It was fodder for innumerable crude jokes, a few awfully goofy skits, and plenty of airplay.

Ironically, considering that I was traveling at a high level of comfort, this was the most uneventful of my record treks. Quite simply, I was used to the drill by now. Everything was better, but nothing was new and that made all the difference. You'd think I'd be filled with grand memories of my days in four-star restaurants and signing autographs for chambermaids who'd left their home numbers under my pillow. But the mind is a remarkably selective little instrument. It doesn't just give you back what you put in—it gives you both more and less than you desire. Which is why only two events from that tour linger. I suspect they endure because they put me in touch with desires I hadn't acknowledged before.

The first revolved around Uncle Mike. I was in D.C. doing an on-air appearance on Melvin Lindsay's "Quiet Storm," that nightly program of ballads that had provided the soundtrack to the lovemaking of Candi Bailey and I. I wondered if she was listening, if she'd heard my song of "Black Sex" and recalled ours. It could have been a melancholy visit if not for Uncle Mike's good cheer.

He came with me to the station and sat in the engineer's booth as Lindsay and I talked and played my favorite love songs. Some were mournful (Smokey's "Tracks of My Tears"), some lustful (Curtis Mayfield's "Give Me Your Love"), and some fell sweetly in between (Stevie Wonder's "Golden Lady"). All the while Uncle Mike just beamed at me as proud as a Poppa. I couldn't imagine my own Pops being as happy. Music for him simply served a function—you have a funeral, you play a sad hymn; you have a party, you play an upbeat one.

Uncle Mike was much more like me. He saw music as some tangible force of nature. I'd heard Pops criticize his brother as a bad and frivolous father. "You got cousins all over," Pops used to say about Uncle Mike's family, "but your aunts are in short supply." This may have been true. But I only had brief glimpses of that Uncle Mike. The one I knew had a cocky, relaxed spirit that I admired and tried to emulate, though I knew the dour, practical spirit of my pops was deep in me.

After the taping Uncle Mike, Edge, and I went over to a Georgetown bistro where they regaled each other with tales of 'Trane and Sonny Rollins, and jazz clubs long buried under storefront churches and Kentucky Fried Chicken franchises. Uncle Mike worked as a security guard at Georgetown University, but his musical erudition and overall coolness made him seem like a less fortunate Edgecombe Lennox. They didn't seem like brothers, but they were truly kindred spirits.

My second powerful recollection of the "Black Sex" promo trek took place in South Beach, Miami. After having little initial impact, music videos were starting to be a factor in the marketing of black music. Crossover acts needed videos to gain MTV exposure. Black Entertainment Television was slowly gaining access to cable outlets in cities with large black populations, while scores of programs featuring r&b and rap videos were popping up on public access, educational stations, and some independent stations.

Taken as a whole, all these outlets didn't yet make hits. Black radio still did that. But once a record was broken, this video exposure would result in sales to more casual consumers. And, in Europe, where American black music faced fewer racial and demographic barriers, a video was essential.

So I spent an absolutely gorgeous early June day cavorting on the beach with Beth Ann. Yeah, Gibbs' Beth Ann. And, nope, Gibbs was not there, nor anywhere else in the area. To hear Beth Ann tell it, "He's got as much chance of getting back with me as shit does smelling like Chanel." Apparently Gibbs' transgressions in Paris had been graver than he'd admitted. She wouldn't go into details, but it was clear Beth Ann had been embarrassed more than once.

Once that discussion was out of the way and I'd said nice things about my ex-roomie, my lust kicked in. Beth Ann may not have been the most beautiful woman I've ever seen—Pam Grier will always wear that crown—but she was pretty close. Tall, lean, and made extra chocolate by the Florida sun, Beth Ann moved with the grace of a dancer and the joy of a child.

As the star of my new video, Beth Ann was either wrapped in my arms or flirting intensely with me for much of the day. I sang to her about "Black Sex" for hours on end. Of course that could have been old real quick. But Beth Ann's stamina, built up through years of modeling gigs, kept me going. She hung on me, basking in my celebrity just as I bathed in her beauty. Still, she managed to avoid being in my trailer alone with me. There was never that moment away from the crew and the camera when anything really sexual could have occurred.

Reality set in as a harvest moon hovered over Miami. I was making muscles with my left arm to illustrate how "firm" I was. Beth Ann squeezed a couple dutifully and then made a muscle herself which, while not nearly as large, was just as hard as mine. This became a little game where I made her touch a part of my body and then I'd touch one of hers. Things were going all right and I was about to pinch her left buttock when Bovine Winslow showed up.

If you're not a basketball fan the name means nothing to you. If you follow the NBA, you know the story. Pat Ewing gets hurt in a second round playoff game against the Bulls. Charles Oakley gets four fouls in the first half. So Bovine Winslow, a late-round draft choice from Virginia Union, came in and racked up 25 points, 15 rebounds and 5 blocks. A monster game that made Bovine, six foot ten inches of strapping twenty-three-year-old, a cult hero.

As he approached, Bovine's biceps flowed out of a tank top like reddish brown melons. When we shook hands, Bovine unintentionally squeezed my fingers red and nearly threw out my shoulder with his rigorous up-and-down shake.

Beth Ann played it cool. She'd met Bovine one night at Nell's, and my man had been in mad pursuit ever since. When the camera was on, Beth Ann was as affectionate with me as before. When the director said "Cut!" Beth Ann gave me space, making it clear to Bovine she wasn't taken. When the shoot wrapped I anticipated Beth Ann would roll off in Bovine's little red Corvette. Instead Beth Ann let it be known she and some of her long-legged friends would be hanging out at the News Cafe—if Bovine or I wanted to stop by.

Bovine was irritated by Beth Ann's strategy, while I quickly reconciled myself to the young lady keeping her options open. I got a driver to take me back to my hotel. According to the music biz rituals, I was supposed to continue sweating my video's leading lady. But, and maybe this was another sign that I didn't have the ego to be a real love man, I had no intention of battling a basketball player for a woman.

"When You Were Mine"

It was late June and I was back in Brooklyn running through Fort Greene Park. "Black Sex" was number 10 with a bullet on the black singles chart and number 62 on the pop chart. My video, with the recurring image of Beth Ann's lovely face pressed against my chest, was playing on BET and VH-1. MTV was thinking about adding it.

I was running up the steps on the Myrtle Avenue side of the park, sweating profusely and pushing myself hard, when someone called my name. Edge stood at the top of the steps, a vision in dark green (suit, shoes, and shirt) with a half-empty Heineken bottle in his right hand. "We've won," he said with an air of self-satisfied triumph. Between breaths I wondered what was up. "We just sold the record to BCR."

"How long have you been negotiating this?"

"They called yesterday to feel us out. This morning they made a serious you-can't-refuse-this offer. I've tried to call you, but I got so excited I had to come tell you myself. You are paid, Derek. Even if you don't sell another record you should clear a couple hundred thousand when all the paperwork's done."

We sat at the top of the steps, enjoying a panoramic view of the Fort Greene projects with the Manhattan skyline in the distance. "So," I wondered after finishing his beer, "how much will you make?"

"Enough to retire on. That's if I want to. Don't know if I do yet. But now my investors will be paid plus interest."

"Just from selling my one record?"

"Well, BCR now distributes Edgey Records."

"Yo, Edge," I said heatedly, "what about all that talk of proving a point and all that."

"I've done that, Derek. You can see that, can't you? Don't think I don't have principles or lack integrity or any of that shit." He sounded genuinely hurt. "But in business, in any business, but especially in this one, flexibility is crucial. I pulled out all the stops on this record. It was the kind of record that deserved it. Now it's time to sell albums and to really capitalize on the excitement. To do that I need a machine. They'll get us a half-million preorders on *Black Sex* the album."

Something in his tone chilled me. "You believe I'm a trick, don't you?" I said bitterly. "You just milked me and once the juice is gone, some time after the record starts dying out, you'll throw me away for another piece of fruit."

He said, "Derek" in that tone that made me a kid again and transformed him back to the man I'd met giving away Millie Jackson singles. "Hits are guaranteed to no one. No one. You may stumble going back down these steps and crack your head open like an egg on a skille·. You may have made a hit record, something that could outlast your life."

"Answer my question."

"I've watched you on this tour. You had a good time, but this ain't what you're hungry for. Something's inside you that's eating you. Everybody's got one demon. Crazy folks got a few. Whatever's feeding on you, it won't be stopped by this experience. You know it. I can tell you know it. By the way, you can only get squeezed out if that one record is all you got, if it's your whole life in those five minutes. If that's all you got, well yeah, you gonna get thrown away."

Two weeks later I was in a conference room at BCR's Sixth Avenue offices. Against one wall was a buffet. In a corner stood a video monitor showing Beth Ann and myself dashing through the Miami surf. Head shots of yours truly decorated the walls. People walked around wearing "Black Sex" T-shirts. I stood taking pictures with Edge, Otis Clyburn, Mayo, Danifa, Doris, and various retailers and radio executives, etc. Everybody's patted my back. Everybody was skinning and grinning.

A month after that party I've got *Billboard*'s number one black single and number ten pop single. "Black Sex" is hotter than a catcher's jock strap in July. MTV's playing the video. I was included in a *Rolling Stone* piece on new jack swing along side Bobby Brown, Keith Sweat, and Al. B. Sure. Dwayne Robinson did a great little review of the single in the *Village Voice*. This should have been the best time in my life. No question, this was the best time of my professional life.

Yet life was not sweet, not sweet at all. I was being sued for plagiarizing myself. Zeke Rider, the sleazy old brother who Vernon Jackson sold "Traveling the Highway to Heaven" to back when we were in high school, was now claiming that "Black Sex" was a rip off of "Highway." And, you know, I'm not sure if the old guy wasn't right. I played the two back-to-back on piano and was frightened by their melodic similarities. "Highway" was the first good song I'd ever written and "Black Sex" was the most commercial. If they were the same song, did that mean, despite all my furious work, that I really had only one good song in me? (Some of Rahiem's associates visited Zeke, Edge told me later, with a check and a Glock .9 millimeter. After that meeting the suit, quite conveniently, was dropped.)

Edge was hard to get a hold of. Once he'd made the deal with BCR, his Broadway office was quickly closed and the answering machine was on constantly over at his Englewood place. Mostly he'd call me from DC, where I could hear the sound of construction in the background. No, he assured, I wasn't being abandoned. "Just got to take care of some stuff down here," he told me. But he was abandoning me again. There was no speech this time. No philosophical rambling. He was just taking care of himself.

If Edge was elusive, Rahiem was intrusive. Edgey Records was now located in BCR's corporate offices and Rahiem, along with his crew, now constituted the staff. My record had put Edgey on the map and, for the first time since he'd gotten arrested in 1983, put Rahiem back in the game. He was in the office daily, furiously signing rap acts and, with Clyburn's encouragement, trying to make Edgey BCR's eqivalent of CBS's Def Jam and MCA's Uptown.

Just as it had during parts of the rap tour, the hip-hop street environment at Edgey made me feel profoundly middle class. Rahiem loved my success, but he didn't really get me, nor I him. It was like I was suddenly recording for Donkey. This cultural gap manifested itself in a battle over my album. He and BCR wanted to concoct a new jack swing collection around me full of shaker sounds, James Brown samples, and break beats that would fit snugly onto playlist with all those Teddy Riley records. I wasn't totally against that. I mean, "Black Sex" tapped into that formula.

But I also wanted the album to reflect my deepest musical yearnings and to have, at least on a few cuts, an old school soul feel. In between promo appearances and interviews, Timmons and I had been cutting more of my songs. In fact, we'd even come up with a name, Unnecessary Noise, for our little r&b duo.

Clyburn liked most of my new songs but wanted younger guys to come in and totally redo the tracks. If he'd suggested some form of collaboration, it would have been cool. But he just wanted to scrap all my tracks and start from scratch. My argument was that I made "Black Sex" a massive hit that confirmed my ability to reach a mass audience. Clyburn, with Rahiem's wholehearted support, wouldn't compromise. He even called in his employee, Doris, to talk to me, but at this point our relationship was so distant, I might as well have been talking to any old label executive.

Even Danifa, politic as always, pointed out that the struggle over the tracks was more about ego than business. As long as I was the album's primary writer I'd be well paid. Moreover, the longer this debate dragged on, the longer it would be before the album came out, and the longer the gap between "Black Sex" the single and *Black Sex* the album, the less successful the latter would be.

I could have compromised again. That worked for me before. I also could have stood my ground and told Clyburn and Rahiem to both kiss my ass. I'd had some success with that technique, too. However, both these options would be moot after my performance at Jack the Rapper.

"The Way You Do the Things You Do"

Maybe it was psychosomatic, but right after the Fourth of July and all through the rest of the month, my throat was scratchy. I tried to play it off. A summer cold I caught on an airplane, I told Edge. Pollen from Fort Greene Park, I told Rahiem. But I knew what it was. It was Jack the Rapper. BCR was throwing the all-night jam this year and I was the closing act. Sometime between midnight and dawn I'd hit the stage in front of the movers and shakers of black music—program directors, music directors, big retailers, promotion people, a&r executives, songwriters, producers, singers, attorneys, managers, and even a few musicians.

Outwardly I played it off. No biggie. Inside I was scared and that fear wrapped itself around my vocal chords. The closer it got to August, Atlanta, and Jack's party, the more I fretted.

"Its not a program, homie," Attak told me one evening in Power Play Station out in Astoria. "You just have to hook up your DAT and you'll be straight."

"I might as well be lip-synching if I use that thing."

"You don't use it on everything, Derek," he explained. "You sing most of it live. You just have to protect yourself on the rough spots. The part of the song where you hit that high note."

"Yeah, toward the end."

"Well, you ain't gonna hit that with a messed-up throat. On the strength, you barely got it in the studio. Am I right?"

"But this is live."

"So, what you saying'?" Attak countered. "That you got better chops in a hotel ballroom than a warm studio? I don't think so. You think people wanna hear you snap, crackle, and pop?" Then he busted out with a big smile. "Yo, homie, remember how I tore that shit up?" I told him I did. "Yeah, that really blew us up in the industry. You listen to me. Get the right equipment and everything will be chill."

Attak was right. Finesse the easy sing-a-along parts, use the DAT as back up, and drink a lot of tea. There were nonsingers all over the place getting over. In fact, there were more nonsingers with hits at this point than singers who could really blow. I was somewhere in the middle. I wasn't Al Green, but I wasn't Lillo Thomas, either. I'd just need a little help, that's all.

It was Thursday and a limo was waiting outside 19 Willoughby to take me to LaGuardia when the phone rang. I'd heard Pops use this voice so many times I assumed he was calling from work and I was right.

"You calling to wish me luck?" I asked hopefully.

"No, son. I don't have any luck to give right now. Your uncle's dead." I put down my garment bag and looked out my front window at the limo driver. I caught his eye and he smiled up at me. Pops continued, "He had diabetes. It runs in our family, but did he take care of himself? Shit, Mike never took care of a thing in his life. Certainly not his health."

In a petulant, adolescent voice I countered, "Well, he always was nice to me."

My Pops sighed. He was exasperated, sad, and in no mood for my foolishness. "That's my brother, all right. Nice to everyone. Nice. Nice. Nice. Nice. Nice." Pops was harsh and insulting, as if I'd fallen into a deep hole of stupidity. "What the fuck do you think this is about? Nice is for people who just want to be led around by the nose! Mike just hung out, got drunk, got pussy, and never took responsibility for his life. Every time he had a chance to dig in some place, he got led off down some other silly ass road."

I stood by the window transfixed and silent. Outside I watched two teenaged black girls talk to the limo driver as he pointed toward my home.

"If you call yourself a man, then you're supposed to be getting people mad at you, you're supposed to have your own mind. You're too old to be calling him 'nice' like that's saying something that means any damn thing. I raised you better than that, didn't I?"

"Yeah, you did Pops."

"I thought so."

"Pops?"

"Yeah."

"I'm sorry Uncle Mike's dead. I know you loved him very much. I know he loved you, too. In the end, that's all that matters."

"Yeah, Derek, that's true."

"Pops, I remember when I was a kid. We were up state at a barbecue. It was the day I learned to shoot a layup—you and Uncle Mike taught me how. Then you and Uncle Mike played against each other, knocking each other upside the head. I was cracking up." The limo driver now stood outside the car, gesturing toward his watch. The two teenaged girls looked up, too, holding pieces of paper the driver had given them. "Do you remember that, Pops?"

After a pause he answered, "Yeah," though I knew he hadn't wanted to.

"It was a great day, Pops, seeing you two play ball and having such a good time together."

"Who won?" he asked. "Who won the game?"

Instead of telling the truth I took a chance and told him, "Uncle Mike won. At least that's what I remember."

"That's right," he agreed. I could hear a smile in his voice. "He always did win. Cheated, too. Mike was always cheating." He laughed lightly, an acknowledgment of familiarity, pain, and love.

"I loved Uncle Mike, Pops."

"I loved him, too."

"And I love you, Pops. I love all the things you've done for me and the way you've lived your life. And I just love you for being you." These words soothed my pops, I could tell right away.

"I love you too, son."

Pops was not embarrassed by the words, but they were definitely hard for him to say and, strangely, for me to hear. His anger, his resigned laughter and statement of love, all constituted more emotion than I believe we'd ever shared. On the ride out to LaGuardia I kept envisioning that day on the basketball court and realized how fruitful a little lie can be.

I drank a lot of Jack Daniel's before I went on Saturday night. It didn't help. I was horrible. My range was more limited than usual. The DAT machine kept coming in and out, so I found myself oversinging when a more measured approach would have been better. No booing, but powerful waves of indifference floated out at me from the crowd. Even the response to "Black Sex" was tepid, as if it was yesterday's news which, in such a trend-conscious industry, I guess it was.

When I got off-stage it was 3:15 A.M. and as I walked through the lobby, past red eyes, gold chains, and the whispers of people being held upright by walls, I knew I was through. Edge put his arm around me and whispered, "You're a real trooper, Derek." Rahiem told me to "Stay strong, we got your back." I heard a rumor that Gibbs was around and I would have liked to talk with him.

Once back in my room I called for a 7:30 A.M. wake-up call and had a block put on the phone.

For the rest of the morning I ignored the knocks on my door and laid atop the bed sheets, arms by my sides, listening to the hotel. Music, shouts, moving feet, and the unmistakable mirth of black folks having a grand old time filled my ears. I listened from a safe distance. My body was still in Atlanta, but my soul was elsewhere.

Seven hours after I bombed in Atlanta I was sitting in a pew at the First Baptist Church of Denbey, Virginia, holding my moms' hand and wiping her tears as Pops stood at the altar and Uncle Mike lay peacefully before him. Dealing with death was his business. I'd seen him handle widows with aplomb, shake screaming children into coherence, and wipe lipstick off cadavers at the request of ancient grandparents. I feared that he couldn't overcome all that to give Uncle Mike his due.

Instead of some perfunctory, perhaps bitter, talk, much like the beginnings of our phone conversation, Pops looked down at me. "At this time, I'd like to ask my son Derek to join me." Bleary eyed and aching

I moved slowly, gracelessly to the altar. He whispered in my ear and I walked over to the organ.

I hadn't played one in years, but I remembered the basics. Then I looked at Pops, nodded my head in that universal signal of readiness, and played the intro to "Traveling the Highway to Heaven." Pops sang the lead. It wasn't gorgeous. It wasn't a performance that would have worried Sam Cooke, but that day Pops and I made a joyful noise. Moms stood up and started waving her hands and the Holy Spirit filled our hearts.

We celebrated life at that moment. We celebrated our love for Uncle Mike, our love for each other and our family. It was a transcendent moment. I felt deep emotion and great clarity, a mix that was almost sexual in its intensity. Pops started crying like a baby and Moms grabbed him, locking him in a bear hug. I just kept playing. I took over the lead. My throat still hurt, yet no one cared because no one was judging me and I wasn't judging myself.

"It's Like That"

It took a while to pull everything together. Of course the biggest part of it was luck. My moms would say it was the Lord's handiwork. God knows she's probably right.

Still, I had to pull apart what I had. But that wasn't hard; it wasn't built to last anyway. The wretched performance in Atlanta sealed the fate of my album. The record came out in October 1988 as part of BCR's Christmas push. Most of my tracks were either wiped clean or remixed at Clyburn's direction. Some good young talent did the work—Civiles & Cole, who'd later start C&C Music Factory, handled several cuts, as did Marley Marl, an innovator of James Brown samples noted for his dusty production.

The album sold about 350,000 copies and would have gone gold if black radio hadn't been so mean to me. "You need 'Black Sex'? What you need is a voice. Ha. Ha. Ha." Jokes of that kind permeated the industry. I hate to admit it, but Milli Vanilli had nothing on me.

Not unexpectedly, Edgey Records didn't pick up my option. I was informed of this during lunch of King Crab, a restaurant on Eighth Avenue just two blocks from Possible 20. But we'd traveled too many miles together for nostalgia. I guess he'd expected me to get emotional. And maybe if I had, he'd have tried to get me a second album with BCR. "Look," I said real chilly, "there's only one thing I need from you and it's not regret or a pat on the back."

"OK, youngblood, talk to me."

"You just make sure BCR pays me what I'm due. Rahiem's straight. You're straight. Danifa will get me my publishing money. But to BCR I'm a one hit wonder. I'm the Cornelius Brothers & Sister Rose, I'm the Dazz Band, I'm Brick. You know what I'm sayin'. So they have no reason to give me all of mine."

"We go back—"

"No. I don't need sentiment. I want my money. You built a house on 'Black Sex.' Well, I want to build something, too." Edge wanted to engage in one of his monologues. One of those fat paragraphs of old-school insight that I'd been charmed by since Mr. Walt's. At this meeting I stopped him before he could get started. The only concession I made to our past was a "Thank you."

"For what?" he asked. "You being so damn hostile, you'd think I ruined your life."

"No, you didn't ruin my life, you just seduced me."

"What?"

"Not sexually. You just made a lot of things possible, just by being you. Not everything I got into was good for me, but that's life. I don't blame you for a thing. But you get me all my money and this circle will be closed and the seduction will be over." Edge didn't like my tone. Made him uncomfortable. Moreover he really didn't understand what I was getting at. To him, I'd always been just a recurring blip on his mental screen. Just another singer. Just another record.

Anyway, he came through. A check came to my attorney for "an estimated advance against royalties" totaling $250,000, along with a note warning me not to expect more.

Not long after that, in the winter of 1988, my cousin Anna, my real estate owning friend Morris, and I drove over to Mr. Walt's where, to Anna's surprise, there were no young men standing in wait by the pay phone outside wanting to score. She said, "It must be a mirage" with the resignation of the newly cynical.

I said, "Get used to it."

Anna looked at me like I was crazy when I smiled. She'd grown used to disappointment. It made me sad to see that in her face—I'd been as guilty of disappointing her as her husband had been—but I was determined not to any more. She'd had the barbershop padlocked. There was graffiti on the outer walls. To my dismay there were several worn, scuffled but still imposing Brothers Black posters splattered over the front window.

Inside, the place wasn't in as bad a shape. Barber chairs were still intact, though the foam was sticking out of a couple. Tiles were loose. A mirror behind one barber chair was shattered. My eye went to the huge space where the record player had been. The wall there was a little brighter, a little cleaner than the rest of the room. I stared at it awhile.

"You really think this is big enough?" Morris' voice pulled me back to reality.

"Well," I said, looking around, "I can get it cheap. It's centrally located—as the crack dealers know—and if we knock down the back wall, we can expand it. Will the city help us?"

"Koch won't," he replied, "but if you contribute to Dinkins' campaign and he wins, I guarantee you the city will help."

"You sure you want to do this?" Anna looked at me anxiously, almost like she was waiting for me to cop out, to say it's all a joke. I asked her if she was gonna open the barbershop again. "Derek, please" was her reply.

"Well, then I'm doing it."

Her question really wasn't about whether I was going to buy the place. I'd already told my parents, Mr. Walt, and a bank that I would. The question was about what would happen after that. I wanted to turn the space into a cultural center where there'd be workshops in music, performance, singing, etc. Everything I'd learned since I'd been in the business would be available to the children of St. Albans and Hollis. I'd teach there. So would Timmons, Attak, and whoever else I could drag in to give up an hour or two.

I didn't have a sharply formed plan, but I was driven to do it. It was my first new dream in years and every time I contemplated it, I felt real whole inside.

"I think he means it, Mrs. Williams." It was straight-arrow, earnest Morris chiming in support. "I haven't known Derek long, but I already know he's a man of his word."

Before Anna could say something cynical, I cut with, "Make sure you call her Anna." Then I leaned over to him and in a mock whisper added, "You know she's divorced."

"Derek."

OK, I may have been a bit obvious about it, but I didn't care. I was hoping to get Morris and Anna hooked up. Little Walt aka Walter aka my cousin-in-law had disappeared in the netherworld of broken dreams, broken families, and broken crack vials that can lead to homelessness. Anna hadn't seen her husband in a year and a half and had divorced him a few months before. It had been very difficult to do, given how her family had just been shattered by her father's death. Still, after Little Walt had taken most of their money, and lots of his father's money, she was compelled to make a permanent break.

Now Morris was no Prince Charming. He was a little stiff and he'd lost his wife to another man. But he was stable and nice in a way no men I met in the record business had been, me included. In fact, he reminded me of Pops, and I hoped that over time Anna would notice that, too.

Pops got it right away. When I brought Morris and Anna over to the house, he bonded with the guy as soon as they started talking real estate. Now this impressed Anna, so I left the three of them in the living room and headed into the kitchen. My moms sat at the table with her glasses on, going over the checkbook. She could have been an accountant. Instead she raised me, nurtured my father, and stayed true to the Lord.

"Come and give me some sugar," she said. After I sat down, I told her about visiting Mr. Walt's and Morris. She peeked into the living room, standing in that same spot Anna and I had years ago to look in on Pops. "Not bad," she observed. When she wondered, "Is he a church goer?" I stifled a laugh and told her she'd better ask him.

"You know that Gibbs, boy? Well, he called this morning looking for you." Hadn't spoken to my old roommate since Los Angeles. He'd called me a couple of times. I'd gotten a message through Attak that he was happy for me when "Black Sex" took off and I'm sure he was in the audience of Jack the Rapper. But somehow our paths hadn't crossed. He would never have tracked me down at my parents' home unless it was important. Important to him, that is.

I set up a meeting at Junior's restaurant, which was a light jog from 19 Willoughby. I got a booth and was ordering the breakfast special when Gibbs and an unannounced guest showed up. Gibbs basically looked the same. He'd put back on a little of the weight he'd lost when he'd first started living large. All that Adidas gear was history and, just like everybody else, he'd joined team Nike.

However it was his companion who commanded most of my attention. Mayo no longer had dreads, no longer wore Army fatigues or that ubiquitous Hendrix button. He wore a turtle neck, a blue blazer, and a fade that Big Daddy Kane would envy.

"Gentlemen. I would say 'What strange bedfellows,' but I figure you two probably aren't fucking." This bit of stupid wit made Gibbs chuckle, but Mayo seemed quite uncomfortable. He chided me for being disrespectful. Not wanting to create any schisms in what had to be a shaky partnership, I cut to the chase. "So, gents, what's up?"

Considering the vocal abilities of both men, the answer could have taken me through lunch. But, like Run-D.M.C. on the intro to "Peter Piper," they traded lines with gusto. The gist was that they were entering into a joint venture with Capitol records to "be for them what Uptown is for MCA," said Gibbs. That was shorthand for mixing r&b melodies with hip-hop beats. "As you know," Mayo said, moving in for the kill, "we've both always respected your writing"—there's nothing as disgusting as professionally insincere people sucking up to you—"and no one has been as successful as you in tapping into this new pulse in black music. We want you to join us. As a writer, producer, even, if you wish, an artist."

"You got the dick head at BCR, Derek." This was Gibbs now. "You and I know it. We'd support you and we'd even kick in a piece of the company."

"There's only one way I'd ever get involved with you two again." I was using that same voice I'd employed with Edge and I was enjoying it. "You guys have to commit to helping build a cultural center in my hood and giving a percentage of every record you sell to the center."

Mayo said, "Hey, I'm in the record biz, not the Fresh Air Fund."

Gibbs asked, "What's this, a tax dodge?"

"No, it's a dream. Personally I don't care whether your company works or not. It's just a vehicle. I have no love for either of you, but if you can help me do my thing, fine. You'll receive a proposal from my attorney. If you want to do it, Kool & the Gang. If you don't want to, that's all right, too."

With that I paid the bill and stepped off. Eventually they got back to me with various uncharitable versions of my original proposal. They thought it was some kind of negotiating ploy on my part. But this deal was not open to negotiation or gamesmanship or any of the stuff Gibbs and Mayo had learned to live by.

The most surprising thing about the meeting and our subsequent contacts was that I'd never asked how those two rascals, once at opposite ends of the r&b spectrum, had gotten together. I guess I didn't have to ask, 'cause I knew. Everything new becomes old, everything trendy and fresh eventually becomes exploited and passé. The business will discard you if it's allowed to. To continue in it you either adapt, becoming an imitator of the new innovations just as you were once copied. Or you barter, using whatever knowledge, wisdom, and guile you've hopefully acquired to woo new talent, new ideas, and, most important, new rhythms into your circle.

Mayo had been the seventies, Gibbs the eighties, and now the nineties were upon us. Both knew it was time to grab onto the next groove or become extinct. Edge knew this, too. I'd actually been in training to be part of this ever-evolving scene since I fell in love with "Charlie Brown."

But in the spring of 1989 I wanted something else. Converting Mr. Walt's was one of the things I needed to do. Jerking Mayo and Gibbs around, while not part of my plans, was quite satisfying, too. Still I needed something else. I needed love and I had no plan for that. Vernon Jackson agreed with me when I told him. He'd already made his move for love.

That spring he showed up back in Queens, back at the First Baptist Church where he'd become a child star and, along with his accompanist Tyrone Baxter, blew the roof off the old, crumbling brick building. That night over pork chops at my parents' house, he admitted that he and his pianist were lovers. Moms acted surprised, but I doubt she was. Pops and I traded so-what-else-is-new looks and cut up our pork.

But if none of us were as shocked as we should have been about Vernon's confession, we were deeply moved by the reasons behind it. "I found myself in a moral dilemma," Vernon began. There was no Rev. Jackson in his voice, just the familiar tones of Vernon. "I love the Lord. I love the mission he's given me to spread his word. And I love Minnie. The conflict between all these things burned in my heart until I used to cry at night. But my connection with Tyrone grew with time until it was clear that my denials only delayed my facing the truth.

"One day I was singing with my daughter—Kenya has such a strong voice, it's amazing to hear her. Well, she started to sing 'Yes, Jesus Loves Me.' A Sunday school song, a simply beautiful song. She asked me about the word 'love' and what it meant. We talked a long time. I kept coming back to honesty. That to be true to your feelings was essential to love. I know that's really a limited view of the word. You could say so much about love. But honesty, it kept creeping up on me. I realized then that I'd never been totally honest with Kenya. Since she'd been born I'd been one way and told her another.

"I had to come out so that she could really know me. Not only had I been cheating on my wife but I'd been lying to my daughter, lying to myself, and lying in the pulpit to the Lord. That was just too much deceit to live with. I love the Lord. But I must love Him as I am."

As you can see 1989 was a year where a lot of things came to a head. Changes were made. Commitments were given. Demons were confronted. Dreams no longer deferred. But I wasn't there yet. Not all the way. I needed some luck. It came my way that June.

I was at the barbershop sweating bullets as I scraped old paint off the walls. On a whim I hopped in my car and did something I hadn't in years—I headed toward Jamaica Avenue. Usually when I came out from Brooklyn I either took the Belt Parkway or drove straight across Atlantic Avenue, avoiding black Queens' main drag. On this day I headed straight there, and it was a mess. They were tearing down the elevated J train and those pillions, the ones I used to grab onto in the frozen snow, were either gone, half removed, or laying sideways on the ground.

As I understood it, the train was going to run underground. It was supposed to revive the avenue. Maybe it would one day, but right now

Jamaica Avenue was nothing but chaos. I parked over by Parsons Boulevard and wandered down toward 165th Street.

Surprisingly the old theater was in decent shape. It was a church now and, while I was glad the building was still alive, no flood of memories engulfed me. It was just a place I used to go to back when Jamaica Avenue was the place to go. I walked to the bus terminal. The depot was as dismal as I remembered, though the donut shop was still there and my honey-dipped treat was quite tasty. I walked outside where the buses and the commuters—housewives, b-boys, school girls, TA workers—were passing time. I was in mid-bite when a woman's voice said sarcastically, "If it isn't D. Harper?"

Since my brief meteoric rise and fall as an African-American sex God, some variation of this question, spoken in the same taunting tone, had become an unfortunate constant in my life. I'd learned to grin and bare it, which I turned to do when the speaker got right in front of me and stuck out her tongue. "I thought they'd done it with trick photography."

"Done what?"

"Given you muscles." Candi stood in front of me as beautiful as my memories of her, yet as different as the Jamaica Avenue landscape. Her hair was cropped short and blond, like that model Toukie Smith. There was a mole on the right side of her mouth. She wore long, silver ear rings that could have passed for weather vanes. Culottes that matched her vibrant crimson lipstick covered her wonderfully sturdy legs, and sandals graced her lovely feet. After laughing at her own joke, Candi embraced me and I squeezed her.

There was so much to talk about. Years of history to catch up on. She wanted to talk about "Black Sex." It was only natural, I guess, but all I wanted to know about was her. The wedding band was on but before giving me her number and boarding the Q33 bus, Candi said, "I'm living back here in Queens." "With your husband?" I asked and she said No and then, "Call me and we'll talk." I watched her bus pull out the depot and fingered her number in my suddenly moist right palm.

My first instinct was to tear it up. My recent experiences with folks from my past had been mixed enough to warrant caution. But my heart was spinning like a break dancer on a cardboard box in front of a

Times Square theater. Hadn't had this feeling in years. Not at Forty-sixth Street, not in Cali, not on my various trips across America.

That night I stopped at a Blockbuster on Flatbush Avenue and picked up *Mahogany*. Hadn't seen it in years. It was still corny with a capital C. But it was also reassuring, like seeing an old friend or, more to the point, like talking to an old lover. You see the changes, yet there is a shared history of smiles and passion. I called Candi right after the closing credits. Her mother answered and she was exceedingly polite—very different from our last conversations years ago. She sounded weak. When she called out to Candi, she did so between thick coughs.

The next night Candi and I sat inside Cino's on DeKalb Avenue, my favorite Fort Greene restaurant, and filled in the gaps. She made me go first and I gave her a very detailed description of my musical career, my dreams for Mr. Walt's, and a carefully edited narrative of my love life. I assumed Candi would approach her narrative with the same level of honesty.

Hers began where our love story ended. Richard Hawkins had been an adjunct professor at Howard. He lectured twice a week on civics. His day job was as a lobbyist for various well-intended health care advocacy groups. Though Richard sounded dull as dirt to me, Candi insisted he "was a marvelous speaker and a really compassionate man." He was mid-thirties, stocky, divorced, and a tenor saxophonist in a jazz combo composed of other lobbyists. On Sunday nights she'd go see him perform at Blues Alley in Georgetown. One thing led to another.

"I know now that I was looking for a father figure and that as much as I cared for you, there was a part of me that needed something else." This was hard to listen to, but I knew an unhappy ending for him was coming, something I took comfort in.

They got married right after she graduated and got a spot in Adams Morgan, DC's multi-culti melting pot. For the first year and a half "it was great. It was everything I could have wished for," she said dreamily. "But one day his ex called saying the business meeting he was at last night was held in her bedroom. And when he got home he didn't deny it, Derek! He basically told me he intended to keep getting with her! He loved us, both, he said. And he wanted me to accept it. DC men, Derek, are spoiled."

I didn't want to laugh, but I had to. Candi tried to give me the evil eye and then she had to laugh, too. "It is funny," I insisted.

"Yeah, you're right. It is funny now. But, Derek, you know it wasn't funny then."

"Did you get my invitation to the concert when I was in DC?"

"That and the fifteen hang-ups. Yeah we got them. You were being real silly that day."

"Yeah, you're right about that." Now it was time to change the tune. "So, am I right in thinking you and your husband are through?"

"My life in DC," she said, "is over. I needed to change everything so I came back home. My mother moved back to St. Albans and I'm staying with her. I feel like I want to start my life all over again."

I explained that I felt the same way, that I'd been all over, "but I needed to get back to something simple and basic."

The past had been dealt with and the future was now on the table. She began by saying, "I'm surprised you're still interested in me. I look a little different, you know."

"Who says I'm interested in you, blondie."

"Well, I guess I was wrong."

I wanted to continue sparring, but my old r&b love song ways just rose up and commandeered my mouth. "No, blondie, you know you're not wrong. I never stopped loving you."

"Oh, yes you did." There was a dark flash of hurt in her face that led me to protest, but she pressed on. "Remember that night in DC?"

"Well," I admitted, "I was mad. No doubt about that. But it was because I was so hurt and so jealous. Now I can't lie—times have gone by without me thinking of you. But not a lot of time." There was an awkward silence at the table that I broke with a question. "So what do you wanna do now?"

"I wanna finish eating."

"No," I said. "You know what I mean."

"Do I now?"

"You know," I said leaning across the table, "I wanna leap across this table and jump on you."

"Well, that would be very immature of you, Derek. Wouldn't it make more sense for you to let me finish eating, buy me two or three more piña coladas, drive me over to your house, and take me to your basement."

"You'd like that better?" I asked. She waved at the waiter and said, "Another piña colada, please."

Our lovemaking was so, so sweet. I spent a long time with her nipples. I was quite fascinated by how straight and firm they were, how they stood at attention every time I saluted them. This was sex long delayed and full of joy. Her voice—that singsong voice—was right at my ear, then against my neck.

But that wasn't the end of the night. There was much to discuss and more to explain. We started by talking about the first time we made love and how goofy, in retrospect, we were. "I was young then," I said.

Smiling, she wondered, "Are you still young?"

"Not as young as I was," I replied, "but I still like to walk hand-in-hand down Sixth Avenue."

"Really? When'd you do it last?"

"About fifteen years ago with you."

"You've certainly gotten a lot smoother."

We hugged up for a while after that. I was feeling sleepy but there was no way I was gonna give in to that. Not tonight. Not with this woman. After a while Candi asked me a strange question. "You remember that Gladys Knight & the Pips song 'If I Were Your Woman'?" Candi knew I did and I told her so. "You know," she continued, "it had that line in it, 'You're like a diamond but she treats you like glass.'"

"Oh, yeah, I remember it well."

"Have you ever written anything that good?"

Without any false humility I said, "Nope."

"Maybe," she said quietly, "you never will."

"Well," I responded defensively, "I haven't yet."

"Maybe you never will," she said again, which really irritated me.

"What's your point?" I spat the question out, trying to make her as uneasy as she was suddenly making me. In reply, her tone was quite even. She wasn't trying to provoke my anger—just my mind. "If you don't, will your life be a waste? I mean, if you never write a song as good as 'If I Were Your Woman,' that wouldn't be so terrible if, you know, you otherwise had a good life. You get what I'm saying?"

I was really tentative and caught quite off-guard by her. I mumbled something. I don't even know what. It made her press on.

"Derek, I'm not questioning that. I was just wondering if songwriting was all you've been about. I mean, have you developed other goals? After 'Black Sex' you could be a great trivia question. In the Jamaica library the other night I saw this book, *One Hit Wonders,* and I thought of you."

"Why," I said very forthrightly, "are you being so mean?"

"Because Richard was so caught up in his day to day that he never looked ahead. I have to admit even before his ex-wife showed up we had some problems. He was so busy with this bill or that Congressman that sometimes when he was home it felt like he was visiting. Are you the kind of man now who'd only visit his home and not live in it?"

I lay there searching to find my words. "I've always felt that if I didn't write a song as good as 'If I Was Your Woman' or 'Tracks of My Tears' or 'If You Don't Know Me By Now,' that, well, I would have failed myself somehow."

"Derek, there's more to you than that. There's more to you than some record in between tire ads."

For some reason I started sobbing. I still don't know why. When I was through, I whispered in her ear that, yes, there was more to me than any single song would ever show. I told her I'd show her that. Not just because I wanted to prove anything but because it was time. It was simply time. I thought that, at least for now, I had settled things. That my tears had made her see where I was really coming from. I said, "You sure tested me. You know that, don't you?"

I expected some sympathy and, hopefully, a return to our earlier passion. But when she looked at me again I knew Candi wasn't through. "What now? Is there more?"

Instead of answering me she reached over and clicked on the lamp next to her side of the bed. She bent down and reached into her pocketbook. I got a sudden flash back to Ruthie Lee and remembered that night of strange surprises. Looking at the back of Candi's blond hair I began to wonder if I'd suddenly gotten in too deep, too quickly. I kept seeing the old Candi, but clearly she'd changed just like I had. Maybe she'd changed too much.

Out of her pocketbook came a little spiral notebook and a black felt-tipped pen. She smiled and then began drawing intersecting horizontal and vertical lines on one sheet. I sat back against my pillow and all my anxiety floated right away. She put the initials C and D at the bottom of the sheet and then asked, "X's or O's?" I told her X's. She put an O down on the sheet and then handed the notebook and the pen to me. "Hey," I said, "there's an extra line on here."

"Well," she said, "we are not exactly kids anymore, you know. It's the same game, just more complicated."

"Something That Will Last"

"When a man's in love, he's only got one story." Lionel Richie wrote that in the lyrics of "Penny Lover" and, after Candi came back into my life, I felt that truer words had never been sung. Being with her was the deepest experience of my thirty-plus years and nothing, not even writing my favorite songs, could compare. We were kids before and subject to the whimsical nature of children. Now we were mature enough to understand that love was not a play thing. We came at each other with the intensity of a Mike Tyson first-round knockout and rolled around the canvas deliciously dazed. Quicker than a 10 count, she'd moved in with me, gotten her divorce, and, over dinner at Jezebel's, agreed to sign on for a lifelong bout.

To say I was happy is to slight the power and richness of my emotions. I was so far beyond happy that I'd have to become a thesaurus of affirmative adjectives to properly convey my feelings. I wrote a song, "Something That Will Last," the night of the day Candi moved in with me, and while I like it all right, it communicates but a thumbnail's worth of my optimism.

"Something That Will Last"

Chorus:
I dream I dream I dream
Of building something.
I dream I dream I dream
Of building something
Something that will last
That will last.

I think of you
When I am lonely
I yearn for you
When I am cold, dear.
But most of all
I know that together (we'll be together)
We'll build something that will last.

Verse two:

I reach for you
In times of sorrow
I smile at you
When I think of tomorrow.
'Cause most of all
I know that together (we'll be together)
We'll build something that will last.

"Pop Life"

There is nothing inherently corrupt about the music business. It is no more corrupt than the trucking business or garment business or the software business. People in all these businesses work hard to carve out a niche, work hard to hold on to what they got, and will rip you off if you're not able to handle yourself. That's just human nature.

The difference is that we don't view singers and songwriters the same way we do truckers or seamstresses. If a truck driver or sweatshop worker cries exploitation, we're certainly sympathetic. We may even clamor for someone to be indicted. But let a recording artist cry "rip off" by a record executive, and people get really righteous, devoting reams of purple prose about the artist's victimization and how the legacy of American music is being undermined, how black artists are taken advantage of, etc., etc., etc.

I try to keep some perspective on things. What's happened to me or any other artist is part of the flow of life. The rich try to play you, they often do play you, and how you deal with that, how you fight back or don't determines your fate. I've had big and small dramas in my career but, looking at the big picture, I've won more than I lost, built a little nest egg, and seen enough to know that nobody always wins, and most folks lose a lot.

In the days before I was to change my life forever I gathered up all my recent *Billboard*s and gave them a quick going over before tossing them in the trash. I skimmed most of Dwayne Robinson's Bass Line columns, which was always black music info central. I noticed that Danifa's publishing company was doing well—one of her young writers had an up-tempo track on Whitney Houston's newest, which would mean a revenue windfall for her. Doris Gilliam, my once lover, now acquaintance, had taken a gig as artist development head of Edgey Records. How she was going to deal with those gangstas I don't know, but, hey, it's not my problem.

Edgey, with Otis Clyburn's blessing, was expanding quickly. My old road managing friend Dirt Bike had been named Edgey's West Coast vice president of a&r. In fact, he'd already signed a couple of rappers from out in Compton who specialized in something folks were calling "gangsta" rap. That active teen molester Donkey had moved down to Atlanta where he was mixing records for the 2 Live Crew and deejaying part-time at a black strip club called Magic City.

I was knocked out when I noticed an item that mentioned Dillon, the bass genius of Jackson High, who was promoting an American blues festival in Paris. He had to be well over thirty now and apparently, just like all of us, had moved on in his life. I wondered if he still picked up his axe, so I called Dwayne Robinson, wondering if he had an address or phone number for Dillon.

He was a little hectic on the phone. Polite but hectic. He was leaving *Billboard*. Turned out he was cashing in on the black film mania and moving out to L.A. to work on a movie. I wished him the best and then inquired about Dillon's number, which, unfortunately, he'd thrown out in a bundle of press releases. Dwayne did, however, have one bit of news for me.

"Did you hear the latest about your man, Edgecombe Lennox?"

When I told him no, he said, "Marion Barry just named him to be the cultural affairs head for the District."

"Cultural affairs?"

"Yup." Dwayne spoke with a satisfied smile in his voice. "You're never dead in this game. There's always another chapter. That's what Edge told me one night a long time ago."

"You know," I said, "he basically told me the same thing."

"Well," Dwayne said, "I'm starting my chapter now."

"Me too."

"Good luck to the both of us."

"Yeah, youngblood," I replied. "And right on, too!"

It was June 1991 and a jeep rolled by the First Baptist Church of St. Albans blasting KRS-One's "The 'P' Is Free" on my wedding day, which made one of my ushers laugh. "Ain't that some shit." He laughed again. "Shit's real."

"But so is this," I said and then straightened Attak's bow tie.

"I guess so, homie."

Then my best man, looking as anxious as a live chicken at a Kentucky Fried Chicken, came in the room. "It's time," he said with well-practiced gravity.

"Yo," Attak said, "this is like going on stage, huh?"

"No," I said quietly, "this is the only time I'm doing this gig."

"I hope so, son." It was my best man again, my pops, my new good buddy, who squeezed me tighter than new money and then led Attak, the always taciturn Timmons, and myself out to the altar. Rev. Vernon Jackson stood there in some nicely flowing robes and hair so meticulously styled the bridesmaids threatened to call their beautician for a refund.

As I wiggled my toes inside the black Guccis I bought for the occasion, I looked out into the pews. The church was filled with record biz types, Queens neighbors, and a few people curious about who the "Black Sex" man was marrying. Danifa was there, but Doris had passed on the invitation, and who could blame her? Morris and Anna were standing next to each other and I smiled at them, hoping one day soon I would be attending their wedding. Moms was crying already and, if I could have, I'd have walked over and held her hand. She wasn't losing her son, I'd told her that morning, she was gaining a whole new family to feed Sunday afternoons. She'd liked that.

Candi had decided to wear white, feeling this was a new beginning despite her previous marriage. Her hair was a bright, white gold and cut so short I could see every curve of her beautiful head as she walked down the aisle. The highlight of the ceremony wasn't the I's and do's but Vernon, who sang "Something That Will Last" like it was written for him. Candi's hand caressed mine as my melody melted in the emotion of Vernon's singing.

And I was satisfied, more satisfied than I'd ever been, more satisfied than I figured I'd ever be again, more satisfied than any one hit wonder had any right to be. And I was looking forward to the moment, the moment after that.